ODDITORIUM

ODDITORIUM

by Hob Broun

HARPER & ROW, PUBLISHERS, New York
Cambridge, Philadelphia, San Francisco, London
Mexico City, São Paulo, Sydney

1817

Grateful acknowledgment is made for permission to reprint: Lyrics from "That's the Way of the World" © 1975 by Blackwood Music Inc. & Eibur Music; used by permission.

All lyrics from "Tropical Hot Dog Night" reprinted with permission of the publisher; words and music written by Don Van Vliet, all words and music copyright © 1978 Don Van Vliet/Singing Ink Music (BMI), all rights reserved, international copyright secured.

FIRST EDITION

Designer: Sidney Feinberg

Library of Congress Cataloging in Publication Data

Broun, Hob.
   Odditorium.
   I. Title.
PS3552.R682403   1983   813'.54   82–48101
ISBN 0–06–015027–0

83 84 85 86 10 9 8 7 6 5 4 3 2 1

FREDA
a little piece always

"ODDITORIUM was launched by Robert L. Ripley to designate an exhibition of oddities at the Chicago World's Fair of 1933–34, but his claim to its invention has been challenged by Allan Walker Read who reports that there was an Odditorium in Kingston-on-Thames, a village outside London, before World War I."

—H. L. Mencken,
The American Language,
Supplement Two

TAKE ONE

Tropical hotdog night
Like two flamingos in a fruit fight

Everything's wrong at the same
time it's right
—*Captain Beefheart (a/k/a Don Van Vliet)*

1

Birds. Dirty birds. Dirty little birds that toddled and pecked at the edge of high weeds. Steep-angled light that was too steady, too bright on a pile of broken bricks. Wind that drove through this dead corner pocket of Hillsborough County like a nasal voice, by the limp clothesline, over a curving neck of pine needles, through saw grass and cattails, and out past the cabbage hammocks to where the water moccasins lived. On the white sill two beetles clambered over each other, fighting or mating or eating. And that goddamn light out there. A nonstop frenzy of it. Windows around here should be dark green. Like sunglasses.

Karl Gables did not know the time of day. His liver worked feverishly to oxidize the last transfusion of Night Train Express while the bubblegum taste went sour in his mouth. A fortified wine, 18 percent alcohol; the kid at the store said junkies used it to taper off with sometimes. Karl picked up the empty bottle, looked through it. It was green and soothed his eyes. Sweat filmed his face and neck, dribbled down his chest, over the delta of his ribs. He was like a fountain.

L & M Shows had cut him loose and he was home in disgrace one more time. So what's the big deal? This sort of thing was sure enough going around. From sea to shining sea folks were being docked, garnisheed, cashiered, laid off and struck from the rolls. Here's the difference, Karl reminded himself: You're chronic.

Last Friday's edition of the *Rocky Mount Courier:*

> A brawl involving some 25 local residents and traveling carnival workers broke out yesterday evening after Koko the Clown and

3

an allegedly drunken man traded epithets at the Firemen's Fair in Gloverville. Police said the fighting started at the fair booth that featured Koko, part of whose act is to insult customers when they fail to dump him into a tank of water by throwing baseballs at a target activating a trapdoor.

Several persons suffered minor injuries. They were treated at Geismar General Hospital and later released. In addition to Karl Gables, 34, who a spokesman for L & M Shows said was filling in as Koko the Clown because another employee was unavailable due to an early morning automobile accident, and the irate patron, Buddy Layne, 52, of Rick's Road, South Newby, police arrested ten others, including two juveniles. All are being held in City Jail until the return of Judge Edwin Geismar, who is said to be on a fishing trip with relatives.

The disturbance began on the fair's "midway" around 7:30 PM and later spread to the parking area.

"Apparently the clown was riding this man pretty good," reported Constable Elvis Dunbar. "He took exception to it, picked up a wooden board and started after him. Before long we had a real fracas going. I had to call in back-up support from the State Police barracks."

One time I get a break from the shit cabins and, pow, right in the head. Must be a curse working on me. Nothing too strong in "Hey, Elephant Ears." Johnny Jugs, the regular Koko, had said a lot worse to people. Stuff about what the missus liked to do with her hair down in the bedroom, real rank stuff. But old J.J. had to clip four posts off a center divider in his Impala. Right. And this rube had to have a sore spot about his frigging ears. And some asshole angel up in Central Control just had to say, Let's give ole Karl Gables' chain another jerk. Oh sure.

At least he wouldn't have to disclose this latest flop to his wife; not quite yet. Tildy was still out on tour, bless her heart, and probably would not come home till late next month. That was good and not so good. On his own in their cinderblock hacienda, alone with his mutilated thoughts, Karl was at times subject to the cold creeps. All was nebulous and dark in these periods, a swirling murk of all-purpose dread, and carrying through the emptiest of days became a bona fide ordeal, like waiting out a volcanic eruption on an island everyone else has left. He would talk to himself, advising calm and patience, the sound of his own voice as monstrous as his passing reflection in a mirror. On a trip to the mailbox, he could panic at the sight of pale undersides of leaves turning in the breeze. He would

4

experience a tightness across the chest, a quickening heartbeat. He would have difficulty swallowing his own saliva.

Down home was down all right. Maybe that explained why, after a week in jail and three hard days' thumbing, he'd felt no relief yesterday on first sight of the place, gazing through the bug-splattered windshield of a delivery truck that had picked him up right outside of Lakeland.

"It ain't *Better Homes & Gardens*, but we like it," Karl said and then, as a pretext, so he would not have to enter the house alone, invited the driver in for a cold one.

"White of you, my friend, white of you. But I gots this 'frigerator to drop off up the road. . . ."

Karl pulled the oilcloth shade, turned from the window and looked upon his hostile friends: sagging sofa-bed with flocked upholstery, coral-colored plastic coffee table, water-stained carpet glued over cement floor, 19-inch black-and-white television in Mediterranean finish wood console stippled with cigarette burns, easy chair supported in front by phone books, white fuzz padding showing through at both arms, magazines in a cardboard box, potted cacti on a buffet tray with folding legs, sunburst clock obtained with six full books of Triple-S Blue Stamps.

Hello, walls. There was an old song that went something like that.

He moved into the kitchen to check supplies, throwing open cabinets covered inside and out with knotty-pine contact paper. Not much more than a week's worth of packaged goods, and only if he skipped lunches. Plenty of pea soup, at least, which was pretty good straight out of the can. A decent amount of Kool Aid and an unopened jar of Skippy with which to make his favorite dish, scrambled eggs and peanut butter. Except there weren't any eggs. But there were berry thickets out in the woods. He could forage, like a bear.

Karl put some water on to boil and examined the booze situation which, it became immediately clear, was only hours away from desperate. The entire inventory consisted of some cooking sherry, a pint of blackberry brandy bottled in cut-rate bond by Palmetto Liquors of Greater Tampa, and two airline vodka nips. After that it was Mayday.

He fixed himself a bowl of rice and white sugar, saucing it up with one of the vodka nips, and ate standing. Then glucose and alcohol clashed in his bloodstream and he had to stretch out on the floor

5

with his head on the overturned bowl. His eyes dropped shut, he listened to the birds and the dripping of the faucet, and within minutes had entered a capricious dream state that was not quite sleep.

. . . The hand-lettered bedsheet banner that trails behind the biplane says BUY WAR BONDS NOW. Waving as he dips low over the crowd, the 17-year-old pilot circles to the rear of the stadium. "His only protection, ladies and gentlemen, a leather helmet and our prayers to a merciful God." A fragile conformation of canvas and wood, the biplane skims over the end zone bleachers, engine roaring, clips off both wings on a pair of carefully placed telephone poles, and makes a shattering pancake landing on the 40-yard line. The pilot jumps free as a Sousa march blares from the public address. The crowd stands as one, shouting, clapping. Take that, Hitler. Our kids don't know what fear is.

Lucky Teter, king of the thrill drivers, knots a white silk scarf around his neck, and fingers the crease in his jodhpurs. He leaves for basic training at Fort Bragg at six o'clock tomorrow. Lucky's wife and his mother are on hand to see his last performance. Strapped into a big black Packard, he is going to shoot up a wooden ramp, soar high over the wreckage of the biplane and come to a dead stop in clouds of dust, directly under the goalposts. Lucky takes a last long drag from a cigarette, then flips it into the grass. It is time now. The ramps have been moved into place, the car is waiting already warmed up, motor running. As Lucky runs onto the field someone from the crew tells him to take it easy, don't push.

He makes one slow lap, working the crowd, building the tension. When it's all lined up he waits, revving out, spitting exhaust, rumbling like a mad bull about to charge. A massive cheer as he lurches forward and bears down on the ramp. Airborne for a second, sunlight all sleek and opaline on its black flanks, the roadster dips, falls short and smashes head-on into the landing ramp; its support beams are laid lengthwise and they thrust forward on impact, impaling Lucky, tearing his head off. Lucky's wife leaps from the stands. Flames have begun to blister paint along the rocker panels and a thin red line widens and extends along the white silk scarf floating out the window. . . .

Karl's head slid down the side of the bowl and met the floor. He turned on his side and drew up his knees at the ambush of nausea.

Then in surflike action, the nausea subsided and something else rolled in: an indefinite sense of wrong, a soft minor chord vibrating along his spine. Lucky Teter had been wearing the face of someone Karl knew well. That laughing face inside the ruined car.

Good Christ, but he needed a drink. He took a firm hold on the bottle of blackberry brandy. The first beams of warmth and peace danced in his abdomen and he whispered across the bottle mouth— creating a kind of flute-like accompaniment—the one and only Bible passage he knew by heart.

"Give strong drink unto him that is ready to perish, and wine unto those that be of heavy hearts. Let him drink and forget his poverty, and remember his misery no more."

So overcome was he by the wisdom and compassion of these words that his jaw began to tremble and his eyes welled with tears. Why couldn't the folks out there show a little understanding? A reassuring hand on the shoulder, a murmur of sympathy; it didn't have to mean anything, just the sound would be enough, some small indication that a drunk was not without his logic. But there were smirks instead, the hard little eyes that seemed to read a permanent plaque on Karl's chest: DAMNED FOREVER.

Like that cozy roadside spot he'd drifted into on the way home, stiff and sore from a night in an irrigation ditch and forty miles in the back of a gas fitter's pickup, looking for nothing more than a little something to rinse the exhaust fumes out of his mouth. The place was called Happy's. They had padded stools and a bumper pool table right by the front window. Working the bar was this sullen granny in a T-shirt. For close to twelve minutes (Karl timed her on a silvery plastic rotating clock advertising a line of canned martinis), she bustled all over, buffing the glass on the cigarette machine, counting empty beer bottles and freshening the bourbon and milk of the only other customer in the joint. It was only after, looking straight at him, she had released some vile perfume from a spray can that she finally asked if he wanted something. And she wouldn't let go of the beer bottle until he'd put some money down.

Yeah, it was that kind of thing. The way people liked to shit on you out there. Even people that knew you, like R.C. Owens right down at the crossroads store. Anytime Karl walked in there, R.C. would come out from behind the counter and follow his every step like he was some spic fruit tramp between harvests; and he'd explained that thing last April a dozen times. How he'd carried those

7

wieners outside because he remembered that he'd left his wallet on top of the Coke machine. But there was no human charity out there. Folks needed their victims.

Karl leaned shakily against the bedroom door, the bottle nestled against his cheek. He yearned miserably for his wife. She could soothe him with her voice, comfort him with a sandwich. So young and lovely, how had he kept her this long? He browsed through hangers in the closet, stroking her clothes, craving the slightest trace of her that might still reside in the fabric. His head swaddled in bunched skirts, jackets and blouses, he haltingly recalled their last time in bed. Crackles of heat lightning on the radio, handcream spilled on the sheets. Difficulty staying firm. Oh well. He wobbled to the floor, sat cross-legged and contemplated Tildy's shoes neatly aligned on the closet floor, each insole dappled with the gray outline of heel and toes like paw prints in sand. It was hell, missing her this way, looking for her in a batch of empty shoes.

He took an enormous hit of brandy as a kind of blunting agent. Real nice, he'd stopped tasting it now. Ought to have just about a full tank by this time—there was an audible sloshing in his belly when he moved—but it didn't seem to be putting him any closer to the hollow stupor he'd been longing to enter for days. And it was into the cooking sherry after this. He was going to need a miracle at this rate, some of that water-into-wine action. Karl tipped back, curled himself at the foot of the bed in the hope that, given a few minutes, he might pass out.

The floor was hard; his left ear throbbed. There were dust balls and odd pillow feathers right next to his eyes when he opened them. Wouldn't mind if the whole house looked like it did under the bed, dark and untouched. Secret. A man could pass out in style in a house like that. Gradually, he extended one arm into the shadows and touched something hairy, more substantial than dust. He closed his hand around . . . It had bulk, there was fur. A dead animal. He would have squawked, probably injured himself with a sudden recoil, but his ganglia were so numbed, his reflexes so torpid, that he pulled weakly and the object skittered into light. It was one of Tildy's slippers. He lifted it out and, cringing at himself even as he did so, kissed the spiky floss of blue orlon. Grit adhered to his lips sticky with blackberry brandy. More shoes, for Chrissakes. Into the slipper's interior, stiff with wifely sweat, went his hand.

"I love you, Karl," he squeaked, pinching the sole of the slipper into a kind of puppet mouth.

8

Inside something skidded under his fingertips. Square, crisp, with sharp corners.

"You got to ask to get," he said in the puppet voice.

He looked at the ceiling, drew out his hand, dropped his eyes again. A fifty-dollar bill folded eight ways. Didn't General Grant look fine, even with a crease right through his eyes!

Sweet, sweet Tildy. There when he needed her even when she wasn't there. She'd been paying the cost to be the boss right from the start; hired Arlo the Aqua Boy to be best man at their wedding. And hadn't the preacher swallowed hard when Arlo handed up the ring in webbed hands.

Karl chugged the brandy dregs and came to his feet shadowboxing, a new man. Flush. He knew just what he was going to do, too. Get hold of that turnip squeezer, R.C. Owens, and order up.

He dialed, waited. "Yo, R.C., this is your day and mine to shine."

"Who in hell is this?"

"Karl Gables, good buddy."

"What you want, thief?"

"No way to talk, R.C. No way at all. I wanna mend fences with you, throw a little business your way. Got some friends coming in for the weekend, gonna need some stuff. Lessee . . . two pounds of olive loaf. Uh-huh. Couple of white breads."

"Listen up. I done told your wife a while back you two ain't got no more line a credit with me."

"This is a straight cash deal here. Greenest greenbacks you'll ever see. Now we got the olive loaf and the bread, yeah, maybe a couple cans of tuna. Need a dozen eggs, and you pack 'em careful, you prick. Then gimme two jugs of that hearty Burgundy . . . you writin' this down?"

"Sure, Gables. In blood."

"Real smart, R.C. Just for that I'll take one case of that Gatortail Ale 'stead of two. Now you get that stuff all together 'cause I'm sendin' my boy for it right quick."

The moment he cradled the phone, Karl found he was overwhelmingly tired, as though he had dispersed his energy through the mouthpiece and along the wires. His knees were quivery, his vision slightly fractured, but he couldn't let himself go just yet. Things to be done still. Had to get Ondray Keyes down here and work out some kind of deal.

The Keyeses were Karl's closest neighbors. There were a lot of them up there; Karl wasn't exactly sure what the total count was.

Amos Keyes worked at a sawmill somewhere inland, but it was an off-and-on thing. Members of the family were constantly off here or there, running down a few days work. Ondray, the second youngest, was sometimes willing to come down the road and do a few things for Karl—run errands for him on his bicycle mostly. He had a basket in front and two saddlebags in back. He'd load up on goodies at the crossroads store, ferry them back, and usually end up keeping Karl's change. Ondray was only in the fourth grade, but sharp, a demon with figures. He looked up at the sky when he talked and never smiled. Hard-ass little kid. And his pricing procedures were too.

Once Ondray had delivered two quarts of beer, hot, nearly explosive from a long trip in the saddlebags, in exchange for a pocket knife with bottle-opener attachment. Frantic for someone to talk to, Karl invited him to stick around. Ondray didn't say a word, just hefted the knife in his small hand and stared at his bike lying on its side in the grass.

"Aw, c'mon, don't be a wallflower," Karl said. Then, in a ruinous stab at joviality. "I really like you, kid. You're the cutest little Sambo I ever saw."

Ondray's markup had taken a truly brutal increase from that moment on. The kid knew what he was doing. He had the only game in town.

There was no telephone up at the Keyes place so in order to call Ondray, Karl had to go out on the front lawn and blow through a conch shell. That was supposed to be the signal. Sometimes Ondray rolled right by, sometimes he came the next day, and sometimes he didn't come at all.

Karl had to rummage through several kitchen drawers before he located the shell, a hefty specimen with the words SOUVENIR OF CABBAGE KEY painted on the outside. He hurried into the front yard with it and sunlight hit him like a bucket of hot soup. He tried shading his eyes, but found both hands were needed to hold the shell steady. His flaccid lips had trouble forming the proper embouchure and the first sounds were like the belches of a housecat. He filled his lungs and tried again. The effort brought considerable pressure to bear on both his head and chest; he felt dizzy and remembered a story he'd once heard about a trumpet player who collapsed and died on the bandstand after a solo. The thought of blacking out in the yard, possibly lying vulnerable there for hours, filled him with such terror that he put his every last reserve behind the next blow and came out with a round bass note that made his ears ring.

With the shell under his arm he ran for the house and away from the light. Sometimes the boy came, sometimes he didn't. Karl would just have to see. He closed his eyes and drained the cooking sherry. Then, sitting on his haunches in a corner of the bedroom, tearing off bits of fingernail and chewing them up, he lay in wait.

Karl Gables was not a habitual underdog looking downriver to the breakup of his life years later. That had already happened.

2

Dense blue-gray clouds floated over the Sergeant Bill Cavaretta Memorial Field. The air crackled with ozone. Brick smokestacks of a knitting mill loomed over the bleachers along the third-base line and behind corrugated tin fencing in the outfield (279 feet to straightaway center). Burdock and pokeweed grew between the ties of an abandoned rail spur. All quiet as the two teams switched positions at the half inning—no claps or cheers, just the low rumble of approaching thunder. Total paid attendance for the Battle of the Sexes Softball Match was 61, not enough to cover expenses.

The lead-off hitter was Clothilde Soileau, a slight but compact woman with tightly curled brown hair and the kind of pale, hearts-and-flowers face that caused temples to vibrate back in 1925. In white lettering on the back of her green uniform shirt over the numeral 1, it said simply, TILDY. She raked the dirt around the batter's box with her spikes, took a few practice cuts, then stepped in, crowding the plate and choking up on the aluminum bat, holding it at a 90-degree angle just behind her right ear. She laid off a hummer at the knees for ball one. Tildy winked at the pitcher, an unemployed roofer with end-stage acne, and laid down a perfect drag bunt that dribbled to a stop in the long grass to the right of the mound. She was standing on first base before the ball had been touched.

Hands on hips, the pitcher talked to his shoes. "The cunt bunts. Real cute." He bounced his next pitch in the dirt and Tildy took off as it skipped all the way to the backstop. The catcher went after it on bow legs as the first raindrops fell, wheeled and sidearmed a wild throw that ricocheted off Tildy's back into short right. She lowered her head and pumped her slender legs, rounding second. Two outfielders reached the ball simultaneously, bumped and elbowed for possession until one of them scooped it back in underhand. Rain came hard and heavy, as from a showerhead with a five-mile diameter; Tildy cut the third base bag and kept on. The catcher waited for her now, a heavy hippo straddling the plate with his mask in one hand, the ball in the other.

She was a dead-sure out and people started running for their cars. Fifteen feet away, Tildy went into her slide, right leg flung above her, flexed at the knee; then her foot sliced out and up, kicking the ball loose, and she sprawled through the wicket of those massive hippo legs.

Lying face down, Tildy smelled fresh, moist earth. She heard the hissing of the rain, but no awestruck ovation from the stands, not even the umpire's safe call. Then she turned onto her knees and saw him through the haze, sprinting for the street along with the rest of her teammates. Tildy leaped up and followed, realizing they'd want to scramble onto that bus and make like a blue streak for the motel before any of the suckers thought to ask for their money back.

From the cork-lined Situation Room of his corporate headquarters in Jacksonville, Peter F.-X. Sparn—past president of the Florida Vending Machine Association, Chairman of the Organizing Committee for the Muscular Dystrophy Bass Tournament at Crescent Lake—oversaw a bustling amusements empire with the help of his loyal staff: Miss Dolly Varden, personal assistant to Mr. Sparn since 1947; and bonehead son, Vinnie, adopted in 1953 after Mrs. Sparn had her third spontaneous abortion.

Sparn's Seminole Star Corporation supplied topless dancers to saloons and army bases up and down the Eastern seaboard; leased juke boxes, pinball machines and video games; and jobbed the finest in candy and confections to movie theaters throughout Nassau and St. John's counties. But the flagship of the operation, the real nonpareil, was Flora Pepper and Her Cougarettes, an all-girl fast-pitch softball team traveling fifteen states and taking on all comers. The mounted sailfish behind his desk didn't make him a sportsman; owning a ball team did. After thirty-eight years of hardheaded entrepreneurship, what had he got? An all-electric home with asphalt drive and in-ground pool. A limousine that sailed down the road like a cloud. A beautifully appointed cabin cruiser drawing ten feet of water. A solid-gold walking stick and a diamond ring insured for over five thousand dollars. But he never wore the ring, kept it in a safety deposit box at the bank. And there you had it. Without sport, without fun, his life was so much gilt-edged paper sitting pointlessly in some darkened vault.

"If fun can be a business," Pete was fond of saying, "then business can be fun."

He'd been around long enough to know that financial success wasn't everything. There were plenty of business wizards around, but damn few sportsmen. Real old-time classy sportsmen, he meant, not the bored board chairmen noodling around on the golf course or flying off on those nitwit hunting trips where drugged animals were herded up to the patio. Sparn's team was much more than a hobby to him, more than a toy to keep him entertained between deals; it was the thing that set him apart and gave him prestige. And so what if his accountants (Pennspar & Kezdekian, of Neptune Street) were unimpressed? What did he care that they said revenues accruing therefrom were inadequate in view of current overall tax judgements? He was a goddamn sportsman.

Every morning, before lifting the smoked Lucite hood of his executive telephone to inaugurate the business day, Sparn read Dolly's impeccably typewritten boxscores, cumulative batting and fielding averages, as well as the expenses and attendance figures. He pored lovingly over these stats, reveling in the pristine, almost mystical flow of the numbers that Vinnie, the Cougarettes' manager, had phoned into Dolly the previous night.

"Another extra base hit for Heidi," Sparn might say. "Let's move her up in the order." Or, "That's three errors this week for Rosie Alonzo. Get her to an optometrist and have her eyes checked."

Dolly Varden made note of these comments, of every grunt and lifted eyebrow, and relayed them to Vinnie at their next phone contact. She did not mind these extra tasks. She did not mind putting in ten- and twelve-hour days, then taking work home to her one-room apartment. Time did not pass for Dolly Varden. She lived in the haunted, unalterable vacuum of a dream. She was a 53-year-old virgin, silently, hopelessly, agonizingly in love with her boss.

In November of 1946, under the name Flossie McCall, she was doing a specialty act at the Cathay Theatre in Brooklyn. To an up-tempo arrangement of "You're the Top," she danced up a flight of steps, leaned over backward from the uppermost stair, picked up a glass of beer in her teeth and drank it down. One evening, after a particularly boffo Saturday matinee, a darkly handsome man came to her dressing room and presented his card. He had eyes like grommets.

"Pete Sparn, personal management. You got a great bit there, sugar."

He took her out for oysters between shows. Dolly was so beguiled that she was unable to swallow her food. When, calling attention to the dessert cart, Sparn touched her bare arm, she felt the membrane surrounding her heart split down the middle, and then a great swelling in her chest, a torrential rush of blood.

So fierce was the heat and excitement within her that at the very next performance she lost her rhythm, plunged from the top of that stairway and broke her back. The doctors said Dolly would never dance again. Confined in a complex traction set-up, she lay in the hospital for weeks, alternately numb and delirious, sometimes afraid to sleep because of the wildly lascivious dreams that would descend on her, leaving her tangled in pulleys and straps, the bedsheets puddled with sweat.

When at least she was released, twenty pounds lighter and using a cane, Dolly had less than ten dollars in the bank and no prospects, but there in the lobby was Sparn with roses, a basket of fruit and the offer of a brand-new career as his personal secretary. The cane clattered to the floor as she grasped his camel's-hair lapels and sobbed her gratitude.

Sparn paid for typing lessons and a fresh wardrobe (an unflattering selection in severe governess grays). He revamped her grooming habits and put her on a diet of steak and shellfish. He brought her bulging cartons of *Billboard* and *Variety* back issues, requiring a daily oral report on what she had read. He coached her in the proper way to behave on the telephone and how to deflect hustlers who came to the office.

"I promised I'd make you into something and I will," he said.

Dolly proved herself an obedient subject, soaking up information like a sponge, memorizing in less than four days the name and hierarchical rank of every talent booker and summer stock producer in town. She grew into the job with astonishing rapidity, slithered through the office in her corrective shoes, the image of placid efficiency from a vocational slide show. Most of all she wanted to become "indispensable," and after a while, largely unbeknownst to Sparn, she did. Dolly cast herself in "Man's Favorite Secretary" as the sympathetic, symbiotic underling who could anticipate the thoughts and wishes of her Boss. But only up to a point, as it turned out.

On the very day when she had at last summoned the courage to invite him home for May wine and sauerbraten by candlelight, Sparn asked her to run down to the engraver's to pick up his wedding invitations.

That night Dolly destroyed much of the contents of her apartment, and did not return to work until the following week. She did not attend the ceremony uniting Sparn and the 16-year-old daughter of Falco Andretti, importer of olive oil and ricotta cheese. She did not attend the elaborate reception held at the Ansonia Hotel with a thousand dollars' worth of white chrysanthemums and entertainment by Red Kingston and his Mellow Fellows. She did not join the bon voyage party catching kisses and paper serpentines launched by Sparn and his bride, bound for a Havana honeymoon, from the railing of the S.S. *Paloma*.

Instead she raged and shivered and wept, living on doughnuts and coffee, sleeping on the linoleum floor of the office and often waking spattered with dried blood from having abused the flesh of her arms and legs during the night with a fountain pen, until that moment when her body became only a body, a pulpy, self-propelled machine, and she did not have to weep ever again.

Now as she stood quietly by his desk awaiting instructions, Dolly did not see a bloated old man, but the handsome Johnny who had come to her dressing room: that smoothly cast face, those black grommet eyes, the swaggering energy she had imagined taking physical form as a crown of cartoon lightbulbs on his head. So much time. So much time that had not passed.

"Think you can clear my calendar for this Friday? Time I sat in on a Cougarettes game."

"I don't see any problem. I always hold the fort for you."

"You're a gem, Dolly, a gem of the first water."

The Cougarettes were in command, leading 4–0 after five innings; several at the far end of the batting order went into the stands to hawk candy bars and the souvenir illustrated programs, fifty cents a copy. Flora was on the cover—a grainy action photo taken when she still bleached her hair and wore it in a ponytail. Flora was on page one—a still grainier picture of her shaking hands with Hector Rosario, a welterweight from Miami, and under it some biographical highlights: 70 no-hitters, 23 perfect games, 4500 strikeouts, a lifetime

E.R.A. of 1.12. The finishing touch was her unique accomplishment of last season, setting a man down on one pitch, a figure-eight wind-mill change-up he'd wiffed at three times.

Flora was also on deck. After replenishing her chaw (mentholated snuff inside a wad of bubble gum), she stepped to the plate and rocked a whistling liner into the gap in left center for an inside-the-park home run.

"That's a Hall-of-Famer, folks. You're looking at a Hall-of-Famer right there." Rhythmic clapping from Coach Vinnie Sparn at his position behind the chicken wire screen. "Five up, let's get some more. . . . Come on, Wanda, little bingle in there."

Right next to Vinnie was a plastic trash barrel of iced beer, one dollar a can. Just another managerial task, keeping the crowd happy. He wore a sun helmet, and around his waist, a canvas apron with his initials on it. As Vinnie made change he looked nervously to his left where his father was sitting. Nodding excitedly to himself, Sparn calculated the biorhythm cycles of the Cougarette players on a specialized, mail-order slide rule, and made notes on a pad.

Dad just loves these unannounced visits, Vinnie thought. The bastard. Not much of a show; no wonder he isn't paying attention.

How Vinnie dreaded the arrival of the old man. It always came at the wrong time. Not last night, when they'd been up against a decent factory team and had pulled in close to a grand, but today, on a crappy Little League field across from a laundromat against a squad of local "All Stars" (a disheveled group Vinnie had recruited in bars and union halls at ten bucks a man). The uniforms they wore came out of a cardboard box in the back of the Cougarettes' bus and fit badly. The crowd was sparse and abusive.

Dad is going to shit a brick, Vinnie thought. I just know it.

Sparn was motioning him over with emphatic swoops of the hand. Vinnie tried to hide under the brim of the sun helmet, but it was too late.

"Good game, huh? A little dry, Dad? Want a brew?"

"How we doing on them? What kind of deal are you getting?"

Vinnie turned around to cheer through cupped hands. "Let's bring another one home, Roxie. Show us some chili pepper up there."

Sparn rapped him on the top of the helmet with his ball-point. "I'm talking to you, Vincent. What I called you over here for is I got to know how many posters you put up last night?"

"Well, see we've been running low on posters and I thought, you know, not to spread yourself too thin and all, so I . . ."

"You're low on posters? So for Christ's sake tell Dolly about it and we'll get some more printed up. What the hell do you think I have you call in for every night, if not so we can stay on top of this thing? Do you read me? Let's communicate, okay?"

"Right, Dad. I'll let you know."

"Great. Beautiful. Let's stay in goddamn touch on this stuff."

Vinnie kicked the dirt, but was inwardly relieved when Roxie Vasquez bounced into a double play to end the inning. Just one more to go, he thought, and we can get out of here.

The room Tildy and Roxie shared was the only one with operational hot water. It was filling up with funky, gritty bodies.

"You better watch your ass, girl."

"Turn your fuckin' face around."

There was some scuffling going on in the shower line. After an eighty-mile bus ride, with windows open since the air conditioning was out, the Cougarettes' collective mood was right nasty.

"How'd you like to eat this shampoo bottle, Wanda?"

Wrapped in a couple of towels, Tildy sat at the head end of the bed turning the pages of a newspaper. Roxie was cross-legged at the other end, searching for tunes on a transistor radio and wedging cotton between her toes before applying a fresh coat of nail polish.

"You just sitting there, Frenchie. You want to use my hairbrush or something?"

"I'd probably break it." Tildy spoke without looking up from her paper. "Haven't touched this hair in years. That's the secret to these great curls."

"You ought to brush once in a while." Roxie shook her head. "You could get spiders living in there."

According to the souvenir program, Roxie was a pearl diver from Corinto, Nicaragua. Actually she could not swim a stroke and came originally from Oakland. One night she had beaten Vinnie up outside a bowling alley and Pete Sparn, on one of his surprise visits at the time, had been so impressed that he fired his left fielder on the spot and gave Roxie the job.

"I can handle a bat, no problem," Roxie said. "I used to be a bouncer at the Hoja Roja in Modesto."

That's-Mary, who was late for everything, came dancing through the door in slippers and a chenille robe. Beer from a paper cup sloshed on her hand as she shimmied to the back of the line.

"Gimme some more volume, Rox. I'm in a party state of mind."

"When haven't you been in a party state of mind?" Tildy asked. "You ought to retire from ball and move to Vegas."

"Thinkin' about it, thinkin' about it . . . Come on, Roxie, make it loud . . . 'Heart's desire creates love desire, goin' higher and higher. . . .' Woo, will you look at that. I just greased these hip joints this morning." That's-Mary slanted forward on the balls of her feet and shook her ass as if it was on fire. "I'm a tiptop bebop can't-stop butt-monger."

"All right, T.M. Get down with it," somebody shouted from the front of the line.

"If you don't watch that beer, Mary, I'll be all over your butt like two miles of wet cement."

That's-Mary patted the wet spot on Wanda's back. "No harm in a little beer. You're headed for the shower, ain't you? We're all headed for the shower. Hell, we ought to bust on in there and have us a shower party, all of us together."

"I ain't into no freak scenes," Wanda said flatly.

Up front, there was growing concern about the hot water supply. They were kicking on the door and yelling. Heidi, who was the youngest and so absorbed with hygiene that she changed panties after every meal, had been in the bathroom for almost ten minutes now.

"Open up, Heidi!"

"Give somebody else a chance, huh? You think we don't sweat just like you?"

Tildy threw down her paper and stood up; the top towel came loose and her conoid breasts popped free, still wrinkled and pink from the steaming water. "Everybody's welcome to shower in my room, but not with this mess going on. If you can't cool down and stop acting like babies, I'm gonna throw everybody out."

"That's fine for you. You already had your shower."

Vinnie, who had been lurking in the hall for some time hoping for a quick flash in the crowd of tit or bush, stepped inside rattling the keys that hung from his belt. "Let's work it out, ladies. What's the problem?"

Tildy made no effort to cover up. "The problem, Vinnie, is this dog-shit motel you booked us into. If we had more than one shower, there wouldn't be a problem."

Vinnie, who could not look at her, feigned interest in the swap-meet landscape painting on the wall. Autumn in Vermont, just like mother used to make.

"We're working on it," he said.

"Mm-hmm." Tildy pulled a T-shirt over her head. "'We're working on it.' You should have that tattooed across your chest."

"Aww, don't be so hard on Coach. His daddy's been after him all day long as it is." That's-Mary, who had bobby-pinned the empty beer cup to her hair as a party hat, twirled over to Vinnie and threw her arm around him. "Let's have some fun, Coach. Wanna play a game with me?"

Vinnie smiled up at her. She's always so nice to me, he thought. No matter what. That's Mary.

It was he who had given her the name. During their first season, Pete had arranged to lease the team bus for a nominal cost with the understanding that free parking-lot tours would be conducted at each game. Patrons were encouraged to avail themselves of a photo opportunity, posing with Flora and the others in front of the sparkling Scenicruiser. One afternoon, at a youth camp outside Cairo, Illinois, Vinnie was conducting an old bat and her three grandkids through the vehicle, demonstrating the multiple settings of the reclining seats, the individual ventilation controls. He was about to throw open the door of the heavily chromed, ultraviolet-flush restroom, when he noticed a figure slumped across the rear seats. After a bottle or two of Tokay and a veal parmesan po'boy, the then Mariellen LoPinto had crawled onto the bus, passed out and vomited all over herself while asleep. The bat reeled back, pressing a hanky to her face and shooing the kids down the aisle.

"Gee, I'm . . . uh, uh . . . that's Mary," Vinnie stammered in explanation.

Now, coming in to score, she would jump on the plate with both feet, spread her arms and shout, "That's Mary!" Pete Sparn liked her grasp of show biz. He called her "That's" for short.

"Wanna scrub my back, Coach?"

She stretched out this last word and Vinnie felt the warm, wet exhaust of her speech on his eyelids. Sweet Lord, did she really mean it? A genuine invitation? Could be, could be. The way her eyes went right to him and the skin went a little white at the crimped corners of her mouth. But not with all these others around. Impossible. They'd eat me alive.

For a few extra seconds Vinnie stood there just watching That's-Mary breathe. Finally he said, "Really thanks, but I've got to go make some calls."

The laughter he heard as he turned away had to do with something Tildy said about Roxie's inability to go to her left, but Vinnie didn't know that. He went down and across the hall to the room he and Pete were in. Sparn had finished his nap and was sitting up in his piped pyjamas playing cards with Ben Salem, the old gink who looked after the equipment, drove the bus, sold the tickets and umpired the games.

"Your old man is sharp as ever," Benny said. "I'm about to lose the ranch here."

"Don't forget, I came into this game owing you ten acres of prime industrial parkland in North Miami."

Vinnie opened a beer, propped himself against the edge of the dresser. "You're playing for imaginary real estate, is that it?"

"Astute, boy, very astute. Real estate's better than cash any day." Sparn pushed the cards over for Benny to shuffle. "That reminds me, you ever get that book I sent you?"

"The one on condominium investments? Very interesting, Dad, but I haven't had a chance to read it yet, we've been so busy. A lot of dates running."

"We're busy all right. Too damn busy. I don't like it."

"Now you want fewer dates?" Vinnie shrugged. "Make up your mind."

"Don't pout. I don't like that either." Pete turned palms up and Benny nodded, dropped the deck in his shirt pocket and got up.

"Maybe after dinner we'll try some Hollywood rummy."

"Wait, you don't have to go, Benny. You're as much a part of this organization as he is. . . . Now what I'm saying to you is that they're stale. I see some lackadaisical play out there, you know what I mean? Lackadaisical play shows at the box office and that's where we're at right now. There are some things we need to get straight.

"People have to wake up to themselves. Maybe it's just a matter of losing sight of our goals, I don't know, but I want to get it straight and it may as well be right now—you round everybody up, Vinnie, and get them in here on the double. I want to have a skull session with these broads."

"Dad, I don't know if this is really the best time for a skull session. The girls need a little time to unwind."

"Fuck that noise." Sparn was out of bed and pacing now. The great General in his tent. And when the General gave an order . . . "If you have to, tell 'em dinner's on me. Just get 'em in here."

Vinnie stared down through the tear-shaped slot in the top of his beer can and saw the foaming darkness of a slow-moving underground river.

"Let's wrap it up and bring it along, ladies." Vinnie rolled into the explicit silence of Tildy's room jangling the big key ring, as much a symbol of his authority as a Bantu chieftain's fly whisk. "Pete's called a team meeting. He wants to see you, like, yesterday."

Heidi, who was flossing her teeth in the mirror, turned and primly expelled a particle of food into the wastebasket. "I don't see why he can't come on in here. Door's right open for him."

"That's right," Tildy said. "We were planning to just sit around here and smoke and read comic books till mealtime."

"He's only right across the street," Vinnie said, but nobody smiled. They didn't seem any happier when he told them Pete was offering to spring for dinner. Then That's-Mary came out from the bathroom trailing vapor and took over for him.

"Go ahead, guys. I promise when it's over, I'll find someplace around here that serves lobster."

That got them moving, but still not everyone was happy. As Wanda Watts filed past, she looked Vinnie up and down and jammed her afro pick half an inch into the wall. Maybe she didn't like lobster.

Still pacing, Sparn chewed on a cellophane-wrapped cigar while his players found seats on the beds and on the floor between them. Then he folded his arms and made a very small bow in greeting.

"Before we get into anything else, I really would like to say how proud I am of the way you're all getting along together. I respect that unity. It's obvious to me that you girls have made some close and lasting friendships on this team." Sparn's pyjamas were dark under the arms. "I'm not going to say we're like a family or any of that crap, but being effective on the field means rooting for each other and I think we all understand that." Sparn looked around the room to see who had giggled, and became alarmed. "Wait a minute . . . I've got my outfield, I've got my infield. Where's Flora? And M.J.?"

Vinnie counted cigarette burns on the dresser top; Ben Salem, cutting cards with himself over behind the teevee, started coughing as fast as he could. Evidently, Sparn was unaware or had forgotten the nature of the post-game activities Flora and her battery mate engaged in after a win.

It was Tildy finally who spoke up. "They're in bed, Pete."

"In bed? The hell they are. I'll go find them myself." And, nudging aside Vinnie, who tried to intercept him at the door, said, "There are no stars on this team."

22

Sparn hurried to the opposite end of the hall where, as always, Flora had her separate accommodations, and tried the door. It was locked. But through it, as the sound of his knock subsided, he heard a bee-like buzzing, steady like a motor. A sort of electric vibrating sound.

When he got back, he told them all to sit tight and Vinnie would call out for some cheeseburgers.

Flora Pepper had always been athletic. Though small as a child, she could outrun her older brothers and beat them up if she felt like it. As a high school junior, she lettered in basketball, volleyball and track; and at an awards dinner honoring young champions from all over northeastern Ohio, broke the nose of the girl who beat her out in the voting for Sprinter of the Year.

There didn't seem to be much else to do, so she became a Phys. Ed. assistant at her alma mater, Girls Normal High. She might still have been there leading calisthenics and breaking up fights in the lunchroom, had it not been for a chance Friday night pickup over the pool table of an Akron dyke bar known as Myrtle's 5 & 10.

The woman's name was Molly Joan Ulasewicz. She drank bourbon and ginger, and called everyone "bunny." She wore a piece of chromed sprocket chain around her wrist. Flora fell deeply and irreparably in love with her after one night.

After three nights, she left Girls Normal and moved into Molly Joan's ramshackle row house on the edge of Little Africa. While her lover wound armatures at an electronics factory during the day, Flora embarked on a rehabilitation program: rehanging doors, puttying windows, sanding the floors and laying down coat after coat of polyurethane. She blew her savings on a waterbed and a set of ritzy china. Pleasing Molly Joan became her exclusive focus, and for the first time in her life she felt calm and balanced.

But on the other side, things were not so rosy. Molly Joan quickly tired of this cozy householdry, the long evenings of beer and adoration. Flora was giving her claustrophobia. Restless and depressed, she fell into savage weekend benders, staring down bikers, and bootcamp studs in the toughest dives in town, vandalizing automobiles, sleeping it off at the bus station.

Early one Sunday morning Molly Joan tumbled in with a caftaned, child-eyed girl whose knapsack had been stolen. She had pale hands and long red hair, and reeked of patchouli oil. Dizzy and emitting foul burps, Molly Joan disappeared upstairs, leaving Flora alone with her catch. The girl said her name was Nebula, that she was on her way to a ginseng farm in Idaho, and that she hadn't eaten anything in two days. Flora gave her some fruit and cottage cheese. Then Molly Joan came down, put some Dixieland on the turntable and summoned them into the living room where, naked, scrubbed and powdered, she offered herself to both, a hungry castaway on an atoll of red satin pillows.

That evening, Flora slashed open her forearms with a broken lightbulb.

It was at this point, with a comely kind of logic, that athletics salvaged the relationship. Molly Joan had just been elected captain of her company softball team and, as a peace offering, took Flora (just returned from the emergency room) to the next practice session instead of leaving her home to sulk and imagine the worst. Flora's natural gifts became obvious within minutes. Her conformation was ideal, with disproportionately long arms and legs for maximum leverage, and good depth through the shoulders. Her long, tapered fingers had no trouble gripping a ball twelve inches around. It was a pointless batting practice because no one could get much wood on the ball, but nobody seemed to mind. The team's coach was ecstatic; this girl could really "bring it." He kissed Flora's pitching hand, ran to the nearest telephone and arranged a soft job with flexible hours for her so she'd be eligible to play in league games.

Flora won her first start on a six-hit shutout and went on to sharpen and refine her raw skills in daily practices with Molly Joan at a local playground. These external relationships of pitcher/catcher and protégé/mentor stabilized their life together; Flora no longer woke up crying in the middle of the night and, as she grew in confidence, recaptured and then surpassed the bliss of those first weeks. But it was Molly Joan who reaped the sweetest harvest. It was like a rebirth for her. Molly Joan who had been diving into brick walls for as long as she could remember, who had driven a cab, operated cranes, waited tables, cut asparagus, pumped gas, hawked rug shampooers door to door and cooked at the Skyway Grill of the Cincinnati airport, had at last found something she loved to do in teaching and guiding her Flora, this beautiful animal with whom she could happily spend the rest of her life.

Flora's amazing pitching performances of that summer, including a string of thirty-five scoreless innings, nearly propelled the Dynaco Sparklers to a national championship. They fell short in extra innings of the second elimination round, but Flora got her picture in a national magazine.

That was how Pete Sparn got wind of her. Just the kind of promotion he'd been looking for. Dolly Varden spent a whole day tracking her down and when Sparn got on the phone he was all honey. He offered to fly Flora to Jacksonville to discuss the possibilities of lucrative barnstorming tours with a team he'd build around her.

"Definitely sounds interesting," Flora said, "but I don't go anywhere without my catcher."

"Fine. Bring her along."

But Sparn wasn't too thrilled when they walked into his office. He visualized a company of sporting stunners, as lovely as they were lithe and swift, and had no desire to mar that overall chorus-line appearance with a chunky member who had a face like a cheese grater and was pushing forty hard. But Flora said there would be no agreement unless Molly Joan was a part of it. The longer they talked, the more obvious it became that this was nonnegotiable. He took the package or he took nothing. In the vocabulary of dealing, this was known as getting boxed.

Unable to curb himself, Sparn was already in the thick of a speech when his star and her lover waddled through the door in matching terry-cloth robes, redolent of sex.

"Go ahead, Mr. Sparn," Flora said hoarsely. "We don't mean to interrupt."

"Yeah. We woulda been here sooner if we'd known there was gonna be chow. Was there any slaw came with this?"

Sparn had prepared two or three sarcastic fusillades, but he swallowed them all. Much as he wanted to publicly chastise those two, his instincts told him now was not the time. There was bad blood flowing, he could tell, and the last thing he wanted to do was spill some of it.

"Okay, we've been talking about spark, or the lack of it. We've been talking about showing emotion and pumping that old adrenaline. You know a man once said that winning wasn't the most important thing, it was the only thing. But I wonder if that really covers it. Frankly, girls, we've got a winning team that's going broke, you hear what I'm saying? It doesn't matter a damn how many games you win if you don't pull the crowds. Is that so hard to understand?

Remember that you're entertainers out there, performers. Those routine plays have got to be more than routine and every game has to be fresh. Now everybody knows that Pete Sparn is not a finger-pointer. I'm not going to single anyone out. But I'll tell you this, when somebody gets a little lazy, a little complacent, well, these things can spread like a virus and infect the whole unit. It's all a question of attitude. Digging down for that extra burst of effort when you've told yourself there's nothing left. Because we all live and die together. I think of this team as a spiderweb, you know? Like many independent strands linked together in a strong, resilient, ummm . . . a strong, ummm, network that is, well . . ."

As Sparn floundered in the muck of this ill-chosen analogy, Tildy slithered between Wanda and That's-Mary to the front of the bed. She had heard enough.

"Pete, you don't know one single thing about what we do and that's for damn sure. We're right there with it day after day after day, and you buzz on out here from Jacksonville to tell us we don't put out? That shit won't float. We play tired and hurt and hungover, anywhere we can get a game. We play at youth camps, in cow pastures, on airplane runways. We play doubleheaders on sandlot fields full of stones and broken glass, and no lights when it starts to get dark so you can't see the ball till it's right up on you and meanwhile the catcher is trying to put his hand in your shorts. Then onto the bus and drive all night to the next date, try to put a few hours sleep together before we play again. A bunch of small-town hotshots who'll never hear the end of it if they get beat by women, and they're looking to tear our heads off. But, Pete, we play the game and we eat the dirt and that's all there is to it. So you take a look right here and tell me whether or not we put out."

Tildy lowered her jeans to reveal a large, ugly raspberry on the outside of her left thigh, souvenir of the slide into home.

"You can check this too while you're at it." That's-Mary thrust forward her leg and pointed to a swollen, purplish ankle.

Heidi displayed her dislocated thumb. Roxie Vasquez showed her bruised calf. And Wanda Watts, just recovering from a pulled hamstring, showed Sparn her middle finger.

Mutinous! Abominable! Sparn would have liked nothing better than to blister each and every one of them with a razor strop, lay on some bruises of his own, instill a little respect the way he used to do with Vinnie, but it was way too late for that. The bad blood he'd wanted to contain was now ankle deep. He would have to back off and make another rush; from a different direction this time.

"Of course you work hard, I don't question that. You have a lot to put up with, fair enough. Don't let's overreact." He sighed heavily and circled to his right, in the general direction of the corner where Flora and M.J. loitered impassively. "You've misunderstood my point. Or maybe I failed to put it in quite the right words."

"We heard you," Heidi said, heartened by the physical closeness of the others and by Tildy's cool palm behind her neck. "Plain as the teats on a sow."

Ignoring her, Sparn kept edging away. He pressed his fingertips together, trying to appear casual but deliberate. "What I'm trying to get across to you, it's not a physical thing. It's an emotional thing. It's not about moving from first to third on a single. It's about moving your audience, getting them excited and getting them involved. Moving them. Making them care."

Several sets of eyes rolled toward the ceiling. With leering ceremony, That's-Mary rolled two wads of a half-eaten chocolate cupcake and used them to plug her ears.

"Drama. Suspense. That's what's missing. Because . . . because we think we're unbeatable. Yes, that's it! Enterprise. Imagination. Emotions. Theatrics. Just as tangible as that welt on Tildy's leg. Let me tell you something. I review the statistics every day and you know what I see? I see dullness. That's right. I see scores like four, zero; five, zero; six, one. Now where the hell is the drama in that? Dull. Cut and dried."

Sparn entered Flora's corner as his speech reached its crescendo. He took her arm, the million-dollar arm, light and whippy, that could fire a fat, rubber-covered sphere at close to ninety miles an hour, and lifted it over his head.

"The greatest," he said solemnly. "Maybe the greatest ever. A young woman who has perfected her craft to such a fine degree that you and I, we can't even understand it. Another realm altogether." He let the arm drop and it bounced on Flora's hip as though she were asleep. "But how do people, ordinary people, feel about that kind of excellence? Think about it. If I announced that tomorrow afternoon at the Knights of Columbus Hall there would be an exhibition by the world's best diamond cutter, how many tickets do you suppose I would sell? Excellence has its drawbacks. It can really put people off." He laid his hand on Flora's cheek. "What you've got to do, honey, is let up just a little bit. Let those bozos on the other side score some runs once in a while."

She flicked away Sparn's damp saurian claw and gazed at him with contempt, as though he had asked her to prepare and consume a melted goat turd sandwich before a gathering of cub scouts. This arrogant, yammering little troll wanted her to intentionally and bloodlessly betray her talent, her sense of professionalism and her love for Molly Joan—because for Flora all these things were bound inextricably together. If it came down to that, she would much rather eat the sandwich.

There followed a long, uncomfortable pause, embroidered by the sound of M.J. chomping french fries. Finally, when Flora had it all worked out in her mind, she tightened the belt of her robe, walked halfway to the door, turned.

"See you at tomorrow's game, Mr. Sparn. Be there."

Carrying a large root beer in which the ice had melted, M.J. followed. Then, without a word or glance to one another, the Cougarettes stood and trooped out of the room past a thunderstruck Peter Sparn with the metered gait of a half-time band.

Sparn's face grew pink, as though he'd been slapped. When he had found his voice, he moved with such speed that Vinnie cringed as he came toward him.

"Jesus fucking Christ, boy. When are you going to learn how to control these girls?"

While his father raved on, Vinnie turned little by little to wax.

Tildy was summoned the next morning to a private breakfast with Sparn at the Magnolia Diner. They sat at a sun-soaked booth next to a window box of plastic ivy. It was after nine o'clock and they were the only customers in the place.

"What'll you have?"

"A large glass of water. Plenty of ice." Tildy adjusted her dark glasses.

"You can do better than that. Have a little something with me, I hate to eat alone."

"I don't like breakfast, I never have."

"You gotta eat to live. Were you always this scrawny?"

"More or less."

Sparn ordered pork chops, eggs and grits. He did tricks with the flatware, flirted with the waitress and generally comported himself like a jolly Uncle Ned. Tildy had known the man for some years and had found little in him to admire. But he had a certain resilience.

28

"So you girls partied pretty late last night, huh? You all gonna turn into zombies?"

"Coffeyville, two o'clock. We'll be ready."

Counting under his breath, Sparn dumped four spoonfuls of sugar into his coffee. "You sure you won't have something with me? I suppose you're sick to here with this diner food."

"It's not so bad. I just always ask for extra gravy."

Sparn slid abruptly forward and pressed her hand. "Where is your life now, Tildy? Are you happy with it?"

Tildy was so surprised she gave a straight answer. "I don't know."

Sparn was making her nervous. Definitely. He has this way of ambushing people, she thought; and recalled an afternoon they'd spent together a few years ago, the day he'd asked her to become a Cougarette.

She was working for Sparn on the topless go-go circuit at the time, and making a fair piece of change. Bare tits were still a big item back then and a bar owner could get five or six bucks for a pitcher of beer from anyone who wanted to see them in action. Tildy was a small, lean, woman, in marked contrast to most of the pneumatic dollies she worked with, but she moved like a snake and the rubes would line up to stuff tips in her G-string. Older men in particular seemed to dig her girl-child body. She was billed as the Ragin' Cajun, Sparn's idea. Tildy was one of his favorites.

He called her one Sunday and invited her to a cruise party on the Saint John's River. They were already out in the channel by the time Tildy discovered they were the only two people aboard the *Big Peter*.

"Look, Pete, if this is one of those fuck-or-swim deals, I'm not doing either one."

Sparn was deeply offended. A soft breeze, sun on the water and two friends sitting down for some pleasant conversation. Where was the harm in that?

"I'm not sure I can buy that."

"But I like talking to you, kid. You got smarts. I'm still trying to figure you out." He poured her a pineapple daiquiri. "Yeah, Tildy Soileau is a very strange item, you know that."

"I've heard it before, if that's what you mean."

"You know, you're the only girl I ever sent out didn't try a little hooking on the side. Hell, you're the only one still using pasties."

"What can I tell you, Pete. It's the way I was brought up."

"No kidding? How'd you get in this business anyway?"

"Just luck."

They anchored in calm water off of Fort Caroline and Sparn went swimming. He did the breaststroke and kept his hat on. Then, with fresh daiquiris, they perched astern on swivel chairs and discussed boating safety, the best places to eat crab and the case of a local attorney on trial for murdering his wife with a nine-iron. Tildy began to relax after Sparn applied suntan oil to himself without asking for help. It was after turkey salad sandwiches and another daiquiri that Pete sprang the ambush.

"You ever play baseball when you were a kid?"

"Who remembers?"

Sparn then ran down the entire Cougarettes scheme to her, talking so fast and excitedly that he spilled his drink. He scurried inside, returned with a sketch pad and showed her the green and gold uniforms he'd designed.

"You're all fired up over this, aren't you, Pete?"

"Aren't you?"

"Not really."

"Did I forget to mention that you're going to be my shortstop?"

"Get out of here. I can't play baseball. I don't even know who won the World Series last year."

"Softball. It's softball. And you'll pick it up real fast, I know you will. First practice is next week."

"Sorry. I've got a gig in Daytona Beach next week. Jerry's Gondola, remember?"

"I canceled it."

There was an argument about that. Tildy threw half a dozen cocktail glasses overboard. But eventually her energy was exhausted and she stood by the mahogany railing, spitting into the water.

"Come on, it's crazy to fight. What a beautiful day this is. Let's fish a little."

Sparn handed her a rod fitted with a large saltwater reel. She looked at it for a moment, then handed it back to him.

"You fish, Pete. I'll cut bait."

Tildy chewed ice and looked out the window to avoid watching Sparn eat. A little boy in the parking lot was writing on the side of someone's car with a piece of charcoal. The car had two flat tires and a blotch of body putty near the door. She knocked on the glass and waved to him, but he went on writing.

When Sparn had picked over the bones, sopped up the last of the grits and egg yolk, he loosened his belt and reached for a toothpick.

"More water?"

"I'm fine."

"Not much to say for yourself this morning. Something bothering you?"

Tildy rolled the icy glass across her forehead. "Just a little drumming behind the eyes."

"I don't know. Seems to me like everybody's cranky and depressed. What is it—all you girls on the rag at once?"

"We're tired, wasted. That's all."

"I don't know. The team is flat as hell. They're bitching, they're dragging their feet. I thought you might know something that's going on. Sometimes—this is going to sound strange, but sometimes I wake up at night with a feeling like the whole operation is coming apart and I don't even know who to blame. You've been around since the start, Tildy. What do you think I should do?"

"You want my advice?"

Sparn nodded earnestly.

"Go home."

On the evidence, Coffeyville was a town with either tremendous civic pride or nothing else to do. An SRO mob had asssembled to cheer and stomp for their team, eight members of the Rotary Club and someone's teenage son. The town supervisor was on hand distributing free ball-point pens advertising his aluminum siding business and his sister had brought her kindergarten class, complete with construction paper name tags. A man in a derby and sleeve garters blew cavalry charges on a dented bugle. A squad of young housewives paraded with homemade signs.

Vinnie was selling an awful lot of beer. Every few minutes a roving Sparn, too worked up to sit still, stopped to pound him on the back or tousle his hair. It was starting to look as though they would be able to clear the entire week's nut off this one show; he was once again Big Pete, the jaunty sportsman, and could dismiss as illusory the image that had possessed him only a few hours earlier, of his Cougarettes sinking into chaos and eventual bankruptcy. On his head at a debonair angle was the gold cap with the big green C.

Although the Cougarettes, powered by two doubles from M.J. in the cleanup spot, were leading 3–0, and the Rotarians had managed but two harmless singles, the Coffeyville crowd maintained its feverish noise level. They were not too partisan, however, to applaud the outrageous play Tildy made to end the sixth inning, a diving stab behind the bag and a snap throw from one knee that beat the runner by a step and a half. But the Coffeyville folks refused to cave in. When they went down in the eighth on two strikeouts and an infield pop-up and the bugle man started to play taps, a fat lady sitting behind him knocked off his derby. Tildy got on on an error in the top of the ninth, stole second and then third on successive pitches. Sparn lit up a victory cigar and Heidi hit a line drive right at the third baseman to end it.

They were all on their feet for the home ninth, clapping rhythmically and whistling. They stayed there when Flora walked the leadoff man on four pitches, then came inside on the next batter and plunked him in the ribs. M.J. called time and went to the mound for a conference. Tildy saw Flora slowly shake her head and point to herself. Flora's next delivery sailed over everyone's heads and the runners advanced.

Ben Salem peeled off his mask and looked at the stands for guidance, but Sparn was dreamily blowing smoke rings and stroking the bill of his cap. The next two weren't even close and there was no way he could call them strikes. The crowd noise remained at a roar as Flora cut the heart of the plate twice for a three–two count. Then she bounced one in the dirt to load the bases. And suddenly Tildy realized what was going to happen.

Coming up next was the kid, who had not had so much as a loud foul off Flora all day long. The other girls slapped their gloves and yelled encouragement, barely audible against the swelling clamor of Coffeyville.

"On the money, baby, on the money."

"Forget it, batter. School's out."

"You git him, big F. Way to shoot, way to chuck."

But Tildy stood with arms loose at her sides, watching, waiting.

The kid was scared, knew he was going to hit into a double play. He plucked at his uniform, spat on his hands, anything to buy a little time. Finally he stepped in. Flora served him a big, juicy lollipop and he slammed it over the fence to end the game.

With a thin smile on her lips and a knot in her chest like a cold hunk of quartz, Flora jogged over and found Sparn pallid and wide-eyed among the jubilant yokels.

"I tried to let up for you, Mr. Sparn," she said. "Was it dramatic enough?"

Fighting his way out of the crush, Sparn stumbled dizzily to the shelter of an oak tree and deposited his breakfast all over its roots.

One hour later he installed Ben Salem as the Cougarettes' new manager.

Then he went home.

3

For the first time in several days, sunlight came blaring through the open blinds, turning everything a rancid yellow, heating a broth of bad smells. Inmates were scattered about the dayroom, some on folding chairs, some on the floor, trying to digest their breakfast of creamed hamburger on toast. They were for the most part too heavily medicated to focus on the television. An interview show was on; a woman was discussing her book on healing through self-hypnosis.

A skinny kid with bruised lips, a new arrival taking only Tofranil, pointed at the blue screen. "Been in a trance all my life, dolly. That's what got me in here."

Oodles, who had been committed by his daughter over the Christmas holidays, was nodded out in his chair. Skeeziks, who had been in the longest, so rumor had it, nibbled a jujube of earwax. His skin was grayish-yellow against the green hospital gown. He sat at attention, arms held rigid in front of him; every few seconds his tongue, chalky and cracked, slithered out in a fly-catcher movement. Skeeziks was exhibiting symptoms of tardive dyskinesia, a common side effect of a prolonged diet of tranquilizers from the phenothiazine group. Boots Malone, a two-year man, was encountering the same syndrome. He stood facing the wall, drenched in sweat, his hands shaking with palsy.

"Bootsie's not looking too good today," said Harris, lighting one cigarette from the end of another. He liked to smoke his entire ration before lunch, then beg the rest of the day.

"No wonder," said Mikie. Mikie weighed 230 pounds and had lost most of his hair by age twenty-eight. "I saw at breakfast. They give him two of those orange bombers, you know. That's almost half a gram."

"Half a gram? Oh, my Lord." Harris tapped ashes onto the back of his hand, smeared them into the shape of a cross. "They're gonna make an eggplant out of him."

"Don't be an eggplant, Boots." Mikie shouted across the room.

Waldo, one of the night attendants, stood in the doorway. He had just finished counting the sharps, making an inventory of every razor, scissors and kitchen utensil on the ward before clocking out.

"That's right, Bootsie. Spit the shit out if you have to." Emboldened by his friend, Harris was shouting too.

Why are these people alert? Waldo asked himself. There is no reason for them to be alert. "Quiet. This is a quiet period."

"Fuck you," Mikie whispered.

"What was that?" Waldo came forward fingering the striped top of an athletic sock that dangled from his hip pocket. Everyone knew there was a cake of laundry soap inside that sock—when Waldo hit you, it was just like a blackjack.

"I didn't say nothing. Just watching teevee here."

"Oh, really?"

"Yeah, we were talking about the broad on the teevee show, that's all." Harris shrugged. "That's all."

"No, you were shouting. You were disrupting. I'm going to have to separate you."

"We'll be good," Mikie said, starting to panic.

"Let's go, asshole."

"No, no. I wanna be with my friend." Waldo yanked Mikie's arm. "Nonono." Harris looked at the linoleum as Mikie and his chair were dragged into the hall. He broke the filter off his next cigarette. Outside Waldo got some bandages out of his jacket and started to tie Mikie's ankles to the chair.

Harris could hear Mikie starting to cry. He got the fresh smoke going and looked around. "Jesus," he said very quietly. Then to himself: Mikie got hijacked out of here and I'm the only one that noticed.

At a low table at the opposite end of the dayroom, another inmate was having an informal interview with his therapist. The inmate had a ten-day growth of beard and thick dark hair that had not been washed in days. He sucked his teeth. The therapist rolled a freshly sharpened pencil between his palms. DR. RECHETTE said his black plastic name tag. "Informal" meant that he didn't take notes.

"Do you want to tell me about yesterday?"

"The thing with Lightbulb Head?"

Rechette sighed gently. "Let's refer to her as Nurse Amato, shall we?"

"Whatever. I didn't make up that name, you know. . . . Okay. Amato and the others are locked in the nurses' station. No scoop there. They're always in there playing cribbage. Sometimes they only come out to get water for the coffee machine."

"No editorials, Jim."

"Didn't I ask you not to call me that?"

"Christo. If that makes you feel more comfortable."

"Right. There's this new admission, anyway. Kid's only been here maybe a week. Yesterday morning he gets this savage migraine attack, doubled over and his face all white. He's got a history of these things, real gut benders. Yes, Marty, I saw it in his file and don't tell me it's against the rules. . . . You want to hear the story, you can't keep jumping in. So . . . The kid is really going through it, but I'm cool. I figure before too long somebody will come out and give him a needle. That's what they're here for, right? But now the kid's wrapped around himself down on the floor, bellowing. I walk over to the station and I suggest—maybe I raised my voice a little—I suggest Amato might want to investigate. Maybe I took a couple of swings at the door, who remembers? Well, Amato wanders out and she's rubbing her eyes like we were dragging her away from a nap. She says, 'Larry is being punished. He's been spoiled by too much easy access to medication and now he has to earn back his privileges.' I got a little hot at that point. Somebody got me in a hammerlock. They wanted to put me in a body bandage, but I talked them out of it."

Rechette shook his head forlornly, dug a thumbnail into the spotless pink eraser at the end of his pencil. "Sometimes you make me want to retire."

Christo reached across the table, jiggled a cigarette out of Rechette's half-empty pack, and said, "How do you feel about that?"

"You think you did something noble, I'm sure, but it was moronic." Rechette narrowed his eyes. "How do you suppose this is going to look when it comes time for your review? I'm greasing all kinds of rails to get you released and you pull a stunt like this. Don't you want to get out of here?"

"More and more."

"Then make yourself invisible for the next ten days. Fortunately

Amato is being transferred to another facility next month so I can probably ease you through. You haven't blown it yet, but don't try again." Rechette stood, smoothed his silk necktie, buttoned his herringbone jacket. He indicated the cigarette pack with a twitch of the head. "You can keep those."

Christo watched him leave: that side-to-side cowpoke walk. He had to admire the way in which Dr. Martin Rechette grabbed life by the balls. The man was not board certified. He was a former urologist practicing psychiatry for the state. He had published an article in the *Journal of Mental Sciences*. He was in a lofty tax bracket. He was also the softest touch Christo had ever come across in thirty years of looking.

Later that day, Christo came upon Inocencia Amato in the corridor. She was bent over the drinking fountain; a hank of black hair had escaped from the pinnings of her cap and hung down past one eye. He crept up behind her and she whirled at the touch of his leg, her clawlike hands, with their long peach-enameled nails, prepared to strike.

"Hiya, Nurse Amato. Is it true that back in the Philippines you eat dog? Beat them to death with bamboo poles to tenderize the meat?"

"Yes." She dried her hands on the front of her skirt.

"I bet puppies are the best."

Amato batted at her loose hair. "You, sir, are wasting the time of everyone in this hospital."

"Well, don't get too excited," Christo said. And when she had disappeared: "You might burn out your tungsten filament."

It was in a cramped second-floor office that Christo's final discharge interview took place. From somewhere nearby came the steady rumble of machinery. Christo adopted a submissive posture in a molded plastic chair from which he could view the parking lot through partially drawn curtains, could be tantalized by the mobility of others: relatives shuffling confusedly across the asphalt having been rebuked, perhaps not even recognized; dishwashers and orderlies still in uniform and hurrying to compact cars that would take them on lunch-hour errands to the bank, the dry cleaner's; the doctors, distinguished Men of Science in British raincoats, padding along a strip of newly replanted grass to their reserved parking spaces as though prowling a parade ground at dawn, some new wrinkle in the elaboration of chemical warfare pricking the conscience.

37

As the last person entered and the door clicked shut behind him, Christo thought of teevee dramas in which the desperate hero dives through a cellophane window, lands nimbly, rolling to his feet, and races untouched into the commercial break. But such crude tactics were not his style. He was fully prepared to smarm his way out.

His panel of inquisitors consisted of Rechette; Monica Fortgang, head of nursing; Dr. Mool Dopesh, a Pakistani behaviorist (who in the last twelve months had received a color television set and a microwave oven from a major pharmaceutical manufacturer in exchange for running evaluation tests of their new drugs on fifty inmates); and the clinic director, an abrasively voluble man in a Santa Claus beard who was seated at a pressed steel desk. The others were bunched in on either side.

Rechette made some preliminary remarks, emphasizing Mr. Christo's sincere desire to remake himself in therapy and the noteworthy progress he had achieved in dealing with such matters as flattened affect, reactive hostility and nihilist delusions.

Dr. Dopesh muttered to himself as he thumbed through the contents of a loose-leaf binder, boosting his volume to mention the patient's original court-ordered detention after a trial on two counts of forgery.

"I was never convicted on that charge," Christo said, regretting the pinch of belligerence in his voice. "And I paid back the money, too."

"Really, Mool, I think that's yesterday's papers," Rechette said hurriedly.

"What papers?" Dopesh was confused, fearful that some bundle of charts, some crucial file, had eluded him.

"A figure of speech, Mool. But I think after six months with us, Mr. Christo is sufficiently mindful of the consequences of antisocial behavior that I don't foresee any repetition."

The director brought a Styrofoam cup to his whisker-hemmed mouth and took little sucking sips of black tea. "Certainly our main concern should be conduct inside the walls of this institution. I'm wondering about this dust-up with Miss Amato two weeks ago."

"Just one of a series," said Monica Fortgang in her wind-up Victrola voice. "Patient has continually shown a marked resentment toward authority, an unwillingness to cooperate and follow orders. He has been a disruptive force on the ward, and frankly I'm far from convinced that there's been the slightest forward movement since he arrived."

Christo felt that the floor was a hydraulic lift pushing him immutably toward the ceiling where, amid the crunch of bone and geysers of blood, he would be mashed against the twin eggbox light fixtures, neatly cube-steaked and ready for boiling. He took a deep breath.

"I deeply regret that incident. Since then I have had an opportunity to apologize personally to Nurse Amato. I've come to realize that however severe the other patient's pain might have been, however much I might have felt that he was being denied the proper attention, it was wrong of me to interfere with staff since they know best how to deal with each patient on an individual basis. I understand now that I was improperly assigning to myself responsibilities I wasn't either capable or eligible to handle."

Monica Fortgang broke the paperclip she had been bending while she relived a year-old incident in which Rechette had accused her, in front of three members of the janitorial staff, of administering a near-fatal dose of Amytal to one of his favorite patients. "Very nice, Marty," she hissed through glistening choppers. "Did you type that up for him?"

"I might point out, Monica, that I have been at this hospital considerably longer than you have. And any intimation that I am attempting to abet Mr. Christo in hoodwinking this committee is totally out of line and an insult to me professionally."

"I'm sure you're quite thorough and expert when it comes to bladder obstructions or cystitis, but this . . . ."

"I fail to see how Monica expects to make a judgement on this case when she is so clearly biased."

"Enough," said the director, striking the desk top with an invisible gavel. "I'd hate to give patient the impression that the review process is in any way a matter of who your friends are."

Dopesh pursed his lips as though he were about to kiss something. "Yes, we are all of integrity here."

"Thank you, Mool." The director, a habitual fisherman who tied his own flies, who had made many a turn with waxed thread around the shanks of Tufted Mites and Red Skimmers, wound the string twice around his tea bag and squeezed out tannic acid. "What about return to the community? Have any arrangements been made?"

Rechette launched into excited accolades for Synergy, a local halfway house and rehab program that had recently secured a sizable grant from Washington, but the director cut him off.

"I think you've said enough already, Marty."

Rechette scanned his face for traces of suspicion or censure—

there was little precedent for his going to bat for a patient in this way—but the director's eyes were as neutral as a snapshot of topsoil.

"I would prefer to hear what patient has to say on this subject."

Moistening his lips, Christo leaned forward in his chair and played straight to the director. "I'd have to say that from what I've heard, I'm pretty enthusiastic about the Synergy program. They stress a very supportive group environment there and I know I'm going to need a lot of help and reinforcement in the first couple of months. Another thing I like is that they have a strong vocational emphasis, and to get through to those final stages of recovery, I'll need a steady, regimented work situation. Something I have to show up for every day, you know, something repetitive. I was thinking possibly about an electronics factory. I used to have a real flair for circuit diagrams in high school. Yeah, basically my goal is to make my life as, you know, as humdrum as possible." He cracked his mouth and tipped his head bashfully to one side.

Bingo. The director was smiling and twirling the edges of his beard.

Christo thought: I'm in, three to one. Which means I'm out.

And: These people are defenseless. If I waited six months to take them, maybe I *am* crazy.

Eighteen hours after his official release, Christo appeared at Rechette's suburban chalet with all his personal effects in a canvas sea bag. These included a memento from Harris (a cigarette lighter "which once belonged to Eddie Fisher"); two clip-on black bow ties; a personally annotated road atlas; his diploma from a mail-order locksmithing school; and a large baggie of blue Valiums. They were a kind of long-term going-away present from Dennis, the social worker upon whom Christo had prevailed to steal in installments over the last couple of months. Dennis wasn't a total loser. He just needed friends. His mother had died over the summer in a boating accident on a private lake outside Rome.

Rechette answered the bell in a velour pullover, designer denims and no shoes. "You never called."

"I couldn't think of anything to say. Going to invite me in?"

Rechette grabbed the sea bag and stepped back. "I was starting to think you might not show."

"I'm not a welsher. At least I try not to be."

Christo followed along to the living room. The carpeting felt like marshmallow. The decorating theme was early-to-mid 70s men's

40

magazine: German stereo components, half-ton glass coffee table, African bronzes and carved wooden masks. He settled into a leather-upholstered sofa and took peanuts out of one dish and a cigarette out of another.

"Real nice layout, as they say in the crime films."

"You look tired. Where have you been?"

"Nowhere. Out and around."

A tingle moved up Rechette's leg, spread an insistent puddle of heat around his hips. He ran his eyes over Christo's hooded face, the round, full arms capable of delivering blows with nonchalance, solidly wedged knuckles twisting against bone.

"Something to drink?"

"Whatever you've got."

Rechette poured brandy from an apothecary jar and brought the glass over on tiptoe, bending as he relinquished it to peer down Christo's shirt.

"You're sleek as an otter."

Christo didn't like the way Rechette was behaving in his home ballpark, all smug in his sportsclothes. His thinning brown hair was wet-combed over his forehead in shaggy Brutus bangs and he gave off a mossy vapor of expensive cologne.

Then, for a moment, he was back in character. "If you're going to put that down on the sofa, please use a coaster."

"Good liquor," Christo said. "The first good liquor I've had in six months."

Rechette sniffed his own glass. "Didn't Waldo sell to you?"

"Garbage. Grapefruit wine, stuff like that."

"There never was anybody on the ward quite like you." Rechette massaged the flesh over his heart. "You were a bloody master."

"And you're a swell host, Marty."

"Come. Get yourself a refill and follow me."

Sliding down a narrow hallway in near darkness, Rechette led him to an airless corner room in the back of the house, with a paint-spattered floor and exposed wiring. Burlap was nailed over the windows. A mattress and corduroy pillows were against one particle-board wall. From a hatrack overhead dangled coils of nylon rope, dog leashes of various lengths, a hot water bottle. Resting on two packing crates in the middle of the floor was a movie projector aimed at a white sheet.

"This must be the maid's room," Christo said.

The soles of Rechette's feet made a swampy noise peeling up

from the floor as he moved to the projector and threaded an 8mm reel. Christo finished his brandy with one stiff-armed toss. It was showtime.

Images fluttered aquatically over the uneven surface of the sheet. A garage. A crew-cut boy with cream-of-wheat skin chained to a grease rack. He was being flogged by a one-eared black man in a studded leather vest and matching jockstrap. Crew-cut bent over. A socket wrench handle dipped in motor oil was inserted into his rectum. Christo listened to the whirr of the tiny fan cooling the projector lamp, to the steady click-click-click of taut celluloid passing over sprockets; and Rechette fell to his knees and, clumsily, urgently, tendons distended at his neck, performed on him an act of oral tribute.

Rechette staggered out to the bathroom to mop up the curds he had squirted inside his pants. For a moment he was inundated with an urge to flee, to break away from the sadly trite cycle of his cravings. He flushed his burning eyes with cold water. When he came back, he looked ten years older than when he'd left.

"King hell, Marty. You look like you need a doctor." Christo had not moved, sat oozing out of his open fly, knees drawn up, head tilted back against the wall.

"Tell me what you see," Rechette croaked, tugging at his belt loops.

"I had a cousin back home who was a cheerleader," Christo adlibbed. "She was just like a painting in her pleated skirt and the little sneakers with the pompom socks. Sweet kid, a bit erratic maybe, but then she only really came to life during football season. Used to practice her cheers in the middle of the night: 'Muscle is muscle and bone is bone, come on, Southern, push it into the zone.' Senior year was very tough on her. Kind of the last waltz, you know? On the bus coming back from the last away game, a six to three win over Collard Polytechnic in a driving rain, she blew the entire first string, offense and defense, and a few of the subs as well. They had to take her to the hospital and pump her stomach."

Rechette had come toward him on hands and knees and was now rubbing his cheek against the instep of Christo's left shoe. Christo sighed, a long, tired sigh with a whistle at the end, and clanked the rim of the empty glass on his teeth.

"Night of the long jives," he said to no one in particular.

For as long as he could, Christo camped out at the Rechette home, sitting tight and fattening himself up. He had his own room with a door that locked from the inside and nothing to do but sleep, eat and work on his juggling. He needed time to depressurize before going back on the game. Casually he drifted through the role of houseboy, with its code of laconic passivity, but it was Rechette who did all the chores, cooking the meals, washing the clothes, emptying the ashtrays. The doctor's desire to serve was unceasing. So were his advances, but he seemed to bask in placid rejections, to relish the indifference showered upon him.

Christo was, however, willing to fulfill his need for mental stimulation and so invented a compliant and correlative past, spinning out anecdotes of a career as a male hustler in Dallas and New Orleans. Gulping vodka and water, Rechette would intersperse hints and clues in a husky drawl—his approximation of black-mirrored boudoir enticement, of the silver screen lovelies from thirty years ago—guiding these vignettes toward his own lust points. The poetry of pain and malevolence. When the heat had risen irreparably and Rechette was knee-deep in the lava of his mind, he would scuttle across the room and nuzzle Christo's groin like a bloodhound. Christo might permit a few minutes agitation of his flaccid penis before shoving him away.

"You just don't do anything for me," he would say, then open a magazine or fix himself a load of pasta with grated cheese.

Ever ready to expand his powers of falsification, Christo withdrew to his room at night to pore over psychiatric bulletins, drug company monographs and the proceedings of various clinical symposia. Additionally, he canvassed the several periodicals to which Rechette subscribed concerning gourmet wine and food. It was debatable to what future use a knowledge of Breton cheeses or the proper technique for poaching quenelles might be put, but Christo did not like to impose limits on his creativity.

Often, Rechette would interrupt these study sessions by scratching at the locked door and begging for attention.

"I need to talk to you."

"Go ahead. I can hear you."

They would go back and forth for a few minutes until Christo, usually clad only in hospital pyjama tops, opened up, blocking the doorway with his body, and threatened Rechette with various types of bodily harm.

"How are you going to explain all those cuts and bruises to Monica Fortgang? She'll want to know."

Cowering in his food-stained kimono, Rechette delightedly received a kick in the shin or a light knock to the ribs, and then a kiss on the forehead before Christo shooed him off to bed.

The performance of these various daily rituals required concentration and an appetite for the dismal. It was beginning to wear Christo down, and on the evening that Rechette, nude and wearing a choke chain, insisted on having his dinner from a doggie bowl on the floor, he determined that things had reached the toxic level and it was time to cut out.

The following morning Christo served his host a cup of breakfast cocoa in which two hundred milligrams of Seconal had been dissolved. Within twenty minutes Rechette was snoring rhythmically on the sofa, arms wrapped around his briefcase. Christo moved easily, taking his time and thinking things through. He filled a suitcase with clothes from Rechette's custom tailor, a former newspaper editor from South Korea. The shirts and jackets were a little tight across the shoulders, a bit short in the sleeves, but the fabrics were elegant and no telling when he might need a quick front. The kind you could slip into in a gas station toilet. From the upstairs study he took samples of a new mood elevator from Smith-Kline, some stationery and prescription pads. There was a small amount of cash in the bedroom and a collection of jewelry as worthless as it was tasteless. He stripped Rechette's wallet of credit cards and driver's license. Downstairs the doctor slept deeply, a thin band of saliva trailing out one corner of his mouth. Christo wrapped the television set in a blanket and carried it out to the car. Finally, as a trophy, he grabbed the fiercest of the African masks, pointed, deep-set eye slits and a gaping mouth bristling with nail-head teeth.

The keys to Rechette's Fiat were where they always were, dangling from a cup hook by the back door. Christo used one of the magnetized *Peanuts* figures to affix a note to the refrigerator door:

leaving tonite for sao paolo   don't wait up   love   C

It took Christo more than one hour to find the place he was looking for, a place he'd heard about from a grizzled old junkie on the ward. The bastard could barely focus his eyes, but he'd been a hard knocker on the street and he knew the city right down to the ground. The place was on a street almost totally abandoned; the only other building that didn't have sheet metal over the windows was a chop suey joint about six doors down. Christo circled twice, parked around the corner and walked back. The green awning was full of holes. Behind steel grates padlocked over the display windows, on step shelving covered in pus-yellow crepe paper, was a jumble of merchandise: plastic animals, dart games, flashlights, party hats, a pile of beer trays stamped with the logo of the Cleveland Cavaliers. A buzzer went off and Christo pushed open the door. It was dark inside, with more of the same. Cases of men's cologne, torn boxes crammed with stockings and pantyhose shoved against the glass counters; crap stacked, stuffed and spilled everywhere so that it was virtually impossible to move. Hovering in the back room near some pipe racks of ladies' sportswear was a tired-eyed fatso with a head full of pomade and a cheek full of tobacco. This would be Keds, the man to see.

Christo nodded, picked up a traveling alarm clock. "How much you getting for these?"

Keds spat in a coffee can between his feet. "You want it?"

Christo shrugged and leaned across the counter. "Nah, I got nothing to get up for."

"If you want something, you want something, but there's no browsing in here."

"So you're Keds, huh?"

"So what?"

"So I heard about you. I talked to a guy."

Keds shifted his wad to the other cheek. "There's lots of places you can talk to a guy. This ain't one of 'em."

"The guy had nice things to say about you, Keds. He really built you up."

"A guy says nice things about me. So I could pour that on cornflakes or something?"

Christo kicked impatiently at a mound of plastic canteens that was slowly collapsing around his ankles. "Look, let's cut through the bullshit. This guy I talked to says you're an honest fence, the squarest in town. You want to do some business or not?"

Keds took a half-step forward and shot a glistening brown gobbet onto the counter less than an inch from Christo's elbow. "Take a walk, kid." And he disappeared into the shadows of the back room.

"Okay, okay," Christo said. "Billy Gaines, the smack head. He was the one who recommended you." Silence. "Billy Gaines—come on, little guy with the hornrims, used to hang out with you at a tavern called Peck Miller's." Still nothing. "Said one night you busted a guy's jaw on the edge of the bar when he tried to unplug the juke box on your quarter."

Keds lumbered into view shaking his head. "You got no fuckin' manners, you know that, kid? No fuckin' manners at all. Now let's see what you got."

As it turned out, Keds was everything Billy Gaines had said. He didn't haggle and gave fair value. Christo even sold him some tools he'd found in the trunk of the Fiat.

His next stop was a pizza shop two blocks south of Aviation Trades High School. There he had a small pie with mushrooms and extra cheese and, out by the dumpster in the parking lot, turned over the Valiums to a grape-eyed fat boy in exchange for sixty-three dollars cash and an underwater watch.

Two hours later, Christo was over the state line. By early evening he had checked into a motor lodge just off the highway. He took a long, steamy shower and stretched out. It felt good to be back on the road, back on the upstroke, but not that good. It had been a grueling day and hospital memories kept tumbling around in his head. He gave up and went for the caffeine. The "complimentary" coffee came out of its foil packet looking like river silt, so he left the empty glass pot on the hot plate until it cracked.

He napped in his clothes until midnight, then placed a call to a comrade in New York.

"Pierce? That you, Pierce . . . ? Turn down the music, why don't you. Yeah, it's Christo."

"Hey, jazzbo, where have you been?"

"Out of action. I got fucked up behind some bad checks, ended up doing six months in the bughouse."

"Bad checks, huh? When are you going to get off the nickel-and-dime treadmill?"

"I don't know, maybe it's in my genes. You got something better for me?"

"You know I just might. Jesus, almost a year I don't hear from you. But it's great you're out in the breeze again. Listen, listen, what kind of line are you on?"

"Motel phone."

"Going through a switchboard?"

"Yeah, but come on, Pierce."

"Go find a pay phone and call me back."

"I really don't feel much like moving."

"So call collect. I mean who just got out, you or me? . . . Oh yeah, bring a pencil and paper."

So Christo laced up his sneakers, promoted writing materials from the night clerk and trudged up the road to an all-night grocery. He enjoyed a late supper—bar-b-q potato chips, two pralines and a bottle of orange soda—inside the phone booth, watching two girls in curlers walk back and forth under the streetlamp waiting for someone to bother them. He lit a postprandial cigarette and dialed.

"I'm back."

"So you are. Think you might want to drive down to Florida and make a pickup for me? The usual percentage. But I can't front you anything, have to be C.O.D."

"I'm right there."

"Fabulous, fabulous. Things have been a bit warm up here, but down in Miami it is really jagged. Street dudes walking into the Sponge Divers National Bank with suitcases full of money. People being blown away in French restaurants. Some of the wheels down there, so I hear, are having their homes electronically scanned for taps, once a week. . . . Anyway, we're channeling through the west coast these days. Naples, Fort Meyers. . . . Get out your pencil and I'll dictate a map."

4

When the tour swung down into Louisiana, Tildy decided it was time to take a few days off and visit her father in Ville Platte. It had been over a year since she'd seen Lucien and he was home from the hospital now. The doctors had thrown in the towel. Nothing could be done to moderate the progress of his disease. Six months at the very outside, they said, but they'd been wrong before. Still, the woman who was looking after him had written twice, hinting strongly that Tildy ought not put the trip off very much longer.

There was, as well, an even more immediate inducement for her to steal away: trouble on the job. Since the debacle in Coffeyville, the Cougarettes had dropped two more games, as many as they'd lost all last season. There had been a fight on the team bus and Wanda now wore a splint on her left hand. Heidi was guzzling her ulcer medicine between innings and threatening to go back to Virginia Beach and get married. That's-Mary was juiced most of the time. Two games ago she had stood with arms folded in foul territory behind first base and watched three consecutive relay throws whiz by. Vinnie, who was fast becoming eligible for the sulker's World Series, crouching off by himself with a stack of detective magazines, was sent in to replace her. On his first chance, he failed to get down on a short hop and was struck in the groin.

When Tildy went to Ben Salem to ask his permission to leave, he consented without argument.

"Sure. Take a whole week if you want. I only wish I was going with you."

"You won't mind fielding eight players for a few days?"

"What the hell difference would it make? Whole thing's turning into a comedy act anyway."

It took Tildy less than five minutes to pack her bag.

The night man at the car rental agency wore a wife-swapper mustache and high-heeled boots that zipped up the side. Spreading his hands on the counter, he confessed that he had left drafting school for this job because he liked the one-to-one contact.

"I'm a people person," he said.

"And I think you're overworked."

He led Tildy by the elbow to a dark green Pinto and flung open both doors. "See what you think. I personally vacuumed out the interior. On my dinner break."

Across the passenger seat and along the console were scaly brown spots which resembled dried blood. But Tildy wrote it off. Just my morbid state of mind, she concluded.

It was late by the time she started south, a profusion of semis on the road making up time. She picked up a hitchhiker a little after one A.M., a soldier heading for his brother-in-law's place on a three-day pass. Thoroughly unnerved at catching a ride with a lone woman, his first ever, he hunched so far forward that his chin brushed the dashboard, mumbling thanks again and again. When Tildy handed him her smokes, asking him to light one for her, his suddenly unresponsive fingers kept tearing sulphur heads against the matchbook staple. His ears were prominent under a lawnmower service haircut and Tildy was positive she saw them turning pink in the gleam of passing headlights.

"They running you pretty ragged at boot camp?"

"They surely are. Yes, ma'am."

"'Right left right. Right left right.' Some kind of life, huh?" Smoke streamed from her nostrils as she turned to face him. "Bet you're glad to get out of there, even for a couple of days."

"S'pose so. But it ain't so bad, not really. They're teachin' me a skill. Gonna be a certified radar technician when I get out."

He looked so familiar, like the boys she used to dance for in the enlisted men's clubs Sparn pitched her to ("Okay, so she's not exactly stacked, but you know what they say: It's not the meat, it's the motion") when he first took her on.

She could remember pumping her hips, flashing her sequined pasties at those avid faces. She could remember their heavy breathing, invariable as a parade cadence. And the way they'd haunt her dressing room afterward, certain that someone who displayed her body for a living would be more than happy to open her arms (and legs) to a fighting man. "You're awful pretty. You know they'll be shippin' me to Nam next week." Tildy tried to be patient with them. She understood how truly innocent they were, how sex was to them a dark and uncharted jungle land, that they were the expeditionary force, full of arrogance and lies about the natives, without a knowledge of the language, or the support of the bigwigs who had sent them.

Tildy swerved to avoid an animal carcass in the road. "Did you enlist or were you drafted?"

"I signed up all right, but it weren't so much my own idea. It was my guidance counselor, she said I'd be wastin' my time in college. Nice lady. She even gimme a ride to the recruiter office."

Two hours later they stopped at his exit ramp. Tildy placed a soft, dry kiss on his cheek and pushed him out the door.

"Watch out for yourself, Harmon. And don't you be taking any more rides with women."

She checked the rearview mirror as she pulled out. There he stood in the liquid glow of a mercury lamp, barrack bunk fantasies unfulfilled, staring pitifully after her.

Tildy reached Ville Platte just after sunrise, the sky smeared with yellow clouds the color of old salve. She cruised back and forth on half-familiar streets, unable to summon up any sensation of nostalgia. This was a place she'd been before, a place where she had passed some time, but it was not home. Like everywhere else, some landmarks had fallen: Mamou's Chicken Shack was boarded up and the movie house was for sale. But she felt no sense of loss, any more than she felt relief to see that the old drugstore was still standing, the one where she'd drunk hundreds of vanilla Cokes as a child. She did not stop in for breakfast. She did not care if there was anyone inside she could recognize, or who might recognize her. After a cup of weak coffee from a vending machine, Tildy headed out LaForche Road to her father's house.

Tildy's olefactory sense had always been highly developed. Her earliest memories were keyed to smells. There had been a period when she was five or six when the smells of road tar or laundry soap, of cellar mold and simmering red beans had registered so powerfully as to be nearly painful. Later on, she learned to do tricks with her nose. From a whiff or two of someone's breath, she could tell them what they'd had for lunch. Led blindfolded into a deserted classroom, she could accurately identify it from the lingering pheromones of the teacher.

Adulthood had dulled her receptors, but still, as she strolled in the parched grass at the side of her father's house, she could smell him through an open window; the stale fumes of his sickness at first, like mist hovering over a poisoned well, and then underneath, his own animal scent as she'd always known it, a sharp blend of vinegar and charred metal. This was the home place, just exactly as she'd left it all those years ago.

Except for the stooped little woman in black tennis shoes standing at the kitchen stove and stirring something in a pot. Her iron gray hair was in a single braid that reached all the way to the base of her spine.

"Don't you be alarmed, honey. Joby Daigle, I'm the one wrote you them letters. Sit yourself down, I'm jes makin' Lucy his breakfast."

"How is he?"

"We takin' it a day at a time. So you're Clothilde, the daughter. I could see it right when you come in that door. You got Lucy's eyes."

Tildy stood awkwardly beside the wicker rocking chair, as unprepared for it all as she'd figured all along. "Thank you for the letters. And thank you for taking care of Papa this way. There's really no way for me to tell you how much I appreciate it."

"Don't you try, honey. I ain't due no thanks. Cared for Mr. Daigle three years before he passed, a good sweet man and partial raised right here in Evangeline Parish. Now I'm carin' for Lucy and seems like that's somethin' I was intentioned for. I take my share of pleasure in it, so I ain't due no thanks."

"Well, thank you just the same," Tildy said. "You're what's keeping him alive."

Mrs. Daigle turned off the stove, emptied gruel into a bowl and swirled in a few tablespoons of molasses. "Lucy's got a terrible sweet tooth. You go on in and see him now, take him his farina. Jes don't be too surprised if he don't know you right off. Lucien, he ain't home no more in here." She pointed to her forehead.

To see if she still knew the house in darkness, Tildy went down the hall with eyes shut, took a sharp left at the stairs, then stood against the doorframe of what had once been her bedroom. She opened her eyes.

Lucien was on his back, the outline of his body, under a tattered wool coverlet, no wider than a light pole. His flickering eyes sat deep in their sockets and all around his hairline and under his jaw the skin was flaky and white. On newspapers carpeting the floor were globs of his viscid black sputum.

Cupped in Tildy's palm, the bowl was hot. She nudged the big spoon slowly around the rim. Now or never if she was going in there.

"Papa. It's me, Papa. Your daughter's come to see you."

Lucien said nothing. He gave no reaction as she knelt, smoothed the covers, kissed his dry, stubbled cheek.

"*As-tu faim, Papa? C'est Clothilde ici.* . . . I can come back later if you want to sleep."

He rotated his head toward her and his eyes snapped open wide. "You have been where?"

"On the road mostly. I've wanted to come and see you."

"I know, yes. Thems doctors out there no let you in. Devils they are, in that disguise of white."

"No, no. *C'est un rêve.* You're home now, Papa. They can't bother you here."

"They know me, yes." Granular mucus clattered in his throat. He braced his elbows against the mattress, legs twitching, as a series of coughs ripped through him. "They come in the night with metal pipes to drain my body. . . . I am so weak from this, me."

"Why don't you eat something, okay?"

"Clothilde, you say? *Ma fille?*" He touched her face.

"Come on, I'll feed you."

"Clothilde?" He eyed her suspiciously. "What is this food?"

There was a face towel draped over the end of the bed which Tildy spread across his chest, resting the bowl on top. She held the spoon against his lips, tilting it slightly onto his lapping tongue, scraping dribbles from his chin.

"Thatta boy," she cooed. "It'll warm you up inside."

Lucien grunted and pinched his lips together, suddenly mulish. Farina slithered down his neck and onto the yellowed collar of his pyjamas.

"Don't. Don't make me cry, Papa."

Lucien Soileau grew up in Pointe Bleu, a small settlement near Lac Saint Jean in the Laurentian Hills of Quebec, the youngest of eight brothers. At the age of ten he went with them into the forests, at first only to carry their tools and water jugs, later to earn his keep at one end of a crosscut saw. He was always the last to eat, the last to get new shoes. After Sunday Mass, his brothers would break out the applejack and take turns beating him up. His father, confident that this battering could only serve to toughen his youngest, a shy and sometimes hysterical boy, stood by shouting encouragement.

Lucien celebrated his fourteenth birthday by stealing fifty dollars from his mother's sewing box—money earned repairing fishermen's nets and earmarked for an eventual pilgrimage to Lourdes—and hopped a bus to Ottawa. For the next two years he bummed around southern Ontario, working when he could, camping in hobo jungles when he could not.

In 1927, in the company of a tramp known only as Stalebread, Lucien traveled to America by boxcar, a move that was to ineluctably alter the direction of his life. In the suburban community of Royal Oak, outside Detroit, he and Stalebread were yanked from the train by bulls in the pay of the Great Northern Railway and walloped with wooden batons. In their jail cell late that night, Stalebread succumbed to the effects of the beating. Lucien saw the spirit leave his partner's body, a billowing acid green nimbus that told him in an echoing voice of the martyrdom of Saint Jude, clubbed to death for his fidelity to Jesus Christ. When the guards came to remove the corpse, Lucien requested a Bible.

By the time of his release, he had read the Book from cover to cover three times. Exulting in his new faith, but stunned and somewhat frightened by the swiftness of its conquering rush, Lucien wandered the streets for days, eating out of garbage cans and awaiting a sign of God's will. It came in the form of a painful kick delivered by one August Hansen, in whose coal bin Lucien was sleeping shielded from a heavy rain. But in an instant Hansen had relented, taking pity on this forlorn boy, offering room and board in return for which Lucien would go to work for him as an apprentice plasterer.

The first time Lucien went on a job by himself he was sent to make some minor repairs at a local radio station. In a cramped, primitive studio with blankets hung on the walls as soundproofing, he met a small, intense priest whose weekly broadcast was the most popular thing on the station. His name was Charles E. Coughlin. Lucien felt an electric charge flow through him as they shook hands. Bolts of fire burst from Coughlin's eyes and danced around the steel rims of his glasses. It was the sign Lucien had been waiting for.

When Coughlin (born in Hamilton, Ontario) found out that Lucien was a fellow Canadian, he invited him to attend services at his church. Lucien was completely devastated by that first visit to the Shrine of the Little Flower and became a fiercely loyal parishioner, taking the host as often as five and six times a week. But it was the sermons he came to hear, fidgeting impatiently through the drone of the liturgy, hoping to be once more dazzled by one of Coughlin's booming orations. He was an angry wind in the pulpit.

Up until that time Lucien's political awareness had been confined to the hatred of the English his father had taught him, a vague desire to avenge the French loss of Quebec at the Plains of Abraham. But now Coughlin opened his eyes to the foul machinations of the Bolshevik Antichrist, a specter that could be traced back to 1776 when a Bavarian called Adam Weishaupt had founded a cult known as the Illuminati, based on principles expounded by medieval rabbis and cabalists. The French Revolution, Coughlin taught, was instigated and controlled by Weishaupt. Marx and Engels had been no more than Illuminati puppets. World affairs were being currently directed by Illuminati bankers in New York and London in collaboration with the Jew commissars in Moscow; and the day would soon arrive when these despotic stewards of Satan would be able to dictate their vile and ghastly terms to every man, woman and child on the planet.

The breadth and enormity of this secret design filled Lucien with terror. It transcended all boundaries, negated all hopes and ambitions. What chance could there be to defeat the Red Serpent when the world's leaders refused even to recognize it?

Lucien left August Hansen, took a room in a flophouse and a part-time job sweeping out the radio station. In order to cleanse himself, he stopped eating, ingesting only fruit salts dissolved in rain water. He conducted all-night prayer vigils in a field behind the municipal car barn, invoking obscure saints and rolling naked in the mud. The weaker he became physically, the stronger was his mental resolve, the greater the inspiration of inner righteousness. On a Sunday just before dawn, weighing one hundred twelve pounds, he rose from aching knees a staunch and fearless soldier in the army of the Lord. He was ready now, ready to battle the Red Serpent until his final breath.

No one was more ravaged when, in 1931, Coughlin's national network hookup was canceled by the Columbia Broadcasting System. In fact, Lucien was so crushed by this Zionist treachery that he left Royal Oak behind, drifting down to Ville Platte, recreating in his own small way the original Acadian migration. But he took with him a personal letter from Father Coughlin appointing him a recruiter for the National Union for Social Justice, the political party Coughlin had formed in alliance with Gerald L. K. Smith and Huey

Long, the senator from Louisiana. Frustrated in his efforts to meet with Long at his Baton Rouge compound, unable to enroll a single member in the party (he was a dreadful speaker and had an innate distrust of strangers), Lucien went to work in a pencil factory, milling graphite, and passed into a friendless and fixated bachelorhood.

During the wicked dementia of the World War, in which he served as a stateside file clerk (receiving an ordinary discharge after one too many efforts to convince his superiors they should leave Hitler alone and get after Stalin), and the silencing of Coughlin by the nabobs of Rome, suggesting as it did Illuminati infiltration of Mother Church—through all of this, Lucien somehow managed to abide. The ensuing years saw many setbacks, the Beast moving ever forward, capturing new territory and new souls, but Lucien's flame burned on. He never lost hope. The day would come—perhaps not in his lifetime, but it would come—when the tide would be reversed and there would be much work for His fiery sword.

As he rankled into middle age, Lucien determined that he would need an heir to carry on the work. In 1953 he met and married Harlene Diggs, an itinerant gospel singer from Grapeland, Texas, who had grown tired of strumming her way along the Gulf Coast and resolved to hitch up with the first blue-eyed man she met. She bore Lucien a daughter by Caesarian section one year later. Harlene took in washing, Lucien worked double shifts at the pencil factory, and before too long they were able to make a down payment on a small farm just outside of town. They plowed some ground for vegetables, planted fruit trees, and traded a dresser and cedar chest for an old milk cow. There was only one thing wrong: Lucien's health. He coughed all the time, was short of breath. Down at the clinic, they told him he had chronic bronchitis. In truth, years of inhaling graphite dust had caused degenerative pulmonary fibrosis, but this condition was not to be discovered until much later.

The weather was mild on Christmas Day of 1958 and the Soileau family went on a picnic by a calm, blue lake ringed with pines. Cold chicken, egg salad, bowls of fruit and nuts were laid out on a lacy embroidered sheet spread over the grass. After the meal Harlene played her guitar and they sang "O Little Town of Bethlehem." Lucien took his daughter for a walk in the woods and made for her a tiny crown out of leaves and plaited twigs.

They returned to find Harlene floating facedown in the water, her skirt fanned out among the reeds, a gingham banner of gall and desolation.

For several months, Lucien did not speak.

"*Pauvre Papa.*" Tildy smoothed his eyebrows with the tip of one finger. "You really ought to eat something, but I can't make you. . . . Remember how we struggled over the fried eggs in the morning? You would stand over me until I cleaned my plate. Those cold, greasy eggs sitting there and I'd tell you I could not eat them, they were like big yellow eyes. But you would stay and stay. You'd be late for work and I'd be late for school, but nobody moved until I choked those eggs down. Do you remember that, Papa?"

"I am bigger than you. Stronger." He lurched, spat a thick wad that crackled on the newspapers. "Jo. Where is Jo? . . . She give me good thumps of the chest when I need."

Lucien rolled to one side, groaning, trying to lift himself, estranged from the mechanics of his own body. Tildy put out her hand; he squeezed it a moment, then pushed it away. Going rigid, covering his eyes, Lucien began to recite a psalm, running words together in a roupy, waning voice.

"Lord all my longing is known to Thee and my sighing is not hidden my wounds are repulsive to me and festering because of my folly I am bent am bowed down all the day I go mourning . . . heart beats fast strength fails me even the lights of eyes I must do without . . . loved ones and friends stand aloof from illness even . . . my kinsmen at a distance . . . and they who seek after my soul . . . lay snares . . . who seek my hurt talk mischief and think . . . up treacheries all day."

Lucien quivered and went limp. Startled, Tildy pushed herself forward, approaching both the bed and the possibility that she had heard last words. Her relief at the thin purl of his breathing, at the vapor left on her ear as she held it to his lips, was boundless. She was here with him now, seeing him, touching him, regaining him, and yet the love she felt for the old man was no less opaque, no less disconnected than it had been an hour ago, a week ago, ten years ago.

Be brave, be brave.

"How'd it go?" Joby Daigle looked up from the teetery metal table where she was pouring herself coffee from a thermos.

"He passed out after a bite or two." Tildy cupped her hands under the running faucet and splashed her face.

"Poor soul. Not much strength left in him. Coffee for you? Brewed it with my own chicory, stuff comes up like a weed."

"Not right now. Mind if I smoke?"

"Suit yourself. . . . Scared you some to see him that way, did it?"

"Something like that."

"Can't be but tore up over it, seein' a man jes about drained empty. Oh but Lucy was quite a man when I first knowed him. Had fire, you know?"

"Fire," Tildy said, turning her back. Her hand was growing numb under the cold water.

"Yep. Used to be all through him so's he kinda glowed. I sure do bless the day I met that man. I was jes driftin', kinda lost. Like to wither right off when Mr. Daigle passed. Got started sendin' out my cards. I'd go through all the papers for the announcements and then I'd send out the get-well cards and the sympathy cards and the happy-graduation cards and the new-baby cards. Did over nine hunnert of 'em and wasn't but twelve people thought to write back and thank me. So right then I says to myself, Joby, you want to help folks, you got to go out and do it. Joined up with this volunteer program for seniors over to the hospital. Met Lucy on the first day. He asked me to read aloud to him from the columnists. Almost three years ago and I hardly missed a day with him since."

"I know. You've done more for him than I have."

Mrs. Daigle fingered the dregs in her empty cup. "Hadn't been for those checks you sent every month, who knows? Don't go throwin' mud on yourself." Her shoulders dropped along with her voice. "I wish sometimes—forgive me, Lord—but I wish sometimes I'd met Lucy a lot sooner. Mr. Daigle, he was good to me but he didn't have no fire. Say there's wheels within wheels, girl. One of 'em had turned a little different, we could be sittin' right here mother and daughter."

"Why not," Tildy said, regretting it. Like swinging at a pitch right up under the chin.

Joby Daigle rose from the table with effort and advanced on Tildy, plucking shyly at the end of her braid. "You and me, we come to an understandin' right off. I like that. We got to be like a team, hear? Lucy's women. Slide on over here and I'll show you my secret jes the two of us be knowin'."

With that she opened the broom closet and dragged out a battered footlocker. Closing her eyes, she mumbled a string of private words before raising the lid. A confusion of sharp smells attacked Tildy's nose. Paper packets, foil-wrapped bundles, bottles and jars of various shapes and sizes were crammed inside the box and as Mrs.

Daigle removed each one, she called out its contents: rose hips, sassafras twigs, hoof powder, allspice berries, burdock root, dried liver flakes, pine pitch, beetle legs, cow moss, milkweed, eucalyptus bark.

"This here's the power of life. Right from nature. Right there for the gatherin'." Mrs. Daigle sat lightly down beside her arrayed pharmacopoeia, flushed with pride and excitement. "It's what brung you and your daddy together."

"Beetle legs?"

"What I'm sayin' to you, child, is this. If Lucy had stayed with the doctors over there, he'd be gone. But I been dosin' him with my secret medicines and he's still here. I got the knowledge." Her knobby fingers encircled Tildy's wrist, an emphatic grip. "I know what he needs, understand? Nothin' funny about it cause it's all from nature. Mother Nature, she can be real generous if you know how to friendly up to her. There's all kinds of life essence out there." Mrs. Daigle pointed out the window.

Tildy followed her finger out to the withered fruit trees and swirling dust. She thought: Lady, you're as crazy as he is.

Mrs. Daigle extracted a few round, yellowish seeds from a vial and popped them in her mouth. "I take these myself," she said. "For gas."

"You got anything for a tired brain?"

"Not exactly, but I know just what you mean." She held up a cork-stoppered pop bottle containing a viscous brown liquid. "My pacifyin' tonic. Chamomile, horehound syrup, licorice root, buckthorn, peach and comfrey leaves. When Lucy gets to wailin' with the hurt and twistin' all over the bed like the devil's tryin' to get a-holt on him, I give him a spoon of this in some weak tea and he curls on up just as sweet as a lamb."

"Could I try some?"

It took time for Tildy to convince Mrs. Daigle that she could handle things on her own.

"Sure, you want some time alone with him," Mrs. Daigle said grudgingly. "But lemme write down my number case you need to reach me. I'll come 'round tomorrow to give him his bath."

Still the woman lingered; puttering aimlessly under the hood of her Nash Rambler, rubbing splattered insects off the windshield with her fingers and casting every few moments an unhappy, squinting look in the direction of Lucien's bedroom. At last, having seen Tildy peering at her from the window, she backed out to the road and rattled slowly away.

"We could be sitting down right here mother and daughter," Tildy repeated, not altogether repelled by the idea at that moment. The only things she could remember about Harlene were that she liked to suck ice and could sleep standing up.

She passed the afternoon at her father's bedside, reading every second or third sentence of the mystery novel she'd brought with her. Lucien floated up into full awareness only twice, each time wheezing out, in his peculiar franglais, a request for white robes and clean straw. Tildy laid a cool washcloth over his eyes. His sleep was tranquil, save for the rattling in his lungs, and when Tildy held his hand it felt as corky and inert as a heel of old bread. She skipped to the closing chapter to find out who the killer was (Carla, the sweet younger sister, with the revolver, in the office above her lover's restaurant) and stole away to pace the sprawling shadows of the house.

Those gloomy, narrow rooms were unchanged, full of the same cheap furniture, the same dust, without the slightest decoration. At the end of a long and contentious life there ought to be trophies and mementoes to pass along. But there were none. No photographs or letters bound with ribbon, no album of pressed flowers, not even the Last Supper rendered on a slab of varnished pine. How dismal it must be to leave the world as bereft as the day you'd arrived.

"*Pauvre Papa,*" Tildy murmured. "I can't even say you've got me."

The sound of her own voice, fluttery and tight, drove her outside for some air. The sun was low on the western horizon now cluttered with water towers and power lines, and the undersides of clouds were tinted orange. She turned, looked toward the scrub behind the house and felt rising within her like bile an urge to take off and run, fighting through brambles and sumac till her legs gave out and she dropped, spent but clear of the area. That instinct for flight that always surged over her when the proceedings turned hard.

In the spring of her tenth-grade year, Tildy was engrossed by the remarkable universe of *Photoplay* and *Modern Screen.* Lucien berated her for reading such trash and burned her first issues. She learned to be more careful, would trek to a clearing in the woods where she could browse undisturbed through styling tips from Sandra Dee's hairdresser.

Auditions were announced for the school's traditional year-end musical, *Annie Get Your Gun* and Tildy set her heart on the title role. At night she pressed her forehead against conjoined fists and prayed for the first time since Harlene had died. Trying once more to conjure up the godly image that had comforted her as a child—balding, white-bearded giant in a blue bathrobe—she promised that if He allowed her to get the part, she would accompany her father to Mass each Sunday for the next six months. But when Lucien on the night before the audition learned of his Clothilde's intention to star in this show, he exploded, bellowing that he would never permit her to frolic around in some scanty costume for a roomful of people. She told him he could go straight to hell. And all the next day, while she cursed and thumped, Lucien kept her locked away in her room.

It was this final gag on the insatiable faith he had tried to instill in her—chasing off friends, confiscating her lipstick and nail polish—that caused her to run away from home, just as her father had done in 1925, heading out right before first light carrying only a couple of crumpled bills.

A mile or two up the road by a house with only a porch light burning, Tildy helped herself to a station wagon with a full tank of gas and the keys inside. She drove nonstop to the outskirts of Biloxi, Mississippi, where the radiator line burst. Leaving the car smoking on the shoulder, she walked into town, to the promenade along the Gulf. Tildy bought her first pack of cigarettes, Lucky Strikes; dangling her legs over the seawall, she taught herself to inhale and spit like a man. Later she frittered away a handful of quarters at a booth where you could win a five-inch lock knife by popping balloons with darts. Finally the gaptooth boy running it slipped her one of the knives on the house.

"I don't need any favors," Tildy said sullenly.

"But I like you," he said. Wayne. His name was stitched over the pocket of his shirt. "Death From Above" was tattooed on his upper arm. "That's some sweet face. You know, if your hair was a little bit lighter, you'd look just like the White Rock girl."

Tildy allowed him to drape his arm over her shoulders as they walked to a nearby café. Wayne bought her shrimp-in-a-basket and a big lemonade and sat there watching her eat.

"Man, oh man," he said. "Look like you ain't had no food in a week."

She told Wayne that she'd been studying dance up in New York, but was forced to leave town due to a broken heart. An English movie director. A possessive bastard.

"Dancin' school, huh?" Wayne nodded and sucked his lips. "You maybe interested in makin' some dough?"

From the sickroom came a low trilling growl like an animal in heat and then Lucien's voice, robust as it had ever been.

"Where that girl . . . Clothilde!"

She scrambled down the hall on cold feet.

"*Viens, Clothilde . . . viens ici.*" He beckoned urgently to her. His skin was terribly white, taut, and the bones of his pelvis seemed about to burst through.

"Take it easy. I'll put the sheet back over you."

Lucien heaved to one side and grasped at her breasts. Just what kind of connection was he making?

"I'm with you, Papa." He was squeezing her painfully. "It's all right. Lie back now."

"*Pas long temps.* They take me out there and no coming back. There are things you must hear now, so come. Give your attention."

"A few minutes. But it's late, we should both be asleep."

Lucien buzzed his lips. "I know how late. So I am telling you . . . *Ecoutes*, my girl. Sit by me and hold this hand. We must speak of your mother, no keeping from you any longer what was done. . . . Always I have my suspicions. All the time I am writing to the police about footprints I see by that lake. You remember the lake?"

She remembered. Water a perfect shade of blue. The ripple of skatebugs. The way Harlene bobbed gently in the water so that until the moment she turned over, Tildy thought she was doing the dog paddle in her clothes.

"There was a great crime on that day. That holy day. I speak with a man who knows of the enemy."

"At the hospital? Your roommate?"

"We live as allies. We share food together. One day I tell him of your mama and how we find her floating there. I see how his face goes tight at this. *Bien sur*, this man can tell me. I look for him every day, me, until he will surrender this truth. The truth as I have always known it. . . . In the college at Baton Rouge there were professors who know of my fight. They are Bolsheviks. *Juifs, tu comprends?* They see how I am exposing them and their plans and the order comes from Moscow I must be destroyed. The assassin is a man named Klein, but he is a coward. He follow me for many weeks, afraid to get close. You remember the fire at work that killed my foreman? No, you were too little, *ma Clothilde*, but this was Klein. There is rage at his failure. Now Klein himself is in danger. So it was that on that day he finds your mama alone, his time for attack has come. He set on her like an animal and crushed her throat in his hands."

"Enough, Papa. You've said enough now."

Lucien lifted her hand from the mattress. "You must be strong before this evil. Now it is in you. You have heard it from my lips and must swear to carry out the vengeance."

Tildy's upper body sagged in glum exasperation. "Forget it. You don't need any visions now. It's long over." And silently: It's your own death you should be thinking about.

"There is no limit in God's sight. Pledge to me."

Tildy looked at this frail chump of a man in raw lamplight who by his madness had denied her access to basic implements of living, who had deposited in her a charged nugget of himself, magnetized for fakery and sorrow. She realized that all he really meant to say was: Can you do me a favor?

"Sure. I promise. I swear."

"*Bien*. It is done."

He relaxed all at once and she was able to pull free. There were round red marks on the back of her hand. Lucien lay quiet for a few moments, then began to retch. He opened his mouth like a bird and hacked up a twisted rope of mucus that fell across the pillow in a tarry black line. Tildy unfolded his body and wiped him up. He was sweating from every pore.

Hard as she tried, Tildy could not fall asleep. By three o'clock her calf muscles were knotted and she'd been grinding her teeth. The kitchen floor felt gritty under her feet. She drank some water and groped back to the sofa. She masturbated coldly and drowsed finally away with one foot on the floor.

Mrs. Daigle shook her out of it around noon.

"You any better, dear?"

"Was I ill?"

"Looked the picture of it to me. That's why I let you rest this late."

Mrs. Daigle left the room but came back five minutes later with a breakfast tray: a segmented grapefruit topped with honey, two slices of dry wheat toast and a mug of some dank herb tea. Tildy dabbed grapefruit juice on her eyelids. From nape to skull, she ached.

Lucien had refused all nourishment. He seemed aware only of large shapes. His friend sat by with a jar of pale green salve that she applied now and then to his chest; and when his wheezing built into an "Oh Jesus," she would repeat after him. Little hands curled against her throat, she turned to face his daughter and told her not to worry, that it would be soon.

It was a sticky hot day, but Tildy went out in it anyway. She took a long, circular drive on back roads where she could run at 25 with nobody behind her. On the way home, driving into the sun, she nearly struck a black dog that leaped out from some hedges; a little girl came screaming out of the driveway and threw a stick at the car. After that she stopped at an air-conditioned bar and without really thinking about it, downed four straight-up bourbons.

Tildy had no sense of how tanked she was until she got back to the house. Swaying through the kitchen, she embraced Joby Daigle and asked her to spend the night.

"You got the shivers and shakes all on you, that's all right," she said, patting Tildy on the shoulder. "You're entitled."

Tildy backed away, stood by the screen door looking out. "It's not that I'm afraid. Not about . . . Maybe it's this house in the dark. I hear things."

"You gonna be fine. We'll have a little fruit salad, play some bid whist if you like. S'posed to cool off later on. We'll make it on through till mornin', long away as that must seem to you. And maybe there'll be peace by then. Did I mention Lucy turned his back on dinner? He was all drawed up in a knot. Like his face was tryin' to meet with his knees."

Tildy pushed the screen door, let it smack shut. Then she did it again. "He's getting himself ready to go. Is that what you think?" Mrs. Daigle didn't say anything. "I do too." She pushed the door again and dodged the backswing as she stepped outside.

But there was no cooling off as the night wore on. Tildy fanned herself with a paper plate. Mrs. Daigle told a long story about a canoe trip she'd taken with her husband in the spring of 1962. Mr. Daigle had been bitten by a turtle. The refrigerator kicked on and made an intermittent noise like someone chewing aluminum foil. Outside, a tow truck, or something like it, went by with its yellow flashers going. Mrs. Daigle recalled the first time she had given

Lucy a bath and how he'd tried to pull her in there with him. Tildy wished she had some more whiskey.

Somewhat later, after the brushing of teeth and the distribution of pillows, they went in for a look at the old man. Slack-jawed, pale tongue jutting, he was only half asleep with the sheet bunched around his middle. Slowly, one by one, his fingers rose and fell as though he was doing a piano exercise.

"You go on ahead, child," Mrs. Daigle said. "I'm gonna make one last try, see if he'll take a little somethin' with tea."

Tildy was first up the following morning. On her way to put on the kettle she peered into her father's room, saw his face waxen and gray, and knew it was over. She awoke Mrs. Daigle, who wept vigorously but quietly. Then she dialed the police. They promised an ambulance within the hour.

"I hope you know," Mrs. Daigle stammered, "you was the only thing in this world he'd admit to lovin'."

What Tildy did not know was that less than twelve hours ago, wanting only to deliver both Lucien and his daughter from further pain, Mrs. Daigle had administered to him, along with the tea, three seeds of the castor bean plant. The seeds contained an extremely toxic substance, called ricin, that brought on circulatory collapse.

The ambulance driver wanted to know where he was supposed to take the body and Tildy didn't know what to tell him. She got out the Ville Platte yellow pages, phoned the mortuary with the largest display ad, and asked what they were charging for a no-frills cremation.

That upset Mrs. Daigle no end.

"You can't do it. That man done lived his whole life in the light of the Church. He held on to that faith all the way through, even when he seen there weren't goin' to be no miracle for him. He's jes got to have the rites. And a proper burial."

"He's dead now. It doesn't matter anymore."

"You ain't meanin' what you say. Grief can cloud the mind."

"If you want to say some words over him, go right ahead. But he was my father and he stays with me." At a low trajectory, Tildy flung herself between the long-ago death and the one newly fetched up; Harlene's floating blue doll-face, Lucien's drawn mummy mask. She had only one offering to make. "When I blow this town, I won't be coming back. And I'm not going to leave him behind."

Tildy followed the ambulance into Ville Platte and completed arrangements for what Mr. LeBeau, the funeral director, referred to as "high temperature carbonization of the remains." At the house that afternoon, she received a call from a real estate agent to whom it seemed Mr. LeBeau was in the habit of supplying information on new vacancies. He wanted to find out her asking price. Tildy said she would not object if he went ahead and got what he could for the place, and gave him her address and phone number in Florida.

Lucien came out of the oven the next morning and Tildy was on her way. Benny and the girls were waiting on her in Lydell, but she was pointed in another direction. They could all go hang. She was headed on home with her daddy riding beside her in a burnished canister of bronze.

5

Strained through low woolpack clouds, sunlight was still intense. It penetrated the dusty windows of the house like a flashlight shined into a laundry hamper. The house was a squat bunker of lime green cinder blocks planted carelessly amid scrub. Tildy was seldom on time with the mortgage payments. From the rear, looking out the kitchen door across the parched yard to a chicken coop now serving insectiverous beasts as cabaña and snack bar, it was easy to believe the world was flat. The overwhelming suggestion was of landlocked terrain, of a desolate outback where old buckaroos went to die.

Gibsonton had been a winter home for circus and carny people since the 1920s when a cookhouse operator named Eddie LeMay pulled off the road one evening just as the sun was setting over the Alafia River. He liked what he saw. "This is it, honey," he told his wife. "Get out the bedrolls."

There wasn't much there at the time: a few shacks, a path through sweetgums to the river, strangler figs growing over everything like flowering pythons. But joined by a handful of colleagues the following year, Eddie persuaded J. B. Gibson, a Tampa land speculator who owned the riverfront where they were squatting, to put in a drainage system and sell off a few lots. The next year a large family of Italian acrobats moved down, and a deaf old man with a pet elephant, and two contortionist sisters who'd once spent a long weekend with P. T. Barnum at a spa in Red Bank, New Jersey.

Each year since, from late October to Thanksgiving, the folks have streamed into Gibsonton—pitchmen, palm readers, barkers, animal trainers, jointees, "human oddities"—to take up residence in their cottages and housetrailers until it's time to go back on the road again in spring. The pace of life is languid, the atmosphere blasé. A man with a pair of miniature legs sprouting from his chest can walk down the street without drawing a second glance, and the town's postmistress, now retired, weighs just over eight hundred pounds.

Karl Gables could smell his own breath, fumes from a derelict cheese works. He was woozy from fourteen hours of sleep and there was a throb in his stomach that fried pimento loaf on toast hadn't been able to muffle. Wearing khaki slacks, rubber sandals and a painter's hat, he sat cross-legged by the kitchen door and drank Bromo Seltzer. A soft breeze came through the screen, played over his face. It felt good. A day like today, he ought to walk down to the river and have a swim.

Karl stuck his head out the door and sniffed. Something warm and sweet, a little like vanilla extract. Uneasily, he wandered into the yard. Brown grass crunched under his feet. A rustling came from somewhere in the underbrush and Karl answered by stomping the ground. Sounds kind of hollow down there, he thought. His stomach puckered and a humming began in his ears, grew louder. The river was just too far.

He jumped back in and latched the door. Then he went to the living room and picked up the book he had passed out with last night, Dr. Herbert J. Wigmore's *Gemology for the Hobbyist.*

STAR OF ESTE
While a relatively small stone, its alleged weight being a mere 25½ carats, the Star of Este is noted for its perfection of form and brilliant quality. It belonged to the Archduke Francis Ferdinand of Austria. Subsequent to his assassination, presumably, it reverted to the Crown and was said to have been in the possession of Emperor Charles, who died in exile in 1922. The later history of this stone is unknown.

Tales of buried treasure had been circulating around Gibsonton for years—pirate booty, smugglers' coves, sea chests crammed with gold or precious stones. Donut Willie, who was forever buttonholing people on the sidewalk, claimed that a few years back his mother had gone to fillet an amberjack and found a ruby the size of a golf ball in its belly. There were lots of stories. In lunch counters, around gas pumps, at the barber shop, old mugs told each other about the fortunes that were out there, the made life waiting for someone who dug in the right place.

Sometime in the late '30s a sword swallower by the name of Stix Morgan, who had been forced into retirement by a chronic allergy that caused him to sneeze suddenly and without warning, was digging along a sandy rise behind the fish hatchery at Bullfrog Creek. The blade of his shovel struck something hard. Stix fell to his knees and began scooping with his hands, already visualizing himself in spats and a vested suit, tooling around Miami in a chauffeur-driven roadster and tossing silver dollars to pedestrians. Something black and round began to emerge from the sand. Its surface was pitted. Stix thought of the pirate coffers in storybook illustrations, the shape of their lids. But when he brought his lantern closer what he saw was a human skull with most of its teeth still in place. Quivering, bathed in cold sweat, he kept on digging. Had he come upon the bones of some long-forgotten buccaneer? Some rapacious fiend who had fled Hispañola with a heavy purse, evading both enemies and history alike? The skeleton was finally excavated. Propped on its worm-eaten breastbone was a rusted metal disk marked with the points of the compass. Rabid with doubloon hunger, Boots grabbed at it without first noticing what it read. The compass needle fell to the ground between his feet.

With a shovel in his hand, Stix Morgan died six months later of a heart attack. He had been at it all night every night, digging up every last inch of that rise, discovering nothing more valuable than an old padlock for which an antique dealer gave him three dollars.

It was only a week or two after he and Tildy moved down to Gibsonton from Virginia, where they had passed the first year of their marriage in noise and trepidation, that Karl heard this story. He laughed until it hurt.

"What a loser, this guy," he said to the barfly who'd told him. "Had it right there in his hand and let it slip."

Not long afterward, in that very same bar, Karl would meet an individual known as Zeke the Freak and eventually become something of a story himself.

From a Cuban chambermaid in a Tampa hotel, Zeke had purchased an old "chart" divulging the location of a fortune in gold bullion. Some legendary rumrunner of Prohibition days had buried a whole shitload of ingots over on Bird Island, a barren lump only a few miles out across the bay. Karl and Zeke went partners on some tools and a small skiff with a six-horsepower Evinrude. Every couple of days they would chug over to the island and dig. Empty-handed after two weeks of this, they were only mildly discouraged. The chart, rather freely rendered on the back of a telegraph blank, was after all a bit vague.

Zeke advocated persistence. "One percent inspiration and ninety-nine percent perspiration. Guy invented the lightbulb said that."

One Friday Karl won a few hands of five-card stud and went on to close the bars. When Zeke came by to pick him up for Saturday's expedition to the island, he begged off.

"I been heaving all night. My gut is killin' me."

That was the day that Zeke, taking five on the beach with a panatela and a bottle of warm beer, caught sight of a large, gray and waxy mass bobbing in the shallows. Long a devotee of nautical fiction, Zeke knew instantly what it was: ambergris, the intestinal secretion of sperm whales valued so highly in the manufacture of perfume. The agent for the New York cosmetics firm who flew down to confirm the discovery speculated that it had originated with a pod of whales off the coast of Africa, floated down to the South Atlantic, then followed a favorable current back up to the North Atlantic and on into the Gulf of Mexico.

"You must be living right," he said, shaking his head and writing Zeke a five-figure check. "Goddamnedest fluke I ever saw."

Karl's share of the deal, excluding the case of Johnnie Walker that Zeke had delivered to the house, was exactly nothing. A couple of weeks later, with the kind of frigid, superfluous irony that tries men's souls, Karl was emptying the last dribbles of Scotch into his morning coffee when the mailman dropped off a postcard from Bimini.

> Who could have thought an old crud like me could win a limbo contest?? Got a suite overlooking the beach and all the snatch I can handle. Everybody around here knows me. The Whale Vomit Man!! I just sit in the lobby and wait for them to come to me. And you know, I ain't tired of telling the story yet. Maybe cause I tell it different every time.
>
> God bless your hangover!!

Love, Zeke.

Karl heard car sounds as he moved between rooms, thinking at first that they came from the teevee. Motor shuddering off, screek of car door opening, thunk of car door closing. Then he saw a movement across the window, a flicker of dark blue. Tildy. She had a pissed-off expression, walked with a slight limp and carried some kind of metal tube. He wanted to go somewhere and hide but there wasn't time.

69

Seconds later she was in the door and looking at the wine jug halfway to his lips, his skewed hat, guilty eyes.

"Honey, I'm home," she said flatly. "What the hell are you doing here?"

"It's a sort of complicated story."

"I think I've heard it already. You got canned, am I right?"

"Yup."

"For God's sake, Karl." She came foreward to gently squeeze, as if it were a clown's shiny red honker, her husband's nose.

Karl was all over her then. "Baby, I missed you so." He sucked her neck, clamped hands behind her thighs and lifted her off the floor. "You got no idea how good it is to see you, darlin'."

"Put me down."

"Okay, okay, but what about you? You ain't supposed to be here neither."

"I'm out of a job myself. Guess I quit." She dropped into a chair. "Amounts to the same thing."

"That's a cold shot, baby. What do we do for money?"

"Not now, Karl."

He lowered his eyes. In spite of the bad vibes, he felt happy. She was back. She'd take care of him. "What's that thing?" He pointed to the tube she rolled between her palms.

"My father. You've never met, have you?" Tildy extended the thing as if Karl was supposed to shake hands with it.

He ran his fingers over the cool curve of metal. "Kinda small, ain't he?"

"He died day before yesterday, Karl. These are his ashes."

Karl blinked and his head seemed to fill like a balloon. He had been but vaguely aware that Tildy had a living parent. He removed his hat, nibbled momentarily on the brim. "Must be some kind of blue for you, baby. I'm real sorry." He started toward her, arms out.

"Freeze right there. Don't you comfort me, damn it. That's not what I want."

"Can I sit next to you on the arm? Would that be okay?"

"If you want. Just don't touch me. I'm booby-trapped."

Utterly dazed, Karl perched next to his wife, hands held in to keep from stroking her. Hairs were erect at the rims of her small ears.

"You're lookin' awful good, considerin'."

"Please don't."

"Forget I'm here then." Karl slid off the chair arm and went to retrieve his jug.

"Poor Karl. Don't try to understand me, it's a waste. . . . I don't mean to be mean, it's just that I'm so tired. And a reunion is not what I'd planned on. I wasn't ready for you, not at all. What I wanted was a decent interval, you know? Deserted house, blank days, some long-distance sleeping. Last few weeks, I've been bounced all around like a basketball. I need to find out where the bruises are."

Karl shrugged, turned up the teevee. "Forget it. Have some wine."

Tildy was mighty tired of tailoring her behavior to outside specifications, wanted merely to burrow like a mole through the black earth, but she left her seat, moved to Karl's side, touched him.

"What's on?" she said.

"You're lookin' at it."

Reclining on a blanket stained with motor oil, Tildy and Karl were silent. Hot dogs crackled on a grill behind them and the portable radio discharged clear channel mood music. Airport rhumba. A crow sailed from the rubbish heap to its mess of a nest high in an overhanging tree. Turning onto his belly, Karl felt the ground with an open hand. He dug through the mat of pine needles and mulch and the smell of earth on his fingers was rich, good enough to eat.

"Another dog?" Tildy said, poking at the coals.

"At least."

There were no buns so they held the hot dogs by their split and blackened skins, dipping them in the mustard jar before biting. Karl poured wine into a common cup.

"How's your season been? Steal a lotta bases?"

"I was playing a little flat actually. Been in a slump, just wasn't seeing the ball real good."

"And Flora? She still mowin' 'em down?"

"More or less."

"I cannot believe you're really finished with those Cougarettes. You're a star, don't you know it?"

"No future there. Don't expect they'll last through the month." Then, anxious to change the subject—"Sun feels awful nice."

"Sure. Sunshine State, it's even on the license plates."

"Looks like you could use some of it, too. Your skin tone is lousy. Been living like an invalid, have you?"

"You know how I get."

"Do I?"

"We talked about it. You never remember." Karl plucked blades of grass for chewing. Cheeks unshaven and slightly puffy, his elongated, loaf-pan face flushed with effort; an effort first to locate Tildy's good graces, then worm his way in. "It's only sometimes. When you're away and I have to go it alone around here. I'm trapped in that house. Little things get to spookin' me. I spring a leak somewhere, start to feel sick every time I set foot outdoors."

"Is that it? Some people might want to call that a little bit crazy."

"So maybe I am. Nothin' I can do about it."

"Except open another bottle."

"Nag, nag, nag." Karl spat green. "I got reasons to drink, sweets, and you're one of 'em. Bet we ain't spent more than two weeks under the same roof so far this year. And when you are around, ain't long before you'll be remindin' me, even when it's not in words, about who's supporting who."

"Oh, shut up." She stood, knocking the radio over; a muffled crescendo of yoyo violins. "For days I watch my team disintegrate into a summer camp revue. I cut loose from there in a rental car for Ville Platte where I watch my father die. Clean up what I can down there, motor nonstop to Jacksonville to retrieve my own wheels, then on in here with an urgent need for peace and quiet only to find my hopeless Karl fired again, moping around like a granny. And within three hours here we are back again on the same old shit as the day I left. Me, I'm going to take a nap."

Karl would have liked to join her, but was afraid to ask.

Tildy dreamed of moonlit jungle alleys, the hushed stalking of pygmy commandos, their faces smeared with ash. They hunted her with devotion, wishing only to dance in her honor. The stillness was broken all at once by the flounderings of a wounded beast . . .

She pushed the pillows away. "Be still."

Thumps and scrapes of Karl battling furniture outside the door, then a splintering of glass and the last coils of sleep came loose from around her.

"Sellerass them auto workers, ain't on my shoulders."

"Shit." Tildy wrapped herself in the sheet, opened the door and looked out.

Karl was halfway bent, gasping like a beaten fighter. His hair was matted and his eyes looked like bottle caps. "Tildy best watch her feet." He chuckled. "Them little white toe's like candy." He pointed to the broken mustard jar on the floor.

Tildy linked her arms around his middle and wrestled him down into a chair though he outweighed her by some sixty pounds. She closed his eyelids with her fingers. "Play dead for a few minutes." Kneeling, she picked out the larger chunks of glass and took up the rest with a spatula and paper towels. "One thing at least, I won't ever need to have children as long as I have you."

"Nobody's daddy, uh-uh." Karl rolled his head from side to side. "Been ten years or more, still get them cards from Shelly. Every Christmas, every Father's Day. What a joke. Three months gone when Jerry married her . . . 'Little Jerry livin' with his grandma while I walk the streets of Detroit. A widow's nights are long ones. Hope you think of us often.' See why I can never get away?"

"You could stop opening the envelopes." She handed him a glass of water and told him to drink, her body taut and hard under the sheet like a statue on somebody's lawn.

In the living room, Tildy surveyed the overturned lamps and strewn cushions fanned out in a totemic design of cowardice and reproach; and she wondered how long he could toss the salad of his brain before it flew over the sides of the bowl.

Karl didn't know how cars worked, but he could drive hell out of them. Won a demolition derby while he was still in high school; tore up the dirt track circuit with his hardass tactics. A housewife with multiple sclerosis started a fan club for him and middle-aged speed nuts with kids his own age squired him for steak at the Elks Club and slipped him "beer money" on the way home.

Then it turned out that the rubbery blonde he'd been innocently shagging was the adopted daughter of the biggest General Motors dealer in the state, a man who could sponsor him for an assault on serious stock car competition. Karl wrecked that first car in time trials, but loyal Margie convinced her dad to ante up again. He made it on his second try at Darlington when the leader blew a piston on the next to last lap. Margie embraced him in the winner's circle, but instead of congratulations, whispered in his ear that she was pregnant. Karl headed straight for the depot and caught the first available long-distance bus.

Out in Bakersfield, things didn't come so easy. Those California boys didn't like him at all. They took him wide in the corners, pinched him back on the straightaways, and one night rode him right off the track into a cotton candy stand. It took a while for his ribs to mend. Karl was running right close to empty on cash and rooting for any kind of work when a pit groupie who adored his backwoods ways ("Oh honey, chew my lips till they bleed") introduced him to a crewman from a thrill show called Jonny Apache's Hell on Wheels.

The folks at Hell on Wheels didn't like him much either, but they'd just lost a man to a poolroom knifing, were about to launch a six-week tour of the Southwest, and needed a driver badly.

"You take dope?" Jonny Apache said, chewing on a quartered lemon.

Karl said no.

"Pack a bag."

So Karl became the number three man behind Jonny and his younger brother, Jerry. He opened the show with a few simple rolls, joined the brothers for some close-order precision driving, weaves and drifts and so on, and returned later to take part in the death-defying Sidewinder Crash. Jerry starred in this stunt, driving a junker with no glass and the door riveted shut. Jonny usually got on the public address himself to work the crowd. He told them how devoted he was to his baby brother and that even an old pro like himself knew fear. He told them that Jerry would not be wearing a helmet, that his only protection would be their prayers. Way up at the far end of the track, Jerry gunned his motor in a final salute. Ahead of him was a blazing firewall of pine boards, a ramp and another junker parked lengthwise beyond it on which he would land. As Jerry began his approach, left hand gripping the roof, a red bandana flapping in his fingers, Karl zoomed out of nowhere, hitting a 360 degree spin just at the far edge of the ramp as Jerry sailed over him and bellied down on that second junker.

It was a low risk stunt so long as the timing was right. Jonny had insisted on many practice runs employing a fifth wheel calibrated to measure delicate shadings of speed. There was a mere half-mile-per-hour tolerance either way. They did it a hundred and thirty-six times without a hitch. Until Flagstaff.

It was an evening show under floodlights and thousands of papery gray moths embroidered the air. Perhaps it was their erratic flight patterns that distracted him, or breasts in the crowd, but Karl lost it halfway through the first revolution and the front of his car swung out into Jerry's descending path. He heard someone scream,

"Look out," then watched in fascination as Jerry's left rear tire bounced on his hood, each serration in the black rubber distinct in that speck of transfixed time, imagining that Jerry could spin on end there forever, a human hood ornament. Karl let go of the wheel, covered his head and smacked into the parked junker, cracking one knee on the steering column. On its side, Jerry's car slid through grass and dirt like the blade of a giant Rototiller, struck the retaining wall belly first and caught fire. Karl just sat there, blood running warm inside his pants leg, as two young studs from the crowd leaped over the wall, pulled Jerry out and smothered his flaming body.

Chaos in the emergency room. Jonny asked an intern to give Jerry's wife a sedative. Shelly was on the floor, slamming a plastic ashtray against her head. And there was that gink from the crew, the one who had hooked Karl up in the first place, pushing past the security guard to announce that with his very own eyes he'd seen Karl pouring gin into his intermission Coke.

The bleakest tragedy of all was that Karl owned up when he didn't have to.

"Jonny, I know how it looks . . ."

He saw the sudden deadening of faces, sensed the collective tensing of muscles, musk in the air, a circle of predators closing around him. . . . Just one little shot. Hardly more than a tablespoon. Not enough to slow his reflexes. Really. His head had been clear. Something just got away. You've got to believe it was an honest mistake.

But could there be such a thing as an honest mistake when a man lay packed in ice, horribly burned over three fourths of his body? When he would remain in pure agony for eleven days and nights before the ultimate relief?

Karl was all played out. Tildy undressed him and coaxed him to bed. Dutifully, without feeling, she stroked his nestled head as he rattled on, mumbling into the mattress as if the disaster was only hours old and he could still secure the forgiveness of that emergency room lynch mob.

Finally, as dawn arrived, he went to sleep. "I don't feel guilty," he said before slipping away. "I feel pursued."

Tildy rallied herself under a hot shower and drank some orange juice with a raw egg whipped into it. Then she put on some clothes and got back in the car.

Nerves of steel in a bed of grease. Tildy walked the streets of

Gibsonton waiting for something to open up. Illogically, the air cooled as daylight advanced. The sky took on the texture of overripe cheese, and mist came in on a westerly breeze. A thunderstorm to start the day? It might be nice, wash away all the muck. Tildy buttoned up her leather jacket.

She crossed and recrossed a vacant lot, gouging divots with her sneakers, then crouched to fill her pockets with stones. Aiming at the ceramic insulators of a telephone pole across the street, she threw them in rapid succession and scored a perfect zero. Her shoulder was tight, would not rotate smoothly.

Of the Cougarette fielders it was generally agreed that Tildy had the most accurate throwing arm, if not the strongest—that distinction belonged to Wanda Watts who had once shattered a shatterproof windshield at fifty yards. On grounders deep in the hole or to her backhand side Tildy could beat most runners by three or four steps, delivering the ball time after time to a perfect chest-high spot so That's-Mary seldom had to move her glove more than an inch in any direction. Distressing to think this ability could have evaporated so fast.

Tildy sprinted awhile, trying to pump out the tar and nicotine with which she had lately been varnishing her lungs. Noticing a splash of light on the pavement ahead, she slowed, entered the Alhambra Diner, climbed on a rotating stool at the counter. The woman who poured her coffee without being asked had a wiry black beard that curved Ahab-style around her prominent jaw. Her husband, covering the grill with bacon strips for the breakfast stockpile, wore the briefest of tank tops, revealing portions of the classical tattoos that covered his torso: Botticelli's *Annunciation*, Gainsborough's *Blue Boy, Diana and her Companions* by Vermeer.

Inscribed glossies hung in clusters on the wall: "Captain Troy and his Amazing Trained Spiders"; "Mongo the African Methuselah"; "The Flying Arnheim Sisters"; "All the best from Apeman Adams, this Missing Link is missing you."

"How's business, Etta?"

"We're holding up pretty well. Paid off that new freezer last month. Albert, give this child a couple pieces of bacon. . . . You look awful washed out, honey. Been getting enough sleep?"

"How much is enough?"

"The heat'll take it right out of you." Patting her chin, "I always give myself a trim this time of year."

Albert lumbered over with some bacon in a folded paper napkin.

"Who was the last National League infielder to be killed in a plane crash?"

"Tell me, Albert."

"Kennie Hubbs of the Chicago Cubs. He was a demon with the glove."

"You were saving that one for me, weren't you?"

The door swung open and a young man in tinted aviator glasses blew in, snapping his fingers and singing.

"It's just half past six
Waiting for rain in some burg in the sticks
So set em up, Joe
I can do it up fast or do it up slow . . ."

"Coffee, mister?"

"Make mine a double." He had black, shoulder-length hair and a face off an old Roman coin. Sitting right next to Tildy, he cocked one eye in Etta's direction and whispered, "Hirsutism. Probably some kind of hormone imbalance."

Feeling crowded, Tildy drew in her elbows, shifted her knees to one side.

"What's the special today? Got any fish cakes?" He touched glances with Tildy, smiled, a lupine retraction of lips from teeth. "Don't mind me, señorita. It's these time-release Dexamyls. I'm stoked up pretty good."

"Hooray for you."

"Come on, don't be that way. Let's be old friends. Can I treat you to some fish cakes or something?"

"I don't think so."

"Okay, okay. Maybe something with a little more visual appeal. Miss, a hot fudge sundae for the señorita here."

Tildy raised her hand. "I think you ought to know about the special diet I'm on. My doctor says I can only take in so much bull-shit per day. If you keep on like this I'm liable to overdose."

He extended his hand. "Marty Rechette, how ya doin'. I'm a doctor myself."

"Really. What's your specialty?"

"Verbal display."

"I mean medically."

"Oh yeah . . . uh, forensic psychiatry. I just finished testifying in a strangulation case down in Key West. I'm in and out of court all the time."

"I'll bet," Tildy said, intrigued despite the outlandish MO.

Etta refilled their coffee cups, said testily, "You want to look at a menu or what?"

"Nah, I'll just have the fish cakes."

Etta threw down her order pad, flounced to a back booth and opened a newspaper.

He followed her with his eyes, caught sight of the pictures on the wall. "Unreal. What kind of place is this anyway?"

"Just what you see," Tildy said.

"What I see is, well . . . I don't know. Some of those people have serious medical problems. Bad taste, bad taste."

"Not in this town."

"Very inbred, huh?"

"No. Carny people live here, lots of them. Abnormal is normal so nobody notices."

Tildy saw that he was examining her body, slowly and section by section, not caring if she noticed. "Nothing the matter with me, if that's what you're thinking."

He removed the smoke-colored glasses and polished the lenses with a napkin. Then he went spinning on the stool and as he slowed like a switched-off phonograph and came to face her again, said, "You don't want to know what I was thinking."

"It's true I'm not a curious person. People comment on it all the time."

Outside, thunderheads were gathering over the supermarket and papers spiraled in a whistling wind. Tildy placed a stack of change next to her saucer and got up.

"It's been an experience, Marty. Let's meet here again next year."

"Wait now, *señorita*." He came after her, looming, and grabbed her hand as it reached for the door. "Hold up a minute. You don't want to skip out now and regret it all day long."

"I have an appointment."

"'I have an appointment.' Come on. You can't scale fish with a rubber knife." He angled his head toward the street. "I know my weather and this storm that's coming is gonna be a good one. A real extravaganza with lightning bolts from one end of the sky to the other. We'll go for a ride in it and you can show me the sights."

Tildy looked down. His hand was cold and surrounded hers like some sightless underwater beast. "Why not."

"That's much better. I'll drive."

Tildy was watching his seesaw hips as they crossed the street. She tripped over the curb and skinned the palms of both hands in breaking her fall.

"You okay?" He pulled her up. "Little blood there."

"It's no big deal," she said, dodging the arm he tried to curl about her waist. "I'm not usually so clumsy."

"I'm not really a doctor." Pushing the Fiat through a stop sign. "And this car is stolen."

"If you're trying to impress me, forget it."

"I'm leveling with you, that's all. I'm on my way to New York to close out a business deal and my real name is Jimmy Christo. No one calls me by my first name, though. It's not allowed."

"Great. You're a real colorful guy. But I'll have to assume that everything you tell me is a lie."

"Okay, let's hear your story. As plausible as you can make it."

"Why don't you just take me back to my car."

"Not yet. I want to hear your side."

Tildy looked out the window, then at the raw spots on her hands. The first submission was always the hardest; they get progressively easier after that. "My name is Tildy. I'm twenty-five years old. I play, or I used to play, shortstop for a traveling softball team. I have a husband who's kind of a basket case, a small birthmark on my stomach and not too much in the bank."

"You're pretty colorful yourself."

And then with a single horrendous crack the storm was upon them. Raindrops the size of hominy rumbled on the roof of the car and ran in overlapping sheets down the windows. The chill came right through the seams of the car. Tildy's teeth chattered and she slid down until her eyes were level with the door handle. They were breathing fog, felt the cold charge of ozone stiffening muscles along spine and calf. Rising off the floor came the heavy odor of a Turkish bath: steam and sweat and scurf and fungal crusts that fed off one another. Abruptly then, something was sucked from the furious core of the storm and it eased, shifted. They were strafed with tiny nuggets of hail now.

"I think you should have turned left back there," Tildy said.

Two-lane blacktop had turned to one-lane gravel. They swayed in the ruts and Christo had to swing sharply right to avoid the limbs of a freshly fallen tree. Soupy mud thrummed in the wheelwells. Christo stopped short and cut the ignition.

"What's the deal?"

He turned to her and wiped his eyes. Tildy stared ahead, shoulders square, arms folded under pointy breasts perfect as two chrome bumper guards.

"This doesn't go anywhere. I think you'd better turn around."

Rain fell softly now and through a meager canopy of trees the sky showed veins of yellow breaking through.

"I sort of like it here. Tranquil."

"Let's go."

Christo watched her hand dip into a pocket of her baggy slacks, reappear holding a pale, slender object which she tapped against the window glass. It was a straight razor.

"What's that for?"

"Protection." She depressed the thumb lever and the blade, spotted with iridescent tarnish, emerged from its mother-of-pearl housing.

"You don't need it from me, Tildy. Relax. Whatever you might be thinking right at the moment, I'm a real get-along guy. Dogs love me."

"You're a thief and a liar, and that's only what you've admitted to. How do I know you're not some maniac who'd like to tie me up and carve his initials in my thigh?"

"You don't, not conclusively. But that's part of my charm."

"This ride was your idea, don't forget, not mine."

"I'd call that coy, but if you put that thing away, I'll agree."

Tildy shoved the razor back in her pocket. "This doesn't mean I trust you."

He swung the door open, put one leg outside. "We're both too jumpy for close quarters. Let's walk."

Separated by a wide corridor of air, they tramped through the drizzle without speaking. The road dipped and turned past a gravel mound, an overgrown rubbish site: tires, jerry cans, rubber pipes, a tilting stove.

"We could make a fire if you want," he said, turning up the collar of her jacket for her, feeling for the first time the sleek texture of her skin as his knuckles grazed her neck.

"With what?"

"I don't know. Money. I read once about some people up in Minnesota who got caught in a blizzard. They burned twenty-dollar bills to keep from getting frostbite."

"Just keep walking," Tildy said, more vehemently than she meant to.

Their shoes squelched with every step. Tildy began purposely to slog through the deepest water she could find, kicking it in all directions. She stopped in a puddle that was shin-deep and brought her foot down hard, splashing Christo's legs. He nodded his head, smiling, and she did it again.

"Okay." He bent, filled cupped hands and emptied them on her chest.

She winced and leaned over, pulling the sodden T-shirt away from her skin. Christo, taking advantage of her poor balance, gave a slight shove and she toppled backward into the slop.

"Thank you," she said. She removed a sneaker, filled it with water and gradually, so as not to spill a drop, swaggered over and poured it on his head; while he was still blinking, she dropped a cold oyster of mud down the front of his pants.

Christo checked them into the Windjammer Motel as Mr. and Mrs. Leif Lucky of Detroit. The room overlooked the parking lot of a discount hardware store. The carpeting was mildewed, the bathtub drain clogged with hair. They showered separately, got under the covers, got nowhere.

"A lot of trouble you took to not get it up," Tildy said, lighting her only dry cigarette.

They stared at cracks in the ceiling, shared the hollow silences and prickly, irregular flushes that accompany sexual nonfeasance. Down below someone was beating his dog.

Christo reached for the cigarette, puffed. "At least we're dry."

"I know I am," Tildy said, delicately probing herself with an index finger.

Christo pressed the disadvantage. "See. I'm no kink, like you said before in the car. No madman from out of the cellar. I didn't scratch you or crank your arms or pound on you like a piece of veal. There's nothing I can't seem to be, but this is your place, right? Abnormal is normal. Can you tell the difference now?"

Tildy rose on the right angle of one lean elbow and drew out from beneath her pillow the razor, balanced it on her palm like a small stick whittled clean. "Just in case. I stashed it while you were in the shower."

"A wrong move or two and I could have been nutless, huh? Jesus." Christo cupped his groin. "Jesus. You're a tough little item, you know that? Ought to wear a bell around your neck."

"It's all right. I wouldn't have cut anywhere below the shoulders."

"You'll just have to excuse me. It's been a long time since I've been in bed with a woman."

She pulled the sheet over her head. This is it, she thought. Here the stale revelations come, the me-matter in all its weary detail from the first jumbled episode of Mom scrubbing his back to that perfect sexless sweetie who wounded his heart. . . . She did not want to know about his past. She did not even want him to have one.

"Listen, it wasn't up to me. They don't give you a whole lot of options in a mental hospital. Dating therapy is one thing they haven't tried yet."

Tildy jumped up, toes digging into the woven loops of the carpet, shouting through a sudden flurry of little stinging tears, "Why do you do it? Why do you tell me these things? Don't you know when it's time to shut up?" She fled into the bathroom.

"Come on out." Christo chattered his nails on the door, thin composition board he could have put his fist right through. "You should feel good. You probably know more about me than a lot of my friends." He heard water running full force in the sink. "Hey, this is a thoroughly cornball scene, me talking through the door and . . . Look. I move around a lot. I do things that are against the law and sometimes when I get jammed up, I have to take a few months in the bin. But there's nothing out of whack in my head. I don't commune with furniture. I don't go around on the freak with rubber bands in my mouth and the end of my necktie hanging out my fly . . . I'm just a small-time outlaw. Where's the harm in that?"

Jerking the door open, Tildy locked eyes with him briefly, then brushed past. Her wild brown curls spilled down her back like a gallon of dead bees. "I think I would like to go home now," she said, stepping into her pants.

"Bullshit." In annoyance Christo took a swipe at her fresh wake, perfumed with pink motel soap. "I interest you and you interest me, why kid around? I've been square with you more or less from the jump, so let's make it even. Home obviously is the last place you want to be. Don't you know I sniffed out your action before I was in that hash house two minutes? You got all the signs, sweetie, and believe me, I've been on the run long enough to recognize somebody else with the same disease. You need to bust the hell out and I think you ought to do it. I think you ought to come to New York with me."

Tildy's head came poking out the neckhole of her T-shirt, brows arching then flattening out, two dark valves above her glinting eyes. "That may be true."

"You know it."

"But don't try those slimy intimidation tactics with me. I'm no plastic dolly and I won't stand still for it. I never have. You don't know how many bozos I've had try and intimidate me into things. All my fucking life. Pushing at me, poking at me . . . 'I know what you want, sister, I got what you need.' "

"Man, but you could boil water with those eyes," Christo said admiringly. He had been dressing while she talked, now buttoned the cuffs of one of Rechette's blue cambric tab-collar shirts, pulled on ribbed black socks of see-through nylon. "I wasn't trying to push you, just keep you honest. We had kind of a saying, too, back there at Milford State: 'Don't mess with a psychotic, you can't win.' "

"You really want me to come to New York?"

"Absolutely. If I'm lyin', I'm dyin'."

"With that load of marijuana you've got in the trunk?"

"Well now, well." Christo fell back on the bed laughing, a slow, low-frequency laugh that had always served him well.

"I have a very sensitive nose."

"I'll say. And I won't insult your intelligence by telling you I've got a little quarter-horse farm up north and it's sweet clover hay you were smelling."

"Lovely. I'm supposed to sign on for a trip to New York with you and a load of dope? Uh-uh. Jump back, Jack. If I can smell it, so can any traffic cop."

"True. Get pulled over, you better talk fast fast fast. That's where the sport comes in for me."

"Well, I don't need any more sport. I'm retired."

In the dank T-shirt that chafed and made her nipples hurt, in stiff pants that rasped against her knees like sailcloth, Tildy moved shakily to the window and tipped her forehead to the glass. A light breeze stirred rain-laundered palm fronds and oily black puddles in the parking lot below. She let go of the pretense that she had any choice. What was the point? It was like the fading trail of a comet that had already passed. Her resistance was based on nothing; a fetish, the mindless twitching of a nerve. Somewhere back there a security violation had taken place, a border had been crossed, and now some dark and possibly terminal scheme had gathered her up. Quivering, rolling, heading straight into the wind and gaining speed. Bon Voyage! . . . And a vision of her immediate future flew by, milky and indistinct, like an animated cartoon projected onto the surface of one of those puddles. New York: a definite spot, at least, on the map.

"Right then. We'll stop by my house and I'll throw some things together."

"No hurry. We'll have lunch and a couple of drinks first and you can tell me about your husband."

"Forget I ever mentioned him."

"If you like. But let's have lunch first anyway."

"Aren't you afraid I'll change my mind?"

Christo just whistled through his teeth.

Parking in the shade, Tildy tossed the car keys in the ashtray.

"Wait here for me. I'll be right out."

"Have you decided what to say to him?"

"Not really."

"Just don't tell the truth. It's poor form."

It was stuffy inside the house, choked, even with the windows open. The furniture seemed shabby, unfamiliar; she felt, moving quickly and uneasily across the hard floor, that with a slight adjustment in the tuning of this signal she could be in the home of a friend she had not seen in years, who had called out of the blue to invite her over.

Karl stood with his back against the far wall eating peanut butter out of the jar.

"Where have you been all day? Car trouble?"

"No, everything's fine." She leaned against him, running her hand back and forth across his shoulders. "I ran into someone, we got to talking. You know."

"I went outside this afternoon," he boasted. "Walked up to Keyeses' and back, saw a blacksnake sunnin' himself in the road."

She shook her head, declining the gob of peanut butter he offered on the end of his finger. "I can't stay."

"What about dinner? Thought we might go out someplace. Had a cravin' for fried chicken and some cream gravy since I got out of bed. Dunno why."

Tildy saw that she would have to jolt him, and wasn't quite up to it. Despite his self-destructive history, the stubborn drag of his missteps and disabilities—or perhaps because of them—she was very loyal to her husband.

She pushed it out all at once. "I need some free time, Karl. This friend I ran into today, we're going up to New York for a while to look into some things. I left some money with R.C. down at the store so you don't have to worry about groceries and stuff. We'll keep in touch by phone and if . . ."

He flung his arms around her, still holding the jar of peanut butter which she felt hard against the small of her back as he squeezed. "You're leavin' me, ain't you."

"Don't dramatize. It's just a trip, no more." She broke away from his cramping, disconsolate hold. "It's no different than if I were back on tour, like Sparn had booked a few dates in the Northeast. You see?"

"No. You goin' off with someone else, that's no job. And I need you here."

"I won't be long."

"If you'd only stay, I'll straighten up and fly right. Promise."

She fixed her mouth on his and slicked her tongue over his lips, tasting something thin and bitter. "I have to go get organized now. He's waiting for me outside."

"You didn't say it was no man."

"I didn't need to."

"Don't do it, baby. Not now. S'like leavin' me out in the desert to burn up with no canteen . . . I'm set to fall in pieces, I can feel it comin' on. You got a responsibility for that."

But she was gone. From where he stood he could see her moving about the bedroom, reaching, leaning. She is slipping in and out. Slippery. Like a bar of soap, he thought. The harder you squeeze, the greater the odds it will fly away from you.

"Didn't always treat me this way," he said, but quietly so she wouldn't hear. "You used to stick by me in the old days."

Leaning inside the closet, the wrinkled white bedsheet that curtained it pushed over one shoulder and falling down her back like a bridal train, Tildy worked through the tangle of hangers one by one. Nothing much appealed. What were they wearing these days in the Big City?

"I wasn't planning to get bogged down in this," she murmured.

Taking her diaphragm from its bed of cornstarch, Tildy held it up to the light to check for tears or pinholes. Fine white powder fell on the sleeves of her jacket. Noises from the front room. Two distinct voices, not just Karl talking back to the teevee set. She hurried out, found them sitting opposite one another drinking beer.

"We're getting acquainted," Christo said, saluting her with his dripping can.

"Didn't I tell you to wait outside?"

"I seem to remember something like that."

"I had reasons for saying it, damn you."

"Curiosity got the best of me."

"Can't see why you wouldn't want us to meet." Karl, suddenly casual, almost smug, sucked foam off his lips. "We gettin' along fine."

"Sure," Tildy snapped. "You'll cozy up to anyone who brings a six-pack in here."

"Some temper."

"Oh yeah. Had that short fuse ever since I knowed her."

"When was that?" Christo slid forward in his chair, one foot jittering up and down at the termination of a crossed leg. "I always like to hear about how couples first met. That's real Americana to me."

"You can both go straight to hell." Tildy threw her jacket in a corner and returned to her packing, but left the door open so she could listen.

"Seems a lot longer ago than it really was. You know how the time can just seem to leak away on you."

"Sieve city. I know what you mean."

"Okay. So I was with this outfit movin' through farm country up there—Michigan, Minnesota, Wisconsin, so on. I was on the crew put up the rides and broke 'em down. There's some good rakeoff on that job, too, 'cause them rides, they design 'em to bounce the suckers all over and shake the money right out their pockets. We used to find all kinds of stuff, rings, watches, fountain pens . . . Say, you mind? I must've got too much sun today 'cause I sure am dry."

"Help yourself."

Karl unzipped a fresh beer, gargled some down. "Anyhow, Tildy. She joined up with us halfway through as a kootch dancer and, man, could she swing it. Make the hairs on your neck stand right up. July heat wave, we played a weekend in some town full of Polacks and what have you, they decided to throw a polka contest, offered a two-hundred-dollar first prize as bait. Naturally they needed some shills in there and me and Tildy got throwed together for it. Now I got a couple of heavy feet, but with her I was spinning around like a feather in the wind, just as sweet and smooth as could be and we copped that first prize. After that I followed her everywhere, carryin' my big hammer and all." Patting the dome at his beltline. "I was in good shape back then, didn't have this beer keg here and I could do hundreds of fingertip push-ups. Oh yeah, I wasn't gonna let that girl get away from me. Like she was my fairy godmother or somethin', like she could give me wings to fly."

Christo, reaching out for a comradely slap at his arm, said, "That young love, it just breaks your heart, doesn't it?"

86

Karl shrugged uncertainly. "We weren't that young. Got married in August in Saginaw with all the carnies there and wasn't that a show. Wish we had some pictures."

"It was Huron." Tildy's voice came cold and tolling from the far end of the house. "And if your dancing had been any better, or I hadn't been so bewildered, it would never have happened."

Karl was doing a few clumsy polka steps, his thumb pressed over the trowel-shaped opening in the can to keep the beer inside, a look of slowly thickening dismay on his face. By the time he sat down, that hatchet face had grown dim again, the small ritual elapsed, the spirit flown from his body with no reminder.

"I done a lot of things on the circuit, a lot of things, but I never put on no damn caveman suit and bit the heads offa snakes. There's some men will turn you low and rotten with half a chance, but I got my protection. I got my protection and I hold on."

Tildy wandered into the room fiddling at the untracked zipper of her suitcase, treating her husband's load of talk like so much jellied silence.

"She tell you what I'm doin' now?"

"No, she didn't."

"I got the donniker. I'm the donniker man."

"Sorry," Christo said. "That goes right past me."

"Donniker is the public toilet on the midway, see. Some of these owners want to go all modern, tell me to call it a personal hygiene station, but you get the picture. Got soap, towels, cologne, combs and hair tonic. And the paper. Got to come to me for your paper. So there I am, head man in the shithouse workin' for tips. How about it?"

"I've heard worse."

"Yeah, it ain't all bad. Nice and quiet in there and nobody I got to answer to. It's got more of a routine to it, most days just like the last one and the one before. But I remember one time, this was last summer in New England somewhere, we had a real big crowd and there was a drug company had these young bimbos passin' out free samples of this laxative thing. Problem was a lot of people took it for chocolate candy and gobbled it right up. You should have seen 'em all lined up with the sun beatin' down, hopping around like rabbits. Oh, I was a rich man that day, mm-hmmm!"

Tildy was the only one not laughing. Her eyes converged at a point high on the spotted gray wall. "I thought I might hardboil some eggs for us to eat in the car."

"What's this? What's this?" Giddy with all the talk of himself,

Karl had apparently forgotten about the trip.

"She's cleared for action," Christo put in. "I think that's what she's getting at."

"New York, is it? . . . What are you gonna do up there?"

"We might introduce Tildy around, maybe put a fresh face on her career. I mean, don't feel scorned or anything like that. Strictly a business venture with me, at least so far."

"What is it you do for work? I was aiming to get with you on that, then she came in about the eggs." Karl, just now beginning to sense some type of bunco activity, was fumbling toward truculence.

"Well, it's not so easy to put a name on what I do. I'm sort of a scout or an agent, free-lance. Maybe 'catalyst' describes it best. You take some energy from over here, put it together with some energy from over there and see if anything happens. Sometimes you get a healthy, profitable mix and sometimes you get third-degree burns. There's no way of telling just how the deal will go down until it does."

Karl appealed blinkingly to Tildy for translation, but she was verging elsewhere.

"Will you go wait in the car now? I need to talk to him alone."

"Tempo, tempo. Don't push the tempo." Christo let his open hands waver down toward the floor, like a pantomime of "Autumn Leaves." "Would you like to know what I think? I think the three of us ought to sit down to a nice candlelight dinner and really get to know each other."

"Yeah, let's do up some chicken and gravy." Karl shot out of his chair, began pulling at Christo's sleeve. "And while we're at the store we can stock up on more beer. . . . *Olé! Olé!*" he shouted; and to himself: This guy's okay, might be simpler if he just moved in.

Outgunned, Tildy sagged into the empty chair still puckered in the shape of Karl's wide hams, still warm with his yeasty, drawling smell, and covered her face with both hands.

Balled-up napkins, intersecting rings left by wet glasses, littered bones, beads of creamy wax and fat. Splayed legs under the table and sounds in the dripping light: teeth sucking and belches and Karl grunting as he touched the place at the corner of his mouth where the bent tine of a fork had repeatedly jabbed him. There was sliced pineapple for dessert and then more beer.

Across the floor moonlight was a steel-colored box within which lay a single spattered shoe, its laces trickling off into the dark. Karl asked that the dishes be cleared away so he and Christo could match muscle in an arm-wrestling bout. They drained their glasses and stooped together, fingers wagging then settling into the gaps between bone, elbows wrapped in dish towels, waiting for Tildy to cue them. But she stood to one side rolling a pill of yellow wax between her palms, radiating indifference. Christo took the edge—"Now!"— and pushed fast and hard so that Karl had to rise out of his seat to avoid an immediate pin. He gained leverage until they were back at a rigid right angle, blue veins popping, eyelids clamped tight, the double fist in a tremor now as Karl leaned, condensed his force, and Christo bent at the wrist. The table shivered under them and Karl's tongue emerged pushing tiny silver bubbles over his lower lip. And then it was over, Christo's arm slapping down backward, rubbery and dead.

"But you gave up? I don't get it."

"I do that sometimes," Christo said, wiping his face with the towel. "It hurt. And you would have won anyway."

While Christo finished the dishes, Karl slept curled like a pet on the floor, hair spiky, a low buzzing of mucus inside his bristly nostrils, an oily sheen on his face, the hem of the blanket Tidly had laid over him wadded in his fists. He had collapsed in the midst of his fourteenth can of Gatortail Ale.

Rebuttoning his shirt, Christo backed away from the sink. "I thought it would be easiest this way. No messy farewell scene. We'll slip out quietly and be gone when he wakes up."

"It's cold, but I suppose you're right. I just wish . . ." Tildy aligned the soap dish beside the sudsy blue sponge, wrapped half a lemon in wax paper. "I just wish what I was doing made a little more sense."

Insects clicked in the wet grass and the sky was punctured with stars as they made their way, hand in hand, to the car. Christo looked up at the bright bulb of the moon, pulled her against him and drummed on the trunk.

"Want to take a look inside? See what we're carrying?"

"No, that's something else I'd rather ignore."

6

Night was a cold black suction at the windows. Their destination was a ruined city. There was exhilaration in the raw, hot smell of gasoline and the whine of the Fiat's six cylinders at maximum stress, in the glow of dashboard lights like prowling jungle eyes. A gospel station faded in and out, jammed by a news broadcast two clicks to the right: *"I'm gonna walk that milky white way some of these days. . . ."* Tildy let the unrolling wilderness contain her. So long as the wheels turned, misgivings were irrelevant.

They passed a pint of Bacardi back and forth, mixing Cuba Libres as best they could: swig of rum, a wedge of lime, a nip from the canned cola balanced on the dash, all swirled in the mouth like dental rinse, then swallowed. Their lips burned and their blood rumbled. Christo, raconteur, riffed on and on.

"There are a million ways to end up in the bughouse. Nobody's exempt. The president of IBM might drop in if it seemed like a good idea for him to disappear temporarily. 'Exhaustion,' they call it. Yeah, it's the closest thing you'll ever see to a classless society in there. Everyone gets fucked just the same. They don't care who you are. There was a kid I knew lost his larynx to cancer, had one of those vibrator gizmos he'd touch to his throat when he wanted to talk. One summer he started going around to radio stations and do, you know, anything, he'd sweep out the studio, it didn't have to be the weather or the traffic report. But he really wanted to get into radio. Unusual, but who could possibly be threatened by it? He's buzzing away at the station manager of one of those all-news operations, making his pitch, when the guy makes one phone call and, wham, that's it. They stamp his papers and throw him in with the rest of the nuts. I collect stories like that. Old gent I met up with this last time. He wasn't just the quiet type, he was the prototype. Lived in a small town all his life, never married, had nothing to do when he retired so he wandered the streets all day shaking hands with whoever. 'Afternoon, good to see you.' It got to be an obsession. He'd dash between cars to get to the other side of the street for a clasp. But some people didn't like the way it looked or something, so they had county welfare put him away. Sound as a drum when he got there, but he'd done two years by the time I checked in and was afraid to tie his own shoelaces. Oh, they get you, one way or another . . . Shit, you can take my own case. Or one of them."

He scissored two fingers, took the cigarette she lit for him, his features glazed orange with the first long drags.

"But let me give you the background first. I was running with this Indian girl in Denver a few years ago. Oglala Sioux. Sixteen years old, and like I always say, you're only as young as the woman you're sleeping with. Silver had long black hair, green eyes, the sweetest disposition. God, was she lovable. We had a real tight game going, went something like this: I'd rent a late-model car for one week, slap fresh plates on it, make out a phony registration form. Silver would put an ad in the paper offering the car at an insanely low price. A mark would be there in no time and he'd find Silver all upset and crying because the landlord was going to put her out on the street unless she got her rent up that day. The mark's getting a steal anyway, a couple minutes with those big, wet eyes and he's happy to help out by paying cash. That night, before he's had a chance to re-register it, I go over to his house with my duplicate keys, drive the bastard away and we start all over again. Not real sophisticated, but we had it tight, doing three or four sales in a good week. We were building up a stake, planning to spend a year in Mexico in a house overlooking the beach. But then I came home one afternoon and it was all gone, Silver, the money. Gone. All she left me was a can opener and the furniture we'd picked off the street. And you know where I'd been all day? Out looking for one perfect thing to give her on her birthday that would make her just light up. It was bitter, all right. I had a soft spot for her, understand? So anyway, I'm sleeping in the park on frozen ground, living on cupcakes and trying to figure my next move. My body can't take that program for long; next thing I know, I'm puking all over my shoes in front of the Brown Palace Hotel, cruiser pulls up and I get popped for vagrancy. On top of all my other grief, this was the fatal dose. I wigged out at the stationhouse, screaming my head off. 'I got important friends'll make you regret this.' They didn't need my aggravation, right? So they packed me off to the state bin and, bingo, case closed. It's the perfect indeterminate sentence."

Tildy touched the rim of his nearest ear. "What was it you bought her for her birthday?"

"Parrot feathers. A ten-pound bag of parrot feathers. Now, do you mind if I make my point? . . . Okay. Clear Creek Hospital, a real warehouse. They had a little of everything in there, like Noah's Ark, and no time to play around. They started breaking you down right from the git-go. Inside of five minutes they'd stripped me down, put me in this flimsy cotton item split up the back, thrown me in a dark lockup. I can't remember how long it was before I got any food. I was reeling, see, and not yet wised up, I wasn't hip to the provocateur element, this on-arrival jolt they hit you with. Shout in your face one minute, pat your head the next, ask you trick questions and call you a liar when you don't give the right answer. There's a lot of browbeating, real humiliating crap. I'm good and whiplashed after a few days of it and they got me doing a little free labor, scrubbing the linoleum floor with a brush. And all of a sudden I could see what they were making me into. But I couldn't see far enough because what I did then was right on schedule. I lost it, completely lost it. Suds all over the place and I'm ripping up sheets, just raving. And that's when they've got you, see? It's all over and those house odds were just too strong: 'Now you see how dangerous and uncontrollable you are. In fact, you may be even sicker than we thought. We will have to drug you and put you in restraints before you hurt someone.' It can be months before they throttle back on the medication and give you a standing eight count."

Tildy shivered, nibbled on lime rind. "I see what you mean," she said. "You've got to watch out for that provocateur element."

Was it possible? Yes. It was possible to say she was having a good time.

OBEY LIMITS
YOUR SPEED MONITORED BY AIRCRAFT

In search of fuel, Christo switched to a secondary road. The gauge had been pinned on E for several miles.

"Rechette will have put out the word on these cards. They should have made the hot sheet by now." One by one Christo removed the celluloid wafers from his wallet and scaled them out the window. "You got to know when to ditch these things. I found that out. But we may latch on to some free gas yet."

Without lights, Christo nosed up an asphalt drive, parked by the adjoining garage and cut the motor. He waited a few minutes, alert for any sound or gleam of light from inside, then stepped out and tried the garage door; it was locked. He went over all four sides of the building, feeling with his hands, hunting for signs of alarm wiring in the thin radiance of a cigarette lighter. Satisfied he ran no risk of setting off bells, he took a set of picks from his jacket, sprang the simple pin lock on his first try and eased the door up carefully on its tracks.

A pair of Cadillac hearses were parked inside, two state-of-the-art beauties fresh from Detroit that model year with hand-rubbed gray finishes, understated chrome trimmings and, in the rear, gauzy white curtains behind smoked glass.

"Delicious. Maybe we should just swap," Christo said. "These babies can do a hundred and ten and you don't even know you're moving."

Tildy yawned. "I don't think you want to blow your cover that badly."

"I guess not. But how about that leg room?"

From the webbing under the driver's seat Christo plucked out a coiled length of transparent rubber tubing. He spun the gas caps off the Fiat and the closer hearse. Inserting one end of the tubing down into the hearse's gas tank, he took a few deep breaths, moistened his lips and commenced sucking on the other end, pulling away to exhale, bending his knees each time to lower the tubing's elevation. Gas traveled gradually up the line, reaching his mouth when the tubing was on an even latitude. He spat furiously and guided the flow into the Fiat's tank.

"Now we let gravity do the work." Spitting again, swabbing at his lips with his shirt-tail. "This was the first game I ever ran. Couldn't have been more than nine, scooting around the neighborhood with milk bottles and four feet of garden hose and all I was after then was enough money to buy mud flaps and a side mirror for my bike. Twenty- two years I been at it and still getting gas in my mouth. Now there's a story with a moral."

"What is it?"

"Beats the shit outta me. Any rum left? This taste really stays with you."

Bolted under the dashboard was a 32-channel CB radio assembled at a runaway shop on the Philippine island of Mindanao. Christo explained that the original owner had installed it. Rechette, he said, was fond of cruising the suburbs listening for distress calls: multi-car fatals or simple fender benders, propane leaks, lost children, angina crises. Rechette was a qualified CPR instructor, a collector of drug abuse bulletins, an amateur mechanic who kept his trunk packed with flares, blankets, first-aid supplies including ampules of Thorazine and of epinephrine (for the treatment of anaphylactic shock), boxes of tools and spare parts, fifty feet of yellow nylon rope, and, of course, a Polaroid camera. "Everyone just take it easy," he would say. "I'm a licensed physician," and he would move gawkers and sobbing relatives aside with the slightest pressure of his vital hands—the cool professional, the humble altruist. And he was hypnotized by glazed eyes, by faces paled with fear and marbled with blood.

"What a ghoul; he showed me some of those pictures and got excited all over again," Christo said as they squealed around a curve, headlights slicing through the trees. "Told me once in so many words that this was a great way to meet people." He seized the handmike, dangled it upside down on its spiraled cord. "Some marketing hero came up with this idea. Expand the machine population, that's always a plus, right? You got your CB dictionaries and your CB clubs with insignia to sew on your CB windbreakers. You got a whole army of yokels talking at each other in the dark like some damn circle jerk."

He pressed the button to transmit. "Who's got their ears on out there? This here is Lonely Lonnie beaming right at you, come on. Hey, nightbirds, do you copy? We pointed north for that Fun City so how's it look up I-95 through Savannah, come on."

"Comin' in strong, Lonely Lonnie." Frog voice through a curtain of static. "You got Daddy Pigtails out of big Gee Ay, the man with the bacon from Macon, come on."

"Get your feet on the floor and your hand on the door, Daddy. I understand there's a real bad infection down your way."

"Mile high negatory . . . What you talkin', boy?"

"Just a random FCC check, sir. I suggest you drive immediately to your nearest emergency room." Christo flipped the toggle switch, replaced the mike on its hook. "These things are a menace to public safety."

But this gaudily professed scorn, Tildy noticed, didn't prevent him from playing along. He couldn't resist those free airwaves. With the urgency of an intermission smoke, he'd grab that mike and start babbling, a new identity each time, a fresh cover story. Self-parody? Protective coloration? She was making an effort, at least, to get the idea.

But there was no idea as such, no underlying sense or motive. There were only the zigzags of dissimulation that Christo had learned—as a mole learns which roots to eat, as a raccoon learns how and when it is safe to topple garbage cans—in order to make his living.

"This is the Rajah Rat running a load of hot spareribs out of Calcutta, India, that there ebony void." And twenty miles later he was Little Ore Bucket and after that, Mad River Gramps as he rambled on about the great gone days of the Model-A Ford and real grass in the ballparks; and the loss of his dear wife to the vampirish thirst of the nation's favorite disease. "Look at your watch. Two minutes from now someone on this planet will die of cancer."

"You're pretty good at this," Tildy said. "You ought to have your own show."

"It's occurred to me."

She opened the vent window, let the wind hit her face full on. Darkness was beginning to erode, a sallow-gray modulation at the edge of the horizon. They had been some ten hours in transit and she felt punchy, a tremolo hum in her ears, a raw spot at the back of her throat. Christo behind the wheel was noisily efficient, in full command. But she'd stayed right with him, hoped this had gained her some leverage. Her steadfast ambition at this stage: to be just one of the guys.

FLASHING LIGHTS MEAN LIFT BRIDGE IN OPERATION

It was nap time in Summerton, South Carolina. Christo was beginning to hallucinate: fallen trees across the road, low-flying aircraft, and finally a scant formation of rocks on his left which he mistook for a jackknifed semitrailer.

"We better stop for a little bit before the road disappears from under me."

They registered at the Blue Bell Motel as Donnie and Connie Bodanski.

"My kid sister," Christo offered. "I'm driving her up to Boston for her freshman year at college."

"Ummm," the desk clerk grunted, a putty-faced old ratbag in an orange muumuu who couldn't be bothered to lift her eyes from a back issue of *Daytime TV Mirror*. "Number twelve. Last door on the left. Coke machine's busted."

Altogether pumped out, they tottered inside, exchanged a few instinctive pleasantries and fell asleep with their clothes on. It was late afternoon when they resurfaced with dim headaches and coated tongues. Tildy was so fogged she forgot to remove the crimped sanibag from the bathroom glass and water glanced off the paper, making cold little shock points on the back of her hand.

She came out rubbing her neck. "I think I should burn these panties."

She shucked off shoes and socks and did a little running in place, some knee bends, finished up with forty push-ups counted aloud. Christo watched leaves of muscle along her back widen and contract. Twenty-eight, twenty-nine. Hair fell across her face, exposing the first percolation of sweat on her neck. Thirty-two, thirty-three.

He roused himself, lit a cigarette, got on the wire with a long-distance operator. He read off a credit card number from the back page of his address book, its binding reinforced with Band-Aids. "This number belongs to Dow Chemical. I use it whenever I can. . . . Hey, Pierce, it's Mr. Christo, your mule."

"Where are you?"

"Cotton country somewhere. One of the Carolinas, I don't know."

"You coming on horseback or what? I was expecting you today."

"I know, I know. Got a little sidetracked down around Tampa, picked up an associate."

"I hope she's over sixteen. Don't want you getting busted for statutory rape and blowing my load."

"No problem. She's not into mating anyway. You got nothing to worry about. We should be there tomorrow, early P.M."

"Call me from Looie's."

"I'm gonna need some cash when I . . . "

But Pierce had hung up.

"Who was that?"

"One of the foremost herb brokers in Manhattan. You're going to like him a lot."

Replete with chicken-fried steak, home fries, and wedges of

96

chocolate chiffon pie, they were back on the track an hour later, Tildy relegated once more to map reading and gazing out the window at passing greenery.

"Whatsa matter? You don't trust me to drive?"

"Not at all. But suppose some cracker lawman were to shake this car down? Then I saw you by the side of the road with your thumb in the air and you don't know a thing about me or what I'm hauling."

"Wish I could believe you were that kindhearted. I really do."

They had arrived at some uncertain, intermediate stage, with not a single thing to say. Tildy counted the corpses of animals who had misjudged a sprint across the road; they were all over the place, losers to speed beyond their understanding. Back home, at the tourist information booths where they gave out free orange juice, there were little warnings posted about alligators who liked to sun themselves on the highway.

Christo chainsucked peppermints, steered with his elbows or his teeth, sang bits of advertising jingles and enjoyed a bout of good old nerve-rattling, mind-prodding paranoia. Every passing motorist wearing a tie was an FBI agent. Every speedwagon with growling tailpipes and wide tires contained some overwound DEA zealot who would just as soon blast you and take the dope. Every dark blotch on the horizon was a roadblock bristling with shotguns. What a nice unadorned target he made out here among the onion fields.

Finally, as dusk approached, they stopped at Nick & Nora's Swim-O-Links for a dip in the pool in rented suits. Tildy's white one-piecer with reinforced bra cups was at least one size too large; it bagged out in back and the shoulder straps kept slipping down. Christo challenged her to a five-lap race and lost, Tildy finishing with a sloshing burst, the suit peeled down around her middle by the rush of water. He paid for the chili dogs as promised, but fared no better at miniature golf. Tildy scored two holes-in-one, the first a shot that just missed the descending blade of a motor-driven Olde Dutch Windmill, the second a miracle putt that wobbled into the mouth of a cement polar bear, dropped through a pipe onto all-weather green carpet and rolled through a clot of dead leaves that altered the path of the ball almost ninety degrees, enabling it to reach the lip of the cup, teeter, fall in.

"I'd say you were a natural born athlete," Christo muttered, tearing the scorecard to shreds.

In northern Virginia they came upon an outgrowth of the Indochinese diaspora. The Ban Dinh Family Restaurant was just across the street from a gas station where Tildy flirted with the attendant while Christo swiped a quart of 30-weight and wiper blades that turned out to be the wrong size.

"How about a late supper with the boat people?"

"I'm not really in the mood for exotic food," Tildy said.

"We'll see. Maybe they've got a steak and lobster combo."

It was warm inside the restaurant, steamy. Thai Airlines posters were tacked over sloppily pasted red wallpaper, blinking Christmas tree lights outlined the rec-room–sized bar, and on each Weldwood table was a cruet holding plastic roses. Except for a golden age couple dressed for a sales award banquet, puttering uncomfortably with the remnants of their meal, Christo and Tildy were the only customers in the place. A slender boy escorted them to a table with great ceremony and a wrinkly, don't-shoot-me smile, laid out menus, withdrew pad and pencil from his designer jeans.

"You choose by number, write down here." The smile was ferocious now, a rictus.

A chunky old woman, probably the kid's grandmother, materialized at Christo's elbow. Her stylized movements and buoyant manner suggested a veteran of service familiar with the ways of white people: Those were grand days in '56 and '57 at the Club Charenton near Saigon. We knew where we stood.

When she spoke, light did strange things on the metal bridgework at the front of her mouth. "Good evening. You would like perhaps a cocktail?"

"A martini for me."

"There are no more olives. So sorry."

"That's okay. Something for you?"

"Just tea," Tildy said.

As they were studying the menus, Tildy murmuring that she'd be happiest with a bowl of plain rice, the other couple passed by on their way to the cash register. The missus loitered near their table, assuming the instant comradeship of compatriots stuck in some dreadful foreign backwater.

"Whatever you do, don't order anything with pork. It tasted flat rancid to me."

Christo nodded thoughtfully, twirled the pencil like a baton.

"No shit. Let me tell you something, lady. These people know what rat meat tastes like. They know that if you stand near a column of napalm smoke it'll suck the air right out of your lungs. So do I. I've seen it happen. In your position I'd be damn grateful there wasn't any strychnine in the food."

She giggled, touched her lips, then felt the icicles of Christo's glare upon her and beat it out to the car.

"You were really over there?" Tildy said, and a nasal voice from the middle recesses of her brain yelled: Sucker!

"Sure, sure. I was a real mudeater. Last of the doomsday grunts. I'd go days without sleep, get myself all smacked up and volunteer for night patrol, go for the big thrills. Maybe a little hand-to-hand combat, unzip some gook and lick the blood off my bayonet."

"Sshhh."

"Don't be dense then. You know induction day was it for me. Ran around the halls dropping my shorts and spreading for anything in a uniform. Man, I had my 1-Y all signed, sealed and delivered inside two hours. It was a lot easier in those early days. Another year or two and they'd seen all kinds of dodges. You had to be a little more creative. Little brother of a guy I used to do street vending with went down with his pet St. Bernard, Rollo. Rollo used to drool all over himself after they spiked his Gravy Train with LSD. But the kid's all smiles, very enthused, ready to ship out to the zone as soon as possible so he can start blowing Commies away. We've got to stop them before they reach Santa Barbara, all that. Just one thing, though. He's got to take his dog along. 'Can't go anywhere without my dog, sir.' Plants a kiss on those slimy chops. 'Me and Rollo, we're closer than brothers. Maybe you could teach him to sniff out land-mines?'"

"Did they go for it?"

"Oh, yeah. The shrink was real impressed. Too bad it didn't end there."

"What happened?"

"It started to come down on him that summer. In buckets. His father died in a hotel fire. His girlfriend went out for ice cream one night and never came back. The band he was with threw him over for another bass player right before they signed a record contract.

And somebody ran over his dog. So what the fuck, he went and enlisted in the marine corps. Got both his legs blown off in Cambodia."

LANE ENDS 1000 FEET

This segment of the north-south artery was a memorial to our most recently murdered Chief of State. The rest area in which Christo and Tildy were parked had been named after the Hon. Elihu S. Robbinet, evidently a worthy Maryland jurisprude of days gone by. Such was immortality in the age of the disposable raincoat and the celebrity golf tournament; in a nation that communicated increasingly via T-shirt and bumper strip.

Christo dozed sporadically, a watch cap pulled down over his eyes, while Tildy chattered on inside the clammy, hermetic little isolation box the Fiat had become.

". . . like the way you stuck it right into that woman back at the restaurant," she was saying. "That's what I'm talking about. I admire that kind of conviction because I don't have it. There's a lot of meanness in me but I don't use it, and that makes me feel so half-assed. I'd like to be a real bullet-nippled bitch but I always fall short. All I can get to are the gestures. Maybe it has something to do with the choices I made a long time ago."

"Timing." Christo scratched his nose, rested his cheek on the steering wheel. "S'all in the timing."

"For God's sake, it's not strategy I'm talking about."

"It's all strategy. And that's all."

"Then why can't I carry it off? Why do I feel like a whore sometimes?"

"Don't bother yourself over nothing. Let's climb in the back seat and get friendly."

"Uh-uh. Crank this thing up and move. I want to get to New York and show you just how much of a bitch I can be."

"Right on, kid. Right on."

UNION CITY, NEW JERSEY
HOME OF THE AMERICAN EMBROIDERY INDUSTRY

Christo leaned on the horn. "Poor, itchy New Jersey, the sick love-slave of New York. And how she loves the pain."

The joy ride was over now. Ten minutes away from the target and Christo was antsy, constantly checking his mirrors, jaw muscles pulsing as he clenched his teeth. There was a taste of brackish water in his mouth, against his hot cheeks the sensation of emery paper. Tildy frittered up and down the AM band; nothing but news and commercials.

"Enough." He slapped her hand away.

They spilled onto the bending, descending ramp to the Lincoln Tunnel and there, beyond the wharves and the viscous gray river, was that notorious skyline depicted on a thousand beer trays, decals, pennants; intaglioed on coffee mugs, woven into beach towels and sweaters. It was the image pilgrims took to bed with them at night: I have been there, to the sizzling core of the Machine. Today, through a thick and striated haze, it seemed to be melting away for good.

"Tally ho," said Tildy.

They had just enough to cover the toll.

Midtown, midafternoon. All manner of faultlessly turned out honeys bombing up and down the pavement; a career-girl carousel. Fueled by Lo-Cal lunches consumed at their desks, they emerged from their warrens carrying briefcases crammed with reports and market research printouts, considered their profiles in shop windows, hailed cabs imperiously, letting the wind whip their layered coifs since, after all, today's woman doesn't live by her looks.

Tildy wondered how she could possibly compete.

"There it is," Christo said. "Hot enough for you?"

Five blocks south of Times Square he curbed the Fiat next to a pay phone, dug around for a dime. But the phone was inoperative: receiver clipped off, coin box disemboweled, and all over everything the felt marker glyphs of pubescent soul writers—

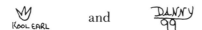

"Wait here for me. If you get bored, just circle the block. I'll catch up with you."

He dialed Looie from a Blarney Stone bar. A woman in rainbow knee socks was wishing herself happy birthday. Three old-timers were arguing with the bartender over program selection on the tube.

"What's shakin', Looie? You ready for a delivery? We're just fifteen minutes north."

"We? No, never mind. Surprise me."

"She's not your type, Looie. Trust me."

"'Trust me,' he says. I didn't even know they'd let you out until a couple days ago. You're in defiance of science, my friend. You'll teach them all humility before it's over."

7

Louis "Chemikazi" Levitski came from rugged Ashkenazic stock. His father was a muscular, taciturn individual who had learned, during a lengthy tour of Eastern Europe's DP camps, that a keen sense of dread was a man's best friend. He was not a family man, preferring to spend all his time behind the counter of his stationery store, sipping schav from a Mason jar, never removing his overcoat. He wanted his son to go into banking or real estate and become "a bigger thief than any of them." Louis's mother, a sickly woman with an erratic temper and a compulsive devotion to the films of John Garfield, wanted him to become a composer of Broadway melodies. "With the royalties, you can buy me a whole hospital," she used to say. But Louis disappointed both of them. He was a genius.

In 1965 he became the youngest student ever to be graduated from the doctoral program of Rensselaer Polytechnic. A multinational corporation offered him a substantial bonus package to sign on and he went immediately to work on a shellfish toxin project funded, through a Liechtenstein holding company, by the CIA. While the project itself was a failure, Louis was not. He was, in fact, the talk of the boardroom. Skipping a few levels of the hierarchy did not endear him to his colleagues (that was fine; he didn't want friends), but a year later he had his own lab, an unlimited budget, and was busily rearranging peptide chains in an effort to develop a neuromuscular blocking agent which, when released into an urban water system, could "neutralize" as many as half a million people in less than twelve hours. He was extremely happy in his work.

Then came the Summer of Love and Louis was ravaged, subverted.

Late one evening he was snuggled in his tiny apartment listening to Ezio Pinza and reading a chemical engineering journal—or trying to. The noise from above was making it very difficult: clangs, thumps, shrill laughter, and what sounded like someone roller-skating from one end of the hall to the other. He went upstairs to complain.

There, in a hot crush of thoroughly unhinged folk who seemed to be emitting smoke from every orifice, a large man inexplicably dressed in Bermuda shorts, a straw boater and the dress tunic of Her Majesty's Coldstream Guards prevailed on him to have a cup of punch and then another and then . . . Yes, he'd been right about the roller-skating. Lovely girl, but her taffy face was, my God, drooping down around her waist. Hmmm, better lay off that punch. Tastes like glue anyway. . . . Getting chilly. Maybe ought to close those portholes, keep the storm at bay. At bay in the Bay, indeed. Louis with the large L, have we met before? Athens, perhaps. Look out for the cactus, look out. . . . Fingers numb. Tingling in scalp area. Blankets, more blankets. I must see the Captain. . . . I'm repelling electrons, buddy, don't get smart with me. . . . You're okay. Just some queasy thing'll pass. I know what I'm doing. Ionization. I'm in solution . . . Wait a minute. Oowooo, there's something in my belly made of jelly and it needs to get out! . . .

This first LSD experience was by no means his last but, in its aftermath at least, was certainly the most transforming. After riding up and down in an elevator with two gay poets and a beagle for an hour and a half; after scampering through soot-black tunnels of the IRT line with a teenage waitress from Babylon, L.I.; after a dawn confrontation with the Angel of Chemistry, a cheap dame wearing all kinds of bead necklaces who spilled maggots from her mouth whenever she opened it; after waking up fully clothed in three inches of bathtub water in the home of a kindly black postal worker who had scooped him off the shoulder of the Cross Bronx Expressway, Looie Levitski had no choice but to start all over again.

He entered his laboratory that afternoon, destroyed all his notes, poured acid over the desks of several vice-presidents, and with his bare hands smashed spectrometers, gas chromatographs and a scintillation counter worth upwards of four hundred thousand dollars.

A fugitive from justice, he fled to Oregon and built himself a cabin overlooking the Rogue River. There he passed the next four years, sturdy and contemplative, with his logger's boots and brier pipe, hewing wood and drawing water, observing birds and wildflowers, casting for steelhead trout and making serene, Tantric love to a series of fragmentary women who came to sample the purest hallucinogenic drugs in the state, the product of Looie's undiminished skills. To his amazement and delight, he discovered that women found him charming. By almost any standard, certainly, he cut a less than dashing figure, so what was it? Perhaps his newly discovered abilities as a chef? His cool acceptance of failure? His distaste for violence of any kind? Or perhaps it was nothing more than his avowed discovery of a vaginal enzyme that prevented tooth decay and his manifest intention never to darken again a dentist's door.

But one day, Looie wandered into the forest to collect pine cones, having left a gas flame on near a beaker of formic ether. The cabin burned to the ground. Everything was lost, including eighty-nine chapters of automatic writing: "Cacaphonous Desperation Versus the Inherent Glide of Starched Mush."

He returned to New York via bicycle. It took him five months.

Looie's loft was on Pearl Street in a part of the city originally laid out with the horse-drawn vehicle in mind and Christo had to jog back and forth on one-way streets. The block was grimy and dismal, a line of vacancy; obsolete workshops of stale-cake brick held together with barbed wire and rusted sheet tin; street pocked with glass, sparkling seeds from which the weeds grew.

Tildy, with narrowed eyes: "Who'd want to live here?"

"You know what they say. Never judge a book by its jacket copy." He made a modified K turn, nosed up to an enameled green steel door. "Actually, I think you'll like this part. It has a certain cinematic tang."

He got out, climbed on a standpipe to press a button high on the wall. The door lifted, revealing a caged freight elevator. Christo pulled the gate and drove them, Fiat and all, aboard, called "All in" up the shaft; they began very slowly to rise. The shakes and shudders gave Tildy the same and she reached for Christo's hand.

"It's all right. This thing can hold a cement mixer."

At last they edged into light. Looie was waiting for them by an already open gate on the third level of this one-time hides and leathers warehouse, a short, thinset being in a velour tracksuit. He had beady black eyes and, except for a small, triangular beard dyed blue, not a hair on his head—this made his prominent nose even more so, like, you could open beer bottles on it. The original-cast album of *Bye, Bye Birdie* was playing and he lip-synced along.

"We're going to park in this guy's living room?"

Christo smiled. "I thought you'd like this part."

But there was no living room as such. The dividers, panels of pebbled plexiglass on overhead tracks, had been drawn to one side; it was one clear-through space so large that details at its farthest depth—some kind of platform, old machinery—were hard to make out. The floor was sanded white, walls stripped back to the brick, tin floral-imprint ceiling, furniture of chrome and suede, warm earth tones, recessed lighting.

Glossy head tilted appraisingly, Looie helped her out of the car.

"Meet my partner, Tildy Soileau."

"*Enchanté.*" His lips skimmed across her knuckles and he embraced Christo, kissing him on both cheeks. "Welcome back. Welcome back to the madhouse without walls."

"You're looking good, Chemikazi, got that glow of health and wealth. And I like the blue beard. It looks a lot better than the green."

"It's been a tough year, a lot of cruelty and fraud out there—you know—people whizzing around like insects, trying to stay clear of the big boot heel coming down. But I just float through it all and never get hit with the debris. I can't explain it. It's a matter of faith. . . . Now, can I get you anything? Ham salad? Fondue? White wine?"

"Later for that. I say we sample up." Christo applied the trunk key, opened one of the garbage bags, tore off great fistfuls of the herb, gummy with resin, dropping them onto an unpleated road map. "Pierce tells me they had a very dry growing season down in Colombia and we have here some tops of the bush pickings. El Primo. He says even an old jade like you will be impressed."

While Christo sat at a butcher-block table rubbing buds through a flour sifter, Looie took Tildy lightly by the arm and showed her around his "barracks." He pointed out rosewood cabinets he'd installed himself, the hand-cranked dumbwaiter where he stored onions and potatoes, a row of pancakes—blueberry, buttermilk, whole wheat—tacked up intact as instant sculpture. He opened a locker of salvaged skins of bear and fox and stoat and made her feel the brittle age in them with her hand.

"Once when I still had hair I shared a lunch of berries with a young grizzly. Tremendous berries in Oregon. Justly famous."

He'd saved the best for last, guiding her now to a window centered in one wall, tiers of green, flashing movement behind the glass. How lovely his touch is, she thought, I know his arm is there but it feels weightless.

"My vivarium," Looie announced. "Not a terrarium or aquarium. It's sort of a country club for reptiles, you know, like the place where the mobsters go. La Costa."

The terraced enclosure was high and deep. Mossy outcroppings and sandy pools were surrounded by wooden sticks (for climbing) and broadleaf vegetation. There were perches and hollows, tunnels through the wet black earth, areas of shade and areas of warm yellow spotlight (the same lamps, Looie said, fast-food places use to keep the french fries warm). Heaped mealworms writhed in the feeding dishes and a ventilation unit hummed quietly.

"Some of these types in here are temperamental or frail. I try to keep it at an even eighty-two degrees. I'm afraid they do get institutionalized after a while, you know, roll onto their backs at the first break in routine."

Tildy indicated two green lumps wedged behind a chunk of lava.

"Korean fire belly toads," he whispered. "I'm going to isolate them soon for breeding. Extremely difficult to obtain in this country. I've been doing some consulting work for a flavors and essences company. They felt they needed help with their mocha and their number-two beef, so I went up to New Rochelle for a week, gave one a few more bass notes and softened the salts in the other. Simple. But it paid for my toads."

With some prompting he got her to distinguish a speckled salamander with gold chip eyes from the dwarf begonias under which it was curled, and explained how an old girlfriend had smuggled it from Africa inside a steam iron.

"How did you get him out?"

"That's nothing. Two friends of mine, brothers, attempted to smuggle marijuana from Yucatán in their scuba tanks. It took them all day to pack it in through half-inch air valve holes. But it only took Customs two hours to unpack."

"*Caramba!*" Christo displayed a wicked cheroot of Rubio de la Costa, Colombia's highest octane strain, tightly and quite symmetrically rolled in a sheet of onionskin paper. "Let's go, boys and girls."

He lit up with an entire book of matches, paper flaring as he inhaled, face barely visible behind clouds of smoke.

"Nice flavor, very nice. Like incense in a Catholic church."

The paper was burning too quickly, ash and seed embers dropping to the floor.

"That's like a taco. You have to do it over something." Looie brought a cookie sheet.

Collecting smoke in cupped hands, he washed his face with it.

106

"Excellent bouquet. Pungent but not too sharp. Almost camphorous." He made the delicate pass with Christo, took small puffs, exhaling rapidly through his nose, then one large one which he swirled, shifted back and forth between pouched cheeks like a wine taster. "Good resin content, no doubt about that. A little harsh on the throat." Lifting a teapot from the table, he sucked cold oolong from the spout. "Any metabolic signs so far?"

"Slight chill in the palms, increased pulse rate . . . and this—this sort of walls-of-stone effect in my sinuses."

"Uh-huh, uh-huh." Looie refilled his lungs.

Then Christo held his face over a smoking hunk that landed on the cookie sheet and sucked through his nose till his eyes watered. They both watched the column of lacy blue smoke undulate toward the ceiling, examining it for omens, nodding learnedly like a couple of Delphic kibitzers.

"Looks like Pierce has done it again," Christo said. Tildy stared into the grain of the table and wobbled her feet; he prodded her. "What about you? Why don't you join me in our test kitchen to sample a new product absolutely free."

"Okay. But I should tell you, strong grass gives me a headache."

She handled the thing, smoking like a flare now, as if it were a cigarette; though her eyes bugged out, she managed not to cough. Christo made encouraging whatta-ya-waitin'-for gestures, and pinched her on the cheek.

"Just fuck off, Jimmy," she choked. Looie shook his head, recalling something once said about not messing with a psychotic. She took a few modest hits, passed. "Don't get pushy, that's all. It provokes me."

"You don't want to come along, don't." Christo shifted, his speech twangy, stressed. "There are some changes really need to be made in Colombia. They're still locked into that coffee economy, and monoculture just destroys the soil. Clear the forest for coffee trees that suck the nutrients out of the ground, before long you have to clear more forest and start again. Now nationalized marijuana plantations would offer a much more favorable foreign exchange situation without the inefficient use of land. It's labor-intensive, you can have staggered planting and harvest times. . . ."

Through gritty casement windows flanking the elevator cage, the sky bled by slow degrees to a duller shade of gray. The only sound in the room now a repetitive hissing: phono needle circling the end-groove of a Bing Crosby album. The humongous joint had been followed by a second, lying crumpled now and half finished on the cookie sheet, generating an atmosphere wrapped heavily with aimlessness. Like waiting for fruit to drop off the tree. In want of hostly energies, Looie snoozed open-eyed amid the fumes of an Indonesian clove cigarette. Christo, trying to do figures in his head, kept losing the handle in the process of rounding them off, but returned doggedly to the starting point. One kilo equals 35.2 ounces. The silence was so commanding, so tightly sealed, that when finally Tildy spoke, the words were like machine-gun fire.

"I think," she said thickly from the depths of a canvas sling chair, "I think those aspirin you gave me are outnumbered."

"I can give you something stronger," Looie said, nearly toppling out of his chair as he reached to test her cheek for fever.

Beginning at the tips of his fingers, a protective urge shot through him. This brittle and uncertain girl thrust suddenly into a wild frontier—for her alone he would draw the wagons into a circle, heat bath water over a buffalo chip fire, pamper her with silk bloomers all the way from Junction City. One so dainty as you, ma'am, out here on the plains . . .

"The three-thousand-dollar kilo," Christo said, discarding his calculations and taking a stab at it. "I think we've reached that plateau. Ought to check in with the boss. Where's your phone?"

Looie pointed into the shadows. "All the way back on your right, next to the sewing machines."

Tildy, for her part, had been sizing Looie up for some time, admiring his sleek contours and the elegance in the movements of his mouth. She imagined now a certain telegraphy between them—perhaps it was nothing more than weed hyperbole—a swift, uncoded message of flesh need. One for the homefolks, Karl in particular. "What'd y'all do up in New York?" Fucked a guy with a blue beard.

Conscious of her watchful eyes, Looie fanned out crackers on a cheeseboard, sliced up a wedge of Emmentaler shot through with cumin seeds, popped open a bottle of sparkling rosé.

"Pierce wasn't home, but I left a message on his machine." Christo appeared as Looie dealt out the glasses, filled one and swirled wine in his cottony mouth. "Ain't nothin' to it but to do it. With a little teamwork we can have this shit bricked up in no time flat."

"What's the hurry?" Looie, to be sure, had other things on his mind.

108

"Fine. You two go ahead and sit there, chew the fat and get drunk. I'll do the work. Don't worry about it." He walked sideways toward the Fiat, hands on hips, as though expecting one of them to jump him from behind. "Don't worry about it at all."

Noisily, he dragged bulging bags across the floor to the kilo press, an apparatus made of planks, pipe, a spring or two, and an automobile jack. The herb would be weighed out on a delicatessen scale, jammed in the mold and formed into bricks to be wrapped in lightly waxed yolk-yellow paper and sealed with gummed labels of Looie's own design: La Cometa Azul   Imported under License to Phillip II of Spain.

Next to the kilo press was a letterpress with which Looie turned out a monthly poetry magazine containing his own punning and shaggy dog works, and those of a varying roster of friends. The May issue's table of contents listed contributions by Mercedes Triumph, Looie's ex-singing teacher; by Feral Hix, a Zen cab driver with a heavy jones for flower imagery; and by a spade kid named John Alonzo (Looie had only seen him once, darting around the corner in white canvas high-tops) whose Koranic pensées scrawled on spiral notebook paper would appear every so often, inside of a magazine or catalogue jammed in the mail slot. It had been years since Looie'd known money worries, and in fact he oversaw, without professional guidance, a small but diversified securities portfolio. But on Sundays, by the fountain across from the Plaza Hotel, Looie peddled his homemade editions at fifty cents per copy, a gesture to the indigent boho past he'd never had.

He flirted rather clumsily now with Tildy as they picked over the cheese remnants. Each had detected the other's lust and their little corner of the room became a vivarium of its own, crowded with hot pinpoint lights and liquid radii flowing between them, while Christo toted his bales, fine-tuned the scale.

Looie told a story: dabbing a professor's tuxedo with an extraordinarily potent moth lure so that when he arrived for the Alumni Banquet, his lapels were a quivering, powdery gray.

Tildy told a story: secretly, while her father slept, listening to Cajun boogie music on the radio—Clint Boudreau and his Zydeco Nightriders.

And when at last Christo looked up from his toils, some thistly remark at the end of his tongue, their chairs were empty. Cracker crumbs, whorls of cheese rind, were on the table, bubbling dregs in two wine glasses—an amateur's tawdry still life, but the message was there. Out of darkness at the back of the room came rustlings, thuds on the wooden platform bed.

Tildy knelt on the mattress, crossed arms pulling the shirt over her head. Confused, flushed by the boldness of it all, Looie watched her and felt, oh my, pressing against him a sleek warm thigh that awaited his kiss. He saw in profile her sharp peewee breasts and something flipflopped inside him like the snap and release of taut elastic. . . . How very young she is, a small bird in the snow.

"It's like an ostrich egg," she whispered tentatively. "Could I do something?"

"Anything."

"Could I, well, sort of run my tongue all over your skull?"

Christo used the fire stairs. He grabbed an evening paper and headed uptown. It was good to be back on the subway again.

Pierce Milbank's Claremont Avenue duplex (which had once belonged to the great blind historian, Duncan Gateshead, when he was a visiting lecturer at Columbia) had three fireplaces, two kitchens and a Jacuzzi. In the front hallway, softly lit by a chandelier, he had hung a framed photograph of himself taken several Easters ago at his late grandmother's home in Connecticut. In a vested tweed suit, the jacket draped over his shoulders à la Sinatra, he stood in front of a cluster of white birches, the last snows of spring withdrawing to sullen patches on the lawn. The only thing missing was a brace of freshly bagged grouse splayed at his feet.

Sure, it was all there, buried somewhere in the faint, granular background of the black and white print. The legendary Boston period, running black opium out of a quiche shop on Mass. Ave., then up to the majors, the fast track: drug casseroles, high-stakes badminton, the tumbling act in his sports car, charcoaling a steak in a men's room sink at the New York Stock Exchange. Levels upon levels of carefully plotted can-you-top-this outrageousness.

Christo lifted the picture off its hook and carried it into the living room where the light was better.

"Like it?" Pierce entered clutching a black gym bag. "My publicity still. Can't you just see it on the cover of the *Times Book Review?*" He pulled the bag's zipper back and showed Christo what was inside.

"Don't you believe in banks?"

"This is just mad money." Pierce counted out thirty one-hun-

110

dred-dollar bills. "You're the last one in on this shipment. I ought to fine you a couple hundred for lateness, but I won't. Seeing as how you've been out of action up till now."

"Thanks, white man."

"Where's the car? Still down at Chemikazi's?"

"Yeah. Ought to be safe there, don't you think?"

"No good. Tomorrow you'll drive it up to Fox Street in the Bronx and leave it there. It'll be stripped or torched within twenty-four hours."

"Whatever you say."

"That's the spirit." Pierce zipped the bag shut and tugged slyly at his blond mustache. It was easy to visualize him behind a carved desk at his family's shipping company, barking memos into a dictaphone. "So where's your friend from Florida? You could've brought her along, that's no breach of security."

"She seemed to be having a good time so I left her down with Looie."

"He's such a gentleman." A click of the tongue. "You're not pressed for time, so why not stick around? I thought I might shake up a few gimlets. Gin or vodka?"

They carried their drinks upstairs to the "conference room," a cork-lined sanctum filled with books and dominated by a long mahogany table surrounded with leather swivel chairs. Heavy glass ashtrays were distributed around the table and a water pitcher and tumblers sat on a tray in the middle. Black velvet curtains eclipsed the windows.

"What is this? You've got stockholders now?"

"You haven't been up here since I renovated, have you? My hermitage. I shut off the phone, come up here to read and think."

"You're in clover, Pierce. What's to think about?"

"Everything. The past. The future. The book I want to write."

"Uh-huh." Christo had heard this bedtime story before. "A little soon for your memoirs, yes?"

"No, no. Something with a broader scope. An extended essay on the ingredients that threaten the most basic structure of our lives: psychiatry, deified technics, the credit economy. I'm calling it *Under the Wheels of History*."

"Sounds like a thriller."

"Be as snide as you like." Pierce's top lip bounced on the rim of the sweating gimlet glass; he took tiny sips as though it was medicine. "But in this business you've got to have an escape route. You must leave yourself some open space, in the same way that it's essential to maintain that distance between yourself and the street."

Christo propped his feet on the table, rolled down his lids. "A little crackerbarrel philosophy?"

"All I'm saying is, stay with the game too long and they grind you up for hamburger. What breaks most guys is their own greed. They go for that one last score and get buried."

"But that won't be you, huh? While those other clowns are sinking out of sight, you'll be dickering movie rights."

"It may not be easy but it can be done. Boston's biggest smack dealer from the sixties is now running a three-thousand-acre Christmas tree ranch in Wyoming. And Denny Sunshine—you might remember him as the man who once dropped ten thousand hits of mescaline into the Fenway Park bleachers from a helicopter—well, Denny retired years ago to a vanilla plantation in Guadeloupe where he weaves rugs and makes babies. So I'm not worried. I'll get clear in time. There's more discipline and prudence in my genes than either of them could even think about."

Though the timing wasn't right, Christo laughed. "Those genes, where would we be without them. And how is Sara? Have you heard from her lately?"

"Holding up pretty well." Pierce looked down, buffing one section of mahogany with the sleeve of his shirt. "She lives on a feminist commune outside Austin. They grow grapefruit there, and not bad. She sends me a crate every couple of months. They look after her down there and she's coming right along. Goes spelunking on the weekends she says—you know, crawling around in caves with a carbide lamp on her head? She was a total claustrophobe when we were kids. Five minutes in a closed car would make her sick and in the dead of winter she slept with all her windows open."

"Really. I didn't know that."

"I haven't forgotten, jazzbo, if that's what you're getting at."

Christo smiled sweetly. "Neither have I."

It was seven or eight years ago. A judge with a crowded calendar had remanded Christo to a state institution for purposes of "observation."

It was while waiting in the hallway for his preliminary hearing on a charge of attempting to redeem stolen traveler's checks that Christo realized he could go somewhere other than prison. In this particular round of The State v. No Fixed Address they had him

112

backed into a corner, but there was no reason why he couldn't take the punches on his arms and shoulders. In the time it took to walk to the water fountain and back, he worked out his maneuvers.

When the Hon. J. Roccia banged the gavel to start things off, Christo grasped his head and dropped to the floor. Before the bailiff could reach him, though, he was back on his feet and circling left behind a straight jab, explaining to the court that the colony of soldier ants inside his skull was often upset by loud noises. Judge Roccia reminded him that it was within his power to order physical restraints. Christo replied that if proof was needed, he would try to coax one of his little guests out the front entrance (defendant here indicated his nose) for cross-examination. He could try for one of the colonels, Christo said, but he was a lot closer to the enlisted men. The Hon. suggested that Christo's attorney make some effort to control his client; at which point Christo, throwing looping hooks as he bulled his way toward the bench, confided that this court-appointed scumbag had made sexual advances to him. The public defender, a young busy-bee only a few months past his bar exam, experienced a jolt of paranoia that caused him to believe a single drunken episode with his wife's older brother was now about to bring an oh-so-promising career down in flames. As he rose to stammer his indignation, Christo backpedaled and began to lead an entire ant battalion in a double-time march across the defense table.

And that was all. Citing the fact that defendant had no previous convictions (That *you* know of, Christo murmured to himself), the Hon. Roccia stated his intention, pending agreement of counsel, of rendering Mr. Christo into the custody of qualified professionals who could determine his mental competency. Whenever that might be.

Plumdale was in several respects an unusual institution. One of its inmates, before amputating his son's penis with a bread knife, had been head chef at Galatoire's in New Orleans and, since he spent all his free time in the hospital kitchen, the food that came out of there was nearly good. The chief administrator of Plumdale actually lived on the premises. He was a 72-year-old Alsatian widower who believed that tobacco was a tranquilizing agent and that the last event that could be truly marked as progress for mankind was the invention of the pop-up toaster. Under his aegis, hydrotherapy, a curative method first codified in the mid-seventeenth century was still practiced on a regular basis at Plumdale.

Subbasement A, two levels below ground, was a huge vaulted room of pastel green tile, fitted with shower stalls and canvas-covered tubs, called the "soup tank." There was a heavily chlorinated wading pool in which the water was piss-warm. There was a sauna that only the staff was allowed to use. Intransigent patients were sometimes strapped into chairs under small-bore pipes from which water poured directly onto their heads. Flow and temperature were controlled from a panel of valves and wheel cocks in an adjoining room that had a long, shatterproof window.

Long a watersports enthusiast, Christo visited the soup tank frequently. Also, this was one of a very few unsegregated activities and afforded the best contact with female inmates. There was one in particular who interested him, an emaciated girl with a white streak in her hair. She was always there, silenty cross-legged in one of the shower stalls with her leotard full of holes. He imagined her to have once worn fashionable clothes and French cologne, to have made witty conversation in ritzy cafés where domestic champagne was never served. It took hours of cajolery to elicit the single fact that her name was Sara.

Christo brought her sourballs and pictures he'd cut out of magazines, which she accepted with a small and wordless smile. But it was not until he slipped on the wet tiles and fell, ripping open his hand on a screwhead not quite flush, that he won her. Sara knelt beside him and applied a shred of her drenched leotard to the wound. She cried as she licked the blood off her fingers. She permitted him to towel her off and comb the knots out of her hair. And she spoke.

More than two years ago, she said, her parents had arrived one night unannounced at the tenement apartment she shared with her lover, a 34-year-old body builder and part-time bouncer. For months they had been bombarding her with letters and phone calls, berating her for the aimless and degenerate life she was leading. But they seemed calmer now, conciliatory. Let's go for a drive, they said. We'll stop somewhere for coffee and a nice long talk. They had a friend waiting downstairs, a member of their tennis club, named Dr. Soberin. After a ten-minute interview in the back seat of the car as they drove to the hospital amid shouted abuse from Dad, waterworks from Mom, he signed Sara's commitment papers. Dr. Soberin listed such symptoms as: sexual acting out, masculine role playing (she was wearing cowboy boots and a denim jacket that night) and refusal to accept responsibility for her actions.

Sara's mother sent her a book on crewel embroidery that Christmas, but that was the last she'd heard. Chuck, the body builder, sent a few letters promising a visit but never showed.

"I'm dead to them I think," Sara said, plucking devotedly at her split ends. "I have a brother and he cares about me. But I'm not allowed to see him or even speak to him on the phone."

"Is that legal?"

"They say he's a negative influence. . . . I don't know, maybe I'll spend the rest of my life here. Sometimes I think about eloping, but I'm not strong enough. Not yet anyway."

"Eloping" was the term inmates used to describe a permanent and unauthorized self-removal from the facility.

"I've been thinking about that ever since I got here," Christo said. "We ought to put our heads together."

Sara fervently agreed but by the following afternoon had retreated into the egregious nullity that was her food and shelter.

Christo moved ahead on his own. He began shining up to a new aide on the ward, a blond smart-mouth he'd instantly pegged as a colleague, a fellow delinquent. The kid had skipped bail in San Diego and the proceeds of a fast drug-store robbery were eaten up on the trip east. Broke, forced to spend his first night in town at a 24-hour laundromat, he'd answered a want ad in the paper.

"Be gone soon as I get a shot at the narcotics closet," he confided.

In exchange for intelligence on who carried master key sets and their lunch hour routines, he told Christo of a little out-of-the-way office where a set of hospital blueprints was on file. Late that night Christo broke into the office with the aid of a nail file stolen from the nurses' lounge.

He studied the blueprints for almost an hour and discovered a serviceable escape path through a series of heating ducts to the ground-level parking garage. Facing budget cuts, the chief administrator had instituted an austerity program; the heating system was shut down from one till five in the morning. The parking garage was at the rear of the hospital facing a narrow residential street. There was one security guard at the gate and if he wasn't asleep, Christo would have to take him out. He'd need a blunt instrument. And clothes. And good breaks.

Early on a Friday morning, when the last portion of the heating system's off cycle coincided with the hour when several of the nurses were wont to gather in a vacant supply room for gossip and cigarettes, Christo slipped down to Sara's ward on pilfered crepe-soled shoes. He carried with him in a pillowcase two janitor uniforms and a steel support bar it had taken less than two minutes to unscrew from his bed.

Sara was fast asleep. Christo peeled back the covers and gently pinched her behind.

"Time to go, Sara."

Her only response was to brush once, twice at her cheek as though a fly had landed there. He whispered urgently, prodding her ribs. But Sara slept on, burrowing deeper into the pillows. He cursed her aloud, convinced she would foul him up, but unwilling to leave without her. One of Sara's roommates sat up in bed, moving her hands in front of her as if she could part the darkness like living room drapes.

"I would like a glass of water, please," she said.

Christo took Sara in his arms and carried her out the door.

"Taking her away for repainting?" said the roommate. "It's fine with me."

Sara came awake as they moved down the hall, kicked feebly and said, "Put me down. I'm sick."

"There's nothing to worry about," Christo said, propping her against the wall. "It's all been figured out for you." He handed her a pair of cracked vinyl slippers he'd found next to her bed. "Here. Put these on. . . . Come on, come on, we have to move fast."

Sara's knees were shaking. With the metal bar, Christo pried off the grate, pointed into the dark mouth of the heating duct.

"I'll go first and you hold on to my ankles. We'll take a left and then our second right. It's a sharp angle so watch out."

"No." Sara shook her head hopelessly. "You go on, I can't. I can't deal with closed spaces like that. I can only say goodbye."

As she swayed forward to kiss him, Christo rapped her upside the head, caught her by the shoulders, shook her. "Listen to me, you cunt. You don't have a choice, understand? I'm taking you. You're going out of here if I have to strap you to my back like a knapsack."

Frightened, doll-like, she obeyed and, only moments after stuffing herself into the cramped and stifling shaft, passed out. Christo heard a diminuendo moan behind him and felt her grip relax. He had to slither down to a junction point, where a smaller pipe fed into the main line, in order to turn himself around and drag her the rest of the way. It was very noisy work—sweaty, too, since the tin walls were still warm—and he was amazed that no one intercepted them at the other end. He kicked out the grate and pulled Sara free; her eyes fluttered open and she looked like a movie star at the finish of a deathbed monologue.

"Can we get a bus from here?"

"Not yet, not yet."

Their pyjamas were soaked through but they were too far behind schedule to change clothes now. They'd have to go for it as they were, even though the white garments would practically glow in the dark. At the end of the narrow, carpeted corridor, through a high window in a heavy brown door, Christo could see light glinting off windshields. He put his arm around Sara's waist and coaxed and carried her forward.

"Use your legs, dammit."

He thought: This is a lot like babysitting.

She snapped to in the cold air of the parking garage, leaned over the hood of a station wagon hyperventilating.

"Wait a minute. . . . Wait a minute."

"Don't fade in the stretch, Sara. We might reach a point where I can't afford you anymore." He took the steel bar out of the pillowcase.

Sara nodded, took his hand. They ran up a cement ramp to the driveway, stopped, looked in unison to right and left like figures in a pedestrian safety film, then briskly but quietly walked across. Christo pulled her down in a bed of ivy; she was trembling. Up ahead, the gate man stared out at the street from his lighted cubicle and puffed on a pipe.

"Wait here and be ready to fly."

With long, low strides, Christo covered the intervening ground in seconds. As the gate man turned toward the sound of his final step with a half smile on his brown, creased face, Christo cocked the bar and brought it down square on the back of his head. The gate man's cap with the shiny badge in front flipped off and hit the ground before he did. A flash as Christo spun away, blood welling over gray crewcut stubble.

"Now, Sara. Now!" And he took off like a deer.

She breathed deep, gathered herself and went after him, her slippers coming off as she sprinted through half-melted snow, the pillowcase swinging wildly at her side.

Shivering, embracing, they climbed into the janitor clothes behind a hedge six blocks away.

"Okay, next phase," Christo said as Sara jumped up and down and crooned at the stars. "Where does your brother live?"

117

"In Boston—oh, you beautiful man. I can't believe I'm out . . . I'm really out. I could never have done it by myself."

"Well, don't tell the neighborhood about it."

"I don't even care if I get frostbite," Sara said, wiggling her bare toes.

"Phase two now, darlin'. Concentrate. You know this town, find us a Western Union."

They walked for endless blocks as a cheerless dawn broke overhead. Sara was manic and couldn't stop talking, even when Christo walked ahead, fingers plugging his ears. He sat, teeth chattering, on a park bench while she wired Pierce collect, asking him to send as much money as he could as soon as he could. The clerk gaped at her in the baggy green work shirt, the impossible balloon pants she had to hold up by the belt loops.

"Spot of trouble?"

"My house burned down," Sara said gravely. "Guess I left the bacon on too long."

A large chunk of money was handed over to her within two hours and Sara alternately wept and apologized for being so sentimental. They spent the remainder of the morning shopping for clothes, lingered over a lunch of lobster salad and cappuccino, and touched down at Logan Airport at dusk. A freshman gofer of Pierce's decked out in chauffeur's livery was there to meet them and, in a long black limousine equipped with stereo and wet bar, to transport them to an all-stops-pulled welcome home party already in progress.

The following day Pierce invited Christo's suggestions as to how he might best demonstrate his gratitude.

"I could use a job."

The exam period preceding spring vacation was but a few days away. Christo was given a car, detailed instructions on how to find five area campuses, a promise of liberal commissions, and a shopping bag full of amphetamines.

"Sweet and soft as butter, that sister of yours." Christo held the stem of his empty glass like a cigarette between middle and index fingers. "I can still see her in that sea-blue gown with the tassels at the waist and the whole room levitating when she'd walk through."

"That party—" Pierce thumped his elbows on the table. "That party cost me over two grand."

"Commerce has made you vulgar, you shithead." Fractured little

118

smile, head going ruefully from side to side. "I've got only one re-gret from that whole thing. One large regret."

"Let's have it then. By all means."

"I never slept with her."

"I don't know about that, jazzbo." Pierce squinted at him and the lamplight was harsh on his yellow, ruling-class hair. "From what she says in her letters, the only type of sex Sara enjoys is with herself."

"You've got a real close family, Pierce. That's nice." He stood, stretched, moved toward the spiral stairs. "But I'm glad I never did."

Pierce spread his arms on the table, seeming to embrace the whole of its dark surface. "You going to retrieve your friend?"

"Nah, let her float awhile. But I ought to get us a hotel."

"Do that anytime." Pierce waved dismissingly. "The kind of ho-tels you like are never full. It's early, for Christ's sake. Stick around and I'll tell you about my book, we'll maybe shoot some dice or something."

"Look, man, I've been on the road a long—"

"But it's early. More gimlets?"

"Yeah, yeah, yeah, more gimlets. You shithead."

8

The telephone was ringing in Room 31 of the Kenilworth Hotel (Transients Welcome). From a thick and muggy sleep Tildy ascended through those first turbid layers of consciousness as in a bubble of gas. She became instantly aware of phlegm dangling like a cord of taffy in her throat, raw from the forty some-odd cigarettes she'd smoked the night before. She forced open her eyes and, bit by bit, pegged her location. Christo. New York. Scumbag hotel. It was impossible to gauge the time of day because the windows were painted the same bile yellow as the walls. Good morning, Naked City, and thanks for everything.

She lifted the receiver and Christo's voice rasped in her ear.

"Hiya, bunny. Ready to roll?"

Her lips moved silently against the holes in the plastic mouthpiece. She belched at him, whispered, "Where are you?"

"Seventy-ninth and Lexington. Been hiking around since eight o'clock. I tried to wake you for breakfast but you kicked me."

"'M sorry."

"Don't worry. I kicked you back. You all right?"

"Feel like dough. A big tub of rancid bread dough."

"Okay, okay. Get yourself in the shower and let it run awhile. Brush your teeth, run a little sandpaper over your face and get into some clothes. You'll be meeting me in one hour outside the Planned Parenthood Thrift Shop at Seventy-fourth and Third. There's doings on for tonight and we need to make some preparations."

"Why?"

"Seventy-fourth and Third. Southeast corner." And he hung up.

120

After retching in the shower, Tildy felt much better. She dosed her dehydrated system with two cans of orange pop from the lobby vending machine and tried to sharpen the focus of her eyes over the morning headlines: a Long Island building contractor had been accused of engaging in deviant sex with members of his scout troop; an off-duty transit cop had shot a Dutch tourist in a dispute over a parking space.

The man at the desk gave her a couple of cigarettes for the road. He spoke just enough English to tell her how to get crosstown but in the 77th Street station she went up the stairs to walk in an adverse northerly direction for several blocks before realizing her mistake.

She arrived at the appointed corner a half hour late. Christo took pains to mime his annoyance, flinging the butt of his hotdog at her as she advanced shading her eyes.

"I thought you'd maybe gone back to sleep."

"Who can sleep with all this excitement?"

"Don't get snotty."

"So I'm here. What's the project?"

Christo reported that he and Pierce had drawn up tentative plans for a joint business venture, something that would move him out of the man-Friday class. "He's finally going to steer me onto something ripe, the bastard. A bit of the long green. After all this time." An evening of revelry had been scheduled to celebrate their new partnership.

"Congratulations. I hope you'll both be very happy, but did I really have to come all this way to hear about it?"

"Right now we're looking for uniforms."

"Uniforms?"

"The Canteen has a very strict dress code."

The Canteen, he went on to explain, was the nightclub sensation of the nouveau hip nation, a "private" pleasure facility with an exclusivity that hardened Manhattan smarties had not yet fully decoded. Housed in an enormous structure occupying half a block on lower Tenth Avenue (it had been in previous incarnations a furniture warehouse, a television studio, and—briefly—a performance space for the Theatre of Last Resort, a dramaturgic cabal following the teachings of the structural anthropologist Claude Fantomas), the Canteen had with great expense and lavish attention to detail been made into a flyboy's furlough wet dream of flash and high times *circa* 1944. In order to have any chance of being admitted, it was necessary to be decked out in scrupulously authentic period costume.

Tennis champs and teevee luminaries with their own line of hair-care products had been turned away for reasons of unsuitable clothing. The management discouraged the patronage of celebs anyway. The Canteen was a place to get away from all that, where status licked the boots of style; no amount of juice, no carefully accrued influences and interfaces of the social powerplant could prevail if one was not "aw-reet" and in the swing with the Swing.

"Marvelous," Tildy grumbled. "I came a thousand miles to play dress-ups."

"Hey, you're welcome to sit around the hotel all night doing crossword puzzles."

The thrift shop aisles were jammed with women on safari for bargains—not that there were any bargains to be had. The shop's volunteer staff, young debs unable to land a situation on the museum/gallery circuit and marking time until that photographic expedition to Ecuador could be finalized ("Daddy knows someone at *National Geographic*"), certainly knew the value of things: three-figure price tags on art deco cocktail sets; dinner gowns with designer labels intact at twice the cost of Orchard Street knockoffs; even crayon-defaced editions of Nancy Drew and the Bobbsey Twins were a dollar and up. But money spent to good effect, when you were helping to defuse the population bomb.

It took them the better part of the afternoon to piece together their wardrobes, flashing in and out of the changing cubicle, posing for one another, rejecting one selection after another. Christo finally chose a headwaiter's holiday suit, light brown with blue pinstripes and wedge lapels; a lemon-yellow shirt; two-tone wingtips and clocked socks; a hand-painted cravat by Al-Hy Haberdashery of Flatbush Avenue; and a rather decrepit snap-brim hat. Tildy, who was terribly hard to fit, was forced to settle for something rather more cutesie than she'd hoped—a flouncy print dress with Mardi Gras dancers on a mottled field of blue and black. With fishnet stockings, red satin wedgies and an orange chiffon scarf at the throat, she'd look like a real chippie. Blow jobs behind the PX. Hey, Joe, you got gum?

Six hours later they were traveling downtown in a Checker cab and drinking rye and ginger out of paper cups.

"Hubba hubba," Christo said, fortifying his drink from the pint. "I just know we're gonna sizzle tonight."

Her feet propped on the jumpseat in front of her, Tildy gazed at the scene unrolling like a scroll past the window. She was amazed by the level of activity at this late hour, the sheer density of bodies on the avenue. In Houston, previously the largest settlement she'd visited, it had been nearly impossible to buy a box of tampons after ten P.M.

"I'm tired," she said. "The last few days have been strange. I feel like I just got out of the hospital after a long series of tests."

"But you're fine, just fine. Look at those nice white muscles. Hubba hubba."

Tildy cranked her window down and emptied her cup on the pavement.

The Canteen was situated in a zone of novelty wholesalers, juke box dealers and distributors of Latin records. The entrance was on a gloomy cross street with its own canopy of smells; spoiled meat, soot, wet newspapers. Tildy breathed through her mouth. In the doorway of a dead luncheonette a man with a bandaged head crooned softly while staring into a brown paper bag.

Tildy slid her arm through Christo's. "Is my lipstick on straight?"

Their clothes passed muster at the door and their "temporary membership" cards were accepted by an Oriental bruiser in a Shore Patrol outfit after examination under an ultraviolet lamp. At the end of a long corridor lined with potted palms, Christo gave a fifty to a combat nurse toying sullenly with her cuticles, and was handed in exchange a book of ration coupons, the only currency recognized inside. They pushed through a pair of tufted leather swinging doors to another checkpoint (a woman in "Rosie the Riveter" masquerade presented Tildy with a heart-shaped box of chocolates, on the house), through a second set of doors, and into the jangle and heat of party time.

From the top of the carpeted stairs the room looked big enough to hold an aircraft carrier. Velvet hangings along the side walls were pulled back to reveal huge smoked mirrors that swallowed the room and spat it out on the opposite side. An all-white gutbucket combo—two brass, two reeds and rhythm—churned through "Bugle Call Rag" atop the terraced black glass stage, riffing away at vein-popping tempo while mucho authentic kittens and kats jitterbugged, lindy-hopped, trucked and pecked on the dance floor. Figures jostled and bounced in the blue backlighting of the large bar, built to resemble the front section of a medium-range bomber in profile, complete with cockpit and bubble canopy. Girls in Red Cross uniforms distributed coffee and doughnuts from stainless steel carts. Waiters in sailor suits glided among the tables (each with its own bowl of roses and shaded lamp throwing shadows across the damask cloth) on rubber-wheeled roller skates; the more ambitious would execute an occasional leap or pirouette, perhaps hoping that some starmaker in the crowd would notice them, perhaps merely happy in their work.

It was several minutes before they finally located Pierce sitting at a shadowy corner table beneath a sepia photograph of Joe Louis twisting Max Schmeling's head around with a right cross. He was negotiating with two rice-powdered dollies who not long ago had made him the target for tonight and, without a word, helped themselves to seats at his table.

Dodie and Charmaine had known each other since junior high. They shared an apartment in the West Village. They worked for competing ad agencies but met each day on their lunch hour to promenade up Madison Avenue sharing a joint. Their one consuming ambition was to escape this urban anchorage for a brand-new hot blood dimension—a world, as Dodie often spoke of it, of Europe and yachts; and their sensitive antennae rated Pierce as someone with access.

"Don't mind the ladies, they're part of the floor show," he said and made perfunctory introductions.

"What a beautiful name." Charmaine slurred her words, having earlier ignored Dodie's admonition that Tuinals did nothing for one's charm. "Are you French?"

Tildy poked at one of the floating roses. "Not yet."

"I was in France once," Charmaine said quietly, unable to remember if this was a true anecdote or one she'd invented. "We flew over for a pâté festival."

Up on stage the drummer broke into a solo. He was a scrawny kid with a pencil mustache, a propeller beanie atop patent-leather hair and a head full of boogie shuffle licks as plain as a dental chart. The audience whooped him on; it was like a pep rally. Even leaning across the table Pierce had to shout to be heard.

"Miss Florida is lovely, a bloody vision. I'm forced to say she looks too good for you."

"Kiss mine."

"Think about it, think about some of the women you were running with in the past. They had the shakes. And black circles around their eyes."

"Well, dig it, the past has passed. Mister Christo will be running on the fast track from now on."

The drummer was into his windup now. Coming out of a tom-tom onslaught, he popped off the stool, keeping the pulse alive on bass and hi-hat, bobbing his head and twirling his sticks. Real gone. He hit a brief mambo rattle on the cowbell and slung the sticks to one side. Only half turned, barely looking up, Tildy speared them both in one hand with two perfectly timed rotations of her wrist.

She faced Dodie and Charmaine with an ingratiating smile, offered them on an open palm like breadsticks. "Souvenirs?"

"Zowie." Dodie clapped both hands to her head. "That was fantastic what you did."

"I was alone a lot as a kid," Tildy said. "Learned to catch insects on the wing."

Charmaine looked on adoringly but turned shyly away when Tildy met her eyes, to stare down her own cleavage, plucking at the rounded collar of her black silk pyjamas right out of a *Terry & The Pirates* panel.

The band returned for a couple of rideout choruses to heavy applause.

"Yeah, thank you. Copacetic." The alto player brought his palms together as he bowed. "We gonna cool off right now, but we'll be back later to sock you and knock you nonstop."

"Hey, black shoes, you oughta hock those instruments." This from a deep voice at the bar.

A lot of dead air among the Milbank party. Pierce stared hard at the dollies, but they held their ground through this obvious exit cue.

"I gather you ladies aren't going to give up without at least one glass of champagne," he said. "Right, then. Champagne for everyone. I feel loose tonight."

He pressed one of the illuminated buttons on a small console under the table and within seconds the sommelier arrived. He was dressed like the best man at a London wedding and wore around his neck a large plastic skeleton key treated with phosphorescent paint.

"Julio, a magnum of the Henzlicht–LaFosse. From Admiral Nimitz' private reserves, and *très sec*, if you please."

"On its way, Mr. Milbank."

Julio wafted off to call the "cellar" on the intercom. There, two craftsmen were kept busy decanting California wine into bottles bearing counterfeit labels. The bottles were then rolled in a trough of wood ashes and finished off with mylar cobwebs sprayed from a device originally contrived by a producer of television commercials.

Slipping off her pumps, Dodie extended one stockinged foot under the table in search of Pierce. "You seem to have a lot of pull. How come we haven't seen you around here before?"

"I was probably playing Scrabble in the back room."

"Do you know Steve personally?" Working her way across Pierce's instep, Dodie turned to fill in the newcomers. "Steve is the spirit behind the Canteen. He's like an independent compass for environmental design."

"Steve is a very beautiful and creative man." Charmaine sighed dreamily. "When he made love to me it felt like I was being sculpted."

"How about that." Christo leaned back in his chair. "Well, I once fucked Johnny Carson all night."

"And what do *you* think about that?" Dodie said challengingly.

"I think I have a nicer asshole," Tildy snapped.

And then, before things could get really ugly, the champagne arrived.

Pierce filled their tulip glasses and proposed a toast to "Our visitor from Dixieland." Tildy permitted him to kiss her hand.

"I'm a great student of accents," Charmaine said. "I'll bet you're from Alabama."

"Nope. I come from Louisiana." Tildy brushed foam off her lip. "With a banjo on my knee."

"I was in New Orleans once," Charmaine offered. This one was for real, a memory all too vivid.

She'd flown down for the weekend with a bartender who was in on a lead-pipe scheme to doctor the ninth race trifecta at Evangeline Downs. Except this kid trainer was wired for sound, and when the payoff man whipped out his envelope, Pinkerton agents were all over him like a blanket. Charmaine spent most of Saturday night tied to the bed with extension cords and woke up in the hallway Sunday morning locked out of the room with nothing but a ripped T-shirt, a black eye and a pair of paper shower slippers. Rule #1: Don't come on to the bartender.

The bandstand receded on worm-geared tracks, was replaced by a back-alley stage set complete with knothole fence, cardboard lamppost and suspended crescent moon. Half a dozen showgirls pranced out to a vamping piano. They wore pink tights with marabou tails appended and pointy ears on their pink berets. They had whiskers grease-penciled on their upper lips; in nasal thirds reminiscent of the Boswell Sisters, they sang,

126

"We're fuzzy little alley cats
In a special kind of heat,
We're all stoked up on catnip
And we love that boogie beat.

"Prowl girls, howl girls
And wag your silky tails . . ."

The piano rumbled and they rendered some rudimentary and
not quite synchronized dance steps.

"Put me up there." Dodie gestured awkwardly with her empty
glass. "Put me up there and I'd show you some moves'd stiffen the
neckties in this dump."

"Dammit." When Pierce's fist hit the table, it rattled the lamp-
shade. "What is it? You crib all your dialogue from comic books or
what? Why don't you just cool your jets for ten minutes and be
ornamental."

The pink kittens gurgled.

"Fish may be our favorite dish
But meat is also yummy . . ."

Tildy felt dizzy and hot. She unknotted her scarf and held it over
her mouth. Christo asked if she was doing okay.

"I'm going to go wash my face," she said.

All eyes at the table turned to watch her go.

"Nice bounce," Pierce commented.

Charmaine, paralyzed with adoration, listened to her own sedat-
ed breathing and wished she were a boy.

Tildy sat in front of a large spotlighted mirror and examined the
flanks of her nose for blackheads. Didn't have the billboard looks of
those two back at the table, but there was something solid there,
something durable. Lucien used to tell her she'd make her way in
the world because there was upright character showing in her face.
Thanks, Dad. You should see me with makeup.

She gathered a ridge of skin between index fingers and squeezed
until a translucent plug of sebum wormed up out of a blocked pore.

"No, never do that. It leaves pits." Charmaine swayed in the
doorway, twisting the orange scarf in her fingers. "I ought to know.
My sophomore year in high school, I had the worst acne in my
homeroom."

"That's all right," Tildy said, dabbing saliva on the red spot. "My face needs a little distinction anyway."

Charmaine moved up to the mirror and plucked at her fawn-colored bangs. "In this city your face is all you've got. I dote on mine. Lemon and egg white every morning . . . But it used to be horrible. I just hid out in my room for months, like I was a leper or something. Then this old Armenian lady who lived next door, one day she gave me some cuttings from a bush she had growing in her yard. Told me to strip the bark, boil it up with the leaves, then soak pieces of cheesecloth in it and tape them to my face before bed. The stains it made. I must have gone through fifteen pairs of pyjamas that summer. But by September my skin was like glass. Better than it is now."

"And it's beautiful now. Egg whites? Is that what you said?"

Charmaine turned her back to the mirror. The scarf was wound around her wrist and diagonally across her palm like an improvised bandage. "It was a transformation all right. Boys started to come after me and my new face. They told me I had a different look, older somehow. They'd touch my cheek like it was something from outer space that glowed. I fell in love with a few of them. I had a baby. A little girl. Tara didn't cry, not ever. She just seemed above it all. Sometimes sitting by her crib watching that face, *I'd* want to cry. It was so soft and white, I almost expected it to come off on my fingers when I touched it. Like powder. She had a mobile hanging over her crib and one night it got twisted around her neck somehow and she stopped breathing. She just lay there with this necklace of toy lambs."

Charmaine wobbled her feet and shrugged. There was regret in her voice, but no grief. It was like anything else: a plush apartment, a snazzy car—you had it for a while and then it was taken.

"That was how you found her? My God."

Tildy meant only to touch her shoulder but it was too long a stretch; her hand came to rest on the upper slope of Charmaine's heavy breast. They looked at each other for a moment and then Charmaine sank to her knees, one arm around the back of Tildy's chair.

"Don't be sad," she said, lowering her head onto Tildy's lap. "It doesn't make any sense to be sad. You can't keep hold of anything in this world. Not even your face." Sitting up, pushing Tildy's hair back. "You ought to show more of your cheekbones, you know." Charmaine caught Tildy's hands and held them against her breasts.

Her eyes glistened. "They're a little tender. I'm about to get my period."

Uh-huh. This was where Tildy always seemed to be coming in.

"Next time," she said, backing away. "Maybe next time."

The stage was empty when Tildy returned. So was the bottle of champagne; so was Dodie's chair. The partners were puffing casually on needle-thin reefers.

"We shook off our little hustler," Pierce said. "You do the same with yours?"

"More or less."

"Fluffheads," Christo grumbled. "But at least they matched the decor." All evening he had been able to think of little beyond his new business horizons. Pierce was free with promises; it was always a bull market with him. He was also someone who needed to be repeatedly pinned down. But Christo could not make his opening, could not find the words. An unfamiliar sensation. "So here we are, just the three of us."

"Just the three of us," Pierce repeated. "We should get cozy." He motioned for them to bring their chairs in closer. "We should just be loose."

Tildy avoided his eyes, focusing instead on the white satin handkerchief spouting like a fountain out of his blazer pocket. She found him, thus far, completely uninteresting.

"So what happened with the entertainment? I like to watch dancers. Used to be one myself."

"Really." Pierce tipped his shoulders forward and she felt his smoky breath on her face. "I might have guessed as much from that physique of yours. Very supple. Like an otter with curves. What was your specialty? Tap? Flamenco? Ballet?"

"Nothing so special. My boogaloo was popular."

Stagelights flashed on and the band members hurried out. They began furiously tuning their instruments.

"Let's have some of those doughnuts."

"Let's order a drink."

"Let's get out of here."

Pierce negotiated his Packard roadster through a flying wedge of taxis.

"Is this yours or did you rent it for the evening?"

Pierce smirked and flicked Tildy under the chin. "This car has been in my family for years."

"Didn't I tell you, kid?" Christo said, pouting in the back seat like a birthday boy who'd gotten nothing but savings bonds. "This guy's a real ruling-class worm. If he hadn't got so wrapped up in the dope business, he'd probably be working for the State Department."

"And doing a superb job. I had three years of Russian, you know."

It finally occurred to Tildy to ask where they were going.

"My place," Pierce answered, and his voice went all rich and silky. Like Bela Lugosi.

A cone of balsam incense smoldered in an ashtray on the desk. Fibrous blue smoke moved through a shaft of lamplight in the slowly shifting patterns of dawn at sea. Pierce bent over a mound of white powder glittering on a mirror.

Only weeks ago, on the eastern slopes of the Peruvian Andes several thousand feet below the altiplano, leaves from the shrub Erythroxylum coca had been harvested. Two Indians wearing cotton sport shirts under their ponchos, murmuring to one another in Quechuan, had dumped the leaves into an old oil drum containing a solution of potash, kerosene and water, and left them to soak. After several days the precious alkaloids had been leeched out in the form of a brown paste left behind when the leaves and their marinade were discarded. A former classmate of Pierce's (at St. Eustatius Prep of Sharon, Connecticut—"It is the Spirit that quickeneth") serving with a Peace Corps agronomic project near Tingo Maria came in a jeep and collected the paste. Packing it in two Zip-lock bags, wrapping it in a thin sheet of lead to circumvent possible fluoroscoping by the Post Office, he dispatched it to Pierce's mail drop, a one-room apartment on Staten Island that contained one mattress, one chair and a clock radio. Back at the duplex, in a makeshift lab installed by Looie, Pierce, using a simple method involving treatment with hydrochloric acid, manufactured three remarkably clean ounces of what had been until 1903, in name only now, a key ingredient in the world's favorite soft drink.

Pierce inserted a piece of drinking straw into first one nostril and then the other, snorting one line into each. "We have lift off. Passing through the stratosphere . . . ionosphere . . . Past gravity pull, beyond the orbit track and into deep space." With a moistened fingertip he gathered adherent crumbs from knife blade and mirror edge, massaged them into his gums.

Christo leaped forward to fill his own nose barrels. "That's a serious freeze," he said, backfiring his sinuses. "Off a few pounds of this

I could go fishing in the Bahamas for four or five years."

"Right. So what're you going to do, a little Rumpelstiltskin magic? Sit down in the basement all night spinning straw into high quality blow? This business is like any other—office machines, aluminum siding—you got to push and push and push. There are no shortcuts, jazzbo. Anybody starts to tell you about one, get a firm grip on your wallet."

"Right, coach." Christo served himself another couple of lines.

"I'll pass," Tildy said when Pierce beckoned to her, his face wreathed in bright hokum like a schoolyard perv trying to lure her into his car with a bag of jawbreakers.

"Listen, sugar, you're not going to come any closer to the unadulterated product. This hasn't been stepped on with procaine or lactose or talcum powder or any of that shit. This is the goddamn sacred bestowal of the Inca sun god right here."

Without looking up: "Have you got some beer in the icebox? Or a bottle of Cold Duck?"

Pierce was not a romantic. His relations with women had always been capricious, diversionary. These recreational contacts (sometimes nearly grudging) were wholly separate from the deadly serious system of male competition that had begun long ago at the core of his life and grown outward, adding layer upon layer until exterior guise and interior pith were indistinguishable. But Tildy was anomalous, that rare species who could thrive outside those boundaries, well beyond the reach of his manipulations. Pierce felt like he was looking at diamonds through the wrong end of a telescope, and did not like it at all. He wanted to impress this woman he barely knew, to draw her in. He wanted a charm to reach her with, a magnet, but he had only the parlor trick of spilling the white flakes into a glass of bleach and water, explaining to her that the speed with which they dissolved demonstrated their purity.

"I believe you. I believe that you're a man with refined tastes and the equipment to back them up. But I would still like a bottle of beer."

Pierce looked to Christo for help, gained no more than a shrug, and left the room in a poorly concealed sulk.

"I think you hurt his feelings," Christo said. "I'm proud of you."

"I thought you said I was going to like him."

"Did I? You're sure I didn't just say you'd like his weed?"

"Yes, I'm sure."

"Well, maybe it's just a city mouse versus country mouse thing."

Tildy came and straddled his knees, put her arms around him. "Do you have to be partners with him? Absolutely have to?"

"It doesn't mean anything. Going into business with him doesn't mean I have to convert."

The gentle breath soothing his temples, the slow lips that touched him were like dry little explosions to his coked-up nerves. He stiffened under her, shifting, turning his head to one side.

"You've come all this way on your own, making your own game. What is it you want to grab so bad you'd change now?"

"That's the kind of thinking keeps people driving tractors all their lives and buying on time."

"What's the matter with that?"

"Plenty. Let's not get sentimental about it." He nudged her off his lap and refilled his nose at the mirror.

"You'll be giving something away if you go in with him and we all know it," Tildy said. And to herself: Why why why do I care?

Pierce stepped in with Canadian ale, a mug chilled in the freezer and renewed aplomb.

"Here we are. A simple brew from the North Woods."

Pierce opened a desk drawer, removed writing materials and a pocket calculator. "I think it's time, jazzbo, that you and I sat down and hacked out some specifics. The kind of move you're looking to do, that ad-lib style of yours just won't cut it."

"Absolutely. I've been itching to get at this all night." Christo's eyes were a shotgun; he fired both barrels at Tildy, but she was watching bubbles burst in the beer foam.

"Itching is just low-level pain," Pierce said. "That's what my grandma taught me the summer she had shingles. All right then, let's say we capitalize this thing for a hundred thousand dollars."

"Hold on."

"Take it easy. This is only for practice, a nice round figure. Now, you've got two cuts to make out of that before you clear this end—" Punching numbers on the calculator.

"Two cuts?"

"Right. The Swede I told you about and then your transshipping back. That's going to be your second cut."

"Isn't there a simpler way to go?"

"Come on, where's your sense of artistry? I mean, shit, we're not in this for the money are we? We're in this to keep from dropping dead with boredom."

"Sure, sure. I've really been looking forward to a trip abroad. But

132

what are we talking about? Maybe twelve and a half percent each way?"

"That seems like a solid figure. So you're at seventy-five thou, and from there we go to your expenses, which are travel, and the car. . . .And some emergency fix-it money—we've got to allow for that."

Tildy, with no appetite for shop talk, slipped out and went looking for a telephone. Incense aromas followed her through the thin, dank air outside the room. She stopped in the dim hallway, noticing the photograph of Pierce, his blond bowl cut melting into the pale background of snow and trees; he had on tinted glasses, the kind state troopers wore. Reminded her of Sparn, a youthful picture of him she'd once seen, all slick and slender, outside some Palm Beach movie house with straw hat tipped low and coat draped over his shoulders in the customary impresario pose.

She supposed there were other similarities between the two, both tacticians with unswerving faith in trappings of every kind, but she was already sufficiently depressed—no need to contemplate them further. Dipping her thumb in beer dregs she drew a large X on the frame's glass.

Next to a ceramic crucifix in the next room Tildy found a wall phone. She pressed a button to activate one of the four lines and punched up a long-distance number; then she wound the cord in her fingers and counted the rings.

"Yeah, who's this?"

"Your wife."

"No shit. Where you at?"

"Still New York."

"So how's it goin' up there, baby? That dude findin' any work for you?"

"Finding work? I don't . . ." Some line Christo must've given him the night they left; she couldn't remember. "No, it's been mostly window shopping and bar hopping, Karl. Not much news to tell. It's only, I don't know, I wanted to hear your voice and make sure you were getting by all right is all."

"Well, ain't you some sweetness. Tell ya, I been shaky some, but then I just sit still and talk to you out loud like you was right here and it calms me down. You always say the right things. And I know you would too if you was really here. See, while you been bar hoppin', ole Karl's been all sober. Ain't had even one drop since you left. How 'bout that?"

"You're serious, aren't you."

"Yes indeed. Like to drown in sweat the first couple days. But ain't I makin' that effort? I'm tryin' to be a good boy for you, so why can't you come back home?"

"I will, you know I will. Just not right now."

"But I need some reward. Even a trained seal when he does his stuff right, they give him a fish. I can't be doin' like you want me to all on my own. You got to throw me a few fish about now."

"I love you Karl and I'm glad I called. Don't make me regret it."

"Well, I'd sure like to know what it is up there that's keepin' you."

"So would I."

"Then why don't you cut loose and come on down for the weekend. We'll go up to Tampa and eat crabs and get rowdy."

"Sounds good, and we'll do it. Just not right now."

"It's just I been missin' you so hard."

"I know. Let me tell you where I'm at in case you need to call."

Karl couldn't find paper, so he wrote on his hand in ink. "I been thinkin' all about you. See, it's like that old song, baby. You're the queen of my heart . . . Baby?"

He was talking to an empty line.

Tildy looked all around, everything so neat and squared off, like a dentist's waiting room. There was a draft and the surfaces of furniture were cold. She cried without moving her face.

Down at the other end of the hall, ice motes oozed through septums and blood pumped thick from triphammer hearts.

9

Warm rays filtering through pine boughs fell at the edge of the marl pit where Ondray Keyes sat holding the last half inch of a cigarette between fingernails, trying to catch a last puff or two without burning himself. His shirt was buttoned to the throat, the collar turned up. It had been chilly all morning, icy dew on his bare feet as he ran to the outhouse, fog on the pop bottles.

A brown bird fluttered out of the scrubwood behind him. It hovered a moment, dive-bombed the pit, skimming over weed-choked water, then floated up into high branches across the way. Ondray kept his eye on the small shape, knowing that if he looked away for only a second he'd lose it in the leaf shadows. He slapped one eye shut and aimed through the clear, soft air. Hook that finger round the trigger, take a breath and hold it steady, then squeeze. Pop. Ondray was saving up to get a BB rifle.

He flipped the cigarette end, hardly more than a coal by now, into the water and walked back to the culvert by the road where he'd hidden his bicycle. He brushed dirt off the seat and adjusted the playing cards clothes-pinned to the rear spokes (they made a bad motor-buzzing sound when the wheel spun). Once he'd climbed on, Ondray unwrapped three sticks of bubblegum and wadded them together before filling his cheek. The flavor went so fast. Then he put his small weight on the pedals and took off down the crown of the road, alert for any gleam in the weeds.

Maybe ride all the way to the big highway. Maybe see what's doing over at that Mr. Gables' house.

Karl answered the door holding a blue towel around his waist. "Ondray, my little pal. What you doin', son?"

"What *you* doin'?"

"Standin' here gettin' my butt cold. Come on in here so's I can close the door."

Ondray moved slowly, sucking on his pink wad. "You sleep all day, man," he said. It was not a question.

"I was up late. Wife called me again from New York last night. Had to sit down and make some plans, you know, stuff I gotta be doin'. A few deals I want to be on top of when she gets back." Karl grinned woozily and padded toward the bedroom. "Put some clothes on and I'll be right out. Should be a Coke in the fridge if you're thirsty."

"Can I keep the bottle?"

"Sure, go ahead. Collectin' 'em are you?"

"That's what we be doin' most every mornin', me and my brother. And splittin' the money half and half."

"So that was Earvin I seen the other day snoopin' along by here with a gunnysack?"

"Coulda been." Ondray pulled open the big white door and found the Coke next to a bowl of something that had fur growing on it. "Coulda been," he said, parking his gum by the sink before drinking.

"That's real good. You boys got some enterprise." Karl emerged in pants and a Louisiana Tech sweatshirt, sat at the kitchen table with socks and sneakers in hand. "If you'd told me before, I woulda been savin' all my empties for you. That's some enterprise all right."

"No, uh-uh. We just be findin' 'em, that's all." Draining the bottle, he jammed it neck first in the back pocket of his dungarees.

"So it's all in the huntin'. Right. All in the huntin'." Karl hummed experimentally while preparing his morning meal: instant coffee and crushed aspirin mixed with hot water from the tap. "You know those ads in the magazines that say 'your song poems wanted.' I was thinkin' I might take a swing at it. Whatta you think, Ondray, you think I could get a hit record?"

Ondray shrugged, replaced his wad.

"Okay, but you might hear my words comin' out a juke box sometime. They're lookin' for new blood, you know. New ideas."

"You gonna eat this banana?"

Ignoring him, Karl peered out the window. "Guess it's a nice day out there," he said, rubbing his eyes. "Maybe you and me could do some huntin' on a day like this."

"We finished that up already and Earvin done went home to eat. He like that fish head soup."

"No, see what I had in mind . . . Lizard huntin'. Remember a couple years ago how we went lizard huntin' right out back here in the slough. Caught some big ones, too, and my wife tied pieces of thread on 'em so you could walk 'em up and back like on a leash. Remember? We got awful muddy, both of us. And you were just a little scrap back then, looked like a piece of devil's-food cake with the frosting all mussed. But we sure had a time of it. Nice kinda day to do it again. We could go right now if you want."

Ondray's mouth was filled with banana so he answered by angling his head and wandering toward the door. Nothing much else to do that he could think of.

Karl walked in front. He wore his painter's cap and carried a shoe box and a couple of glass jars. Ondray scuffed along after him, eating a jelly sandwich. As they reached the trees, Karl cautioned him about making noise. A hunter, he said, had to move as softly as a breeze. They walked several minutes through thick woods with clouds of gnats hanging over their heads. A bread crust slipped from Ondray's fingers and tiny brown ants instantly swarmed on it. He bent down to watch them.

Karl, who'd gone ahead, came thrashing back through stalks and saplings. "Come on, we got to stay together out here," he said urgently. "You can't tell what might be lurkin' around."

"Sure, man."

The trees thinned out and the ground became uneven, exposed roots and grassy little hummocks. A smell of warm rot reached them.

"Couldn't get me out here by night at the wrong end of a gun," Karl said. "That's when the swamp cats come out and big bears'd tear your head clean off with one swipe."

"Ain't no bears," Ondray said impatiently.

Up ahead, light hit the stagnant water like a fist.

"There's snakes though. They good to eat."

Karl moved back out of the sun. Sweat was dripping down his neck and water had begun to seep through his sneakers. The coffee was pressing at the neck of his bladder but he didn't want to let it out. He had this crazy thought that if he took his cock out, some creature would jump up and take a bite out of it. Crazy. But every time he'd reach for that zipper, he'd imagine what they'd feel like, those little wet teeth, and it was so real his stomach would drop. Hey. Settle down now.

He was duckwalking by the edge of a puddle flecked with scum when he saw one and froze. A black salamander with yellow spots. It was basking with eyes closed and forefeet just touching the water. Karl balanced, set his weight back on his heels, moved his open hand very slowly until it was directly over the target, and then he swooped. Mud and water in his fist and, yes, a little something cold and wriggling, a dark head emerging from between his fingers. He felt behind him for the jar, fascinated by the struggling movements, the shiny jaws widening. He thought he heard a tiny squeak and then there was a new sensation, something warm. He loosened his grip, looked. In his excitement he had squeezed so hard that the salamander's belly had ruptured and its purplish viscera were all over his palm.

Karl flung the body away, churned his hand in the water, wiped it on the grass. And then he stopped. Ondray was gone and he was completely alone in the cruel emptiness and heat of the slough. Here it came again, that panic of broad daylight that he knew well enough to recognize at its first shifty approach. The trees closed off his route of escape and the sun descended on him from above.

He wanted to call for Ondray but his throat would open only for the thinnest stream of air. No sound came out. His head felt like a sponge full of wet plaster. If he'd had the strength he might have dug a safe hole in the earth. But all Karl could do was curl up in the mud and pray his lungs and heart would keep working.

"Man, you funny. You come out here to sleep."

"God almighty but I told you. Don't you ever walk off and leave me that way. I told you we had to stay together."

"Yeah, okay. But be cool, jes be cool." Ondray backed up, alarmed by the wild-eyed mudman who wavered toward him. "I found some good stuff back in them reeds."

He held up his collecting jar; it was filled with clear jelly speckled black.

"What the hell?"

"Frog eggs."

"You little bastard."

"Good stuff. These don't die on the way, I be farmin' frogs."

Karl recovered with an ice pack and some afternoon teevee. His favorite show came on at three, *I Married Joan* ("What a girl, what a whirl, what a life!") with Joan Davis and Jim Backus as Brad.

Joan Davis was no stunner. She had a big nose, almost no chin and a rubbery face that could have been a man's. But there was something about her that brought the heat to Karl's balls. He would picture her sprawled across a bed, skirt up around her waist. Conical tits, legs and arms so thin, so helpless. He imagined himself pushing them here and there like a doll's, grasping that helmet of glossy blond hair and pulling her face close to his. He lay back on the sofa and masturbated, thinking of Joan Davis, of Tildy, of a little girl who let him pee into her hands in third grade; and at the end, as usual, he thought of Jerry Apache's wife in the emergency room, her dirty sandals and red toenails, her face distorted with grief, tears and mucus running, her knees buckling as she slid down the white tiled wall and fell in a heap on the floor.

He ejected his semen onto a torn magazine. Just as quickly he began to recede. That moment's appeasement faded into the slack afternoon; his nerves twitched, frantic for something more, and went numb. A droplet fell from his deflated penis, cold and gray on the edge of his thigh.

He reached behind him for distraction, pulling old issues of *Rockhound, Prospector's World,* and *True Treasure Tales* from the tumbling pile in the corner. He knew parts of them by heart, favorite passages he would reread at times of dejection like verses from the Bible. Ah yes, here was the one about the man who discovered a 28-carat diamond while pitching horseshoes with his nephew. There was inspiration in these yellowed pages. All things were possible. One revelatory moment, a fast dig in the right piece of ground, was all it took to turn your life around. Rebirth. Rebirth as a man of means.

Opening a three-year-old copy of *True Treasure Tales,* Karl looked at the pictures and read the advertisements. Then he found an article in the back which, after hurrying through the first few paragraphs, he could not remember having ever seen before. It was written by someone called J. Frank Robey (Former NYPD Consultant). The title was "Jazzman's Fortune."

> . . . The diminutive, hunchbacked Webb overcame his handicaps and went on to become one of the premier jazz drummers of his era. Connoisseurs of Negro music still speak in tones of awe about the great bands he led in the 20's and 30's at the Savoy Ballroom in New York's Harlem. Many famous musicians graduated from Webb's band and made names for themselves elsewhere. Included among these would be Ella Fitzgerald, the great vocalist who's still making records today and who, as a shy orphan from Baltimore, debuted with Webb's band in the early 30's.
>
> Unlike many jazzmen of the time who squandered their money on cars, clothes, liquor, and fast women, Chick Webb was a

shrewd businessman who made sound investments and managed them carefully. So it was that shortly after his death, the Harlem rumor mill was alive with stories of a fortune in cash and jewels secreted somewhere in Webb's sumptuous townhouse. Mounted police were called in on several occasions to control wild mobs trying to break into the property. Over the next few years amateur treasure hunters, as well as some out-and-out criminals, tore the place apart, but nothing of significance was ever found.

The end of the story? Maybe not. Says one-time nightclub owner Dixie Diggs, "Chick sank a lot of money into real estate. He was ahead of his time. He had buildings all over Harlem. Sugar Hill, Morningside Heights. There could be a floor safe or a secret room in one of those places that nobody's stumbled on yet."

But what are the chances that the treasure ever really existed? Is it only a myth? A relic of that tumultuous period in our history when the nation's heart beat in Swing time and men and women danced all night to forget their worries? Dixie Diggs thinks not.

"Chick was always pretty tight with a dollar. It would have been just like him to stash his dough where no one could find it."

Naturally, Webb's real estate holdings have long since passed into other hands and tracing them would be a difficult task. But then, who ever said treasure hunting was easy! Maybe that floor safe or secret room is still waiting to be discovered. With some careful research and a little luck, the jazzman's fortune may yet be found.

New York. A city that big must be full of hidden treasures, and Tildy, who wouldn't know where to look, had gone without him. He closed his eyes and tried to visualize the New York he knew from the movies—blinding neon, overflowing sidewalks. And thousands upon thousands of buildings. It would take a lifetime to search even half of them. Was it really all in the hunting?

Karl went back to the beginning and tracked the story again. He was so absorbed in this second reading that he barely heard the rapping at the door and the rattle of the knob.

"Yo. Yo in there."

Karl fastened his pants, peeked through the curtains at a man in a polyester suit who turned to one side as he lit a brown cigarette. He straightened, flicking the dead match away, and Karl saw his tense face, with bits of green toilet paper pasted over shaving cuts. He looked too nervous and shaggy to be much of a threat. Probably had the wrong address anyway. Karl puffed himself up and opened the door.

"Karl Gables," the man said, reading from a slip of paper.

"You're lookin' at him."

"I'd like to speak with your wife, Karl. Is she around?"

"No sir, she ain't."

"That is her car parked over there, license number 5Y 213?"

"But she ain't in it."

The man smiled abruptly and one of the paper bits dropped off his chin. "What it is, I'm a friend of Tildy's. I'm associated with her employer, the Seminole Star Corporation of Jacksonville. I'd like to come in and ask you a few questions, if you don't mind. Get a few things cleared up."

Karl looked at the heavy gold chain around his neck and the grime on his shirt cuffs. "You got a business card or something?"

"Gee, you know I'm fresh out. But I really am a good friend of your wife's. I know her well enough to tell you she likes mustard on a baked potato."

"Yeah, okay. That's good enough," Karl said, stepping back.

"Fine. Great. Just a few minutes' conversation, I mean I'm not going to screw up your day, Karl. And I'll tell you what, I've got a bottle of six-year-old bourbon in my car. Good thing to carry when you spend as much time in motels as I do, know what I mean? We'll have a couple of nips and I'm sure the time will pass quite pleasantly for both of us, okay?"

"Yeah, why not. I'll get some glasses."

The visitor was back a minute later with the bottle. He shopped the chairs in the room, chose one, and filled Karl's glass. "Actually, I think I'll hold off a couple minutes till I get my breath back. Been humping all around trying to find this place."

"We like it out here." Karl sucked bourbon fumes through his nose, upended the glass. "Real mellow. You carry good whiskey. . . . Say, I don't even know your name."

Settling deeper into his chair the visitor removed a leatherette memo book and a mechanical pencil from his breast pocket. "They call me Buck, and so can you."

"Thanks, Buck. How about a refill?"

"No problem." The visitor filled Karl's glass three quarters full this time, still poured nothing for himself. "Is Tildy going to be here later? Are you expecting her at any special time?"

"Nope."

"We figured to have heard from her by now. She left us in kind of a hurry, you know. Not a word."

"So you work for the ball team, is that it?"

"The corporation has many different interests." The visitor looked at his watch. "You think I might be able to talk to her, umm, say tomorrow?"

"Not likely. Tildy, see, she's on kind of a vacation. Her old man croaked just a while ago and she's been wound pretty tight over that."

"Yeah, Tildy's a sensitive girl." Scribbling something on the pad. "So maybe this isn't the best time to bother her, but we do owe her some back pay and we'd like to settle up as soon as possible, no hard feelings. You tell me where she's staying and I can get that check to her right away."

Karl tried to speak in mid-gulp and spilled bourbon down inside his shirt. "Damn surprise check, huh? Now you talkin'. And we can use the money, yes sir. I just knew there was somethin' fine all ready to pop up like that today. You know how every once in a while you'll wake up with a feelin'? Like maybe you had a dream was meant to show you . . . ."

"Where do I find her." The pencil hovered.

"Tell you what. Seein' as how you all'd like to get your paperwork squared away, whyn't you let me have the check right now and be done with it? I could hold it for her till she gets back."

The visitor flinched, doodled interlocking circles on his pad. "Well, it's not . . . It's not that simple. Before I can, umm, actually. . . Before I can write anything up I have to discuss a few minor details with her. Per diem expenses, that kind of thing." The circles expanding now, moving unevenly across the page. "I mean, it's not that I don't trust you in terms of holding the money. But . . . I think I will have one with you." He grabbed at the bottle.

"Come on ahead, amigo. I'll go get the radio from the other room and we can listen to some tunes."

"No, that's okay." Shivering at his first sip.

"No trouble. I'll just plug her in over there."

"I'd rather you didn't. Really."

"Sure. I was only thinkin' we might have a little party. Got a ways to go on that bottle yet."

The visitor looked disconsolately at what remained in his glass. "If you don't mind an observation on my part, Karl, you seem a little nervous."

"No shit. Mite keyed up, huh? Probably just lonesome is all, cooped up in here."

142

"Have you heard from Tildy at all? A postcard?"

"Nah. We don't get much in the way of mail around here."

"I hope you won't get hot, but I have to ask this: Has your wife left you? Did she take a walk on you, Karl?"

"You're pissin' on the wrong hydrant there, Buck." Karl lurched out of his chair, gestured sloshingly with his glass. "You got business with Tildy, you wanna ask me some questions, I don't mind. But don't you go pullin' my chain. I got as much dignity as the next sucker. Goddamn right. Now both of us on the road, me and Tildy been separated a lot, but we got a solid understandin' and we got plans. Hell, she called me from New York last night just to hear my voice."

The visitor leaned back and arranged his hair, catching his reflected profile in the windowpane. "She give you the address of the hotel?"

A vague sense that he had left the door to the lion cage open flapped at the outskirts of Karl's mind. "Never said she was at no hotel."

"Didn't you?" The visitor topped up Karl's glass.

Lounging amid shadows and smoke at the Kenilworth, Tildy and Christo argued over where to go for dinner.

"Anyway, I don't like Greek food," Tildy said. "It's too greasy."

"I heard you the first time."

She stretched herself across the bed until her palms were resting on the warped brown floorboards. She wore a green baseball cap, flowered panties and a plastic lei rescued from a garbage can.

"I love these little pork chops," Christo said, petting her shoulder blades.

A photographic rendering of this scene, the kind of grainy enlargement brought into a courtroom and mounted on an easel, might be advanced as the image of two young citizens in a state of postcoital entrancement. That would be an unscrupulous frame-up. In truth, bodily contact had been negligible. Tildy was bewildered, having expected more, some show of possessiveness after she'd spent a second night at the Chemikazi loft.

"How about seafood? You got to like shrimp."

Tildy jumped up, shook herself. Balanced on the balls of her feet, one arm shielding her breasts, she scanned the twilight street framed by the open window.

That New York mystique had thus far escaped her. Another city just like the others; bigger, with each rudiment carried to a further extreme, but adding up to not very much. A cannon and a peashooter, were pretty much the same.

"What are we doing in this fleabag anyway?" Tildy wanted to know. "There's all the money from Pierce for the grass we brought up, but then you hole up here like you just got out on parole."

"What is it you want, a place with a view of the park? I can send you on a tour to the Statue of Liberty tomorrow, if that's what you're after."

"Don't strain yourself missing the point, Jimmy. This was supposed to be a holiday. I left all my aches and pains to go on a spree, but here I am with the mildewed room and the cold hamburgers and I might as well be back on the road with the Cougarettes. So what's the story? Am I being punished for getting it on with Looie?"

"We got no ties. You don't owe me one little crumb of fidelity. And don't call me Jimmy." Christo spoke in freeze-dried tones. "Far as the money goes, that's my business, my score. It's capital. Always I'd build a little roll, then fritter it away, but this time I'm going to make the right moves. Nothing to do with you one way or the other."

"So you're a pretty conventional asshole after all. You make with that gaudy outlaw routine, but it's all a shuck."

"Wish you could see how you look coming on all righteous in panties and a plastic lei."

"Get bent."

There followed several minutes of arctic, high-tension silence. Then Christo gently asked if she still wanted to go out and eat. Tildy replied that in her present mood whether they huddled mutely in the room or went for an all-night hike, stopping for beer and pretzels in every bar en route, was of no interest at all to her.

Before Christo could counterpunch, there came a vehement pounding at the door. Just as glad of the interruption, he slid off the bed. "Probably room service with our lobster Newburg."

Tildy buttoned herself into Christo's denim jacket as the door opened. A pop-eyed individual in a rumpled trench coat darted into the room and pointed his finger like a gun.

"Bingo. How's the little shortstop getting along?"

"Vinnie." She spoke the name with tired, unsurprised disgust.

"Vinnie?"

"Vinnie Sparn, ex-manager of the Cougarettes."

"Want me to bounce him?"

Vinnie backed toward the window, staking out some territory. "I see I came at a bad time. Sorry to spoil the party but it can't be helped. Sure, I could come back later, but think how I'd feel having to start all over again 'cause you'd skipped out in the meantime. After coming all this way to find you."

"If this is a social call . . ."

"Hey, do yourself a favor, Johnny. Put on your pants and get out of here. She won't be turning any more tricks tonight."

Christo bore down on him, looking from side to side for a heavy object. "I think I would like to drop you out the window."

"Stay out of my way, Johnny."

They were inches apart and breathing on one another, but Tildy interposed herself, pressing a shoulder into Christo's chest and pushing him back.

"Butt out. I can cope with this flunky."

"Hey, watch that talk."

Pulling at the brim of her cap, "Don't play like you came on your own. What does Pete want from me?"

"An apology to start. When you jumped the team like that it really hurt his feelings. We looked after you and we gave you whatever you wanted. Didn't I always let you bat leadoff? And then you go AWOL in the middle of the season. The ingratitude really got under Dad's skin. He's just that kind of guy. Dad believes in a kind of basic decency and when it's flouted he gets very upset. That kind of stress isn't good for a man his age, you follow me?"

"I'll write him a letter."

"Okay. You had your screen time, asshole. Now beat it." Christo had edged back within striking distance.

"I said I'd handle it. It's my problem."

"And a letter just won't cover it. Not nearly." Vinnie stroked his sideburns, glowered. "It gets into a legal and moral area. Dad sees the idea of the contract as very crucial to our society. It's not just a piece of paper, it's a symbol of something much bigger, a complex system of cooperation and mutual trust. When you break a contract with Dad it's kind of like spitting in church, you know what I mean? No, I'm afraid you're going to have to come back to Florida and work this out with him face to face."

"This is a joke, right? Are you really going to these lengths because Pete couldn't turn out one of his girls as a shortstop?"

"I think I've explained it."

"Not at all. You can start by explaining how you tracked me down."

When he smirked, Vinnie's eyes became little slashes in his sandpaper face. "No big miracle really. A pretty short order once I talked to your husband. A real good old boy, by the way. A great sport. We sat around and had a few and he let slip you were up here. In another little while I was able to make him see it would be to everyone's advantage to be a little more specific. Then I caught the first plane out. Nice. I got prime rib and a movie."

"You knocked him around. You leaned on him, didn't you, fuckface." Tildy hurled a glass ashtray; it whistled past Vinnie's ear and exploded against the wall.

Vinnie swept ashes from his lapel and popped his lips. "I hoped things wouldn't develop this way. I hoped you'd come with me voluntarily." He slipped one hand inside the trench coat and came out with a snubnosed .45.

"Lovely." Christo subsided onto the bed and took a cigarette from behind his ear. "I used to have one just like it. Got it by selling a hundred and twelve tins of White Clover Salve."

"Go fry your head, Johnny." Though he'd practiced all his moves in front of a mirror, Vinnie was close to wetting himself.

"You don't remember White Clover Salve? Used to advertise on the back page of the comic books. They sent you a consignment and depending on how much you could unload you'd get an archery set or a pair of binoculars or a model airplane or a cheezy little tin bank that was supposed to be like a miniature safe with this plastic combination dial—"

"Shut up! You shut up." Vinnie hopped from one foot to the other, gesticulated meaninglessly with the barrel of the gun. "Come on, Soileau, shake it. We got a plane to catch at LaGuardia in two hours."

"Vinnie, this is really too ridiculous. And I'm not getting on any plane with you."

"Don't push me." Vinnie thumbed back the hammer and the three of them played eyeball billiards.

"Okay, you win," Tildy finally said.

"Wait a minute."

But she scuttled to the bed and held Christo down. "I'd better do it. He's more afraid of his father than anything else."

"Who the fuck is his father?"

146

"Enough!" Vinnie released the hammer, circled around to the door. A votary of private-eye novels, there was a deep invigoration for him in bringing the timeworn gestures to life. The gun felt warm and comforting in his hand, like a baby animal. He could almost hear background music, bongos and walking bass: Vinnie's Theme. "Hurry it up."

"Sure, Vinnie. I'll just put on some makeup and get my stuff together, okay?" She backed toward the bathroom, her movements slow and easy, her smile placating, as if dealing with a maniac bent on swallowing lye. "Don't get all worked up now. I'll just be in the bathroom getting ready."

"You got five minutes." Maintaining pistol position, Vinnie took out one of his miniature cigars, but didn't have enough hands to light it with. "You, Johnny, you lay back easy on that bed and don't try and be a hero. You'll just end up making a mess on the floor."

"Sometimes it's hard to tell what I'll do, even for me." Christo plucked thoughtfully at his lower lip. "I been in and out of the psycho ward pretty near all my life, Vinnie. I think that's something you ought to know right at this moment. I've been declared a SCUT three or four different times. Schizophrenic, Chronic, Undifferentiated Type. That's how they label the real savages, Vinnie, the ones even drugs can't touch. You know I once bit an orderly's nose clean off his face, and after that they used to cut cards to see who had to bring me my meals. So you can't tell. You can't ever tell what I might do."

There was hissing and knocking from the pipes as Tildy opened the taps full.

The little cigar jigged at the corner of Vinnie's mouth. "You're all noise, Johnny. You don't worry me."

"How many feet from the end of the bed to where you're standing? Eight, ten maybe? I could be on you in one jump."

"You want your ass in a sling?"

"You're losing it, hotshot. Little by little you're losing it."

"One more word." Vinnie snapped into firing position, both hands on the pistol grip and arms stiffened. "I don't need any more reasons to blow you right through the wall."

Tildy materialized from the bathroom trailing steam. Tightly, down behind her leg, she held the bronze canister of her father's ashes, the last thing wedged into the suitcase back in Gibsonton on the chance she might find a becoming place to scatter them somewhere along the way.

"Vinnie, should I wear this beige skirt or something more formal?"

He turned to face her and, with the quick release that had started countless double plays, sidearming across her body, she threw the canister at a crucial point between his navel and his kneecaps and hit it dead on. Clutching his groin, Vinnie collapsed like a marionette and the gun skittered free. Christo sprang from the bed, scooped up the weapon and drove his heel into Vinnie's liver.

"A great throw," he said. "An honest-to-God, Hall-of-Fame throw."

"Been wanting to do that for two years. I only wish I'd had something heavier, like a thirty-six-ounce bat."

"You want me to kill him?" Christo spun the cylinder, stepped back. "Christ. It's not even loaded. You shmuck, I ought to break this thing down and make you eat it piece by piece."

Vinnie sucked air, unable even to whimper.

"Let's just tie him up and get out of here."

"I'm with you. Tear that bedsheet into strips and soak them in water so they'll hold good and tight."

Tildy stood immobile, suddenly chilled, her skin broken out in goose pimples.

"Ease up now, girl, it's finished. You did great, just great."

"A lot of help you were."

He came and pulled Tildy against him, talked into the soft mat of her hair that smelled faintly of smoke. "Do you really think I would have let him take you? No way. I was working on him the whole time, playing with his head." He moved his fingers up and down the column of her neck until she softened, her arms went loose and her face nestled into his.

Ten minutes later, with Vinnie securely trussed and gagged on the floor, Tildy was preparing a snug nest for Lucien in the deepest recesses of her bag. She stroked the cool, curving metal with her hand and said, "You go back to sleep, Papa." Then she snapped the bag shut, stepped over Vinnie and out the door.

By midnight they had consumed large quantities of shellfish, listened to a 67-year-old pianist play boogie-woogie in a penthouse bar and checked into a fresh hotel near Washington Square. The room had wall-to-wall carpet, air conditioning and a color teevee.

"There," Christo said. "Is this what you wanted?"

In darkness they watched a Jock Mahoney western (saddle tramp befriends young widow, saves ranch from foreclosure) and blankly,

148

wordlessly, Tildy drew out his damp, curled penis. The dilatory rhythm of her pumping hand did not increase even at the last. His come was cold on her knuckles by the time she went looking for a towel.

10

Men of affairs get up early and begin striving right after breakfast. While time may not be money, they often race in the same colors; and in the words of a young blood who tried to sell Christo a hot watch at five A.M. in the Detroit Greyhound terminal: "Ain't never too early to be hustlin'." It's not so much a question of getting a jump on the other guy as it is of tilting your mind to precisely the right angle, like the morning prayers of Benedictine monks.

Replete with brioche and black coffee, Christo and Pierce sat at the dining table counting and stacking bills and discussing the state of the market.

"You don't see so much of that good black hash these days," Pierce was saying. "Some fairly substantial quantities were being moved out of Lahore a year or two back, but I haven't heard of anything lately. Nothing that's reached New York at any rate."

"How much would that bring per pound on a quantity basis?"

"Hard to say. Hash is moving into that premium area right now, so you might, depending on the variables, be able to hit eleven or twelve hundred."

Christo reached for a paper clip, tossed another bundle of twenties onto the growing centerpiece beside the coffee pot. "I wish we could figure something that didn't involve my leaving the country."

"Poor methodology, jazzbo. You want to maximize every advantage, buying at the overseas market value and then selling back here. It's called transfer pricing."

"Whatever. It's still a bit early in the day for that textbook material."

"You should just meditate for a while. Get in contact with those bills."

Pierce had suggested the ritual money counting. Clearly, their putative dope scam would require more capital than Christo was in any position to supply and so to increase his bankroll, Pierce had gotten him a seat in a no-limit poker game starting up in a few hours. He had suggested the counting as a kind of preparatory workout, a way of tuning in to those ethereal cash frequencies; the motions of gathering, riffling, folding and unfolding, the tactile sensations, all magnetizing Christo for those monster pots.

"I've got my mystical side," Pierce had said.

"Uh-huh. Pass the sugar, will you?"

The game was run out of the East Side apartment of an all-purpose middleman named Ernest Freed. Back in the late '60s Freed had almost cracked the best-seller list with an espionage novel called *The Abramowitz Integer*, but his next one had flopped badly and he hadn't been in hardcover since. The last piece of writing he'd done was the script for a movie about lesbian stock car drivers that was never produced. Now he ran his little gambling operation, introduced his friends to very amiable "fashion models" (the friends, in turn, would occasionally alert him to an upcoming stock manipulation), and dabbled in ghetto real estate. When pressed, he would admit to having a literary project in the works, but indicated the media overlords would never let it see the light of day since it would "blow the lid off their whole lousy game."

Freed's game didn't need a steerer. He kept to a select clientele, cosmopolites and professional people who wouldn't get ugly if they dropped a few thousand, for whom it was better to be stone broke than uncool. He made generous contributions to the police department's bulletproof-vest fund and kept the hard boys away with monthly payments and the understanding that if he booked any sports bets, he'd lay them off with some new talent they were bringing along, a decertified osteopath over in Jersey who was just coming off a three-year bit for Medicaid fraud.

"So what is it you've gotten me into?" Christo asked. "I mean, I'm not going up against pros I hope. I'd hate to get sandbagged all the way back to square one."

"Would I lead you into that kind of spot? Hey, you should be able to put four walls and a roof around this type of competition. They're lightweights, believe me. It's only a game to them and to you it's a job. It's not a question of whether you'll win, but how much."

"Then what the hell is all this for?" Christo pointed to the piles of money and the packs of cards.

"I want you to be in your best fighting trim, that's all. A little science, a little superstition. Remember what I said about maximizing your advantages? Now then, I'm going to deal you some straight flushes and I want you to really concentrate on a visual image of those cards."

"This is a cash-only game. No checks, no IOUs." Freed wore loafers without socks, satin jogging shorts and a white shirt open to his sternum. "We play no-limit table stakes here with check and raise permitted. It's a fixed five-dollar ante, dealer calls the game and I take five percent out of every pot."

Christo nodded. "Then I guess we'll have to try to keep the pots small."

"There's an open bar." Freed had the rote geniality of a tour guide. "Please help yourselves."

Pierce poured himself a large neat Scotch. Christo opted for plain soda with a chunk of lemon.

"Who's that?" Nodding to the brown colossus standing by the door.

"Security. This is his summer job. Rest of the time he's what they call a nonteaching assistant at some vocational school in Brooklyn. Used to be a pro wrestler, the Mighty Bobo."

"I thought these guys were supposed to be well-mannered. Family men."

"You'll see."

Then Pierce introduced him to the other players: Steve, the record producer; Randy, who owned a couple of Japanese restaurants; Dennis, the lawyer; and Maury, from Wall Street. They shook hands and went back to arranging their money—fifties, hundreds, great sheaves of them. Freed tore the cellophane off two factory fresh decks, spread them out on the spotless green baize.

"You fellas don't use the jokers, huh?" Christo said as all four were removed and torn in half.

"Where are you from anyway?"

"Newport, Kentucky. Fast horses, beautiful women, and plenty of side meat with greens."

"Swell. A tourist."

"Welcome to actionland, pal."

"Come on, come on. First jack deals."

On the first hand he stayed with all the way, Christo got sandwiched between an ace-high flush and queens full, and lost a little

152

over four hundred dollars. Maury from Wall Street had whipped the pot skillfully and didn't seem like any lightweight from where Christo was sitting. He glanced at Pierce with raised eyebrows.

"Early yet," his partner said. "Pace yourself."

Then he cut the cards for the new deal and his face said: I brought you to the zone, but now you're on your own.

Tildy, too, was on her own and this was a day weighted with gloom from the moment she'd opened her eyes. In the note he'd left her, Christo suggested she take in a movie or visit the Botanical Gardens, as he'd be tied up all day. Thank you very much. Tildy could accommodate solitude—that was a skill she'd picked up early in life—but not this way, not now. For the very first time, she felt a real need of him, of the reassurance his mere hereness would bring.

She missed the cramped sameness of home and adoring Karl, childish but unquestioning. She wanted to loll in the warm smells of her own bed and hear the mice chittering under the floorboards. And she wondered if she wasn't just playing out a long string of blunders reaching all the way back to . . .

Half awake, she sat in a murky barroom drinking amaretto and coffee and watching the Bowery Boys on television. The woman behind the bar talked to herself. She counted beer coasters and swizzle sticks and wiped the same glasses over and over. Her black hair was teased and lacquered, her long red fingernails meticulously shaped; they clinked on every bottle and glass she touched. Every few minutes she would glance up at the gray screen, then at the clock on the opposite wall. Her gestures hurried and anxious as if she were waiting for someone who was late, she would take a cigarette out of her purse and light it, and then grind it out underfoot after two or three hissing puffs.

"I'd like another when you get a chance."

"When I get a chance? That's a good one. When the hell did I ever have a chance? I'm just living the life I got handed." In the time it took to bark these four short sentences, she had filled the shot glass to the rim, realigned the amaretto bottle and grabbed the coffeepot from the warmer. "You taking cream with that?"

"No, I'm fine."

"Yeah? You married, honey?"

"Yes. I just don't wear the ring."

"I know, I know. Why discourage them? Right after the tits it's your hands they look over. And a girl your age—well, my advice

153

would be to get out of it as soon as you can. It's slow death, honey, the slowest there is. Marriage'll eat away at your insides till there's nothing left but the water and the fat and you're no damn use to anybody."

"You must have had a pretty bad experience."

"Me? Uh-uh. Fuck 'em and forget 'em is my motto. But I've got eyes to see what goes on with people, and sooner or later, young and old, they just about all end up here."

Behind her, through a blizzard of static, Leo Gorcey tugged at his bow tie and said, "Don't bother me with that noise. What's for dinner?"

Tildy left her change on the bar and wobbled into the light.

At 59th Street she bought a bag of popcorn and entered Central Park. Exhausted, she sat down on a bench that looked out over a small pond, and within half a minute, a squad of pigeons had gathered expectantly at her feet. Christo had told her that they were carriers of several varieties of parasitic disease and that every few months some desperate soul would be admitted to the hospital after making a meal of one. "When they say there's no such thing as a free lunch, they mean it." Tildy munched a few handfuls of popcorn, then emptied the rest of the bag on the cement. The pigeons went at it so furiously they didn't even notice a few sparrows who sneaked into the feeding circle. When Tildy left, they were tearing up the bag.

She continued up a gentle rise to a meadow where stretched out before her were a dozen baseball diamonds. The grass was withered, chewed up, and all but two of the diamonds were vacant, their emptiness almost spooky with the late sun flaring on wire backstops. But at the one nearest her, a father served up fat balloon pitches to his small son who, swing after swing, grimacing, hit nothing but air.

Down in one corner there was somewhat more advanced activity going on and Tildy went toward it, shielding her eyes: street types in a pickup softball game, shirtless outfielders, a pitcher with a transistor radio blaring in his back pocket. As she drew closer, circling around behind first base, the centerfielder sprinted and dove for a humpbacked liner, but the ball skipped by him and three runs scored. His teammates cursed him, loosed insults at him that were in no way playful, and when he finally picked himself up, chest speckled with dirt and dead grass, Tildy saw that he was fighting back tears. Evidently a more serious game than it looked; maybe there was money riding.

154

The inning ended without further damage, the other team took the field, and their first baseman tossed a few warm-up grounders. He was olive-skinned, tall, with pectorals swelling under a T-shirt that had his name felt-markered across the back: Silvio. A high throw kicked off the heel of his glove and, instinctively, Tildy trotted after it.

"Bring it here, Mommy." He had stunning black eyes.

Tildy looked at the slightly misshapen ball, squeezed it, weighed it, rolled it around her palm. They were all watching her, smirking. She let it drop, bouncing it twice off her toes like a soccer ball, scooped it between her legs, caught it with her other hand and flipped it over her back. She took it on the one bounce and in the same motion launched a throw that trailed smoke as it rose from her shoe tops and whistled toward Silvio's head. Ducking down and away at the last second, he threw up his glove and the impact of the arriving ball spun him halfway around. He whirled on her, features tense and sharp, but realized in another moment that to lose his temper in front of the others, and at the provocation of this scrawny little *bruja*, would also be to lose face.

"What position you play, Butch?"

"Shortstop."

"Okay, Butch. You show us what you can do. Chombo! You go in the outfield."

Silvio borrowed a mitt that was slightly too big for her hand and she felt suddenly haggard, ungainly as she took her position, rubbed dirt on her hands. She had not won his respect, only his curiosity. . . . Check the freak, boys. This ought to be good.

Her first chance was a slow roller that trickled past the mound. She charged, barehanded it and leaped high on the throw, scissoring her legs. The man was out by eight feet. He stood for a moment, hands on hips, and then spat.

"Get down with it, Butch."

"In his face."

The chatter felt good to her, a warming incantation. She caught a soft pop-up, backpedaling, to end the inning and scooted off the field with her head down to conceal the grin that forced itself on her. She flopped down under a tree and Silvio came and sat next to her, rubbing his back against the knobby trunk.

"You blow some minds out there, Butch." He shook his head. "Where you learn to play ball, in the joint?"

"No, I just fell into it."

155

"What else you do, Butch?"

The hand he had placed on her leg conversationally was still there. Did she imagine a slow, deliberate increase in its pressure? Then he shifted so that the outer curve of his hip melded with hers and there was no mistaking the heat that flowed between them. She felt an odd serenity with this stranger touching her, a soft abatement of her protective reflexes. They gazed into space, said nothing, while his fingers splayed and met, splayed and met, taking small pinching folds in the fabric of her pants.

"You're up now," he whispered. "Go hit a homerun for me."

But with men on first and second, Tildy struck out on three pitches, her mind totally preoccupied with imaginings of what Silvio looked like without clothes. She came away from the plate blushing.

The game ended two innings later on a disputed play at the plate. Silvio ushered her away from the contracting circle of screams and threats, saying he knew a real nice spot where they could go have some beers. This was not an invitation, but an accomplished fact. He was going to take her without even asking what she wanted. It was the kind of arrogance that would normally have inflamed her, but she went along, her silent presence beside him all the consent he required. And when, as they walked, he slung an arm around her waist, she responded instantly (knowing him to be an operator, a man without underwear who carried shiny white knife scars with pride) by crossing her arm over his damp back and smiling into those black, still eyes. She amazed herself.

Orphan Annie's was an airless, close-fitting bar that smelled of roach poison. It might have been the noise, the press of the crowd, the urgent, wheedling faces lunging at one another, but for whatever reason the new setting pierced the vacuum in which she had been afloat. That echoing, dreamlike serenity was gone and a sour unease took its place. Drinks with a bastard and in another fifteen minutes, back to his place.

Picking at the label of her beer bottle, Tildy wondered how she had ever gotten herself into such a box. Was it boredom? Feckless curiosity? Anger at Christo for leaving her alone? It didn't amount to a damn. For if there was one truth to which she held fast it was that reasons were the province of the doomed; that only results mattered.

And so a few minutes later when Silvio danced off to the men's room, she bolted for the door and ran. Full out. For blocks and blocks.

Down and dirty. Pierce dealt the final hole cards with care, sliding each one across the table with his finger, detouring around the green mountain in the center. Christo checked his pair of kings and Steve the Record Producer blew a few blasé smoke rings. He had four spades to the ace showing.

"I'll go two thousand," ironing the bills with the back of his hand, laying them delicately on the crest of the mountain.

It was two big ones to Randy Restaurants, a heavy loser all afternoon who'd been annoying everyone with such irrelevancies as the stale tale of screenwriter Ellie Sebring dropping dead at his sushi bar. He stalled, picking his eyebrows, massaging his overbite, and finally dropped.

"Yeah, what suspense," said Dennis the Lawyer, throwing in yet another busted straight. "I can't catch pneumonia here."

Playing with the jogtrot conservatism of a loan officer from the Corn Belt, Pierce had been drifting back and forth across the break-even mark all day long. Now, true to form, he dropped without even looking at his seventh card.

That brought it around to Eddie the Agent, a big, silk-suited noisemaker from the William Morris office who'd bought in only an hour or so ago and immediately lost four big pots in a row. He was showing paired eights and a couple of junk cards.

"So Steve is hot to trot with his spades, eh? And ace high, too. Fuck, is this déjà vu or what?"

"You really ought to put out some more face towels, Ernie." Maury from Wall Street was just now returning from a pit stop in Freed's black tiled bathroom. "The one I used was all wet. . . . Say, this looks like our biggest pot so far."

"Shut up, Maury."

"Yeah. If you're out of the hand, stay out. What're you up to, Eddie?"

"This is so exciting I just have to call."

"Then I have to raise," Christo said, counting three thousand into the pot.

Steve the Record Producer exhaled very slowly. "And two more. That's three grand to you, Eddie."

"Well, that's damn exciting, but . . . But I don't think I can stick around for the showdown."

"You and me," Christo said. "Let's see it."

Slamming the edge of the table, Steve the Record Producer

157

threw open his hand in disgust. He had three red cards down and a second ace. Christo turned kings over nines and drew in the pot on the blade of his arm.

"Outstanding read," breathed Maury from Wall Street. "Hell of an outstanding read."

"Fucking ridiculous is what it is." Steve the Record Producer was going a little pink about the ears. "There's no possible way you can raise into me and then call me out with two cocksucking pair."

"It was easy once he folded the winning hand. Trip eights, wasn't it?"

Eddie the Agent shrugged helplessly.

"I must thank both of you." Christo looked for a moment into the bursting silver bubbles of his club soda. "You did exactly what I wanted you to."

"And your buddy was dealing, too. What did you do with the rest of the spades, Milbank, swallow 'em?"

"Back off, Steve." Freed was behind him and kneading his shoulders. "It's history, babe," he said gravely, the wise old infantry sergeant who's seen men die a hundred different ways.

As discreetly as he could with all eyes on him, Christo counted his money, he found that he was roughly thirty-one thousand dollars ahead. "Gee, I'd buy a round of drinks for everybody but they're already free."

He was not making friends.

"New cards," said Eddie the Agent. "New cards coming out."

So a few rounds later, in a gut-out five-card stud hand, a couple thou in revenge was extracted by Steve the Record Producer; and when things went no better over the next half hour, Christo began to suspect that he'd blown it, failed to recognize his peak and bail out before traveling the inevitable downside of the curve. Eddie the Agent was being dealt out while he "made some calls," Dennis the Lawyer had tapped out and left, and Pierce was folding most opening bets, acting bored: Now was the perfect time to push the game into breakup and run with the profits. But on the other hand, there was still a great deal of money on the table that wasn't his.

"So what's the story?" Maury from Wall Street, peering over his Ben Franklins. "Are we all taking a nap?"

"Deal cards. Deal cards."

"What time is it?"

"Dinner time," Pierce said, "Hey, Freed, why don't you open a restaurant in here? Some of that new light-on-the-mind cuisine, you know, raw fish wrapped in seaweed and eight-dollar salads. Maybe the publishing people would start coming here for lunch, you might do yourself some good."

"What would you know about it?" Freed growled.

"I'm a writer myself, Freed. I know what it's like to face that blank white sheet."

"Do you wanna play cards or would you rather smartass?" Steve the Record Producer was by now getting after everyone.

"Sure, sure. Why don't you deal something really challenging like Anaconda or Spit in the Ocean?"

But the game was draw, jacks or better. Christo's five-hundred opening was called around, even by Pierce. Christo rapped on the table, passed one hand over his cards. Pat. Everyone but Pierce came right on into him, but his straight to the eight was mortally locked in.

Christo pushed his tightly fanned cards into the middle of the table. "Dealt," pointing across to Steve the Record Producer and then, with the rude leer of someone tipping a Reno blackjack dealer for her cleavage, throwing a folded ten-dollar bill to him.

"Motherfucker."

Impossible to say who came across the table first. Christo landed the first and last real punch, a chopping right to the side of the neck. A pawing uppercut was the best Steve could do before Freed's rented muscle was all over him with a hammerlock.

Maury from Wall Street was yelling at the top of his lungs. "Bloody idiots. Bloody idiots."

"You'd best take your damn seat, turkey," Mr. Hercules said, shoving Christo with his free hand. "Or two seconds after I break his arm I'll be breaking yours." Then, curving the other's body with a slight twist and tug, "Seems you and me already been to this movie, eh little Stevie? Little Stevie Wonder. I'm gonna have to kick your ass up around your collar if you don't learn how to behave." Something he often said after confiscating a blade in the halls of Printing Trades High.

And then Freed stepped in to mediate the money situation, boundaries between individual stakes having been obscured in the commotion.

"Now who had the brand-new fifties?"

"I did," Christo said. "But where's his ten? Let's find Little Stevie's ten first."

Freed stuck a hand inside his shirt, somewhere near his heart. He looked at Pierce and clicked his tongue. "You get the man's money together and then you get him the fuck out of here."

In came Eddie the Agent massaging his receiver ear. "Hey, what's happening, beautiful people?"

Warm rain had come with darkness into the streets. Night walkers kept close to the buildings, rushing along with heads down, jostling as they passed. Cabs poured down the wide avenues with wipers slapping and the bleeding edges of distant traffic lights, taillights were sucked up into particles of mist—sweat mixed with steam, steam with soot.

Christo shadowboxed his way past a restaurant window, college girls inside blowing on their soup. His pockets bulged. "Man, but I put out their lights."

"Sometimes," Pierce said, "sometimes I wonder why I have anything to do with you."

"What's your problem now? It was like printing my own money. I cleaned up on those ginks and now I'm ready to invest."

"But, jazz, you burned the game down. You fucked me up with those people and some of them are customers."

"The hell with them. We got a whole new operation, partner. New worlds to conquer. With my radar I can put us on to most of the psychiatric shoppers in this city, doctors and patients both. Who needs drugs more than they do?"

Pierce caught him by the belt loops, pulled him out of the path of an oncoming bicyclist. "Why don't we go stash that in my safe at home before it works its way out of your pockets?"

"No, I want to feel it and look at it and spend it. Let's go get some cocktails and a few pounds of meat. I'm paying."

Christo had never tasted a Rio Rumba before. It contained absinthe and three different kinds of rum. He had four of them before dinner and had to have someone cut up his sirloin for him. Just outside they'd run into some people Pierce knew, an AP radio reporter and her husband. She was small and aggressive and undernourished. He had a couple of children back in Venezuela and had married her to keep from being deported.

"Come on. You have to line your stomach with something if we're all going to make a night of it."

She was carving his meat and feeding it to him. Nice action. He ought to find out her name.

They bar-hopped their way down Second Avenue in the general direction of a birthday party. Some fanatic in a plastic derby started buying drinks in a place by the Queensboro Bridge, so they lingered there awhile. Largely drowned out by Irish reels from the juke box, Pierce tried to talk politics with the husband. Christo and Monique (the name he'd given her for the evening) slipped out of their shoes, chalked the floor and played hopscotch. By the time they made the party it was well past midnight and running steady. The lights were off and the music was loud and it smelled like the inside of a rain boot. Monique danced until the sweat ran in her eyes. She had Christo up against the side of the refrigerator, groping with one hand, tugging at her pantyhose. She whispered something unintelligible in his ear and then a light blinked on, blinding white. The refrigerator door was open, someone saying, "Where's the damn beer?"

Later Christo got into an ugly, window-rattling argument with a woman, both of whose parents were psychiatrists, who became so angry she spat in the host's fish tank. They left the party by popular demand and visited a few more bars. Things went entirely out of focus. Somewhere in there as the morning wore on they landed in an after-hours Italian social club, Pierce and Monique shooting an endless eight-ball game while her husband slept on his arms at the bar and Christo belched gingerly, sipped expresso. Monique dropped ashes on the pool table and laughed like an idiot. But finally, inevitably, everyone got crashed out and depressed and went home.

Christo had to really lean on the bell before anyone came to unlock the lobby door. The night porter didn't see any reason for anyone to be awake at this hour. Christo gave him a carton of Italian cigarettes he found under one arm. The porter accepted and kept grumbling. Christo stood in the motionless elevator with the door closed for some time before he remembered to push the button.

He was going to beat all over the door, but Tildy answered right away.

"Morning."

"Is it?"

"Okay if I come in?"

"Sorry."

He brought up his arms and she dodged away from him. "You mad with me?"

"Not particularly."

"You can't be mad with this." He emptied his pockets one after another, greasy, misshapen doughnuts of money piling up on the bed.

"You've been wobbling around all night with that on you?"

"Yeah, I could just kiss myself."

"And how soon will the cops be here?"

"No, baby, I made those cards fly tonight and it's mine. Coulda made 'em swim if I wanted." He reached for her again, fell forward, steadied himself on the bed. "What is . . . What is this about?"

There under all the green paper, tidily lined up with the stripes on the coverlet, were Tildy's clothes all folded and ready for packing.

"I'm through," she said, turning her back and looking for a cigarette. "I'm off."

"Hold it there. We'll have to talk about this."

"I'd really rather not go into it."

"Too cold." Christo sat roughly on the floor. "It's panic and I'm not even sure I like you."

She bent and clasped her cold hands behind his neck. "Has nothing to do with you, so don't feel bad."

"But I was thinking we could be . . . ." His head was so heavy and slow; he pressed hard on the bone between his eyes. "Partners."

"You're better off." He caught her wrist when she tried to get up. "But you're too drunk, Jimmy. I'm not going to try and follow your eyes and pound words into you. It's like writing in sand."

"I'm down, I'm all the way down. So talk to me. You can call me Jimmy, but just talk to me, tell me the story."

She flopped down in surrender with that cigarette still unlit. "Not a very interesting story, a girl stuck in neutral . . . I came up here with you to get away, right? But nothing happened. I had three tosses for my quarter and didn't score. That's when you walk away. You go home and take care of your husband and wait on tables like any other ordinary broad."

"But that's all wrong. You don't belong with that chump. And you don't want to play hauling pitchers of beer and getting your ass pinched by guys in canvas hats."

"Forget about Karl. You don't know what that is."

"But you're wasting it all, we both know it. It's easy to say: 'This is not how I pictured it. Not at all.' Sure, easy. Everyone knows how to give up, but is that really what you want? To just fade into the wallpaper?"

"Very nice, Jimmy. But I've heard all the stories, I've been hearing them since I was sixteen. And time just keeps roaring by. A lot of years people have been hitting on me. The circuit should have made me tough enough to get what I wanted on the 'outside,' seems like it

162

just wore me out instead. When I close my eyes all I see are, are these, what—landscapes from some distant, unreal past. I feel this dull, maybe I should *be* dull. So I guess you're right, I guess I do want to fade into the wallpaper."

Christo was stumped. He asked for a drink of water. Tildy filled a glass in the bathroom. When she gave it to him, words stuck in his throat like wool waste in a clogged oil line.

Now she lit the cigarette. "But didn't I tell you? Didn't I say I'd show you just how much of a bitch I could be?"

On her way to the airport Tildy had the cabbie stop at a far-fetched downtown address. She told him to wait. What the hell, Christo was paying. Looie was waiting for her as she came off the elevator cage unbuttoning her blouse.

"I don't have a lot of time," she said, moving for the rear of the loft. "Roll me a joint."

TAKE TWO

It may be that happiness lies
in the conviction that one has lost
happiness irremediably.

—*Maria-Luisa Bombal*

11

Dim and muffled music of the seasons. The moon half asleep in its phases. But even in the tropic zone there is winter, a collective downturn: Citizens put on weight, slept longer, reacted with unconscious gloom to the early arrival of darkness. Even lifetime residents who had never salted a driveway dreamed of toddies by a crackling fire and sleigh bells in the snow. Up and down the Sunshine State, people ringing in the New Year with banana daquiris.

But there was a hollowness that nagged here, a sense of borrowed mythology, like the canned apple juice and paper oak leaves of a New Mexico Thanksgiving.

Karl Gables wobbled down the gangway of the *Miss Jenny Lee III* holding one end of a cooler packed with fillets: Yellowtail, mutton snapper. Oscar Alvarado, retired tattoo artist, held the other end, and following close behind came Cocoa Jerry with a blood and fish scale-spattered baseball cap turned sideways on his head. Cocoa Jerry was drinking "shark repellent," half vodka and half instant coffee. They'd been on an all-night charter party and everyone, including the captain, was pretty well plotzed. Everyone except Karl, who'd confined himself to ginger ale, saltines and, when no one was looking, a few chunks of bait.

Walking up the pier they argued over how to split the catch. Alvarado pointed out that it was his cooler. Cocoa Jerry pointed out that he'd supplied the ice and done all the gutting and cutting. Karl, who had boated only a few small ladyfish, kept his mouth shut.

"How about we roll dice?" Cocoa Jerry suggested. "Winner take all."

Alvarado said he'd rather eat steak anyway and why didn't they go on over to Bummy's, see what they could peddle to the early morning jar heads.

Winter in Gibsonton meant party time. The carnies were on hiatus, filling dead time with noise and fast motion. There were card games, pancake suppers, dances at the Independent Showman's Hall. And there was drinking, lots of it. The bars were always full of glowing folks exchanging lies and confessions, sighs and professions of love. Marriages broke and reformed in a matter of hours, lives were threatened and memories erased. Uncoverable wagers were made on the eye color of the next person to come through the door. And if all else failed, there was always shop talk, prospects for the upcoming season to be discussed and, inevitably, lamented. "When I came up there was two, three times as many shows goin' as now. It's the damn television that's killin' us."

Bummy's jukebox was sending out steel guitar breakfast music as Alvarado tugged the cooler inside and sat down on top of it, his head in his hands. Doc up in Tampa had told him he'd better slow down or one day his valves would blow out.

Karl arrived with a roll of aluminum foil (he'd left Cocoa Jerry heaving into the dumpster behind the market) and the two of them worked their way from stool to stool down the bar, hawking fillets.

"Not outta the water two hours," Karl said, wrapping four pieces of snapper for Elsa Spitz, Queen of the Midgets. "Got all your vitamins."

"I'm buying for my cats," Elsa said, raking him with the same imperious sneer she gave the gawks from her little linoleum platform in the freak tent of Yester's Family Circus.

"I been up all night, don't go busting my chops now." Alvarado was getting hassled over price a few feet down the line.

"It's fuckin' food is all, ain't no investment. I'll give you five bucks for that lot."

"We didn't catch these babies off the rocks, amigo. Kearny don't take you out to the deep water for nothing, you know what I'm saying?"

"Ah . . . You dickhead." But he came up with the seven fifty out of his change on the bar.

Bummy took foil packages, etched the proper initials on them with his thumbnail and shoved them in with the bottled beer. None of these rummys was going anyplace for a while yet.

George Beasle, who'd run for mayor back in the '50s on a bars-

168

never-close platform, announced that Mrs. Beasle made a superb fish chowder and he'd buy up whatever was left. The woman next to him pointed out that Mrs. Beasle had died of throat cancer well over a year ago.

"Thanks for squashing my deal, honey," Alvarado barked.

"What are you, sick?"

"Shit, I would have thrown in my own cooler here for an extra ten bucks. Sound good, George?"

Beasle's face spread out in a smile that was like time-lapse film of a blooming rose. "That's right! She bought it, didn't she? Well, damn, a round of drinks on that, Bummy."

When Karl declared that all he wanted was a glass of plain soda with maybe a squeeze of lemon, there was widespread disbelief.

"Karl takin' plain soda?"

"Karl Gables, the ferry man on the whiskey river?"

"Maybe it's somebody just looks like him."

"Nope, this is me," he said. "But I done stared temptation down. I'm like that old horse you can lead to water, you know?"

"So what's the story, Karl? Did you have a talk with Jesus or something?"

"Just the love of a good woman," laying one hand over his heart. "A pearl of a girl."

"Yes. Just this morning I purchased from your wife some bunion pads." Elsa Spitz held up a stapled paper bag for all to see. "To me she looked run-down."

A few blocks to the south, at the Medi Quik, Tildy examined herself in the antitheft mirror: wan and pulpy, skin like the white of an egg. What she needed was some prolonged exposure at the beach, a new haircut. Or maybe, maybe it's an allergic reaction to all these beauty products, to the terminally sleek fashion faces of the merchandising displays, the bright package graphics.

Six and a half hours until quitting time. She moved down the aisle with her clipboard, taking inventory. . . . Q-Tips, cotton balls, eyewash, mouthwash, lip gloss, dental floss. She felt disapproving eyes on her. Ray Holstein, store manager, whose duodenal ulcer had forced his retirement as Oceola High basketball coach, was checking through the previous day's receipts and hoping to find a mistake.

"Cindy. Cindy, can you hear me?" He could never get her name right. "You'll have to step it up. I need that inventory by twelve thirty. I'm having lunch with the district supervisor."

Hallelujah. Lunch with the D.S. would be the highlight of Holstein's week. Not that he lacked suitable fear of a company superior, but the D.S. was someone with whom he could feel affinity, rapport. (Rapport—wasn't that what team sports were all about?) They shared interests, could gab all afternoon about target shooting, marketing, home video equipment. They had the same tastes in sportswear. Holstein was desperately hungry for this kind of thing. He hated Gibtown and the people who lived there. He felt isolated, a lone sentinel of decent reality among stooges, chiselers, fast-talkers, the mentally and physically deformed. Every single one of them breaking some kind of rule: moral, behavioral, genetic. Holstein was a true believer in rules. He had once bounced his top play-making guard right off the team for wearing unmatched socks to a game.

Tildy rattled her pen on permalloy shelf supports to get his attention. "Did you reorder those party supplies? The paper hats and all that?"

Hand going to the knot in his tie. "What about it?"

"We've still got everything from last month."

"It wasn't my idea, got a memo on it from the central office. They must be stuck with a whole warehouse." Looking away, into the green digital readout of the cash register. "So what are you worrying about it for, Cindy? All you have to do is fill in the boxes on your inventory forms. Somebody else will take care of decision-making."

"Sorry, Mr. H. I guess I got carried away."

Eight hours a day with this weasel couldn't be too good for her either. All for three ten an hour and whatever lipsticks and candy bars she could sneak out in her shoulder bag. A jalapeño milkshake to toast the perforation of your stomach, bossman. Go digest yourself.

Tildy's fifth job in as many months and by no means the worst. The first gig after she got back from New York had lasted less than a week. She got into a rhubarb with some regular patrons ("What is it makin' your nipples so hard, sweetie?") and bopped one of them with a beer mug. After that she cleaned motel rooms. A month and a half with the flannel rags and the Ajax and the plastic bags—and an occasional startling discovery: a turd in the middle of the bed, an abandoned chihuahua tied to the sink with a shoe lace. There was even a kind of eloquence in empty liquor bottles grouped just so on an ash-strewn table. Tildy became increasingly sensitized to the things revealed in people's trash and soiled leavings. Her appetite for such material kept on growing. Scenarios of sleaze began to dominate her every waking moment and finally enough was enough. Curiosity was one thing and fascination quite another. After that her friends at the Alhambra Diner took her on for the dinner shift, but Karl complained about being left alone at night.

Manically sober Karl. He was so much more alive off the juice, and on the muscle these days, wanting more and more from her. There was greater energy between them now than at any time since their first year, beating the bushes with a bus-and-truck show, never flying off to Bermuda like they planned, and not caring. There was clear improvement in the mechanics of romance. Karl's newborn energy flared brightest in the bedroom and their sex was better than ever. She had even come several times. He was playful, like a little boy sometimes, and would curl around her in the dark, stroking her to sleep. But still she was restless: Is this *my* compulsion, or something to do with hormones? Assuming there's a difference.

Karl felt strong and solid, like a newly installed king. He placed his empty coffee cup on the tank behind him, shifted forward on the cool toilet seat and listened to the gurgling of his intestines. The king makes music! All morning long the pressure had been building in the lower regions of his belly and now there was release.

Refreshed in recent weeks by the new domestic harmony (he was a husband again, with all those privileges), by good feelings seltzering through his bloodstream, Karl had become preoccupied with the smallest details of physical action. He went about the most mundane tasks attentively, watching his soapy fingers circle the rim of a dish, measuring the exact extension of his muscles as he reached for some object, relishing the way in which the smooth pistol-grip handle of the metal detector Tildy had given him for Christmas fit in his palm, the easy action of thumbwheel controls.

Now he felt the contours of a smoldering cigarette, rolling it against his fingertips, applying that certain degree of lip pressure that would draw smoke through the cellulose filter. Things could be so easy if you only let them.

"Easy," he said, and snapped his fingers.

He took a last drag, flipped the cigarette between his legs into the bowl. The orange coal grazed his scrotum, the pain signal reaching his brain at the same moment the butt hit the water with a hiss. Despite the sudden sharpness of the pain, he did not even wince.

Years ago. A dewy, languid morning, early summer. Sitting in his grandma's two-hole privy with birds squeaking outside, digging with his toes at the earth floor; and that summer peace ripped open by a mean, searing pain behind his little hairless balls. He exploded through the door, ran screaming for the house holding his pants up with both hands, then stopped dead, knees knocking, at the sight of a yellowed curtain flapping in an upstairs window. He knew how Grandma would fuss, wanting to examine the disgraceful hurt, to handle him and touch and poke. So, terrified and ashamed, he bolted into the woods and pressed cool moss to the burning spot, threw his arms around a tree and sobbed. The bark was rough and cold, but it was something to hug.

There he lay for a small boy's eternity, quivering and filmed with sweat while a new pain engulfed him, an agony in his stomach that pulsed like a drum. Only the grown-ups could save him now. Would he die twitching in the dirt like a fish? For there was no doubt that he must die from a wound received in the midst of such a filthy act, from a punishment some evil toilet god had directed at the most wicked part of his body.

But he made it, stumbled crimson-faced into Grandma's bony arms, and the first thing he did, with saliva running from his mouth and tears from his eyes, was apologize.

"I'm sorry, Grandma. I hurt myself making kaka. I'm sorry."

She threw him in the back of the DeSoto and they flew down the hill, across the causeway to the army hospital. At first they thought it was acute appendicitis and were prepping him for surgery when a nurse noticed the lesion on his perineum. She said it looked like an insect bite. The doctors muttered and fiddled around in their white coat pockets. Black widow spiders were not unknown in this part of the country. The females often spun their webs beneath outhouses and their bite introduced a deadly nerve poison into the system.

By the time they hit him up with a jumbo dose of antivenin, Karl was teetering right on the edge. For some hours there was very real doubt as to whether he would recover. When two days later he did, he refused to go home. They tied him up in a sheet and carried him out to the DeSoto. For months Grandma had to lock him in his room to keep him from running away.

The moral of the story was that you were never safe. Each tiny fraction of a second held the possibility of pain and death; and something was always lurking. Always.

All aquiver, sphincter wound tight as a tow-truck winch, Karl got to his feet. He put his head in the sink and let the cold water run

172

and run. Then he turned fast, so as not to see himself in the mirror, and got the hell out of that bathroom. Air, he needed fresh air. He'd take a little stroll by the mailbox, see what was waiting for him there.

That same sample box of fabric softener was hanging from the post in a plastic bag. Been there near two weeks now, had a look of bad luck about it. Karl tore it loose and flung it into the thicket across the road; then he pulled back the mailbox door and peeked inside. Pine needles, gray bits of old wasp nest and, yep, something pale way in the back. But don't be no fool and stick your hand in. Karl flicked the letter out with a stick.

You were never safe. Never ever. He recognized the sharply angled handwriting, the way his name was written in red. His hands were shaking so badly he had to open the envelope with his teeth. This is what the letter said:

> A big hello from Motor City. Sorry you missed your Christmas card this year, but I was busy recuperating from major surgery and just couldn't find the time. I know how you enjoy news of Little Jerry and me. The streets are covered with ice now and the car won't run, but we're pushing on ahead and who needed a set of ovaries anyway? I'm running my own massage studio, living in an apartment upstairs with a view of the switching yards. Little Jerry is with me and a constant inspiration these days. Did you know he wants to be a race driver just like his Dad! Isn't that sweet?
>
> Many happy returns,
> Shelly

There wasn't a single thing to drink in the house. . . . Except for this dusty bottle of grain alcohol under the kitchen sink. Was that the stuff that made you deaf or blind or something? Just the smell of it made his eyes water. How bad could it be? He remembered a gobbling geek named Suggs who used to drink shoe polish strained through a felt hat; but then, after biting the heads off mice every time he could muster a good crowd, probably anything would do.

Still, no skull-and-bones on the label. Just a little taste then. A tablespoon dispersed in grapefruit juice, one dose of tonic for his nerves.

When Tildy returned home that evening she did not find her husband sprawled across the floor like a bag of laundry. She did not find him at all; just an empty glass on the kitchen table, a disarrangement of solvents and cleansers on the floor.

Nothing to be alarmed about. She heated a can of soup and filed her nails. Maybe he was lurking in a closet, waiting for her to pass so he could jump out and scare her breathless. Like a little boy sometimes. Then she heard the siren wail outside. She listened hard, wanting it to go on and on and fade in the far distance. But it stopped close by, as she somehow knew it would.

She ran out to the road and stopped. Voices yowling through the trees, a smell of smoke. Something dire going down at the Keyes place. Tildy broke into a sprint, knees pumping high, sneakers slapping hard on the pavement. Up ahead, an undulating orange glow. Down the bending driveway she could see the pump truck setting up, playing out hose. The Keyes outhouse, swaddled in flames, was tipping backward, igniting refuse and scrap lumber stacked around it. Cars flashed by her, volunteer firemen with their domelights spinning. Watching impassively from a bowed front porch, Mrs. Keyes sipped on a beer and shooed her children inside. Just as quickly one of them would pop back through the hole in the screen door and scramble with excitement back and forth along the railing. Water churned out the nozzle now, blowing a hole in the blazing outhouse wall. The firemen cheered themselves.

Then, from some deeper region of darkness, came a more familiar voice—Karl's. "Black widows," he screamed. "You can't even burn 'em out."

Tildy had to take an advance on her salary to cover the costs, a couple hundred to cool the Keyeses' anger and persuade them not to press charges, and another seventy or eighty for building materials. Karl, on Tildy's orders, had agreed to rebuild the privy himself.

"I can't think of anyone more qualified," she said, driving him home from jail on Saturday afternoon. "I mean that's your business. Isn't it, donniker man?"

"Okay, okay. Don't jump salty on me. I know I deserve it but . . ." Karl looked down, digging into a seam of the upholstery with his fingers. "But it wasn't really me did it. It was like me standing outside my body and watching."

"Just a bad dream, huh?" Tildy tromped on the gas pedal and the Galaxie roared through the intersection streaming blue smoke.

But she couldn't stay mad at him long. With the wind out of his sails he was bobbing and drifting like an innertube, her fumbling old sad sack again. He moped and whimpered and fawned, promising

174

he'd never go near alcohol again. Oh yes, he should be whipped for treating her this way, putting shame and botheration on her when every week she brought the bacon home. Tildy listened quietly with her eyes half shut. It was almost comforting, this noise, like the lowing of cows.

They had cold cuts and macaroni salad for lunch, then a short nap, with Karl corkscrewing around the mattress but not daring to touch her. Finally, she took his hand and held it.

"Either keep still or get out of bed."

From under a bulwark of pillows she heard his retreating steps and a thick, low voice as the radio snapped on, low and steady as wind, more soothing than music.

Tildy suction-cupped a sign to the inside of the door—BACK AT in fat white letters and a clock face underneath with movable tin hands. Nudging them forward to 11:15, generously allowing herself a full half hour, she turned the lock, went back to the stockroom and lit up a joint. The very last crumbs of the bag Looie had pressed on her as a memento of their passion. Dear sweet Looie, and she could barely remember the contours of his face. It was good dope, though. Two or three drags and there was that tightness across her chest, a twitching in her brain like an old motor coming to life. Tildy held the smoke in her lungs until she was dizzy, and then, letting go, could hear for a few seconds the tomtom rhythm of her pumping blood before it faded out like the end of a record. An easy mark for distraction now, reading along the wall of a box—STORE AWAY FROM HEAT PACKED AT CENTRAL DIST. CTR. FAIRMEADOW, INDIANA—wondering what Fairmeadow looked like, factory town with an endless strip of muffler shops and fried-chicken stands and not a meadow in sight.

The joint had gone out in her fingers, a blackened stem she stashed for later in the cellophane of her cigarette pack. Envelope glue was what her dry mouth tasted like; and it was suddenly spooky back there with the cartons and shredded paper, an interrogation room. She went and sat behind the register, sucking mints and scratching pictures on a ledger pad: palm trees, a sofa, free-floating breasts.

Someone banging on the door. Only five after but they wouldn't go away. Tildy stumbled coming off the stool and banged her hip on the edge of the counter. A skinny woman peered through the glass, deep acne scars, lavender eye shadow and pencil marks on upper and lower lids like sun rays in a child's drawing, stringy blond hair that hung down past her shoulder blades. Tildy stood blinking, rubbing her hip.

"Come on, come on. I really need some stuff."

My time is your time. Shrugging, Tildy pulled the door open, kicked a rubber wedge under it to let the breeze in. A little late. The woman sniffed ostentatiously, winked.

"I'll find what I need. You go on back to whatever you were doing."

She had chains around her neck, bracelets crowded on both wrists and every time she moved it was like somebody shaking a jar of nails. Tildy hung there beside her, rising and falling on the balls of her feet and staring like an imbecile. The woman backed away, tugging at the sleeves of her black cowboy shirt.

"I'd take five if I was you, honey. Your eyes look like silver dollars."

Nobody asked you, but okay. Tildy climbed onto the stool and tried to look busy pushing papers around. Flitting among the shelves the woman studied bottles and spray cans intently, lips moving as she read the labels; and then her eyes would roll to one side and catch Tildy doing it too. They were watching each other, appraising. Tildy wanted to start a conversation, but felt timid and blocked. What the hell was going on? All the shivery tension of a blind date.

"I'm looking for a conditioner."

"What?"

"It's just so lifeless." Raking fingers down her scalp. "I should have it cut off. . . . But if it's all right, lemme ask what you use on your hair."

"Nothing."

"Well, nothing really works for you. It's got a kind of innocent look, like, I don't know, some silent-movie star."

Not very surreptitiously, the woman ripped open a bag of malted milk balls and ate a few. She browsed at the magazine rack and tried on several pairs of rubber sandals. Squatting on the floor and talking to herself, she experimented with different hues of nail polish, didn't bother to screw the caps back on the bottles. Tildy didn't bother to camouflage her amazement, either. She envied this one's gall.

Finally, in one concerted sweep, the woman filled her arms with products and swaggered over to dump them on the counter: tampons, foot powder, wart remover, orange sticks, baby oil, a toy air-

176

plane, and three of the magazines that Holstein, left to himself, would never have stocked in the first place.

"You ever check out these pussy books you got? They make the girls too pretty if you ask me. It's better with all the hair, dirt under the nails and maybe a pimple here and there."

"So maybe they should leave the faces blank altogether." Tildy was ringing up her items very slowly, peeling the price tags off.

"But it's got to be real, see?"

"Yeah, I used to be a stripper about a hundred years ago. Worked three straight nights at this place with a terrible case of hives. They loved me. On the fourth night they wanted to paint them on."

"No shit, you really did that? How was it?"

"Lousy. But I liked the hours."

The woman dug into her greasy jeans, spilled a hash of bills and coins on the counter. "Hope I got enough."

Tildy took a crumpled five. "Tell you what. Pay me for what's already on the machine and we'll call it even."

Shown in a wide smile, the woman's teeth were small and gray. "I can have the rest for nothing? You sure?"

"Doesn't matter to me. I'm not working for commissions."

"Well, *muchas gracias.* You're damn good down-with-it people, you know that . . . uh, Tildy," reading the plastic name tag, then hooking a thumb at herself. "DaVita. Big D, small a, big V. My mom wanted something unusual, the old cow, and I guess she got it. Yeah, down with it. So what time you get off here, Tildy? I'd like to buy you a drink."

"Around six. But I . . ."

"Cool, cool. Can you meet me then at the Paddle Wheel? It's down Route 17, just past Sears. I'll wait for you in the parking lot and we can go in together."

"Why not."

But when Tildy found her perched on the hood of someone's jeep around by the rear entrance, DaVita had already been inside. There was a table waiting for them.

"I know the bartender," DaVita said.

She seemed to know everyone at the Paddle Wheel. As they were sitting down, an older woman in an orange caftan rushed over and threw a drunken sloppy kiss on DaVita's chin.

"This little girl is just so full of life," she yipped at Tildy. "I just love her right to death. So full of life. Wisht I could be your age again."

"Really needs a man, that one," DaVita reported as the woman shouldered her way back to the bar. "Hasn't been off work more than forty-five minutes and already she's sloshed out of her old head. So what do you do for fun, Tildy?"

"Could I get a glass of rum with no ice?"

"Sure. Let me catch my breath a minute. Whoo, but this shit can become a way of life, like Donnie says I should just go on and move in here, all the time I spend. Him and the two kids there in a house-trailer, so if I don't get out regularly—you know—I got to flip out from all that time boxed up. You married?"

"Seven days a week."

"Mmm-hmmm. It can get that way. Men seem to move a whole lot slower, that's what I've noticed. They're like lizards or something around the house. Where's the fun? Like, Donnie just came off the work farm. Some bank guy came to take the car back and Donnie punched him around. So he pulls three months on the farm and what does he want to do his first day out? Drink beer and fuck me while he watches television. That's the most fun he can think up in three whole months. Moves too slow for me, that's all."

Tildy nodded; she knew about the slowness. "He doesn't try and keep you home?"

"No point in that. Besides, Donnie weighs close to three hundred pounds. How many times is a guy like that going to get lucky? Once, and I'm it. . . . But what about you? What do you get into on the weekends?"

"Not a lot. Drive to Tampa and eat out."

"I know you're bluffing, a fox like you. Think about it some more and I'll be back with drinks."

Not much to think about—that was the problem. Tildy was embarrassed at her own dullness. Playing catch with Karl on a typical off-work day, hitting a few fungos just to watch the ball sail; sometimes going off on a treasure expedition, but unable to share Karl's rudimentary excitement at digging up a high school ring near a roadside picnic table or a few black Mercury dimes at a demolition site. If she weren't so perverted, could make the quick, animating choice instead of turning from it, she'd still be in New York and shacked up with Looie. No one to blame, sweets, but yourself.

DaVita showed up with two drinks, two men, and an unsettling gleam in her eye. They all four shoved in around a table for two and it was instant kneesies.

"Tildy, I'd like for you to meet Leroy and Bob. Leroy runs the security for Sears and Bob manages . . . What is it, Bob, sporting goods?"

"Affirmative. That's my area, rods and balls." Beefy Bob chortled through his mustache and his elbow pressed into Tildy's left breast.

Leroy, squinting over the rim of his Bloody Mary said, "How about it for sports? Do you do tennis? Horseback riding?" Leroy was tall and pop-eyed, his hair cut in early Beatles fashion, sort of a Merseybeat Ichabod Crane. His arm went around DaVita and squeezed. "Now DaVita, she loves to go four or five miles on a stallion, right?"

"Don't let these boys startle you," DaVita cautioned. "That's just what they're after."

"Not at all, not at all." Bob sadly puffed his lips at the extent to which they'd been misconstrued. "I mean would we be making the money we make and looking how we do if we weren't a couple of straight arrows?"

"I'd like another," Tildy said.

DaVita emptied her glass. "Me too," she said with her mouth full of ice cubes.

"Okay, this is my round," Leroy volunteered. "Let's get the party going."

While he was off seeing to refills Bob stuttered his chair to a strategic angle and dropped his hand in Tildy's lap. She tossed it back. With the sudden downshift of a telethon emcee going from toilet joke to fund appeal, Bob came on all chumpy and sincere.

"Hey, I'm really sorry. Don't get ticked off, okay? I'm not always this crude but sometimes I get so nervous, you know, nervous around women that I act like a dumb high school kid."

"No whispering, Bobby." DaVita waggled a finger at him. "This is a party. You gotta be loud."

Tildy smiled at her, but it was hard to tell if she and DaVita were allies or not.

Then Leroy was back and it was time for a toast to Mother's beaten biscuits, dancing by moonlight, and, for all present, the peace and contentment of a sow on her belly in a bog. They all touched glasses and drank. Leroy, who seemed deeply moved by his own words, had to be cajoled into sitting back down. DaVita tickled under his chin and told him he had poetry in his soul.

"Don't worry about it," Bob said. "He got that off a record jacket."

"Bullshit." Leroy sent a fine spray of tomato juice across the table.

"Lighten up now, both of you. This is a party." DaVita made them all touch glasses again.

Trying to ignore everything but what was in her glass, Tildy was struck by the sudden inspiration that separately or together DaVita had already fucked these clowns about a dozen times. This better not be a setup, she thought.

Bob, meanwhile, had returned with a vengeance to his original tack. Tildy jumped when he pinched her thigh, drinks sloshed all over the table and now it was Bob's turn to buy a round. Leroy went off to empty his bladder, leaving the girls alone to discuss developments.

"What's cooking here?" Tildy wanted to know.

"Bob's pestering you? So you'll sit next to Leroy when they get back. He's much easier to handle."

"Then you know these two from before?"

"Oh hell, yes. We're like long-term buddies, drank ourselves unconscious in here many a time. Couple of sad guys, really. Snakebit. Mrs. Leroy, she lost her arm last summer. Driving down the road with her arm out the window, truck went by with a two-by-four sticking out and tore it right off at the shoulder." DaVita mimed the impact, the expression of horror and revulsion, seeing your arm all mashed on the highway like somebody's dead cat. "And Bobby's so cranked up most of the time it's pathetic, like a disaster just waiting to happen. But they're totally harmless, believe me."

Tildy needed subtitles, something to translate all this bar palaver into words of one syllable. "You and I were going to have a quick beer," she said lamely. Was she being encouraged to come across with a charity fuck for one of these "sad guys"?

DaVita reached for Tildy's hand with sisterly reassurance and her grip was soft, insinuating. "Oooh, your fingers are like icicles. You need to relax a little. I don't think that job of yours is worth it if it makes you so uptight."

"You've got advice for everyone, don't you?"

"Know what I do? I've got these special breathing exercises. There's a rhythm you have to master, but after that it's easy. You get those lungs working smooth and steady and soon all your bullshit problems just float away. I'll show you sometime."

Bob arrived with a tray of highballs and an angry waitress at his heels. She windmilled her arms and screamed that he had no right taking her customers away like she wasn't fit to carry drinks ten feet across a room, and he'd better give the tray back before she had him bounced the hell out. Bob was serving all the while with deep, smirking bows, throwing little scalloped napkins down to catch the frost-drip from the glasses. When he was through he flipped the tray at her like a pie plate and tried clumsily to jam a five-dollar bill into her modest cleavage. The girl took the money, but she was crying.

Tildy slid back as Bob melted into his chair. "What was that for? Do you get a jolt out of wiping your feet on people?" She was hot and cool at the same time.

"So don't get all in a sweat over nothing. She got a nice fat tip out of it." To DaVita, with a snide, shimmying delivery, "This is the stripper you told us about? So what's with the goody-goody bit?"

Tildy turned flame-thrower eyes on DaVita and saw in her face sheepishness but no apology. "You've got it all wrong. There's been a misunderstanding. I was a stripper, true, but in my uncle's antique shop in New Orleans, the French Quarter. I stripped the paint off furniture."

DaVita's bracelets jangled in the bubble of uneasy silence. The evening, the party, had quietly slipped its bonds and was beyond capture, free to roam as it liked. Leroy loomed up with the orange caftan lady on his arm and offered to take the whole crew out for bar-b-que at some nigger spot back in the woods. There were no takers. Bob slurped from every available glass and looked ready to hit someone. Asking plaintively why, with the world so overpopulated, folks had to go on being lonely, the caftan lady wept inconsolably. DaVita chewed her split ends and asked if anyone would like to buy her a pack of cigarettes. There were no takers.

Even Leroy could pick up these vibes. "Hey, what happened, guys? Did I miss the boat or something?"

"Totally," Tildy said.

"Well, fuck you, people." And Leroy led his sobbing comrade away to a quiet venue near the restrooms where they could get to know each other better.

"Just the three of us now," Bob said. "Ain't that cozy." He changed moods like paper hats.

Tildy slowly twisted to face him, lips flirtatiously slack, dampened by a sliding tongue. "As cozy as you want to make it." Fingers darting inside his rayon shirt to tug at coiled chest hairs.

Bob flinched. "Don't burn your fingers, baby."

"You'd really like to get into my pants, wouldn't you?"

"I surely would. Whatta you think?"

"I think one asshole in these pants is enough."

She stood, tipping the ashtray onto Bob's blossoming erection and, without so much as a glance in DaVita's direction, headed for the exit.

It was a beautiful night. A beautiful night for a secret thought or a hanging. She heard DaVita's jewelry sounds behind her.

"You're mad, you're mad." DaVita moved as though there were a hot griddle under her feet. "I should never have mentioned to those tired rejects about your being a stripper. I know that."

"Why are you following me?"

"I feel bad."

"Yeah, don't we all." With a flat hand Tildy swept water beads off the car and onto DaVita's chest.

"Hey, come on. So you got naked on stage. So what."

"So," pointing inside, "so you don't tempt a hungry man with a steak."

"You think I was pimping you? Well, honey, that just ain't fair. It wasn't that way at all. Those guys are drinkers, not doers, I'm here to tell you. I thought we'd have a little fun with 'em, tease 'em along, get a few free belts, but that's it. Shit, I'm hurt you could think anything else."

"Who invited them over? Not me."

DaVita tugged at her wilting hair in frustration. "How could I know it's going to turn into an ugly scene."

DaVita was eager to please. Tildy softened a bit, regaining a sense of—was it proportion? "You shouldn't have waited until now to tell me the score."

"You're right, of course you're right. A little bit late, that's chronic with me. So I still owe you, don't I?"

"Never mind."

"But I want to make it up to you." DaVita was pleading; she looked pale and wasted in the rain. "We'll go out Saturday and I'll show you my secret beach. No one ever goes there so we'll have it all to ourselves. Some days it's good for body surfing and you can pick up nice shells if you want, they're all over. I make necklaces and sell them." Touching her throat, "I don't have one on to show you but . . ."

Tildy opened the car door and threw in her bag. "Let's just call it a draw and forget it."

"No. I really like you, Tildy. I mean, I don't even know who you are, but it's one of those gut things." DaVita shivered. Her vehemence was mysterious but compelling. "It would be good for me right now to have a girlfriend."

"Agreed." Tildy slid behind the wheel, turned the key. "A little sun, a little sand. I'll meet you in front of the store at around eleven."

"Cool, cool. And I'll bring my kids along, I want you to meet them. They're real sweet. I wouldn't lie and say I'm happy to have 'em around all the time, but they're my kids and I love 'em. Okay? So you drive careful now and don't worry about me. I can hitch my way home, done it hundreds of times."

Tildy activated the wipers, waved quickly, backed out.

"Don't worry about me," DaVita murmured into the headlights. "I'll just put out my thumb and get soaked."

The children were shy and pretty with hair of seaweed black. Robbie was five, Gina was three, and they held tightly to one another's hands, moved cautiously onto the back seat with their dripping popsicles.

"Don't you go making a mess back there," DaVita said gently.

"Yes ma'am." Robbie's lips were tinted wild cherry. Kneeling, one hand braced on his sister's head, he pushed in the chrome knobs to lock both doors.

DaVita pushed a ragged straw bag between them. "You have to both be watching this for me 'cause our sandwiches and everything are in here. That'll be your job, okay?"

"Yes ma'am."

But Robbie pushed the bag into one corner, Gina clambered over the transmission hump, and they sat close, clasping sticky hands.

Tildy was not in the best frame of mind for a weekend drive. It was hot and growing hotter and DaVita unbuttoned her shirt; a lacy scar curved out from under her bikini top. She snooped restlessly through debris in the glove compartment.

"Can't you go any faster? We're liable to miss the prime tanning period."

"It's an old car."

But Tildy put a hair's extra pressure on the accelerator. A delivery van zoomed past, honking. She checked the odometer, then the rearview mirror; 12.7 miles and still not a word out of those kids.

They reached the coast and turned south past fruit stands and reptile museums and pastel stucco bunkers offering live crabs by the bag. Tildy rolled her window down to catch some of that salt breeze, but all she could smell was diesel smoke. Jammed up behind a laboring trailer truck, they passed slowly by a tongue-shaped inlet where men were wading waist-deep and scooping great weed balls into olive-drab buckets on shore. A guard sat nearby on a camp chair, shotgun across his knees. His bald head was red and peeling.

"Water hyacinth," DaVita explained. "It fucks up boat propellers so they rip it out, chop it up, spray it with molasses and use it for cattle feed."

"I'm impressed. Where'd you pick all that up?"

"Those are boys from the farm. Little bit ago you coulda seen Donnie out there pulling twice as much as anyone else."

Robbie broke his vow of silence: "My dad's so big he could pull a train."

DaVita howled with laughter, reached over to squeeze a little baby fat leg. "But he couldn't be the caboose, could he?"

"No ma'am."

Past a line of palms, through a couple of S curves, and DaVita said, "Take a right, your next available right."

They rumbled down a sandy trail descending gently toward water that was dirty green with shreds of white over the surface where the wind kicked it up. With a long sweep of sky behind it, the silvery beach was right out of an airline magazine. The only problem was the barbed wire they would have to climb to reach it; and the big red NO TRESSPASSING signs every ten feet. To the left, where the shore swelled out round and fat like the toe of a sadist's boot, was a power generating station. If anything was coming out of the monstrous stacks it was colorless.

"Park right here and you'll be invisible from the road."

"'Violators subject to fine and imprisonment'?"

"It's all right. I've been here lots of times and it's always deserted. We won't have to bother about suits."

DaVita padded the top strands of wire with folded towels, boosted Tildy up, then lifted the children over to her. With a vault and a spin she cleared the wire herself, landing gracefully with arms

184

spread as in the finish of a tap routine. They picked a spot below small dunes tufted with sawgrass and laid a blanket down. Robbie took the plastic pail, Gina the matching shovel, and they wandered off along the hot sand.

"They're independent," DaVita said. "I like that. You been married a few years, how come you don't have any kids?"

"It never came up really, we were both away so much. Now? Who needs one more thing to fail at. I don't have so much confidence in myself as a mother."

"That didn't stop me. Fuck it, I know I don't do all the things I should, but they're tough and they'll get by—or not—regardless of what I do."

DaVita peeled off her clothes, then her bikini, and stood hipshot, humming softly, challenging Tildy to look.

"You think I got a good body?"

The scar was a tilted capital C under one tiny breast and her sloping crotch was shaved. She pinched her thighs, slapped at them, thrust herself forward with palms on her ass.

"Too much bone, you know. You can count every rib I've got."

Staring at this scrawny, breakable woman, Tildy did not know what she felt, but it was sitting heavily in the pit of her stomach.

"For a man my tits are too small but I like them just the way they are, and like I tell Donnie, anything over a mouthful is wasted. I think you maybe got a little more up here. Come on, let's see. Let's see who's bigger."

Tildy looked down at the chipped pink polish on DaVita's toenails, then over at the surf sliding in, frothing, bouncing up in little wedge-shaped waves. Whatever the spirit was, wherever it was leading, she'd get with it. Was this what DaVita meant by toughness? With stunning speed, she got naked.

"Zowie." DaVita whistled through her teeth. "You got gorgeous lines. Yeah, everything tapers just right. But when you get right down to it I'd say we were about even. My breasts are firmer, see, the way you hang just makes them look bigger. I bottle-fed my kids from day one 'cause I didn't want that droop."

"I'm a thirty-two B. How about you?"

"I take an A cup myself, but I still say we're even."

This seemed to satisfy DaVita and she lay back on the blanket brushing hair out of her face, a fine web of sweat along her collarbone.

"Can you see the kids? Are they okay?"

"I guess so."

Tildy stretched out on her stomach. Hot as it was, there were goose bumps all up and down her legs. She shifted from side to side, digging herself a hollow in the sand. The itch of the blanket was not unpleasant. After a while she felt her flesh soften, her muscles relax. The sun was directly overhead and the still air seemed to hum with its clean yellow fire.

"I love the heat." DaVita sat up and began to anoint herself with olive oil from a glass jar. "Mmm, that's good," massaging her breasts, scissoring her fingers on shiny, tumid nipples. "I hope I'm not making you uptight. When I'm close to the ocean like this with the sun on me I feel like the first woman on earth."

Tildy ducked her head and said nothing.

"Don't you want some of this? You'll get an evil burn without it. I've never seen skin so white."

Tildy felt cool glass against her hand. "Not yet. Not just yet."

"Demon heat."

DaVita's squelching hands moved in wider and wider circles as she opened her legs and Tildy became aware of layered fragrances, the slightly rancid oil, something sharp and gaseous released from DaVita's body. She pressed her eyes harder into the crook of her arm and there were blinking yellow dots in the blackness behind them. This is ridiculous, Tildy told herself. You want to look, she wants you to look. So go ahead and look.

DaVita had three fingers of one hand jammed up into herself, the other hand softly pivoting at the top of her hairless seam. Tildy was not aroused by what she saw, not physically; but DaVita bit down on her lip, Tildy looked into a face that was a fixed animal mask of something resembling pain, and was moved. Moved by a raw tenderness. This frantic, despairing woman inches away with every nerve exposed. It was touching and sweetly sad and almost like looking at herself.

"Oooh, I'm coming, coming."

And quickly Tildy pushed DaVita's hand aside and replaced it with her own. Her fingers were numb, a set of tools; she felt everything with her eyes.

Heaving, DaVita flipped onto her side and hugged her knees. "Thank you," she whispered.

The wrong thing to say. Those two words of gratitude, and the deadly confusion behind them, pushed outside the magic circle, destroyed illusion like a long knife slicing through the center of a movie screen.

Tildy whispered back, "I'm going to swim," and zipped off with sand spraying out behind her.

Motionless, Gina and her brother watched the sea. Tildy's hand on her tiny shoulder, soft as putty, didn't startle; Gina remained straight and still, not looking up at the woman whose name she did not know.

"Is it time for lunch?"

"Later for that. Would you like to go in the water with me? I'll hold you tight so you won't go under."

"We're not allowed," Robbie said. "You go in. We'll be your lifeguards."

Tildy waded out, arms floating on the easy swell, and rinsed her mouth with stinging salt water. She bowed herself backward, dunking her face and bringing it back out to the sun, then swam out beyond the breakers with short, hitched strokes, her eyes burning, the water a slow-motion tongue on her body. She dove under the choppy surface and frog-kicked along until her lungs were ready to split, broke the surface sputtering, gasping for breath, and looked back.

The figures on the beach were small and stick-like, discernible only because of the white background. They could just as easily be clumps of driftwood. A wavelet smacked her in the back of the head. She turned and swam on, stirring up bubbles with her chopping arms. Cold began to penetrate her tightened skin. Tildy's head swiveled out of the water to inhale on every other stroke now, and it was as if she'd entered a different atmosphere where the oxygen was thinner. She was clenching her teeth, squeezing shut her eyes as she battled the thick water, and her whole faced ached with the tension. She tried to relax and slow her pace, to glide easily and relieve the stiffness in her legs. Smaller movements, no wasted effort. But her arms felt limp and heavy and her entire body throbbed with the cold. It was time to turn back.

Heading for shore with renewed energy, Tildy pulled up after a few minutes to check her progress and found she wasn't any closer. Only the power station loomed larger, interlocking cubes of white concrete. Could she, in the confusion of fatigue, have been swimming parallel to the beach? Or drifting on some lateral current with a pull stronger than her own? No wonder they called it the crawl.

Treading water, she sighted her course and plunged forward, counting to a hundred before she raised her head again. From the look of it, she wasn't getting anywhere. Fear traveled like an electric current down the length of her shivering body and there was a smell of iodine on the wind.

She waved her arms and yelled, hoping DaVita would hear her. But panic was fatal; that was how people drowned, clawing wildly and hopelessly at the water, flailing away in one spot until they exhausted themselves and disappeared. She reminded herself of the natural buoyancy of salt water. If she surrendered to it totally, would it cup her like a hand and carry her to safety? She flipped onto her back, buying time, staying afloat by virtue of scissoring legs while her arms rested, trailing along at her sides. The sound of the water rushing by was like a lullaby and the sun was warm on her breasts that jutted into the air like two volcanic islands. The pain in her shoulders lightened and a dreamy torpor spread over her. It felt so good to rest, to snooze in the bobbing rhythm of the waves. A rolling liquid cradle.

Then came the moment when Tildy gave in to it, stopped moving altogether and dropped below. She fought her way back up coughing and gagging, and stared in dismay at the silent, smooth expanse of beach that was still so far away. Steady, steady. But she could sense her body hardening with cold and fear. Darkness awaited her if she lost another second.

She swam ten strokes and rested; another ten strokes, another rest. Easy now, go easy. Push down through the water, don't slap at it. Ten strokes and rest. Ten strokes and rest. Treading water was now as hard as swimming through it, but the pain abated just enough each time, only to begin again on the very first stroke. She did not look up, certain that knowledge of the distance yet to cover would defeat her. Every tendon and muscle, every flap of tissue, was in flames. She swallowed water, groaned aloud with each rotation of her arms. Now she could manage only five strokes before a rest, five pitiful, paddling strokes with limbs that would soon be useless. Her ears pounded, her nose ran and her heart thundered like an overloaded motor about to shake itself apart.

Her foot scraped across a rock and she went limp, submerged, gripped the bottom with her toes, lurched and stumbled forward till she fell, retching, trembling, and ground the bits of rock and broken shell against her skin. Land.

Tildy lay there for a very long time with the surf washing peacefully over her, no longer the enemy. Her knees gave way each time she tried to stand and so it was on all fours that she scrabbled up the beach, calling for DaVita but drawing no answer.

Painfully and slowly she dressed. The foot that had scraped the rock was bleeding, the nail of its second toe torn partway off. She wrapped it in a napkin from her pocket before easing into shoes and hobbling over the dunes.

No particular surprise in finding the car gone. Nothing to do but get on the road and start walking. With any luck she'd catch a couple of rides and be in Gibsonton before dark. That made her think of Christo. Of Silvio. Now DaVita. And emphatically she told herself: I've got to stop picking up strangers.

If only there were some shade to sit in. She hadn't been walking long, only two cars had passed her by, but with each step the top of her sneaker rasped against the mauled foot. Crouched down, fumbling with the laces, she heard squealing tires behind her, turned to see gleaming chrome grillework and a bulge of blue hood.

"Oh my God, you're alive." DaVita's voice. "You're alive." She tumbled out of the car, ran around and crushed Tildy in her arms. "You're alive and I thought you were dead."

"So you figured to leave me for the crabs to pick over and took off in my car."

"Try and understand."

"Understand! Fuck you."

DaVita reached in, brought out the car keys, and as Tildy went to snap them up, caught her behind the neck and drove her rubbery mouth against the thin red line of Tildy's lips. One manic, grappling kiss and she retreated, pulling hair in front of her face.

"There's no way to explain it. I just freaked out, that's all. You were out there so long and we lost sight of you. Up and down the beach, up and down, staring out till my eyes blurred. I didn't know whether to stay or whether to go somewhere and call the police or the Coast Guard. I didn't know what to do, so I just freaked."

"Get in the car."

Tildy slammed the door, rammed in the key and the engine knocked and roared. She felt a tug on her hair; it was Robbie, his gray eyes wide and clear. Next to him on the back seat, Gina was wrapped in a towel and fast asleep with thumb in mouth.

"Mommy said you couldn't hear us underwater."

Just then a thought dropped into Tildy's mind, plop, like a honeydew melon tossed out of a third story window. "You don't know how to swim, do you?"

"Not a lick." DaVita nodded. "I know a lot of other things, like how to change a set of sparkplugs or how to make jambalaya or how to keep a man from shooting off too quick or how to stay up all night without watching teevee or listening to the radio, but I don't know a damn thing to do around water."

"You should have mentioned that before, DaVita. You really should have mentioned that before."

The return trip passed in stunning silence.

Pulling up at the entrance to DaVita's trailer park, Tildy left the motor running.

"Why don't you come on in and I'll make us something to eat. You like pig feet?"

"Just go."

DaVita leaned against the open door looking scrawny and beat and pawed at her scarred face; a ruined child who'd been missing the point all her life, soon to trap herself inside a brand-new shape, the imperviously smashed oval of inertia without end.

"Will I see you again?"

Tildy smiled in spite of herself, pulled the door shut and drove.

Karl was in the backyard bouncing a tennis ball off the wall of the house.

"What happened to your foot?"

"Banged it up on a rock," Tildy said.

He showed her the gauze on the back of his hand. "Sliced it open on a saw up at Keyeses'. Guess it's been that kind of day all around. But I got the side pieces up, ought to be finished by Monday."

He underhanded the fuzzless gray ball to her but she didn't reach; it skittered into the weeds.

"You ain't up for a catch, huh?"

"I'm exhausted, Karl, and sick to my stomach."

"Too much sun probably."

"Much too much."

"Come on, darlin', I'll squeeze a dozen oranges for you."

Tildy lay in bed with a cool cloth over her eyes and soft pillows under her head. In her stomach all that salt water she'd swallowed could not escape the influence of the tides. Up and back it rolled, up and back, up and back.

190

"Here. You don't have to sit up." Karl guided a straw between her lips. "I left a little of the pulp in. Just the way you like it."

"Fine. Put it there and I'll have it later."

"You goin' right off to sleep?"

"Sleeping or just lying still. I don't know."

Karl touched her naked instep with a cautious finger and she jumped. "Hush now, little sweetness. I'm only thinkin' you ought to have a bath, give this foot a little soakin'. It'll soften up the nail so she comes off nice and easy."

"I don't want to get up."

"Don't you worry."

Karl filled the tub, undressed her, carried her in and lowered her into the water. Hot, safe water that welcomed her. He bent down very gradually and brushed her lips with his. A dry, fleeting, sober kiss, but the sweetest she'd ever had. She purred softly while he soaped her.

"Lord, it's so good to be home," she said.

And meant it.

12

Landing in Tangier at six in the morning, stiff-necked and bleary with trepidation, Christo was hard-pressed to accept the reality of African soil beneath him and the game now beginning in earnest.

Twelve hours ago, in a Midtown delicatessen lined with celebrity photographs, Pierce had given him a single piece of parting advice: "Be alert." No problem. Nestled at the bottom of his cigarette pack were two little methamphetamine footballs; a green rabbit's foot sat in his pocket. He'd be alert all right, at critical mass. He chain-smoked by the baggage carousel and his eyes moved like automatic cameras in a bank, checking every face.

The customs inspection was perfunctory—a heft of his bag, a fast dig around the sides, a squiggle of chalk on top. His phony passport was glanced over, duly stamped by a civil servant with a prosthetic hand. A real work of art, the passport, handcrafted by a woman who had married briefly into the Milbank family, who ran a design studio turning out corporate logos at ten thousand dollars a pop. The new identity was Arno Bester, Professor of Biochemistry, and in a tweed one-button with elbow patches, baggy slacks and bow tie, Christo was trying to look the part.

In the small café by the observation deck he ordered a pot of coffee and turned to the smuggler's basic activity: waiting. The coffee was strong and thick and made his stomach pucker along with his mouth. Or was that anxiety twisting in him like a parasitic worm?

He took out the Polaroid of his local contact. In front of a wattle-and-daub hut, a brawny, heavy-boned individual with blond whiskers posed, wearing a cable-knit sweater and a bicycle racer's cap with the bill turned up. He stood at attention, an expressionless mug-book figurine under a sky whose marine hue probably had more to do with developer chemicals than any quality of North African light. Tomas Ulrich was the name. He was a Swedish expatriate who'd had a long and (to insiders) renowned career as an arms deal-er: AK-47s to the Turkish Cypriots, grenade launchers to the Pre-toria-backed faction in Angola, plastique to the IRA, and on and on. But he was retired now, ran an auto body shop in the heart of the city.

"Tommy's an absolute no-bullshit pro. A heavyweight," Pierce had promised. "If there's any trouble it won't come from him."

But Christo didn't much care for the idea that his envoy and broker, the hinge on which the deal would swing, was a weapons man. Gunrunning, it was agreed even among the hardened, was an unusually demented business. It attracted men interested in more than money, taught them that anyone, even a partner, was ripe for the picking.

Already Christo needed help. He did not want to leave the con-soling anonymity of the airport. They'd taught him about synthetic spirit on the inside, where time was measured by the clattering of pills in the bottom of tiny paper cups. He shook out one of the foot-balls and medicated himself. There now. The moment after swal-lowing, he felt more hopeful about the task ahead; like starting down the road with a full tank of gas.

He taxied to the American Express office where he converted traveler's checks into Moroccan francs. In the men's room of a near-by hotel, he packed everything into a money belt, a thick and cum-bersome going-away gift from Pierce that reminded him of the pro-tective crotch gear boxers wore. Bomblets of speed lunacy went off in his head as he prowled the lobby full of international citizens with their guidebooks and cameras, their contented-cow stolidity he now envied. His mouth felt full of sand. It was all coming up too fast, too suddenly. The scam was too big for him. In hurried misjudgement, he was going to give himself the hustler's bends.

Okay, okay. Just a little stage fright. Deal with it. He sat on the edge of a Naugahyde chair and lectured himself. Now was the time to flush out his system; there'd be no place for this kind of thing later on. Any sign of it and they'd shred him like a classified docu-ment. Keep moving, just keep moving. Let yourself go. Half the pressure, twice the quickness. And finally, because there was no other way out, he pulled himself as tight as the money belt and went on to his next appointment.

The purchase of the Land Rover had been prearranged with transatlantic phone calls and a money order. The salesman wanted very much to take him out for a test run, but Christo dissuaded him. He said he had to be immediately on his way to a meeting with government agronomists in Tetuán, and the lie had a tonic effect. Falling back into the old skills centered him. That's it, just keep moving. He pulled out his Arno Bester driver's license, signed half a dozen forms, and the salesman handed over the keys along with a complimentary map of the city.

The noon heat was insidious despite the ocean breeze, and Christo shrugged out of his jacket, removed the clip-on tie. Following the written instructions, he went down to the abrupt end of a palm-lined avenue and jogged right. Slow-moving chaos closed in, jumbled buildings and people layered like compost along the brown walls. He gripped the wheel hard. Nasty birdcage voices poured with sticky air through the Rover's windows. The breeze was cut off here, the salt fragrance replaced by something heavy and unplaceable, though spoiled melon came close. Someone on a motorbike made a sudden U turn in front of him, and Christo trod on the brake, banged his knee on the edge of the metal dash. He considered the grisly upshot of a pedestrian under his wheels: pulled from the driver's seat and devoured by a raging native mob.

The fright was on him again. He watched bunched faces passing, brown complexions like camouflage, eyes angling toward him. Enough turbulence out there beneath the steady, sullen surface to drown in. He'd been against a foreign venue all along, but Pierce had insisted. Fine for him, Pierce was the strategic whiz who never left headquarters. Christo was smack-dab and defenseless in this human overflow, his only weapon—language—useless here. Hold on and move through it. Keep moving.

Then in a blink, the way was empty, like an eerie curfew zone. These walls were whitewashed and topped with broken glass; doors were armored with black wrought iron. It seemed that the air had thinned, the heat lessened, but Christo did not know whether to trust even his own senses. He was so intent on monitoring himself that he nearly missed his turn.

The street had narrowed, gone rough under him, by the time he located the shop. Tomas stood in the doorway sucking on a pipe and looking like a retired fisherman surveying the sea.

Christo parked in the entryway and hopped down. "Hey, partner, J. D. Christo from the New York office."

Teeth clenched around the pipestem in what might have been a smile, Tomas sidled over and patted Christo's back, sides, hips—an overt frisk. "Just a reflex," he said apologetically. His English was without accent. "New York is full of statues."

"But there are never enough heroes to go around," Christo replied, fulfilling the witless password requirement.

"Come on, then." Tomas emptied his pipe on the street and, as Christo steered the Rover inside, pulled a corrugated steel door down behind them.

Not much action under the low concrete ceiling. Two wiry men in newspaper hats squatted on either side of an upended crate playing dominoes. A pie-faced boy in sandals and a canvas jumper drowsily taped over a car's windows prior to spray painting. An equally drowsy blues sax came out of a stripped-down speaker cone balanced on the disfigured rear end of a Peugeot, accentuating the junk-sick bunker atmosphere.

Tomas bobbed his big blond head, shuffled to the beat. "Your only decent export, jazz. The mighty tree that grew from the death culture. You dig Horace Silver?"

"The most."

Christo was thrown hopelessly off stride, having expected a razor-sharp pro, finding instead this solemn boho who poked him now, called his attention to the piano passage coming up.

"You hear the genius? It makes me think of a rain forest."

Solid, Pops. Just as Christo focused his concentration on the skittering chords, Tomas broke away, all business.

"She is brand new, eh? With all the papers?" Without awaiting an answer, Tomas spoke to the pie-face in mongrel Berber French. Stroking the Rover's flanks, rapping on it here and there, the boy grunted something back. "Abdel is my best man," Tomas said paternally. "A born engineer."

"That's good to know." Christo could feel himself twitching.

"You're in some kind of hurry?" Tomas made a treadmill motion with his hands.

"Well, I didn't come to see the sights."

"All right. Commerce on an empty stomach, then." Tomas pulled him around to the rear of the car. "We will cut down through here, you see? By my estimation we will need eight cubic feet of space. If necessary, we can squeeze more up here behind the firewall. Also, a few modifications so that the final weight will tally with what is on your manifest. Abdel will take care. And once the load is in, he will seal up, putty, sand, repaint and you will be ready to go."

Christo looked suspiciously at the vapid pie face.

"Don't worry," Tomas said. "He is paid from my share."

Feeling tentative, Christo examined oil stains on the floor, listened to the men slapping down their dominoes. "So when do we go to meet the man?"

Tomas had cupped one ear, absorbed in the sound track again. Christo repeated himself, an obstreperous buzz in his voice that hung in the dead air that followed.

Tomas winced. Then, shaking his head as the band picked up its chorus, he growled, "Right away then. But I suggest you calm down on the way. I don't like strain."

Calm down, quiet. It was good advice, except the speed had Christo ready to run through walls, his ganglia red-hot and smoking. Get any more alert and he'd crack like a candy egg. But still he needed the friction, knew he operated best that way.

By the time they reached the village, there were indentations in Christo's thumb from the nails at the end of the rabbit's foot he'd been squeezing reflexively. He was sweating under a heavy woolen djellabah. The long, tentlike garment made him claustrophobic, but Tomas had insisted.

"No use looking any more conspicuous than you have to. And keep the hood up, it will hide your face."

Now, as they crossed the dirt road with sun angling over tile roofs and into their faces, he cautioned, "Keep watch on yourself and show respect for these people. Remember, we're infidels."

The Swede was calling all the shots; Christo accepted his own docility. He simply wasn't prepared. It was like an inescapable dream where everything took him by surprise. He felt as helpless as a cork on rough water and more than willing to be led.

They passed under a stone arch furrowed by several hundred years of windblown sand and entered the souk. It was a scene in suspension and the only sound was the buzzing of flies. Goats nosed around in the dust, too listless to need tethering. The more prosperous merchants had been able to put together stalls of lumber rescued from cooking fires and rubbish heaps, while the rest just sat on the ground with a few articles before them on a cloth—one woman with henna-stained palms offered a rusted flywheel, assorted nuts and bolts, a pile of tiny airline soap bars. Next to her, a crippled boy had loose cigarettes and a half-dead chicken that twitched feebly at the edge of his ragged blanket, its feet bound with reeds.

Christo felt a queer internal tremor as he realized there were no other customers.

"Don't be fooled by what shows," Tomas murmured as he stopped to purchase ten centimes' worth of dried chick peas. "This one here, his real business is in virgin boys."

Christo lurched as an olive vendor tugged his flapping sleeve. Tomas smiled thinly and said it might be wise for him to buy.

"Good will?"

"A gesture. Gestures and ceremony, these things are paramount here."

"Back home we call it public relations." Christo thought: A clever line, I must be doing better.

With olive juice dripping down his arm from the paper cone, Christo followed his guide into a hut that smelled like wet dog. The counter was a plank laid across two kegs, and the little girl behind it (she could not have been more then ten) had a whore's tired, smirking face. She opened two warm Cokes without being asked, listened with meandering eyes as Tomas instructed her, then dropped the coins he gave her in a cloth sack that hung under her skirts.

Back outside, Christo tossed away his olives and collapsed against the wall, caught by the sensation of a mental fissure through which dizziness rushed in a torrent. He was marinated in sweat.

Tomas gulped Coke, wiped his mouth. "These Arabs love the sugar. That's why most of them have brass teeth."

Christo rocked on his heels, touched the crease in his trousers for reassurance. "What now?" he managed.

"Nothing now. We wait. The girl will take my message and after a while they will come for us. For now we just sit."

"Sorry. I must have left my patience on the plane."

Christo closed his eyes to the glare and tried to fold his arms and legs into a napping posture. But recent images whiplashed across his inner eye: Tomas's dank garage, the threatening clutter of the city, aboriginal faces self-righteously blank.

"*Maktub*," Tomas said.

"What?"

"Fate. What will be, will be."

Yes, Christo silently commented, that's just what I'm afraid of.

A noise like an electric shaver cut the air followed in a burst by music from the other side of the wall: dolorous yodeling embroidered by an epileptic clarinet. In the thin belt of shadow that intersected the square, boys had been playing a game with round stones; now they broke away and moved briskly in a pack.

"*Hashish? Monsieur pour hashish?*"

"English? *Deutsch?* Good dope for you. *Ich haben.*"

Christo rose to his feet as they pressed in, but Tomas pulled him back down. "Don't encourage them."

More and more came, as if a chemical signal had been released drawing them like insects to a food source, Christo felt waves of sour boy-breath on his face as they shoved and clamored, cried their incantation: "Hashish! Hashish!"

Slapping heads, an older boy thrust his way to the front. "You waste your time with these filthy childs. I take you somewhere no big noise. You sit, have tea, smoke best hashish all you want, no problem. Listen all new tapes just flown in. Bob Dylan, Rolling Stones."

"*Cessez donc!*" Tomas cocked his fist "*Cessez.*"

They recoiled momentarily, then surged forward, giggling and aping Tomas—"*Cessez!*"—in shrill, taunting voices. The first brave hands shot out to poke and tug; the first rumble of animal menace rose like heat from the ground.

Tomas stood quickly. "Let's walk." They drove through wild puppy furor, but were clear for only a few seconds before it reformed around them in a circular dance that combined entreaty and defiance.

It was eerie, the way they froze all at once, went mute. Christo tensed, expecting the worst, but the pack began to dismantle, boys drifting away in bashful groups of three and four. From the direction in which they carefully did not look, it was possible to detect the cause of their submission.

He was tall and elegantly slim in his Western clothes, his dark face dominated by eyes like a pair of ray-gun apertures, one sweep of them more than enough; a terrible power quickly flashed. Just from the way he set himself, it was clear he had the juice, that he would be a chieftain of the streets anywhere—Bedji or Lima or Chicago.

"Ibrahim." Tomas approached him. "*Salaam aleikum.*"

"*Aleikum salaam.*"

They grasped wrists in a kind of Indian-wrestle greeting. Christo was introduced as an "American businessman." Ibrahim bowed deeply, emitting a powerful fume of bay rum.

"You come yourself to meet us," Tomas intoned. "We are most honored."

"We in turn are honored by your visit." Ibrahim had a rolling, staff-announcer's baritone. "This way please, and we shall ride."

The car was long and black, and pitted by rust and by the sharp stones that were everywhere. It had to be the only Oldsmobile in town. Ibrahim drove at cortege speed through several miles of dismal countryside, gray-green succulents and disintegrating rock. Tomas whispered urgent cultural lore.

"From now on, we are in the care of the family. They will dictate the atmosphere. They will decide how and when to complete the transaction. In Islam, the most important thing is how one provides or accepts hospitality."

"Okay, okay," Christo said irritably. And to himself: Good manners? Something else I don't have.

Turning off the main road and passing through a chicken-wire gate, they pulled up at a low, oblong warehouse with a shining tin roof. Ibrahim's curt horn beeps fetched out a fervently obsequious little man who opened doors and ushered them inside; where his nose should have been, there was a tan hole.

Everyone wore sunglasses except Ali Mustafa, the patriarch, a generous dumpling of a man in a crisp linen tunic, who soaked up deference with the careless inveteracy of a mullah. Clearly, he was running the show. Welcoming his guests to a fragrant sanctum where carpets had been laid over the floor, he bade them recline among the cushions that encircled a brass table. He snapped his fingers and a tray of sweet mint tea in glasses was brought. Christo took his cues from Tomas during the long Arabic toast. The tea was like syrup and made him sweat even more profusely inside the djellabah. The glasses were replenished and a young relative played a halting version of "My Blue Heaven" on the flageolet. Ali Mustafa beamed.

"We thank you for your long trip," he said.

"Yeah, great to be here," Christo said, like someone on a talk show.

"Your wisdom in coming is to your credit. It pleases me much to open my doors for citizens of the world. Since I am a child and my father teaches me to sift kif through horsehair, I am dedicated to a search for better and better ways to make and preserve hashish.

Please to come now with me and see for yourself."

More sunglasses, more relatives. They were busy as beavers in the processing room. Ali Mustafa knelt beside one of his cleaners, dipped into the man's wide metal pan and rubbed fine powder through his fingers.

"Just to touch our hashish is a pleasurable thing." He opened his hand to display the resinous globules that adhered. "And you will see the color, how dark. These plants, my friend, *extraordinaire*. Most we pick before the strong winds come, but these we grow terraced behind a mountain and protected. We wait and wait to pick, and the ripeness is so sweet to make perfume in the valley at night. You see now how it takes form."

From one of the gallon cans, Ali Mustafa scooped an expertly exact amount of his product onto a square of cellophane, laid a second square on top and placed this sandwich in the lower plate of a hand press.

"My grandsons invent this machine. The heat is inside, by electricity. No flame." He turned a small black dial, activating the scavenged element of a steam iron, then spun the crankshaft; the plates clamped together. "Now is the beauty. The spirit of hashish, *comme on dit* . . .It unites. The essence set free in the heat."

The slab he removed moments later was fudge brown, smooth and sealed airtight in cellophane.

"This," holding the slab over his heart, "this is the pride of Ali Mustafa."

Once more around the brass table, they waited in reverent silence while the narghile was prepared. Made of cut green glass, it had four flexible, gold-embroidered smoking tubes attached to amber mouthpieces. The urn-shaped bowl was filled to the rim with alternating layers of black tobacco and hashish, a hot coal nestled on top.

Ali Mustafa leaned close to present one of the mouthpieces and Christo saw his eyes were milky and brown like an old dog's. Suspicion churned inside, stirring up from Christo's cloudy bottom the urge to see conspiracy. Their cunning scheme: banish his vigilance to an island of smoke, fill his head with hash anarchy, then ambush with curved blades. A piece of throat for every family member. Something now at his ribs.

But it was Tomas nudging him. All right, if only for protocol. Christo inhaled, water bubbling and rebounding off the glass, smoke jetting into his lungs. A kick in the chest from a mule. He clapped his hand over nose and mouth to hold down the coughs.

"Very smooth," Tomas offered, blue smoke billowing from his nostrils. "And the taste, very fresh. Your skill is unique, Ali."

Christo could only nod agreement. He had exhaled by now, but articulate speech was beyond him. His eyes were tearing and his throat rippled upward. He took another toke, more cautiously this time, but still felt that mule kick.

"Superb," he rasped. Protocol.

Ali Mustafa chuckled, tossed another chunk of hashish onto the hissing embers. "Superb, my traveling friend, *mais oui*. Your pleasure is mine also."

Christo inhaled through clenched teeth, rocked back with eyes closed.

"He flies now, you see? He pilots the magic carpet."

As Christo sank deeper into the cushions, puffing steadily, he recognized that he was conquered, could no more lift an arm to ward off imminent disaster. He saw Tomas and Ali Mustafa conversing under white corollas, their mouths moving wetly, their hands punctuating the air. The sounds came to him, but none of the words. Let them do their worst, then. Let his uneasy life seep away into these cushions. He could repudiate it all.

Ibrahim looming above him then, a cold presence, and Tomas pulling him upright.

"It's time for the money."

"Hmm?"

Ali Mustafa knitted his sausage fingers. "I know you are men of honor."

"The money," Tomas hissed. "Show them the bloody money."

Through bunched cloth Christo felt along his waist where the heavy belt had chafed him. Staggering to his feet, smiling hazily, he dropped his pants.

Casa Nocturne, the villa the Ulrichs were subletting from a British rocket engineer, had a sweeping view of the harbor from its tiled patio. Christo slouched in a canvas chair, his feet propped on the balustrade, and gazed down at a berthed cruise ship, which was strung with lights and gave off faint twitters of cocktail music. Acacia leaves fluttered overhead in a breeze that pushed ahead of itself the aroma of deep-fried seafood.

Tomas had been furious with Christo's inept comportment. A wonder they hadn't both been left in a gully, he said. Back at the garage, once they'd finished loading the Rover's carefully padded deadspace, Christo had thrown Tomas his cut like a bag of giblets.

"Milbank sends me his office boy." Tomas had folded his arms, struck a pose of pedagogic disdain. "It's not worth getting angry about."

Office boy? Maybe. Christo shifted his eyes from the harbor to the Beaujolais in his glass. He imagined Tomas hemmed in by ski-masked zealots, on his knees before a crate of rifles packed in cosmoline. That much of a pro, he thought, I don't need to be.

"More wine?" Inge Ulrich stepped onto the patio, surfer-blond bangs fringing over her brow like a torn hat.

"Sure. I'll take a splash."

"Such a lovely moon from here. And the ships."

Christo had been presented to her in his biochemist's guise; he was supposed to be on his way to a university lectureship in Accra. Inge, her husband explained, was deeply concerned with physical health and purity.

"No mention can be made of your business here. It would be extremely unpleasant if she found out I am involved in something she considers destructive. But she never objected to my arms business. 'Just machines,' she would say. 'I have nothing against machines.' Does that make sense?"

But Inge had always lived on contradiction; and in ways Tomas knew nothing about.

Years ago in Stockholm she was a prostitute, an addict. She was tough enough to keep the pimps off her back, but she was afraid of the dark and kept a crucifix under her pillow. Her steadiest customer was a physician whose wife had been maimed in a train derailment. He paid Inge generously to put on rubber boots and defecate over a glass coffee table while he lay underneath. On the promise that she service him exclusively, he installed her in a deluxe apartment, supplied her with ampules of morphine that she stored in the egg tray of the refrigerator. But Inge's promise was as empty as her merchant's heart. A private detective reported that she was seeing as many as five clients a day.

The physician was distraught, bent on revenge. He took her to his chalet on Lake Vattern and handcuffed her to steel rings in the attic floor. For five days he denied her food and sleep, beat her with hemlock boughs and pierced her with heated safety pins. This was behavior modification of the crudest type, but when at last he freed her, dumping her scab-covered body in a roadside snowbank, Inge felt immeasurably cleansed. From that day forward, she had not touched so much as an aspirin and, until her marriage to Tomas, was doggedly celibate.

Inge had learned that truth extended no farther than the surface of her skin, that flesh and bone were all the wealth she'd ever have. Now she drank no water that had not been boiled first, and confined her diet to vegetables and whole grains. She douched with ginseng vinegar and all day long gobbled papaya enzyme and bee pollen tablets mailed to her from London.

After dinner, Inge served refreshments in the living room—coffee for the men, chamomile tea for herself. Her hair was pulled back in a ponytail and she smelled harshly of laundry soap. Tomas, suddenly the mellow host, showed off his up-to-the-minute sound system.

"These tapes are very rare. Live broadcasts from the ballroom of a Kansas City hotel."

But his sermon on the martyrdom of Charlie Parker was interrupted by a phone call.

"A Frenchman," Inge reported. "Something to do with business."

She lowered herself to the floor near Christo, now supine and awash in Beaujolais. Smiling tightly, she wiggled her naked toes on the rug, hugged her knees.

"Where were you born?"

"Flint, Michigan. That's up north."

"We have been in the States. Did he tell you?"

"Not that I recall."

"It depressed me. A crumbling empire, you know? And the people are so insecure. So desperate for heroes, don't you think?"

"Not desperate." Christo rolled onto his side. "Just fickle."

"Everything is treated like a pair of shoes." Inge was flushed with vehemence. "What life is there for artists? You see all the musicians who must go abroad for appreciation while the people worship athletes and television stars."

Right. Next, Christo supposed, she'll be asking me if Malcolm X was murdered by the oil companies. "We need a lot of tranquilizing, that's all. Nothing special."

Inge squinted at him, stretched out her legs. "Do you mind?" Already her feet were wedged up against his thigh. "I have poor circulation and they get so very cold."

They were clammy, too, pressing under him and up, digging in like a couple of baby fists. He looked at sea-green veins distinct along her ankle, then into her steady eyes.

"I think in America you must be a beggar or a king and nothing in between," Inge said, and tiptoed up to the fork in his legs.

"That must be why I left."

The laundry soap smell was hypnotic, a rhinal drug like the perfume dumped into department-store ventilation systems. Without the least hint of anything on her face, she massaged the root behind his balls with an icy big toe. The most artless pass ever thrown at him, but they were both breathing hard. Crazy situation, ferociously dreamy, brainless, but under wraps somehow. Strangers when we meet. He noticed a saliva bubble in a crevice between her teeth.

"We must stop." She flipped her bangs, looked away.

Hearing footsteps, Christo rolled over to hide his erection.

A bad morning, Christo faltering out of hermetic sleep and into the shower, rolling his clogged head under the spray until the hot water ran out. Tomas seemed edgy as they walked to the shop, glancing over his shoulder and nibbling the end of his tongue. The paint was dry on the Rover and Abdel, who'd been up all night, had gauze bandages wrapped around one hand. Tomas told him he could take the rest of the day off.

"No hard feelings?" Christo said.

"No feelings, none." Tomas drew a flat line in the air with his pipe. "I close the book on this thing and then no more. You tell New York what I say. No more."

"Well, thanks for the dinner. Next time you and Inge will have to come over to my place."

Christo drove along the waterfront checking pier numbers. The *Sombra*, a freighter under Liberian registry, was a sorry-looking item, algae blots along the waterline, its red stacks barred with soot. White sunlight gave it the complexion of a disaster ship. Christo imagined a Taiwanese mate gone berserk with a fire axe, alone by morning on a rudderless vessel lost in the garbage currents. Oh well. *Maktub*, as they say hereabouts. It was out of his hands.

He signed clearance papers, a stack of traveler's checks. Then, on his way to find a cab to the airport, he let loose his rabbit's foot and watched it fall, an offering to the sea.

Pierce at the wheel of the Packard was a jolly welcome-wagoneer, rocking from side to side as he hummed selections from *On the*

Town. He'd been a few hours late picking Christo up at the terminal, but presumably had needed the extra time to deck out in the belted camel's-hair coat, pinstripe three-piecer, taupe gloves, to grab the feel of this event and then describe it in clothes.

"So our ship comes in on the sixteenth and everything is everything. I never doubted your aptitude, jazzbo, not for a second."

He announced they were bound for Pine Hill, Connecticut, and the Milbank family retreat. It was a proclamation rather than an invitation and Christo chafed at his lack of choice. Back behind the lines, mission accomplished, and still he was following orders. There they were, bombing up the Taconic Parkway with the top down and the threat of snow in the air. They sipped warmth from a pewter hipflask while naked trees whipped by in stripes of gray and brown, a frugal winter plaid.

Minutes from the state line, a police cruiser came up alongside and ran even with them, door handle to door handle. Every few seconds the bruiser inside would turn and stare at them out of his dark eyeholes.

"Fucking yokel," Pierce said. "I should put him away. Done one twenty in this thing against a headwind."

"No special effects." Christo touched his arm. "Please."

It was just the sort of challenge Pierce would hand himself, one more small stone in the legend he was building. But he just smiled and waved, hissing through his teeth, "Your mother's head in a plastic bag, Nazi."

The cruiser peeled back, U-turned across marshy median grass.

By the time Pierce turned onto the gravel drive that led through dark and aromatic woods to the house (erected in 1909 by his great-grandfather with the proceeds from a cotton mill and two tuberculosis sanatoria in the Adirondacks), snow had begun to fall. He coasted around the last curve, leaned back and let woolly flakes melt on his face. With its exposed rafter ends, incised shutters and jigsawed eaves, the house looked like a huge chocolate cuckoo clock.

"Like going back in time, isn't it?" Pierce surveyed his patrimony from the running board. "To the golden age of the robber barons."

Inside, Christo stared at his reflection in the dusty glass bell sheltering a stuffed canary while Pierce chased around turning on lights and thermostats. The furnace kicked on, blowing musty fumes, and Christo said he needed some coffee. Badly.

Improbably shiny copper pans and utensils hung from the kitchen beams. Pierce filled the kettle and got French roast beans out of the freezer. The coffee maker took paper filters but none could be found, so Pierce substituted a scarf that had belonged to his grandmother. The resultant brew had a faintly iridescent surface. Christo lifted his cup, blew, sipped.

"Mmmm." He smacked his lips. "Tastes like old neck."

It was in an upstairs corner room, at a slate billiard table with mother-of-pearl inlay and ball-and-claw feet, that Pierce and Christo convened to discuss the Morocco operation. They puffed stale cigars and played Chicago rotation by the light of frosted candleflame bulbs.

"Give me your assessment on quality," Pierce said, lining up a knotty three-ball combination.

"Devastating. Couldn't see my hand in front of my face."

"You brought a sample?"

"Fuck no. I went out of there clean, baby. An investment like that, I wasn't going to get popped at the airport for a couple of measly ounces."

"That's not like you."

"Maybe not. You're disappointed I didn't screw up?"

"Hey, you're my hot prospect, my rookie phee-nom. Would I let you fall short?"

Christo flubbed a delicate onion slice on the ten ball. "Not so far."

"You're sitting right smack on top of the biggest score of your life, so cheer the hell up. Show a little faith in yourself."

"Tell it to the Swede."

"What about him?"

"We were what you call incompatible."

"Really?" Pierce appraised the end of his cigar, began to pace. "Maybe it figures. The man has the battle stars and he's been through some hard campaigns. But I have to say I didn't fill you in all the way on Tommy Ulrich before you left."

"Let's have it."

"I heard—from a highly impeachable source, mind you—that he had a breakdown three years ago, burned out some circuits."

"Shit." Christo flung cue chalk across the room. "So you sent me over there without a map."

"Take it easy. I didn't want you to get, as it were, psyched out."

"Thanks a lot. So who told you?"

"His wife."

A sickening gyroscope spinning around his brain, Christo slumped onto the window seat. Always the last to know when the joke's on you. Outside thinly layered snow had turned ghost blue under the moon. He pressed his fingers to the cold pane, then his eyes.

"You all right?" Pierce meant to be solicitous, but sounded annoyed.

"Relax. I'm not going to bleed on the furniture." Forebodings were best left where they were. Trite phrases would do: "I'm tired out is all. Overworked."

"Country air will take care of that. A respite among the evergreens, that's my prescription."

Christo moved his eyes slowly over the shadowy room. "I don't know about this place. Too much gloom, too many spooks."

"Exactly. That's why I come here. The sacred ground of the ancestors. They're my people, those spooks, and I need to get in touch, replenish the spirit now and then. Great uncle Lydon who owned half of Nova Scotia at one time and held the state record for brown trout up until the fifties. My grandfather, who appeared drunk before the Supreme Court. And Granny Syl, she gave me the money to swing my first major dope deal. I told her I needed something to live on while I wrote a novel. But they're all gone now and I'm the only one holding on. My parents come here for a week every summer and bitch about the property taxes. So it's me. Everything flows into me. The magic fucking power of the ancestors and I'm the only one who sees how valuable it is."

"How valuable it is," Christo repeated. "I despise the rich."

They dined on a muddy goulash of canned goods and went early to bed.

These rooms were glacial with gentility, outlined in trickery and clutter, overfed on the trivial seductions of the past—yachting trophies on the mantel, seashells in a reed basket, a fez set rakishly atop a bust of Longfellow. Christo could only react to it as a job site. He'd been checking the layout all morning, conjecturing what ought to be taken and what left behind: the thief's triage. And he was watched every step of the way by the brushstroke eyes of china statuettes, the faces in countless photographs whose posed implications were as unbending as noon light on rich wood surfaces all around, brown in a dozen languages.

On the porch in his overcoat, Pierce hunched over his typewriter, banging away at preliminary notes for a detective story. No title yet, but it would involve treachery on the international commodities market and plutonium secreted in someone's toothpaste.

Over the last few days they had not been getting along well. Tension and close quarters: a recipe for spite. Pierce didn't help matters any by making a point of competition—gin rummy, backgammon, twenty questions, even Candyland and Lotto, children's board games dredged up out of musty drawers.

"Enough," Christo protested. "Even boredom is better than this."

"We just need to find a game you can win at."

In the evenings Pierce would fry potatoes, broil some previously thawed chops, uncork yet another bottle of wine. Afterward they'd listen to the radio or to hissing 78's of Paul Whiteman, Vincent Lopez and his Hotel Pennsylvania Orchestra. Then finally, one of them would cross out another box on the calendar; one less hindrance in the way of Hash Wednesday on the sixteenth.

While Christo displayed classic cabin fever symptoms, wandering aimlessly from room to room and talking to himself, Pierce grew increasingly preoccupied. He disappeared for hours into glassy contemplation, spoke cursorily, and only when prompted, of their deal. Would the turnover take long? Had he lined up buyers in advance? Pierce would mumble and shrug, treating the whole thing as an intrusion on his pensive vigil. Christo saw this aspect of his partner's personality both as a surprise and as something he should already have guessed. Here, in the blunt context of Bleak House (the apt name Christo had found on the tooled spine of a book), was the truth for which Pierce had been overcompensating all along. He was not so very different from his sister, no more removed than she from the onerous requirements of Family. Christo wondered whether he had ever considered suicide.

"Writing is no better than factory work," Pierce said now, shivering as he came in from the porch. "How about some lunch?"

"We just had breakfast two hours ago."

"If there's something you'd rather do than eat, let's hear it."

So, while Pierce made busy with skillet and spatula, Christo sat acquiescently at the big oak table. He toyed with a wooden napkin holder in the shape of a turtle. Probably made in some blazer-school shop class and wrapped up for Christmas. Granny had developed a fixation for turtles; they were all over the place, in needlepoint, on coffee cups. One more compulsory tradition.

"I was thinking this morning I might move up permanently." Pierce served a tunafish-and-green-bean omelet. "Somehow I feel a lot closer to reality here."

"You'll get over it."

"It's more than a passing mood." Pierce pointed with his fork. "You don't come from anywhere, that's your problem."

"You're pulling rank on me now?"

"I only mean to tell myself not to waste explanations on you."

Christo pushed away from the table. "This tastes like soap." His scalp tingled with exasperation.

Pierce had to be dragged from under the blankets on Wednesday morning. All the way down in the car he complained of swollen glands.

"You want to stop at a diner for chicken soup?"

"No, let's get this thing over with."

But by the time they reached the customs terminal in Port Elizabeth, Pierce had regained his urban gloss and laughed at his own jokes. After all that down time on the Milbank acres, Christo found the industrial landscape soothing and was able to dismiss the vague unease that had been plaguing him. All cut and dried, really. The hard part was already done; the rest was mere processing. Documents in hand, he went to claim his property.

All omens were good. The *Sombra* had arrived slightly ahead of schedule and the off-loading was already done. The sun was shining and the customs agents looked tired and complacent. Still, he noticed, they're wearing sidearms.

"Lived in New York long, sir?"

"I hear these babies don't get the good gas mileage."

Inspecting the Rover from front to back, they small-talked him, the usual testing for nerves. Christo answered placidly, in no hurry. Then they brought out the German shepherd. No problem, he reminded himself. That's why we layered red pepper on top. At a whistled command, the dog bounded into the front seat, sniffed busily with ears pricked and tail wagging.

"Okay, Rusty." The agent snapped his leash back on, slipped him a biscuit. "Follow me please, sir."

The voice was dry, uninflected; handcuffs jingling on the agent's belt were astonishingly loud. Christo felt monentarily that all was lost and it was too late to run. But all they wanted from him inside was his signature on a few more forms.

With Pierce leading the way in the Packard, he headed at last for snug harbor in lower Manhattan.

Looie met them at the elevator gate with a coil of yellow extension cord in one hand and a circular saw in the other.

"Could we get started right away? I'm hosting a poetry reading tonight."

He put on a scuba mask to protect his face from flying particles and went to work on the Rover's rear panel, careful not to push the saw too deep and tear up the merchandise. Pierce was doing figures out loud, lauding their profits-to-be. Christo was holding his stomach. Something was wrong with the noise of the saw. When Looie started cutting the second leg of the rectangle, the bottom edge dipped, meeting no resistance.

"Hold it."

Looie shut off the saw and drew back.

"What the hell?" Pierce, sensing the alarm.

Christo padded his hand with his shirttail. They watched as he worked under the crack and pried up.

Air. And down at the bottom, a few make-weight bags of cement.

Christo saw spots. Like stepping on the teeth of a rake, taking the handle full on the nose.

"I stood right there."

Looie walked in a circle, massaging his sweating head. "Imported cement," he said. And again, "Imported cement."

"I did." Speech made Christo gag, as though he had alphabet blocks in the throat. "I stood right there and helped load."

Pierce took three long steps and drove a left hook into the wall.

Looie lay back on the floor. "I've walked into one of Aesop's fables," he sighed. All Christo could do to keep the vertigo at bay was continue to stare down the hole.

The elevator began to descend. As Pierce disappeared from view, they heard him say he'd be back. Right now he was going to find an emergency room and have a cast put on his hand.

13

Days lengthening like rye grass, bold new movements along the river, mating calls from out of the trees. Yeah, it was spring all right, and the shows were starting up again, siphoning folks out of Gibtown for another season. Time to shake off the long, idle winter. Jam auctioneers were limbering up with tongue twisters, human oddities working out new poses in front of the mirror.

Karl sat dejected by the telephone. He'd been calling around all morning, pleading with anyone he could reach to help him latch on somewhere. He wasn't an analyzer, a student of self, but Karl understood his own cycles and rhythms. He had to get out on the road again, just had to. But Bert Banion, who ran a fried clam concession for Worldwide, had just told him it was hopeless.

"Nobody wants to touch you after that riot you started last year," said Bert, ever blunt. "The manager of L & M has put the word out on you. Gables is poison. So forget about it, you'll have to find chump work this year."

So he'd be a worthless outcast, a prisoner of the summer, and probably get crazy with boredom or resentment by July. Tildy would finally give up on him, and he'd be a marked man on the street reduced to picking over trash, and kids would throw rocks at him and dogs would pee on him as he slept at night on pieces of cardboard.

Sweet Jesus.

He pulled the newspaper over and went through the classifieds: dental receptionist. Mortgage officer. Typesetter. Karl tapped the side of his nose with a pencil. Were you really expecting there'd be an ad for bathroom attendant?

He turned pages slowly, looking for crime stories, found one headlined WIFE GETS THE FREEZE.

A spokeswoman for the County Sheriff's Department announced today that a charge of murder would be brought against Lester Clines of Miami, described as a "three-foot four-inch midget" who had recently been working as a drummer at a Coconut Grove strip club.

While living in Miami for the past four years, Clines continued to pay rent on a bungalow on Gardenville Road in Gibsonton up until December of last year. When his checks stopped coming, the landlord initiated eviction proceedings, which resulted in the charge being filed against the 56-year-old Clines, who is alleged to have clubbed his wife to death and then stuffed her into a 2½-cubic-foot freezer sometime in 1976.

Sheriff's deputies were removing furniture from the Gardenville Road house last week, the spokeswoman announced, when they discovered the freezer.

"It had a slight odor to it. We were hoping it was spoiled meat but it turned out to be a body," she added.

Sources close to the Coroner's Office report that it took three days for the body to thaw sufficiently to permit a positive identification.

Karl had trouble picturing the body as a solid block cast in the shape of a freezer compartment, frost in the eyelashes, arms and legs all contorted to fit in the small space. Mrs. Clines must have been a petite woman. Maybe even an all-out miniature like her husband.

He turned more pages, browsing through an item on a pharmacist's attempt to cross the Pacific in a rowboat, a recipe for stuffed cabbage. But he couldn't stop thinking about Lester Clines, the little drummer boy. It was really a comedy story if you looked at it hard—this midget laying down a bump-and-grind rhythm, while miles away his wife slept forever with her head on an ice tray.

It happened then, the slight turn of the wheel, the click. Karl remembered an article from one of his treasure magazines about a tiny coon bandleader with a hump on his back, a drummer, too, who'd stashed away a fortune. Drumming midgets, secret hiding places. It was a sign for sure, unmistakable as a thunderbolt.

He rushed to the shelf where he kept his back issues hearing wind in his ears, feeling like a mystery force had him by the nostrils

212

and was pulling him on. It didn't take long to find what he was looking for: "Jazzman's Fortune." There was a muddy picture of Chick Webb; small all right, nothing but a nappy little head visible above his drum kit.

". . . Harlem rumor mill was alive with stories of a fortune in cash and jewels secreted somewhere in Webb's sumptuous townhouse."

With a pair of scissors Karl snipped out both articles, reread them while he brewed a pot of coffee. He sharpened his pencil, found paper to write on and sat down with a hot cup and the sense of profuse anticipation that comes only to the chosen, to begin research.

He drew a line down the center of the page, opposed facts and guesses at facts on either side. This is how it looked:

LESTER CLINES	CHICK WEBB
Drummer in band	Ditto
Midget	Small with deformity
Murdered wife	Unmarried (?)
Miami	New York (Born down South?)
Rental property	Owned own home, real estate investor
Secretive	Ditto
Possible coon (?)	Definite coon

So what? In frustration Karl snapped the pencil in half. But he was no less convinced that he'd been sent a message, that there was a reason these two stories had fused in his mind. He was messing around at the dry surface of things, that was the problem. These men were like elves who came in the night to take his hand and lead him to a pot of gold. Elves were mischievous; they liked to tease. They didn't just give their secrets away, but made you jump through hoops and solve riddles. He'd need a fresh approach. He'd need to attack at a deeper level. If he opened himself up, stayed quiet and passive, something might come to him.

Karl decided to sleep on it. Literally. Sandwiching the snipped-out pages around his lucky silver dollar, he sealed them in an envelope which he put under his pillow.

"Come on, elves," he whispered, "come on into my sleep. . . . And bring your drums along."

He thumbed his eyes shut and counted to a hundred. And as he'd done as a kid, when from the dim refuge of his narrow bunk he'd whirled around the Indy track like a fireball and drunk champagne

213

from smooth white breasts in Victory Lane, Karl dreamed what he wanted to. . . .

Old gray house. Moonlight on waxy leaves. Giggling in the hedges and small, dark animal shapes coming at him in the dark, Chick and Lester on all fours. They roll on the ground like they're scratching fleas, poke at him with silver drumsticks. Chick is like an old eggplant, wrinkled and bulbous and black. Lester has colorless eyes and tiny hands. He stomp-dances while Chick limps. They say, "Don't be afraid of the peewees," and pull him inside the house where floors are slanted and stairs end in midair. They beat a rolling rumble on the baseboard with their sticks. Chick stands on his head; his hump is a searchlight shining into a corner where walls meet at an impossible angle. Lester pulls him back outside through a window, makes trilling bird noises. Chick is tapping out a waltz on his own head and they sing:

> Ask us where is this there
> We say not up our sleeves
> We say down in the leaves

The sticks leave their hands like bullets, making phosphorescent trails in the air. Giggling again, the peewees somersault away into the black . . .

Good cash flow today, an upsurge in the seasonal trade. Kids had been coming in all afternoon to buy water pistols and baseball cards and bubblegum shaped like little running shoes. This kind of brisk selling was a natural mood-elevator for Ray Holstein.

"I know kids," he said around a mouthful of peanut brittle. "Been in their vicinity near all my life. You expect they'll get wild when the end of the school year comes in sight. But this, this . . . You know how much we could do with a minimal lunch counter setup? Those little termites would be in here every day chewing up hot dogs and soda and cupcakes. Dollar here, fifty cents there, ice cream, maybe even some little microwave pizzas. We could double the gross, I'm telling you. I know these kids. You can study them like the weather."

Tildy came away from the window where she'd been evaluating her reflection with several brown-to-purple shades of lip gloss that had just come in. "Instead of telling me, Ray, you should just do it."

"Would that I could, Soileau, would that I could. But I'm just the caretaker here and got no right to make any modifications. Follow

214

the plan, that's all the home office people want from me."

"And you never get tired of that."

"Whatever you think, I'm no damn robot, Soileau. I got ideas of my own. Why the hell not? I got a college degree and I read the papers. Just driving along in my car or loading the dishwasher and I'll get an idea about something. Maybe I've been working up to it all along, but it'll just come into my mind, you know?"

"So you've been having ideas." The way Tildy rocked her head, fingered her throat, made it seem like she was talking about a medical condition. "What *is* on your mind, Ray?"

Holstein started fiddling with things on the counter, lining them up, pressing down with the palm of his hand. "Sure, make a joke out of it. Everybody's a skeptic today. Leave town for a few days and your wife assumes you were banging some chick. Tell a kid about work, improving himself, being part of a team, and he laughs in your face." Crushing the cardboard pop-up display over a tray of disposable lighters. "Everybody's got a sneer on and they wonder why things don't work. Maybe if there was a little more faith in people we could finally get out from under all this shit we live with."

"Ray, you shouldn't do this to yourself."

He was heading straight for the milk of magnesia.

She drove home with the windows open and a bottle of beer in her lap. The air was soft, wrapped around her like the finest mosquito netting. She took the long road that skirted the Alafia River, passed quietly humming power lines marching through sand and scrub pine, and it all looked good to her.

Karl had thrown away the pillows in his sleep, kicked off the sheet. One forearm was curled under him while the other twitched spasmodically. He groaned once and opened his eyes halfway.

"Miss me?" Tildy said, changing into pants.

"What . . . What time is it?"

"Anytime." She danced toward him, twirling invisible tassels.

He sat up and probed furiously behind the bed; a crackle of paper and he slumped back cradling an envelope. "Yes, baby, we almost there. We gonna be so rich you won't recognize us."

Saturday dawned cloudy and cool. By seven thirty Karl had packed his tools—crowbar, pickaxe, three sizes of shovel—into the car, tested the metal detector's batteries, unplugged its six-inch loop and replaced it with a twelve-incher, going for maximum depth penetration over pinpoint accuracy. He was loaded for bear.

Cautiously, just after eight, he went in to wake Tildy. She had reacted with surprising annoyance to his plan, but this hadn't flustered him. He'd read the pertinent texts aloud to her, patiently explained the connections he'd succeeded in making between them, the subsequent implications of his dream.

"What is this about?"

"You don't see how I asked for a sign and it came?"

"This doesn't make a damn bit of sense," she'd said fiercely.

"Don't have to make sense," he replied. "It ain't a map, it's an inspiration."

Forcing down a piece of raisin toast, Tildy was more despondent than before, and tangled in questions. Had Karl become truly demented, past all hope? Did he belong in a hospital? Was humoring him this way really the kindest choice? And why, when he'd said to her, "You don't even *want* to believe in me," had this accusation been so painful?

By nine they were parked at the head of Gardenville Road, shivering in silence marred only by the idling motor. Karl sat slumped against the dashboard, fists pressed into his eye sockets, communing with who knew what. His lips were moving. A last prayer? Tildy wished she had it in her to say one too.

"Okay, sugar, let's move out."

He was so jaunty it made her want to cry.

"Take it nice and slow. I'll know it when I see it."

Like an eager dog Karl thrust head and shoulders out the window, investigating the air with an elevated nose. Mist formed on the windshield. They passed a mobile home park, a chicken farm, the ruins of a church or one-room school.

"Hold it. Yeah, back her on up."

A wedge of sloping roof visible through the trees, a dormer window with three of four panes broken out, a pair of weedy ruts angling out of sight.

"We're gettin' real warm. Can you feel it?"

There were signs of recent activity: fresh tire tracks, saplings bent and broken. Karl scrambled out of the car and searched the brush for further spoor. He found a crushed box, the kind used for takeout sandwiches. The mustard splotch on it was still fresh, hadn't yet completely hardened. A few feet away, pressed into soft earth and disfigured by bootprints, was a paper sign that said: CRIME SCENE AREA   DO NOT ENTER. He held it up for Tildy to read. He shim-

216

mied and kicked, a dance to celebrate his vindication.

"Maybe we should come back when it's dark," she said, wondering if they were being watched.

"Fuck no." He was yanking her out the door, pawing her up and down. "I been waitin' thirty-four years for my big moment. I always knowed a man couldn't live the life of Karl Gables without some damn compensation comin' to him. Now here I am after thirty-four years and I ain't about to wait even another five minutes to finally get my end of the seesaw offa the ground."

This is going to break his heart, Tildy thought, swaying through the ruts with Karl running in front of her, an awkwardly suspended figure in the frame of the windshield. She cut the engine and waited, listened almost hopefully for the crashing footfalls of the stake-out team sweeping down to intercept them before they got any closer. But there was only a faint sandpapering of wind, the overlapping chirps of two birds contesting territory.

"Come on. I need you to help carry things."

She took a pick and shovel and a canvas sack they normally used for dirty laundry ("the swag bag," Karl called it now), and followed helplessly along.

The color and texture of driftwood, the house looked like the setting for a Halloween cartoon. The front door dangled on a single hinge; a few scattered wads of newspaper stood out against the spongy darkness, nothing more. Karl ripped up one of the buckled porch slats and dropped to his haunches, studying the heavy skies. He dug around with the stick at the edges of the foundation, crumbled a chunk of earth in his hand, sifted it.

"They told me, 'down in the leaves.' No point messin' in there." He threw the stick into the black mouth of the doorway. "Somewhere under us," and he put his ear to the ground.

Tildy shivered and buttoned up her sweater. This would be a vigil. She had turned away; Karl's arms curled around her from behind, his nose cold on the back of her neck.

"Don't be mad with me, baby. You'll see."

He clapped on the earphones, fiddled briefly with the tuning and volume controls, and began a preliminary sweep with his metal detector. Ten feet from the porch, beeps came loud and fast. He made a few circles of the area, homing in on where the signal was loudest, then took up the smaller shovel and began digging. Minutes later, he pulled out the bottom part of a kerosene lamp; an earthworm hung from its rust-chewed edge.

"At least you know the machine's working right," Tildy said helpfully.

But two hours later her supply of comforting words was running low. There were holes in front of the house, in back of the house, along the sides. Karl had worked painstakingly at first, scooping out round, smooth-edged cavities and mounding dirt neatly to one side, but the last ragged few looked like shell craters with dirt flung in all directions. The booty so far included a screwdriver, two spoons, a paint can and a faucet. The chill had settled in for the day, but Karl was perspiring heavily and had peeled down to his undershirt.

"In the leaves," he muttered.

She could not bring herself to look at him.

He stood with one foot resting on the edge of the porch, leaning over with his chest supported on the bent knee. "The man that won't be beaten can't be beaten." He was gasping for air. "And I won't. No, I won't."

Karl sprang onto the porch, took one step toward that yawning door and his foot crashed through rotten wood. Foundering, he landed on his side, twisted, and splinter-teeth gouged his ankle. Tildy rushed to him, but he diverted her with a ferocious snarl, and turning very slowly lifted the foot free. Red blood seeped through a torn white sock, and lodged by its stem under crisscrossed shoelaces, a thin round of dead brown—a leaf.

Karl pitched his head back and yodeled with joy. "See that? I'm right on top of it."

"What? What?"

"There's a leaf on my shoe." Reaching for it with quivering fingers, "Lord, I'm gonna kiss this leaf."

And so he did, with the hungry gratitude of a man saved from drowning. Then he reached into the hole his foot had made and tossed up a great profusion of leaves that sailed and propellered down the air to land all around him like banknotes at the climax of a crime film.

"Down in the leaves, boys, I hear you now. We red-hot, boys. We got the goods."

Tildy was frightened by the passion in his voice.

"Get the crowbar. Bring them things over here and we'll rip this porch right up till we find what's underneath."

Raving. Delirious. He was like a man who'd been chasing a mirage across the desert for too long. She wanted to blanket him with her body, cover his parched mouth and burning eyes and lure him into sleep. But it was much too late for that. So she worked alongside him, trying not to think of anything but the cadence of her pickaxe swings. Steady as a metronome. Wood breaking apart, flying. Ground opening up to light it hadn't seen in years . . . *Clang.* Pick point hitting something that was also metal. A shorter stroke, another clang. She reached down and felt smooth cold sides meeting in a rounded edge, little knobs up and down. She flopped on her stomach and peered down. It was a steamer trunk.

"Karl," she said with cobwebs on her face. "Over here, Karl."

He kissed her hands once he'd looked, very calm now, balanced. "You did it, babe. My good-luck charm, like always."

They levered and lifted and heaved and there it was, a simple box reinforced with studded iron strips, scraps of railway and hotel decals grafted to its filthy skin. They stood looking at it, at each other, for a long time.

"Ready?"

As Karl worked the crowbar under the lock, Tildy thought: Maybe it's just another body. Trunk murder. He wiped his hands, hesitated slyly and lifted the lid. The money was not neatly bundled but lay there in a frozen whirlpool of fives and tens and twenties.

"I love you," and she held him tight.

It was not the sight of money that caused this welling up but a vast relief. He was not lost to her after all. Victory instead of lunacy. Karl had won.

"Let's see what else we got."

He went to his knees and pushed through the layer of paper. The first coffee can he opened was stuffed with gold turnip watches.

In the days that followed Karl found it hard to sleep. There were dark raccoon circles around his eyes. He floated through the house in a glowing envelope of bliss, the only nourishment he needed. He played on the floor like a child with the rings and stickpins, the gold coins and gold toothpicks and gold cigar cutters. He picked necklaces for Tildy like wildflowers, topaz and emerald and sapphire. A strange reserve played across his face. It was as if he had popped through a celestial warp into another dimension and nothing, not even the news of Lester Clines's jailhouse suicide, could touch him. He was happy just to play, but Tildy couldn't be so just watching.

Her initial elation had worn off; the impact of their discovery had left bruises. But she breezed off to work each morning, spent the day making change, helping ladies decide which pair of cheap earrings to buy; and the absurdity of the situation offered no comfort. While Karl was on a bender, reeling with visions of a new life that changed hourly, she saw only how much coping she'd have to do; she saw that this sudden blessing of theirs could just as easily be a curse, a machine to manufacture worries. Sooner rather than later, Karl would want to broadcast news of their discovery all over town—she worried about that. True, Lester Clines had discouraged further investigation by hanging himself with his own trousers, but still they were holding evidence in a murder case—she worried about that. They were holding a few thousand in cash and an array of nonnegotiable but traceable items that would have to be fenced somehow—she worried about that, too.

"It's too much for me to handle. I'm afraid."

Tildy repeated and repeated these words like a mantra in the vain hope that an admission of fear would in some way strengthen her. "I'm afraid," she would whisper, to which her only response was, "Yes, you certainly are."

"Let's buy a boat and sail around the world," Karl said to her one afternoon as she arrived home early from the Medi Quik. "Let's buy a farm and raise racehorses."

Tildy scooped up the cufflinks he'd been sorting through and shook them in his face. "You can't buy anything with this, it's not money. Do you understand me? That's not a treasure chest we've got, it's a toy chest. So play with your fucking toys and leave me alone."

She went into the bedroom and slammed the door. All Tildy had in mind was stashing herself in that little box of a room and shutting down her tired brain. But she was about to uncover one more false theory, about to prove that desperation, not necessity, was the mother of invention. She pulled off her shoes, flung them one after the other at the back of the closet; and she thought of Sparn.

Sparn the fixer, the Big Peter who could always get into dark and unseen places. He knew all the angles and how to play them. He knew all the pipelines, where they began and where they emptied. She needed outside help to turn toys into money and he could give it. Sparn was a businessman first and always, and last year's grievances wouldn't count for much if she could bring him a deal.

Before her emotions could get in the way, Tildy went to the telephone and dialed his office.

Dolly Varden answered. "Good afternoon, Seminole Star."

"I want to talk to Pete."

"I'm sorry, he's on another line. May I . . ."

"He gonna be in tomorrow? I'm coming to see him."

". . . ask who's calling?"

"Tildy Soileau. He knows me."

"Yes. The one who walked out on us." Dolly dropped her Southern accent for the hard nasality of her hometown. "You better not be looking for work, sister. We make it a policy not to involve ourselves with people like you. People who betray us and spit on our trust."

"Well, I didn't get a Christmas card from you either. Tell him I'll be there in the afternoon."

"Mr. Sparn will be quite busy all day tomorrow."

"Fine. Just tell him."

Tildy set out for Jacksonville at six the next morning, alone. Karl had instructions to phone Holstein and tell him she had some "personal business" to attend to. There were good reasons for excluding Karl from this trip. She was embarking on an expedition that was perilous enough; she'd need all her warning systems and couldn't afford to keep one eye on him. But the road was white and peaceful in the morning sun and when she stopped outside of Hoppachula for a new radiator hose, the old man gave it to her for nothing because she reminded him of his daughter who'd moved to Oregon. She made excellent time, had succulent fried catfish for lunch and actually arrived in Jacksonville with a tinge of confidence.

The Seminole Star office was frigid, air conditioners running at maximum output. The sweat on Tildy's face and neck dried instantly, drawing her skin tight. Roosting behind an enormous desk, Dolly Varden suggested she come back later, Pete was tied up in a meeting. Tildy sat down with an old copy of *Boxoffice* magazine and tried to listen through the door. A woman's husky voice: ". . . and in 1975 I was named Miss Inland Waterways." Staring with tight, fierce eyes, Dolly turned her radio up loud and that was that.

Four songs and a news broadcast later, the woman emerged clutching a stack of 8x10 glossies. She was an unbewildering Sparn selection in red boots and smoky glasses, her nosecone breasts jutting against a rayon shirt. Pete, gliding close behind her, whirled when he saw Tildy, and then smirked, folding his arms.

"You look like hell, kid. Been up all night?" Then, "Leave your pictures, honey. Dolly, coffee please." He took Tildy by the hand

221

and led her into his office; the furniture had been reupholstered in beige velour. "So tell me what you think of Crystal. Scrumptious, huh?"

"If you say so."

"Crystal's a dancer and a cake popper. You know, bachelor parties, birthdays, conventions. A real piece of talent. Tells me she gets so turned on to an audience when she works that she actually comes."

"An act you can book with pride."

Pete sank into his swivel chair, picked up one of the plastic puzzles he liked to fool with when talking on the phone. "You got a world of nerve, I'll give you that. Went AWOL on me in the middle of a tour, attacked my son when he came to straighten things out and nearly jeopardized his ability to have children, and yet you can blow in here without an appointment and crack wise about a girl who's got twice your sex appeal. You do have a strong supply of nerve, I surely will stipulate to that."

"Thanks, Pete, even though you didn't intend a compliment." She kept her eyes off his, tore dead skin from her lower lip. "I was hoping we could stay off the past and concentrate on business. I don't want to waste your valuable time."

She placed the round package she'd brought atop his IN basket.

"So what's this, a bomb?"

"You could say that."

Dolly came in with mugs on a tray and from her expression, she'd put rat poison in one of them. She threw down some packets of nondairy whitener and said, "You've got a three o'clock with that new candy salesman."

"The one who wanted me to put granola health bars into all my drive-ins? Fuck him. He can wait."

Outside, Dolly slammed drawers and spun the dial on her radio.

Sparn held the package to his ear. "Anyway, it's not ticking." Tinny thumps when he shook it.

"Take a look inside, Pete. Something pretty."

He cut the twine with scissors, separated petals of brown paper, lifted out a rusted coffee can. "You sure this won't go off in my face?"

"Promise."

Slowly, he prized off the lid; inside was a nest of glinting shellfish, antique watches all of gold. He showed her his poker face, bent over the desk blotter to study a diamond chip monogram, a carved hunting scene, ruby numerals and enameled hands.

"Lovely. People had more time for time in the old days." Sparn pulled a whiskey bottle out of a bottom drawer. "I like my coffee with a stick in it. Join me?"

Tildy shook her head and pushed the words out. "I want to fence them, Pete. Do you know anybody?"

He smiled lewdly at her and stroked his necktie. "Where'd you get them?"

"Let's say they were a gift from a friend, an old man who thinks he has a crush on me."

"Hell of a gift, he must dream about you every night. Just how old is this old fool?"

"I don't know. In his seventies I suppose."

Sparn sipped from the bottle before pouring a shot into his mug. "You got some strange birds down there in Gibtown, no doubt about it. Whole town's kinky when you come right down to it, but I guess you've gotten used to that by now. Some strange birds, though. . . . Just recently I was reading about this ole boy, Les Clines, did for himself right there in the hoosegow. Heard about it?"

"I seem to remember something."

"Yeah, that Lester was quite an item. He ran with the carnies for years, but thieving was always his first profession. Had his own mob for a time, the fox, and did real well according to some of the old timers. There was a big beast of a roustabout named Thunder who supplied the muscle, and the Diropolous brothers had the finesse. They were safecracking Siamese twins and real artists. Never once blew a box open, so it's told. But Clines, he was the brains of the operation and picked all the marks. No better place to read people than at the fairgrounds, but I don't have to tell you that, do I? See, he used to work one of those guess-your-age-and-occupation gimmicks and he'd find out all sorts of interesting things about the town doctor and the local lawyer and so on. Les was scrupulous. He kept all his info in a card file and then they'd hit these people on getaway night, just as quiet as a summer breeze. This was years ago but . . . Am I boring you?"

Tildy felt a rubber ball bouncing in her stomach. "Not at all, Pete. The taller the tale, the better I like it."

Sparn poured himself another shot. "To departed friends and colleagues," knocking it back in one go. "Funny thing about all this . . . Well, must have been three, four years ago I heard that Thunder passed. Working on his car when it slipped off the jack and crushed him. Now the Diropolous brothers, they were down in Sarasota. Worked in a supermarket. One was a cashier and the other one bagged the groceries. I'm on the phone with a client of mine down there and he happens to mention in passing how both of them drowned in the bathtub. Probably fighting over the soap or something. Real sad. Now here's old Lester with his name in the paper, he's checked himself out, and that's all four. Kind of ties it up with ribbon, if you see what I mean."

"I'm fascinated, Pete, but I'm also on a schedule. So . . . "

"I know, I know. I'm really an old cornball, yammering away about those old guys. But, man, they used to tell some stories. Late-night stories when you'd have that glow on, just a round or two short of toppling off the barstool. They'd talk about all the yummies Lester was supposed to have put in the ground and how one day we'd have to put our heads together and go looking for them. Saw in the paper where they found a block of ice at his place turned out to be Mrs. Clines. Wonder what else they might have dug up around there."

"If it was anything interesting," Tildy said with a kind of paralyzed composure, "they've certainly been quiet about it." Her mouth was very dry, but she wouldn't touch that coffee. "But those watches, beautiful as they are, I need to turn them over. You can help me if you want to. Will you help me or not?"

"Sure, kid. I can call around, talk to some guys. I'm willing to forgive and forget so long as everything's on the table. I have this thing about secrets, it's almost like an allergy with me."

"I'm not keeping any. Guy's a little weird for me, I need ready cash, you're a man who can do favors. Pretty basic. No secrets."

"I'm so glad. Help is much easier to give when I feel comfortable. . . . And about that friend of yours. Think he might be good for some more gifts anytime soon?"

"Possibly." Tildy looked at her wrist where there was no watch and got up. She had to get out of here right away, before Sparn brought out the thumb screws. "Possibly."

"Let's stay in touch then, kid. If you've got a problem, any kind of problem, I'm always ready to talk."

She trembled in the elevator and stumbled in the lobby. Back to the heat in the street, where she felt stupid and girlish. This exploratory trip, contacting Sparn at all, had been a mistake—that was obvious as a neon sign. But it didn't have to be an enormous mistake, only a modest one. Despite his lumbering innuendo, Sparn had noth-

224

ing conclusive to go on, no way to make the connections definite. Still, he'd laid out those connections so readily that he must have been working from a script formulated in advance. Which meant what? Surely nothing good. Keen temptation notwithstanding, it was never wise to underestimate Sparn, particularly where money was involved. Maybe he'd even sent someone to follow her?

Driving home through thickening darkness, all Tildy saw were dim and scabby faces staring back at her from stoops and alleyways, the circuit bums who flocked to Jacksonville each year to wait out cold weather up north, men with corroded vision and the cowering instincts of dogs systematically abused. Tildy sat feebly in her car as shadows deepened, filled with the realization that she was as defenseless as they were. The more she told herself to stop thinking about probabilities, the more relentlessly her mind turned and turned on the knot of her troubles, making the same progress as a canvas drill bit. Facts were facts. Sparn had her in his crosshairs, Karl was a refugee in fantasyland, there was a trunkload of secret wampum to take care of, and everything teetered over her head. Tildy had the frantic wish of someone who had just lost fingers in an industrial accident: If I could only go back in time; back to before.

She knew exactly where she'd go, too. Back to a night not unlike this one, enclosed in a speeding car, but with the animal presence of Christo next to her on the first leg of that journey to New York that had been so alive with possibilities . . . Yes, Christo next to her. He'd know how to fence the jewelry, how to deal with Sparn and his ticklish suspicions, the whole squalid mess. This sort of thing wasn't merely in Christo's territory, it defined that territory. Amazed and sorry that she hadn't thought of this before, Tildy stopped at the next rest area and went to the telephone.

This had nothing to do with desire or nostalgia, she reminded herself, piling coins on the chewed-up yellow pages. You're only looking for guidance. There's no reason for the stiffness in your fingers. She got Pierce's number out of her handbag, threw in a bunch of quarters and shuffled her feet listening to the rings.

'Hi. I'm not here right now, but if you leave your name and number at the sound of the tone, I'll get back to you just as soon as I can."

Tildy left the receiver dangling and backed away.

Karl was waiting up for her. He took the sack of diner food from her hand and mashed her in his arms.

"Take it easy. I've only been gone since this morning."

"Yeah, but I had these bad feelin's once it got dark, could see pickin' up that phone and there'd be a cop or a doctor on the other end."

They tore into lukewarm hamburgers, dribbling ketchup and fat on the bedspread. Tildy ate so fast that she bit down on the inside of her cheek, a salty taste of blood seasoning the food.

"Gonna tell me what come off with Sparn or do I have to guess?"

"Nothing much. We talked about old times, what some of the girls were up to, stuff like that."

"You know I'm talkin' about the gold. What's that old turnip bleeder gonna do about it?"

Good question. His big lie-to-me eyes were looking at her across the bed. "Well, I don't expect he'll be much help. We'll be on our own. Independent, like it or not."

"That's a long way to go, and I ain't just talkin' Jacksonville and back, to come away with so little. You all right, baby? You look bone tired."

To fill him in would be the decent thing, let him hear what she'd heard in that cold room with the velour furniture. Sometimes decency served no purpose; dead echoes, an alarm shouted into a cavern miles long.

"You're right, I'm beat. But before I get in bed I'd like to wash this dirty trip off in the shower."

"Can I come with you?"

Waiting for something to happen, Tildy called in sick to work the next couple of days. It rained very hard the first night, exposing two separate leaks in the roof. Inexplicably, a tape-recorded lecture on estate planning was delivered to them in the mail. Karl jabbered incessantly about the set of drums he wanted to buy. Ondray Keyes fell off his bicycle and broke his wrist. But nothing happened.

When Tildy showed up at the Medi Quick on Friday morning, Holstein asked what she was doing there.

"I work here, Ray."

"Not anymore."

She turned and looked to the back of the store where he was pointing with his chin. DaVita was buttoning herself into the red and blue company smock. She had a lavender bruise on her face and her hair was much shorter.

"Hey, wow . . . This is very embarrassing and all. I came in looking for you a couple of times 'cause I wanted to talk and finally he asked me if . . . You gotta understand. Dennis cracked up the car and the kids were coming out of the bottom of their shoes and we been living on macaroni and lunch meat the last few weeks. I'm sorry, I'm real sorry."

"You two know each other?" Holstein was crushed.

Tildy's eyes pinned him. "Does the Pope shit in the woods? Sure, Ray, we were turning tricks together in high school." She tugged at her belt, extruded a sliver of tongue.

Holstein just stared with mouth open as if watching a hardcore loop.

DaVita, her mouth going white at the corners, lunged forward and grabbed Tildy's hands. "Don't, don't," she stage-whispered. "I know you must be sore and everything, but don't mess this up for me. Those kids, you just don't know. I can't deal them off like an old washing machine and Donnie's no good to us out in the street all day and they won't let me on the welfare and I *need* this job."

Tildy pulled free and for one small moment laid her palm on DaVita's bruised cheek. "You can have it. I don't want it."

DaVita looked amazedly at the hand that had just touched her. On its third finger was a fat emerald ring that Karl had put there during breakfast.

"That's so beautiful."

"This?" Tildy smiled thinly and turned. "I grow them from seeds."

Then she went up the street and drank herself into a thunderous high-noon headache.

14

Disappointment—sharp, precise and direct—is a good sign of native intelligence. After the humiliating failure of his one and only big-time move, Christo had to get back to basics. A man who doesn't know his limits is a man forever doomed to doing things the hard way.

Christo chose a doctor's name at random from the telephone listings, checking the address to determine which banks were in the neighborhood. He called the office and, posing as a patient, told the receptionist he'd just received a check for overpayment from the doctor and wanted to make sure it was correct. They had a very cheerful conversation. The receptionist was an effusive woman. Her father was the mayor of a town in Nebraska, but the stench of the feedlot had been too much for her; she was studying the guitar at night. Christo found out where the doctor banked.

He got a haircut, put on a Milbank topcoat, went to the bank and filled out a credit card application, using the doctor's name and estimating his income. These things were tiresomely mechanized, he understood, but would it be possible to pick up the card within twenty-four hours? He was leaving the following night for Bonn to attend an international symposium on childhood leukemia. Symposium in Bonn, the clerk repeated gratefully—it was the most unusual thing he'd heard all week. He promised to expedite matters.

Christo collected the card during the next day's lunchtime crush. Four hours later he was back on the road again.

He spent three days at a sedate hotel in Annapolis, stuffing himself with oysters and crabs from the Chesapeake Bay. In the bar one evening he became friendly with the parents of a first-year student at the naval academy; they'd come all the way from Hartford for a weekend visit. The boy was having trouble making the adjustment. His childhood stammer had returned. Christo was invited upstairs for a nightcap. Mom kicked off her heels and turned on the color teevee. Dad put on his lounging robe. Christo checked out of the hotel a bit later with Dad's Rolex and two hundred in cash from Mom's alligator bag.

Smooth as cream, nothing noticed until Dad awoke and fumbled around the nightstand for his watch. By the time he sat down tight-lipped and meek to be interviewed by the police, Christo was having a liquid breakfast in a place called the Clown Town Bar with an old hound from the *Racing Form* who'd just finished clocking morning workouts at the Shenandoah Downs racetrack across the street.

The clocker's name was Sanifer and he got pretty intimate after six apricot brandies. Friends? No such animal in this game, and he'd seen all there was to see since the tender age of nine when he held his first shank. But anyone who'd pick up the bar tab, a young desperado who could obviously use a boost in unfamiliar territory (here he grabbed Christo behind the neck and pinched)—with him, Bill Sanifer would share a good thing in the fifth.

"They been pulling this horse so hard he can barely straighten his neck out. . . . Just look here at his lines." Sanifer spread the *Form* out. "Dead last against these dogmeat claimers at Latonia. Same thing here at forty to one. And here's his last out, see where he breaks on top before the jock can get a wrap on him, then backs up to get beat thirty-six lengths. Yeah, they set this one up perfect and today they turn him loose. Go get cash for your car, kid, and bring it back here for the fifth. He'll run away and hide today."

Christo couldn't move his rental car, but sold the Rolex to a leather-suited man in the clubhouse who'd just hit the daily double. Mister Tuffy opened at 60–1 and plummeted to 18–1 within a few minutes. Great. Real shrewd to dump the money in right away. Soon every pinhead on the grounds could smell the feast and they ran right to it, shoving each other to get at the windows. Mister Tuffy closed out at 9–2.

The speedball that figured broke on the lead and ran clear for the first half mile with Tuffy laboring well back. He made a move on the inside, got boxed on the turn, swung wide as they came down the stretch, and finished an even fourth, the jockey doing everything with the whip but shove it up his ass. The kid looked terrified when he came back to the scales to weigh out. Someone had to take the blame; they'd probably take him behind the stable, grab both his legs and break him like a wishbone.

Christo found a crap game in the parking lot, got rid of his last remnants of cash. He felt fine and unencumbered as he drove north toward Pittsburgh. Who needed money when you had plastic? But he slept poorly that night, his dreams full of menace, the painfully frequent spells of wakefulness laden with reminders of his hashish fiasco, Tomas Ulrich's empty face floating like a joke balloon in the blackness of his motel room.

He dressed while it was still dark, drove more than a hundred angry miles and purposely ran out of gas. He let the air out of all four tires and started walking.

"I've been in again, man. Twice. Things have been rough."

"It's not easy to break away from those old tendencies, Milo. I know all about it."

"I'm trying to get on disability now, but they keep putting me off."

"So life is a shit sandwich and every day we take another bite, what else is new. But we'll sit around and talk and we'll both feel better, I guarantee."

"Listen, Jim, this is a real small place. I mean I'd love for you to stay and all . . ."

"I'll take care of everything, Milo, you're not listening. What's your shirt size?"

"I wear a sixteen collar."

"Sixteen collar, right. And how about that waist measurement?"

Christo left his duffel bag in the telephone booth. He bought three hundred dollars worth of clothes on the plastic at a ritzy men's store, and then panhandled carfare.

Milo, in his upper thirties now, had been a college student all of his adult life. He'd been working on a master's thesis in Slavic languages when he and Christo had roomed together at the Greene County Hospital. Milo had theosophical hallucinations. Saintly voices addressed him from his kitchen faucet. He denounced his faculty advisor as a sulfurous agent of Moloch, a devourer of children. In the spring of 1975, God sat down next to Milo in the balcony of a suburban movie house. He wore a crackling silver cape, His breath

230

smelled like lily of the valley, and He said, "Much too late, Milo. I've given up on you." A few hours later a woman called the police to say that there was a man outside howling and bashing his head on a mailbox. The doctors at Greene County would not allow Milo to read the Bible.

The apartment was small and shabby as promised. Everywhere there were votive candles.

"Really, I'm much better about that spiritual stuff," Milo said. "I just can't afford the utilities."

He was much heavier than he'd been on the ward, but it was the pale, suety look that tokened inactivity rather than improved conditions. With tiny movements in his eyes, he behaved like a dog waiting for its master to discover the turds on the carpet, cried a little when Christo opened boxes and peeled back the tissue paper.

"Things really have been awfully rough," Milo croaked, sliding his fingers over a sea-green turtleneck.

Christo put his arm lightly around him. "And they probably won't be getting better anytime soon. But like you always told us hardheads, if you can't get used to suffering you'll die before your time."

As a young man, Milo had planned to enter the seminary. He imagined eventually joining a monastic order situated in some remote locale, perhaps a Greek island, where he would spend quiet days meditating in the garden, illuminating manuscripts or polishing censers. He would live a peaceful, seamless life and acquire wisdom naturally, like white hairs. But Milo never went to the seminary and, speaking of this period now, was unable to cite any reason for his inertia.

"I don't even remember what happened. But I believe that this sense of noncompletion has been making me crazy ever since."

"Which doesn't leave you much room to operate." Christo lowered a full spoon into his coffee, watched sugar granules turn brown.

"What can one do?" Milo studied his reflection in the napkin dispenser. "Ambivalence is a disease. All Catholics have it."

Christo had other things bothering his mind, making his molars grind. So much for the cushioning distractions of Life on the Road. The Morocco thing just wouldn't leave him alone, or he it. Even Pierce, to his ample surprise, had advised him to forget it, to chalk it up to experience or kismet and move on. But this seemed beyond him, an infection he could not shake. The money was one thing, that he could stand to lose; but to lose—all right, yes—his honor to that simpering hippie fool was intolerable. Ulrich with all his snotty lectures on protocol and attitudes, his cushy villa on the water and wife on the make, had simply hung him out to dry.

"Hey, Milo, do you believe in a just God?"

"I'm trying not to believe in any of that crap anymore. So don't get me all dizzy on that metaphysical ether. It's cruel, man, like giving a reformed alcoholic a fifth of Scotch on his birthday."

"Sure, understood. What I mean is, do you think things balance out in the end? Take care of themselves?"

Milo flicked his paper-napkin bird off the end of the table; it nosedived to the floor. "Me either, comrade. Me either."

Helpless and unshaped as Milo was, he had, if only by example, helped Christo to reach a decision. Unfinished business could finish you. Christo didn't want to grope through summer and fall plagued by that "sense of noncompletion." He'd make the return trip to Tangier and prove himself. He would see the stalled process through to its orderly end.

Destructively cerebral as Milo was, he had helped Christo to give revenge a fancy name.

"What things would you like to have?"

Milo looked startled. "Should I say peace on earth? An end to hunger? Why are you quizzing me this way?"

"No, no. Things. Household objects, appliances."

"Things, yes. Well . . . I think it would be healthy for me to have a radio to keep the silence away. And for my body, I don't know. Barbells? Or maybe a juicer so I could be sure and get my daily vitamins."

"Now you're talking. We'll stop at a department store on the way to the train station."

"Faust." Milo shook his head. "This is reminding me of Faust."

A passport, fresh underwear, pills and a pint of brandy (preventive medicine)—the needs of a traveling man are few. The New York weather was clear and calm, perfect for takeoffs, and Christo (a.k.a. Arno Bester) was eager to go.

"Mission improbable," Pierce observed, making a grudging withdrawal from the petty cash drawer in his office. "A waste of time and energy like this puts my back up. It must be my New England heritage."

"Fuck you and your heritage, too. This whole damn swindle may be a tax write-off to you, but it's what my life is all about."

"That's your heritage, your conditioning. Same difference."

"What does this have to do with growing up in half a dozen mining towns in Michigan and getting high before gym class?"

"It's not for me to say." Behind his impeccable desk, Pierce in blue blazer and tie looked ready to have his picture taken for *Business Week*. "But I hope you're not in over your head. I don't want to sound like an alarmist, but you might want to consider carrying some sort of weapon."

Christo tapped his cranium. "This has been good enough so far."

"Suit yourself. Just don't forget to take the safety off."

They had gimlets and changed the subject. Pierce had been shopping for a literary agent, with no luck up to this point.

"I want to do essays, social history, but nobody wants essays now. It's a dead form, like chamber music or the sonnet."

"Social history, huh? Right, you figure you can peddle your theories like you've been peddling dope. To a grateful public. Jesus, and you think I'm crazy for wanting to regain my self-respect?"

"I'll match my delusions with yours any time, jazzbo."

"Best of luck."

"Same to you."

They drained their glasses and parted without another word.

Christo walked round and round a small park near Casa Nocturne wondering how he could have come this far without evolving a plan. He'd wasted all his time on the plane thinking of Tomas in various states of humiliation; a series of disconnected images, coherent maybe, but like a pornographic collage, too trivial and predictable to inspire the brain. He'd left himself only one choice then: the tactic of no tactics. The hell with timing, the hell with fine points and the integrity of the performance—he'd just have to go in there and get it done. Geronimo!

But if you don't simmer down, Christo warned himself, you're liable to fuck up all over again. He waited a few minutes, chewing grass and tilting his face to the sun, then jogged downhill to the house.

Inge answered the bell in a rumpled bathrobe. Her hair was pinned up and she smelled of sleep.

"I couldn't stay away."

"Tomas is not here now."

"So I'd hoped."

"You lost your job?"

233

"It's a long story."

She shrugged and motioned him in. "I don't try to understand things."

"That's the spirit, Inge. All men are liars. Old European proverb."

Inge smiled and played with the dangling ends of the sash that held her robe closed. She hovered at the foot of the stairs, apparently undecided as to where to go. Her pupils were little black nailheads. She pulled the robe around herself more tightly and retied the sash. It was easy to see there was nothing underneath it. The breasts from which the entire family had drunk sagged halfway down her torso. Christo liked that; that Inge's flesh should be as doughy as her self.

"I was sewing just now." And she went up the stairs, leaving damp spots on the banister which Christo slid over with his own hand as he followed.

"You're not afraid to be alone with me?" He brushed against her on the landing, drew knuckles over the soft knobs of her spine.

"You shouldn't ask me," she said indifferently, disappearing into a room down the hall, a cramped room with no windows.

Christo slithered through the open door, enjoying this game. Ironing board, sewing machine, bolts of fabric and cardboard boxes piled high—Inge's little playroom. She picked up a long piece of orange velvet.

"I am just starting this. A vest for Tomas."

"Nice color," Christo said dryly. "Go ahead and work if you want. I won't mind watching."

She sighed. "No, I am interrupted now." Laying the velvet across the ironing board, she smoothed it with her hands, picked off lint and bits of thread that weren't there.

"You could show me the other rooms."

"To see what?"

For a long minute they observed one another across an invisible frontier, Inge breathing through her mouth, fingers at rest now on the cloth and slightly curled. He noticed a brown speck on her upper lip, a crumb of food possibly, and this one compromising of her laundered paleness made his belly tighten. Her hands slid down the velvet, dropped at her sides. Otherwise, she was still as a mannequin and her eyes would not respond, not with scorn, desire, anticipation. She was like an ornament, a woman about whom other women would whisper.

234

"I can do you," Christo said.

He crossed the frontier in two strides and came at her from the side. He pushed the loose hair back behind her ear, and his hand continued down the side of her neck, over her shoulder, followed the line of the collar down and down until he reached the knot, pulled it, and tore the robe open. Inge did not move, but made a noise like she'd been punched in the stomach. A warm draft rose from between her legs, a flowering scent of coastal mud. He jerked the robe off her shoulders, away from her arms, and except for a pair of heavy socks, she was all white radiating skin.

Christo flicked that brown crumb away and, holding her behind the neck, very slowly explored the inside of her mouth with his fingers, gum ridges, slippery linings of lip and cheek; pushed deeper, pressed on the back of her tongue so that she gagged. But even this did not unlock her passivity.

He pulled her down the hall and into the bedroom—bare white walls, a narrow strip of sun. The bed was carefully made and littered with round pillows. Christo swept them to the floor, ripped off the covers, threw Inge onto her back. Her eyes were alive now; her hips dimpled in tempo as she flexed pelvic muscles.

"Take off your socks."

"My feet are cold."

"Yeah, I remember."

He pulled her by the ankles to the edge of the bed and knelt to the salt lick, went at her roughly with teeth unshielded. Urging him deeper, she tugged at his ears, gurgled. Christo stood up and got out of his clothes. Inge was the dream of an after-midnight Weimar cabaret as she followed his snapped commands, clambering onto her knees, pulling her buttocks apart, anointing herself with her own saliva. He came to her with his erection swinging in front of him like a piece of industrial machinery. He told her he was a thief, spoke her name like a curse, fit himself to the slick, reddened knot, paused—a tense, drawn-out moment of threat with a loaded weapon—and drove to the neck of her uterus in one stroke. It was over almost instantly.

"You are a monster." Inge touched herself gingerly. "You make me burn there."

Christo lit a cigarette and walked out of the room. So far, so good, but it was only the beginning. He roamed through the house breaking lightbulbs and emptying drawers onto the floor. In the kitchen he smeared the walls with raw eggs and ketchup, drank a leisurely beer while he watched the mural dribble and run. He took a bowl of fruit back upstairs with him and found Inge tightly curled in a facsimile of sleep. Removing one of her socks, he tickled experimentally and she smiled without opening her eyes. The shiny skin of her sole was delicately crackled like the bed of a dry lake.

Inge turned her head and sucked air. "It's so late. Tomas is coming home now."

"Don't speak."

"But it's true. He could come in any . . ."

"Shut up."

He bent her leg, forced it back and to the side, and she suckled obediently on her toes.

"You don't know your husband is a dope runner, do you?" Pressing down, jamming her mouth with foot, "Don't say anything, just hear what I tell you. The first time I came through here it was to put together a large-scale drug deal with your quiet little housepet man. Thought he'd cleaned himself up, didn't you? Well, he's dirtier than old diapers, sugar. He jobbed me, understand? Ripped me off for the whole motherfucking load so he could sell it off himself. That's a little bedtime story for you."

Christo released her and picked out a nectarine. Puffy lips quivering, head rolling from side to side Inge righted herself. He waited for sobs, for invective or the protest that he was lying, but none came. Grapes splattering on her clavicle got a reaction. She shrieked, clawed out as he leaped on her, smashed another handful between her breasts. Juice ran down and pooled on her belly. Inge slapped his head and he pitched over, caught himself, left a gruesome print on the sheet, murderous fingers outlined in purple. He twisted her hair and reached back for fresh supplies to slather on her neck. She bucked furiously in an effort to dislodge him, but he had a forearm across her throat, a knee in her crotch. Sputtering, pawing at his chest, she dug her heels into the mattress to gain leverage. Christo leaned in and spat an explosion of chewed grapes onto her face.

Inge went limp and her tongue wiggled out, pleading for suction. They rolled around the bed dripping syrup, locked in a reeking, soggy mating embrace as old as the dinosaur. Laughing uncontrollably, she cupped his balls and mounted him. Her pubic ridge blasted down on him, bone against bone, and she guided his hands to her behind.

His head at the foot of the bed, Christo had an inverted view of the white door as it swung open, of Tomas as he poked inside.

"What's happening in here?"

236

Her laughter rising an octave, Inge kept whacking away. She yelped a few Swedish words and Tomas answered back.

Then, smoothing his hair in back, "I'll be in the big room downstairs." He pulled the door shut with a subdued click.

Inge was corkscrewing her hips, whipping her head to and fro, but Christo, already going soft, pushed her away and slithered off the bed.

"I wanted him to find us, and that's all I wanted."

He showered off, dressed, and made his way downstairs. Lodged in a chair, Tomas was flipping through a magazine, casually brought his eyes up when he heard Christo's heels on the wood floor.

"So you're back." He tugged appraisingly at his beard.

"And you know why."

"Do I? I don't recall inviting you."

Up on his toes with weight not overcommitted, Christo inched forward anticipating a lunge. "But you fucking mugged me, ace. And when I cut into that empty car back in New York, I was invited to put my head between my knees and feel like a natural-born moron. See, I just can't let that kind of atrocious shit pass, no shot. Get up outta that chair."

"I know nothing," Tomas said flatly. "Once you drove away from my place, I finished with the whole business. What happens later is not my responsibility."

"You can't know how much I had invested in that deal, but you're about to make good on all of it. Be certain of that."

Tomas spoke with exaggerated patience. "I do not understand what problems you had with the shipment and I do not even care. An amateur in such business is a risk to everyone, but most of all to himself. Perhaps it was expensive to find this out. May I suggest that once you are home you find something else to do, something that suits you. Go to work in a factory. Pour drinks for the happy animals in a bar. Those are the ones who can be manipulated and bullied, not me."

Christo stood within striking distance now, and his hand gestures measured the space. "Ain't you blasé. That's some attitude, ace. You know I'm here to rumble, but you sit in that chair and shake hands with yourself. I spent the last two hours drilling your wife, but you don't care. You just sit there and take it."

"If Inge was able to find some pleasure in it, then I agree."

No more stalling. Christo ripped the magazine out of Tomas's hands. "Come on, ace. Let's get down."

"You think you are in the movies?"

Christo rammed the chair, tipped Tomas onto the floor and stepped back, making room. "Come at me," he demanded.

Tomas adjusted himself and sat calmly, treating this as some unfortunate psychodrama. "You see, the things that impress my wife have no effect on me. I won't fight."

There was an empty wine bottle on the table. Christo smashed it against the edge, waved the sawtooth neck. "Fucked her and I'll fuck you, too."

Tomas retreated through sliding glass doors to the patio. "I give you one last chance to go." He thought of simpler, better times when he'd never been without a gun.

"I'm not going and neither are you." Christo stepped into the heat of the patio and slid the door shut, sealing them off. "Unless you can fly."

"I won't fight," Tomas repeated.

Christo feinted once with the bottleneck, then put all he had behind a left hook to the viscera. A tinkling of glass and Christo held out his empty hands. "Even up, ace. You and me."

Tomas could barely see, but he kicked out, catching Christo on the shin, and came roaring off the tiles. Two simultaneous grunts as they collided, Tomas butting like a ram, Christo driving an elbow to his neck. They grappled and clinched like a pair of Apache dancers, bounced short punches off each other's ribs. Tomas pulled away, missed a looping right, and they collided again, dragging, swaying, buttons popping and cloth tearing as if they were trying to undress each other. Gathering himself for a finishing blitz, Christo let up a moment; sensing this, Tomas lurched in and pinched Christo's wrists under his arms, immobilizing his weaponry. Growling, red-faced, he sank his teeth into the meat of Christo's shoulder, snapped his head to one side and felt a spurt on his lips of coppery-tasting blood. Christo's howl bounced from rooftop to rooftop and he stomped on Tomas's instep; his head came up as Christo pulled an arm free, then popped a jab straight into that slim Nordic nose.

Tomas zigzagged away, hand cupped under his demolished nostrils, recognizing this first serious blow of the fight just as he received the second, a fast kick to the groin that doubled him over. Christo had time to gauge and fully design a swooping uppercut to the chin which landed with the sound of two boards slapped together. Tomas flew back against the railing, tipped, hung a moment in miraculous horizontal balance; in that millisecond's space a debate in Christo's mind (Should I let him go or try to catch him by the

238

heels?) was drowned out by vivid sensation: the texture of Tomas's suede moccasins as they slipped off his fingertips. Tomas dropped like a cliff diver onto the roadway below.

Christo turned to muffled pounding behind him. Her nude body splashed with purple, Inge stood riven and horror-struck, breasts pressed against the glass.

"Stay there." He knew a crowd was already forming around the corpse in the street, but he moved slowly, wanting to defuse her if possible. "Can you hear me? Stay where you are."

Not much time to take care of her; someone in a uniform would probably hit the scene in just a few minutes. Was this what experts had in mind when they warned about failures in long-range planning? Inge fell against him when he eased the door open. He felt the latent frenzy in her hard flesh.

"I'm sorry," he said ritually, a lie.

"What happened? Where is he?"

"It's done. You can't help now." He righted the overturned chair and guided her into it.

Inge quivered like an overworked lab animal as he plucked grape skins from her hair, humming softly.

Then she pushed his hands away. "No no . . . I've got to make it real," and darted past him.

"Trust me, you don't want to look." Inge flashed across the patio, arms out like wings. "Okay, do it your way, but I can't stick around."

He grabbed his jacket off the banister, moved coolly but briskly out the door and down the street. After another hundred yards he began to run. He ran away from the harbor as fast as his residual energies would allow, dodging through traffic, knocking over a man with a cane, stumbling uphill. Blood trickling down his arm seemed to spread the pain of his chewed shoulder.

Dread and exhaustion. Christo stood in the entranceway of a mosque, near the pile of shoes left behind by the faithful who had gone inside to pray. The wind that whistled through the open corridors and tumbled gutter rubbish was as cold as the deep blue aura that was starting to replace the shadows of afternoon.

The longer he waited, the greater his risk of arrest; but he was so tired, so disablingly tired. Inge had surely given the cops his description by now. No time to clean up, she'd be huddled in the kitchen with her strange warpainted face, telling all she knew to a man with a notebook. Thank God it wasn't much. Still, they would be waiting at the airport, checking the passenger lists. He had to get out of here, go find a cab. If it wasn't already too late, it soon would be. The chances were good that later on, in the depths of night, he'd be ringed by vulture faces in some tiny underground room with sweating walls, the shadow of a rubber hose across his face and a hot wire taped to his balls. Maybe. He didn't really care. The only things that mattered now were the pain that burned in his shoulder and the vindication that glowed in his heart.

He walked deliberately, keeping his eyes on the pavement.

All was serene when Christo finally reached the airport. He got the last seat on a flight to Madrid, where he'd have to make his own connections. The ticket agent wished him a pleasant journey. So did the man who passed him through the boarding area after a cursory glance at his passport. Ominous. On the plane, Christo sweated out an interminable and unexplained delay. He could not sneak a cigarette and risk drawing attention to himself. He could not read the safety pamphlet because the little stick figures depicted all seemed to be assuming postures of surrender. He could not look out the window because every blinking light he saw represented an oncoming police vehicle.

By the time the jet finally lifted off the runway, Christo was virtually paralyzed. It was at least fifteen minutes before he could bring himself to speak. He asked a stewardess for some aspirin and whiskey to wash them down.

What Christo did not know was that he had already provided for his own safety. His scorn and violence had propelled Inge into total regression; shortly before he boarded the plane, she confessed.

My husband was viciously drunk, she said. He abused me all afternoon, forced me to commit acts of unspeakable perversity. When he went downstairs to open another bottle, I followed. There was an argument on the patio. You know the rest.

The chief detective nodded, sucked on his mustache, gave Mrs. Ulrich his own handkerchief with which to mop her tears. An assistant passed him a note saying that the victim was on file as a dealer in contraband. He nodded again. From one point of view, the woman had provided a valuable service.

Inge understood the pressures that would come to bear. The expense of a trial. Press coverage. Perhaps there was a simpler solution? She was a very sick woman. She asked only to be returned to

Stockholm where she would put herself in the care of a certain physician who operated a private clinic on Lake Vattern.

The detective pretended to smile while removing a small black hair from the end of his tongue. Still, he had to admit the woman made a great deal of sense.

"Champagne and orange juice, as promised."

"Are we celebrating something?"

Pierce, who'd been at a gallery opening all afternoon and was half in the bag already, leaned across the table to tousle Christo's hair. "Why not? You evidently have walked away scot-free from a killing. Doesn't that call for champagne?"

"Why don't you say it a little louder so the guys in the kitchen can hear?"

"Relax, relax. We're all killers in here."

Christo looked all over the bar of the no-longer-posh Excelsior Hotel (where the ballroom was now a *prix fixe* Hungarian restaurant), but the only person he saw who looked at all capable of snuffing someone was a busboy with nail polish. "It wasn't like that anyway. Not the way you talk it. More personal, uglier. More human. Wish you could have been there. Made a great floor show."

"I should hope so. It cost me enough." Pierce had a nasty pitch to his voice. When tense, not sleeping well, insatiably bothered, he became a bad drunk.

"So which is worse? Losing all at once or little by little? And what are you sulking about? I had a damn sight more than money invested. That deal was supposed to be my shot to move up in the ratings, be a contender."

"So what, so what. No difference between a hit or a miss. The deals that work and the ones that blow up, it's all the same pointless, stupefying shit."

"Have another drink."

Pierce somberly, with one eye closed: "You may think I'm blowing wind, but I'm not."

"I think you're in a frame of mind to bitch, that's all. So bitch all you want. Go on ahead, it's your party."

"Things become obsolete . . ." Pierce faded into clicking teeth, rearranged orange pulp inside his glass. "Things become joyless."

"You should set this to music."

"What's your fucking problem?" Pierce slammed the table and the room went quiet. "I don't need all this condescending garbage from you today. Christ, treat people like they're all like you and everything's a spiel. So maybe Tomas Ulrich robbed you just for being so snotty, if you can get to that. Tommy can be that way."

"Not anymore," Christo mumbled, telling Pierce to cool it with a downward motion of hands.

"See . . ." Pierce grimaced, his train of thought rumbling unalterably along, "I have to change the attitude while I still can. It is possible to reach a point of no return, the terminal stage. And I'm beginning to show signs. I wonder if there's a bug planted in the bedpost. The Con Ed man in the lobby, I think he's really a narc taking notes on my every move. And the van parked outside is filming me with a zoom lens. I hear about a friend who's taken a bust and the first thing that occurs to me is, will he trade me for a lighter sentence? The whole scene just wears you down to nothing after a while. It feels like you've been ushering in a theater where the movie never changes."

"That's fine, very literate. But I've heard it before and that's the tip-off. When you're really ready, you'll stop talking about it. We both know the day's a long way off when you can let the business totally alone. There's no defeating that heritage, so why try?"

"But I mean it this time. I've got a boat coming in from Colombia in a week or so and it's finished after that. I'm out. Move on up to Connecticut and take the typewriter to bed with me."

Christo was laughing too hard to speak.

"You need a demonstration? I'll give you one." Pierce was furious, he threw some crumpled bills around, dragged Christo outside and threw him in a cab. Once inside the duplex, he sat Christo down in the office and began methodically taking it apart.

"I mean it this time."

He tore up the contents of file drawers, hammered his answering machine to bits with a marble paperweight, pulled the pharmaceutical bulletins down from the walls, the color photos of a Jamaican ganja field. He stormed through the equipment closet, laying waste rolls of plastic bags, boxes of gelatin capsules, tools for cutting and measuring. As a finale he filled a roasting pan with ten-dollar bills from his personal bank and threw in a match.

They watched smoke plume toward the ceiling and Christo said, "I'd be a lot more impressed if I thought it was only me you were trying to convince."

Pierce was exhausted. "There's no pleasing you," he grunted, and threw open a window. Smoke drifted out to the airshaft and swirled up.

242

"It just seems ludicrous to burn money." Christo pushed hair out of his eyes and sighed. "When you could give it to me instead."

"Is that it? You want me to keep the business alive so you won't lose a meal ticket, huh?"

"Maybe you are getting a little paranoid." Pulling fingers down the sides of the desk with the sadly resigned bearing of someone rowing to an island funeral: "I'm planning to quit this evil town within twenty-four hours."

"You didn't tell me that."

"I wasn't going to say anything. I was just going to do it."

"Well. That does alter the landscape some. Where to, jazzbo?"

"South."

"Just South. Back to that hit and run stuff, eh?"

"More or less."

"Why move backward where you've already been? I don't want to jinx you, but . . . "

"That's good. I don't want you to either."

"But don't you worry about falling into the grinder this time around? You're way overdue."

Christo rotated the desk chair, reached down and placed his hand over the edge of the roasting pan. "See that? I know how to burn my fingers. I'll be all right."

From the desk's bottom drawer Pierce removed a tape player, slapped in a cassette he'd been carrying in his pocket. "This came in yesterday's mail."

Looie's voice was harsh and excited: "*Start. Initial draft,* A Guide to Automotive Landscape Painting. *Introduction . . . The magic kinship of man and earth is at the core of all visual art. Period. In adapting this principle to a mechanized age, comma, the depiction of landscapes has become the province of photography. Period. But we are a species in constant motion, comma, madly covering ground in a world of blurred image formations, semicolon, thus there is no fixed moment in which the shutter can close.*

"*New paragraph . . . Imagine all elements in the heat of our motion. Period. Trees are made of butter. Period. Buildings are soft cakes. Period. Only the roadway is solid and continuous . . .* "

"Bloody maniac." Pierce hit the "fast-forward" button.

"I kind of like it so far."

"But he's like a kid who never learned to read. He doesn't know where the boundaries are. Wheeling along the Richmond Parkway, for Christ's sake, with a canvas tied to the dashboard and a brush in one hand . . . Just listen. It's coming up."

Looie again, over varying traffic sounds: "*At forty-five miles per hour I make my first stroke outlining the hills. Not the hills I am passing now, not the hills from two miles back or those two miles ahead, but all of them together. All motion/time images distilled to an essence of hills . . . Keep the wrist loose as you work, move the brush smoothly. As you grow used to these operations you will begin to see yourself as in a film, moving with grace and ease . . . Accelerating through a curve now, I mix a lighter shade of green . . .*"

It began with a single small cry, the bleat of a surprised sheep, then clustered thuds and clatters as the machine sheered off to become part of the landscape, a final implosion of metal meshing with itself.

Christo, standing now, leaned horrified over the speaker. "Did he make it?"

"Barely." Pierce extinguished and ejected the cassette. "He's off the critical list now, but there was a lot of internal bleeding and they still haven't assessed the damage completely."

"Have you seen him?"

"Nobody has. He won't allow visitors."

"The rites of spring . . . Jesus, this has been a bad year." Splaying his burned fingers, holding them away from his body like spoiled sausages, Christo made for the door. "We've got to get out of here."

"Yeah, let's move to the conference room upstairs. It's time for more drinks."

"You're not hearing me, man. I'll repeat it. We've got to get out of *here.*"

And Christo, with curved arms, made a gesture so wide that it seemed to encompass not just the city, but the hemisphere itself.

15

Among the Seminoles of south Florida there was respect for the rattlesnake, a respect based on fear; they believed that the soul of a dead snake would incite its brothers to take revenge on men. By the late 1970s, while there were places in Tampa that would pay four dollars apiece for dead rattlers in order to remove their poison sacs for research, fear (according to popular psychology experts) was a major obstacle to personal fulfillment. But some people began to find that just as they ceased to be frightened and their lives appeared to smooth out, they lost a kind of invisible protection: Events took on a monstrous finality and snowballed out of all control.

The air was so thick and heavy it felt like clothing, the kind of atmosphere that caused fruit to swell and sea worms to rise. Tildy, in a straw bonnet, made shallow grooves with her finger in a corner of the garden plot and planted cucumber seeds. Suspended between two trees in a canvas hammock he'd made himself, Karl leafed through a history of the Hispañola pirates, making notes in the margin with a pencil. A serene little scene, two dolls happily posed. When the telephone rang, it felt like a gunshot.

Tildy ran out from under her bonnet as she went to answer. Joby Daigle was calling from Ville Platte, too excited to bother with hello.

"Don't like to disturb a person out of the clear blue but here it's been so many months with the old place just standin' there all empty and sad when you drive by. There's that For Sale sign still up and it keeps prodding a spot in an old woman's brain. . . ."

"Mrs. Daigle? You're calling about my father's place?"

"That's it exactly, hon. See I met some new folks down here,

245

some of 'em your age, and they're real interested in what we call the healin' arts. We been talkin' about why not start up a clinic that would be for all the people, but where to put it with costs so high. It dawned on me there's Lucy's place, God bless him and keep him, so I got up my nerve to call you."

"You'd like to know my price?"

"Oh my, but you're makin' this so easy on me. I want you to know how hard we'd work to do it up as a fittin' memorial to Lucy. We been goin' out after the contributions to make you at least a little downpayment and there's a fella in town says he can draw up the legal papers. . . . "

"Fine. However you want to do it. Send whatever you like."

Tildy stood stiff for some time, metallic bubblings from the receiver that dangled against her skirt, before she hung up. From a rag-lined shoebox at the bottom of the closet she removed the bronze canister and held it to her ear. It made a sound like sand in a gourd when she shook it. God bless him and keep him.

The treasure trunk sat uselessly under the bed, not one mumbling word from Sparn on fencing the contents. A cruel kind of wealth that wouldn't buy a thing, another devil's prank on Karl. So this new windfall—however small—came just in time. Karl's teeth were bothering him and the Galaxie needed new brakes.

Out in the yard again, Tildy put her bonnet on, drawing it down over her eyes like a riverboat gambler's.

"Who was that?"

"A social call."

"Yeah?"

"An old lady who likes to talk about plants. No one you know."

She knelt in prickly grass and, using a souvenir soup spoon with a dolphin on the handle, worked her father's ashes into a part of the garden where she was planning to put some sweet peas in the not-too-distant future.

After dinner that night—T-bones fried in bacon fat, tomatoes stewed in milk—Tildy sat on the steps and watched the bats swoop as she smoked. Urgent music trickled out the door. Karl had something called *King Solomon's Mines* on the teevee, so wrapped up in it he'd barely touched his food. Tildy thought maybe she'd go to bed early, sleep late.

High beams came arcing past the front of the house, over the grass. She heard the sounds of engine afterrun, a low, cracked voice she knew she ought to recognize.

White sneakers, white slacks, then a white face. There was Flora Pepper grinning ardently, and M.J. right behind her with hair so short she looked like a recovering chemotherapy patient.

"Evening, ladies. Run out of gas?"

Flora kissed the top of Tildy's head. "Damn, but it's good to see you. Been too long. We been on a motor trip, M.J. and me. Left Dayton last month and been on the road ever since, just goofing around, seeing what's out there. But we figured before heading up to Jayville to get ready for the tour, we ought to come by and visit. Gonna be a long season without you."

"Got a college girl to take your place," M.J. growled. "Pete picked her up at a pinball tournament. Great reflexes, he says."

Flora kicked the ground. "You can substitute for someone like Tildy, but you don't ever replace her."

Nothing left but to invite them in. Karl waved incuriously and pulled in closer to the glowing screen. Tildy passed out beer and cleared debris off the sofa. A long time since she'd entertained. There were wives who did it all the time, had the neighbors in for ice cream with cordial poured over it, thought up conversational topics in advance. But she was flummoxed by her guests. Had they really come all this way just to chum around?

"So what the hell have you been doing with yourself?"

"Taking it easy, Flora. Just resting and digesting. Worked at a drugstore for a few months, that was okay."

"Looks like you're in great shape."

"I still do my pushups after breakfast, sometimes me and Karl throw a ball around, but that's about it."

"M.J. got me on weight training this winter. Put some more meat on my upper body, increased my leg strength; I ought to have ten percent more velocity this year. Mow 'em on down like crabgrass, won't I?"

"They won't even touch you, sugar. Our girls can just lay back and sunbathe."

Flora stroked her pitching arm. "All the same, I took some night classes at Dayton Community. Auto mechanics. I want something I can fall back on, you know? I'm on the down side of thirty and it's time to think practical."

"Don't let on to Pete," Tildy said. "He's got no show without you."

"He already knows. We renegotiated my contract and he's giving me an interest-free loan so I can buy my own garage. A garage with maybe a little store tacked on. Beer and fishing tackle and novelty key rings, that kind of thing. So what we been doing the last few weeks is scouting around for the right spot. Somewhere me and M.J. could live quiet, sit out in the sun by the pumps when it's not too busy, and watch the traffic go by."

"He agreed to all that? On paper?"

"We got a good understanding with Pete," M.J. said. "Just a matter of learning to speak his language."

"He still hasn't forgiven you for skipping out. He'd probably throw a tantrum if he knew we were here."

"For sure." M.J. went tap-tap-tap on her aluminum can.

Karl shouted, "They found them diamonds," and patted the teevee like a dog.

"Say, I could use a little something to nibble on. Pretzels maybe? Anything really to help soak up this beer. You know I've never been much of a drinker."

"I'll look, Flora."

Karl joined her in the kitchen during commercials. "What're those lezzies here for? You goin' back on the team?"

"Not in this lifetime. Just slice up the cheese for me, okay?"

"You shouldn't always keep me in the dark on what's what. Man and wife's supposed to hold each other up."

Pitcher and catcher were nuzzling on the sofa, exhaling sweet nothings back and forth. Karl cursed them under his breath.

Flora jumped up. "This is such a cute house. I'd love for you to show me around."

"What there is to see you've seen."

But Flora wanted to talk about color combinations and closet space, to peer behind the furniture for electrical sockets. Tildy hung at her heels, absorbing all this women's-page chat with an increasing sense of misdirection.

"I used to try and picture how it was, your place," Flora said confessionally. She seemed to be counting the plates in the drip rack. "I'm like that with people, trying to get a bead on them. I thought of something a little more, you know, funky. But this here is nice. Like one of those little cottages in the old songs."

Tildy doubted the profession of curiosity; on past evidence, Flora's interest remained within the usual star's boundaries. But none of this was bothering her exactly until they reentered the living room and she saw video images flickering on Karl's sulking face like firelight and felt one of those sad maternal pangs that kept her both with him and irritated at her own forebearance.

248

She swiveled around on Flora. "So how long were you planning to stay?"

"Only a day or so," M.J. said behind her. "We won't disrupt you."

"But we only have the one bed."

"Don't you worry none about that." M.J. came up off the sofa like someone had asked her to dance. "We'll sleep out in the car. The rear seat folds down and it's real comfy, so don't you give it a second thought."

Second thoughts? Always. Tildy looked at Flora, blinking repeatedly, at M.J. moving forward with her stolid catcher's waddle. She said, "Actually, we're a little busy with, with a project right now." And she thought: I'm overmatched again; another fishbone in the throat.

M.J.'s fingers, disfigured by a thousand foul tips, came to rest for a moment on Tildy's cheek. "We know how to entertain ourselves."

"Roadwork," Flora chimed in. "We do miles of it."

Karl, while pretending not to, listened with every nerve. On screen in front of him were the Technicolor plains of Africa, and Tildy thought of small creatures huddled in the tall, wavering grass, alert but still, and waiting out a passing menace.

Briskly, M.J. withdrew a toothbrush from the pocket of her shirt. "Now, if I could just borrow your sink."

Tildy said, "Oh. Sure. Of course."

Karl prodded her in heavy darkness, both hands scrubbing over her belly. Ripped away from a dream of snow and rifles, Tildy came quiveringly awake.

"Something inside," he hissed. "Can't you listen?"

"Stop." She pushed away his hands.

No missing the noise though; a steady thunk-thunk that seemed to flow across the floor and under the door like water. Tildy sucked in her breath. She felt surrounded by jelly, distanced from the thunking, the clicks of the cheap clock behind her on the sill, Karl's feet pushing and pushing.

"Baby. You got to go and see."

"Leave off."

She'd spoken sharply and whatever was out there had heard, went quiet now. Karl sat up, holding a pillow in front of him like a shield, but went no further.

"There, it's gone," Tildy said.

But the hush squeezed and squeezed like a tourniquet. It was the sensation of veins backing up, of tendons approaching rupture that made Tildy dash out and yank on the door. There came, in sequence, her own instinctive yowl, a metallic crash, one short syllable jerked out of Karl. Her hand slapped the light switch.

By the stove in a long raincoat, pots still rolling at her naked feet, Flora was transfixed.

"Dammit it to hell!"

"I didn't . . . Please. I needed a glass of water. An aspirin. I needed a glass of water for an aspirin. I was feeling my way."

"There's a hose outside."

"How could I know? I'm sorry. . . . "

"Here, have a glass." Tildy opened the refrigerator. "Have a carton of milk. Go on."

Flora looked grateful as a starving child, hugged the coat around herself and slunk away. Tildy watched from the front window. The domelight flashed on in the car and M.J. reared up in the sleeping bag, asking questions with her hands.

Tomorrow, Tildy promised herself. I'll get rid of them tomorrow.

But by morning, stupor had come in with the cloud cover. Maybe it would rain, maybe it would not. Things would have to take care of themselves.

"Honey?" Flora gestured with a toasted half of hot dog bun.

"Try jam."

"Where?"

"Cupboard."

Tildy was busy with a load of what they called shrimper's coffee in Ville Platte—coarse grounds boiled hard with salt, eggshells and a few drops of Tabasco. Karl slumped over the table, flirting with sleep. He did not look up when M.J. came in from calisthenics, coughing deeply.

"How about a beer?" she said.

"Go on then." Flora cranked open the window, tapped with her bun on the screen. "What's that little colored boy I see up the way?"

"They live here." Tildy was filling the cups now, holding the grounds in the pot with a big spoon. "You've got the milk in the car," she told Flora.

"Oh. Well."

"I'll sure have a fucking beer." Karl swung the refrigerator door into M.J.'s back, said, "Chicken-n-n-shit," when he didn't find what he wanted, stomped outside and flopped on his stomach in the grass.

"He's not usually so cranky," Tildy said.

"Men are very insecure these days." Flora looked at her coffee, black as swamp water, and tasted some on the end of her finger. "Mmm. Yeah, I'll get that milk."

Tildy lit a cigarette at the gas ring and singed her hair.

"You're wrecking yourself with those things," M.J. said after Flora left the room.

"Not me, just my lungs."

Alone, the two of them, and it felt prickly. Their eyes went all over the room, finally stopped, and the way they looked at one another was a little much for this hour of the day. Neighborhood rivals behind the stadium.

"So I don't get no beer, huh?"

"We can make a run later."

M.J. hefted her left breast like a machine part. "You ought to cut yourself loose from that beat-up hound," pointing outside with her chin. "He can't do you no good."

"Hidden qualities," Tildy said, moving her finger through warm grounds. "Below the surface."

"I'll just bet."

Flora came flapping in, milkless, with a hornet sting puffing up behind her wrist. She whimpered and swore, gyrated as M.J. attempted an exam.

"Watch it, watch it. That's my good hand."

"Don't baby it up."

Too much noise. Tildy opened the freezer. "Ice," she said, and drifted out to the yard where Karl was pulling grass like it was hair on his head. She knelt beside him, put a calming hand on his back.

"Nice day for weeding," she said.

"Mmm." Painstakingly, he tied a long green strand around her ring finger, clipped off the dangling ends with his thumbnail. "Too tight?"

"No, perfect. You have good taste in jewelry."

"I should open a store." He frowned and let go of her hand. "So what's all that moanin' I heard in there?"

"Nature taking its course. Pay no mind."

"Couple of sickos if you want my view, but go on back and babysit 'em if you want. Don't worry 'bout me, I'll just doze off in my hammock."

"It's not exactly what I want."

"Then you shouldn'ta invited 'em in the first place."

"I didn't."

"Shit." Karl pawed the air. "I naturally figured . . . They just showed up like strays you mean?"

"Strays." Tildy pondered that one. "Maybe not."

"Point is, you didn't ask 'em and that's a different-colored horse. I don't like their sniffin' around. Not one bit." He stood purposefully, mopped his face, made for the hammock. "What you should do is help 'em decide to clear off."

"I already had that idea. But today, I don't know, I can't seem to wake up."

Later on, though, Tildy roused herself to take the girls for a drive. She had mad notions of abandoning them out in the piney woods to starve away like a couple of unwanted puppies. Wheeling up the gravel road, past where mailboxes gave out, she saw their rag-wound apparitions ducking from tree to tree. A monotonous hissing in the air out here; earth that would soon disguise anything you dumped. But the endless chatter in the car drubbed her back to reality. A couple of plain Janes who wanted to run a gas station.

Tildy doubled back to R.C.'s; it was all delusion, another by-product of the day's stupor. Motion rather than action. Anyway, M.J. and Flora were no worse than reminders of past lapses, past injuries. Still, the vision of swallowing woods pursued her. She parked with a lurch and pressed her forehead to the steering wheel, taking shallow breaths. Flora asked if something was bothering her.

"Nothing new."

Inside the store, you could hear the coolers humming. No signs of life. But Tildy remembered seeing a car outside, an army surplus Jeep. She called out.

"Back here," a childlike voice came back.

She was clicking away with a price gun in the beverage section. Pleated brown wattles hung from her neck and pebbled growths ran down the flanks of her huge nose and across her cheekbones. Her chin seemed boneless, a slack bag like the dress she wore. She had frozen orange juice cans in her hair for curlers.

"Liddie." Tildy waved. "I'm just gonna grab a couple six-packs of Gatortail and leave them up front while I get my other stuff together."

"Call when you need me."

252

M.J. stole a backward look, spoke furtively, as though her teeth had locked. "You know that beast?"

"Lydia Estes," Tildy said at normal volume. "Used to be Rhino Girl at the Ripley's Believe It Or Not Museum in St. Pete. She's retired now."

"Yeah, right. There's a call I have to make." Flora retreated, fluffing her hair. "I'll meet you out by the booth."

Tildy grabbed a red plastic basket from the stack and started filling it at random with the first can or box her hand would fall on. Plums in heavy syrup. Instant spaghetti sauce.

"Here. We don't look to freeload." M.J. palmed her a greasy twenty. "I'll be outside."

Tildy nodded expressionlessly and picked up a carton of cigarettes for herself. They're afraid of Lydia, she thought; couldn't bear standing near her while she rang everything up. Flora wasn't really calling anyone.

But they were both coming out of the phone booth when Tildy looked through the window. And as she started the car, revved it to keep from stalling, backed out, there wasn't the slightest chatter from either one. Sunlight glared on the tin Bunny Bread sign over R.C.'s door.

Karl greeted them effusively in the driveway. "It's lookin' like a real party." He put the six-packs under his arm and walked ahead, pulling Tildy after him. He dug at her ribs. "Guess who's here."

"The chief of police."

"It's that Crisco guy took you off to New York last year."

Dizzying, the way things converged. Most of all she wanted to run, but where? No time to think or compose because there was that dark head erupting from a window. His gaze was sheepish and tender and she hated him for it.

"Say somethin'." Karl caught the grocery sack as it began to slide from her hands.

Christo pressed his palms together and made a deep bow as Tildy approached. Their faces swayed inches apart in tentative reconnaissance, and for a moment they were old friends, old lovers queasy with regret at a thing not done wrong, but hardly at all. It passed.

"Don't mess with a psychotic." She sighed. "You can't win."

"I missed you too."

"I never expected to see you again."

"And how do you like it so far?"

Tildy sensed the others looking on and half turned. "Well, I suppose the least I can do is give you lunch."

So she went in the kitchen and started making sandwiches as fast as she could. Simple, repetitive work was just the ticket. She was in no state to put things together and draw a conclusion from them.

That left Karl to make introductions and try to get his party off the ground. In being up to the task he was all by himself. Even physical positioning was awkward, furniture suddenly in everyone's way. The sizing-up was surly; no one came within handshake range. The women turned down repeated offers of beer and stood watching the floor like they were at a train station.

"So, Crisco, how's business? Been promoting anything lately?"

"You're confusing me with the shortening."

"How's that?"

"You're confusing me . . ."

"All the same, it's sure good to have another man around. I was gettin' to feel outnumbered."

"No problem. The cavalry's here."

Christo leaned to one side of the chair but Karl, determined to keep his attention by standing directly in front of him, blocked the view. Christo could only see Tildy's hands whirring over the mayonnaise jar and the stack of olive loaf. Another minute for her to arrange her mind and he was going in there, get a few things straight. The astonishing elation that came just from looking at her also forced him to admit what a gamble he'd taken in coming.

Karl searched desperately in his head for an ice-breaker, but came up empty and chose retreat. "I'll go on and see what's keepin' the eats."

Tildy had made close to a dozen sandwiches, but hadn't touched the head of lettuce in front of her. "Quiet out there," she said.

"They don't say nothin'. It's like a row of headstones."

"Take the food. At least they'll have something to do with their hands," Tildy said.

"What about you?"

"Go. I'll make coffee." Anything to stay hidden.

"Big help." Karl snapped his fingers. "All right then. Less you have any objection to make, I'm goin' out there, get myself sauced and fuck all the rest of it."

Fine, she thought. Just keep everyone eating and drinking and we'll get through this. Eventually someone will get fed up and leave. Maybe me.

"No appetite?"

That dark head again. Oh well, you've got to trust someone. "Too rattled," and Tildy kissed him quickly, found something to do at the sink.

"With you, I could never tell." Christo smiled encouragingly.

"Sure. Talk is cheap." But she smiled back. "Anyway, you have no reason to care. You're supposed to be in the fast cash and flying first class by now. I know, you came in a cab from Tampa. You're on your way to check on some overseas investments."

"I got news for you. I'm flat broke and on foot. The last few miles anyway."

"Damn you." The scarred white plate left her hand and broke against the faucet. She whirled on him. "If you came down here looking for assistance, you can fucking well get in line with the rest of us."

Christo didn't flinch, but he looked as deadpan as she could ever remember. "Believe me, I didn't scope it out that way. I only knew I had to move and move fast. I had that booby-trapped feeling, and unless I got going I'd be staring at another set of hospital walls. And maybe this time when they finally let me out it would be too late." He rolled his eyes back, let his tongue droop out. "Vegetable soup."

"You couldn't handle city life anymore, eh?"

"That's safe to say."

"And the big score you were planning, what happened to that?"

Christo waved it away. "Jinxed. The black cat had kittens."

"I'm sorry. But I don't have room for one more sad story."

Christo had let the moment escape. He wanted to confront their unfinished emotional business, wanted to let all the rest of it slide and talk about that elusive part of her he'd come chasing after. Then Flora poked her head in and asked to borrow some olive oil, she and M.J. were going to do some sunbathing.

"What a good idea," Tildy said cheerfully. "But it'll have to be margarine, that's all I have."

"Never mind. We'll risk a burn."

In her eagerness to get her former teammates out the door, Tildy practically pushed them through it.

"Maybe you'd like to join us," M.J. said provokingly.

"You go establish a beachhead and maybe later we'll all come along." And Tildy bustled her along with towels and pillows and a net bag of navel oranges.

Christo thought: God she looks divine, my little shortstop, but she can't keep me out of the hospital if I'm really ready to go.

Meddlers. Filthy deviates. Karl watched with disgust from the window as they stripped to their underwear, lay down on a checkerwork of towels right next to their car. He remembered with untinged delight emptying the box of grape Jello-O into the gas tank while they were out shopping with Tildy. Five or ten miles and that motor would seize up forever. He popped a fresh beer on that, saluting his genius.

"Want 'em out of here by dark." He belched. "You got to handle it. I'm gettin' sauced, remember?"

"Yes, dear," Tildy singsonged.

Then Christo pulled her aside and breathed into her ear, "There are enough kinky vibes floating around to choke a shrink. You ready to fill me in now?"

She nodded, turned to her husband. "We're going to have a little business meeting in the other room. It's for your benefit too, so just sit tight and go easy on the beer."

"Okay. But if I pass out, don't tie my shoelaces together."

Christo saw consolation just ahead as Tildy ushered him into the bedroom and closed the door.

"I wish there was a lock on it," she said.

His skin tightened like a drum head. "Risk always adds a little something," he said, reaching for her.

Tildy dodged away, crackling with annoyance. "If that's what you're expecting, forget it."

His fingers brushed lightly against her contracted face. "Haven't you been thinking about me since New York?"

"Not that way. No more than a couple of times." She turned away, leaned her sudden weight on the dresser like a seasick passenger at a ship's railing. "If you drifted down here looking to bolster yourself somehow, I'm sorry. It's the wrong time, I'm the wrong girl. The list goes on and on."

"A wishful misunderstanding then. No harm, no foul."

There was an odd delicacy about him now. And Tildy appreciated it, even if it meant he'd been pounded in the last few months, tenderized like a piece of veal.

"How is it for you when the booby trap goes off? Does gravity get stronger? Do you withdraw?"

256

"Sometimes. Sometimes I take all the drugs they'll give out and I'm just a cloud of vapor inside pyjamas."

"How do you feel right now?"

"Strong as an ox, but that could change."

"The weather's never right," Tildy lamented. "Why the hell couldn't you have shown up weeks ago when I really needed you?"

"I thought about it. I thought about you all along."

"So much for telepathy." Tildy went to her knees, lifted a flap of bedspread and reached underneath. "You want to be filled in? I'd love to." She tugged and scuffled until the trunk was clear and she could raise the lid. "But this is the only thing I'm sure about."

At first sight, the conglomerate sheen of nuggets and metal was like a cold draft on the eyes. Christo flinched and there wavered in his brain, if only for a moment, the urge for flight. Then envy took over, then apprehension. He stammered.

"Gorgeous. It's a . . . sweet Jesus . . . It's trouble."

"Pandora's box," Tildy said.

"And I'm not hallucinating?"

"I wish you were. That I could handle."

Christo took her hand and pulled her up. He stared into her flat eyes. "Who did you rob?"

The story she had to tell did not lend itself to synopsis and the deeper into it she got, the more blurred it became, the little men in Karl's dream as outlandish as the real-life characters. She lost her hold on the precise sequence of events. By the time she arrived at the collision in Sparn's office, the words were baffled and running together.

"Throttle back a minute. Your old boss, he figured out where this bonanza came from?"

"That's what I thought. But he hasn't contacted me, hasn't made a move since."

"Your dyke friends out there? How much do they know?"

"Maybe nothing. Maybe everything. That's what I mean. I can't handle it. Don't you see? It's too much weight for me to carry, far too much. Dammit, I'm just a stupid small-town housewife."

"And all you needed me for was my criminal expertise?"

Tildy instantly repented of any appeal she had let slip. "It's not your problem. You're free to disappear. Go on, I'm not asking you to stay."

He kicked the trunk lid shut. "You already did. The moment you showed me what was inside." Walk away from a score this size? he thought. Not a snowball's chance in hell. He pressed her reluctant head to his shoulder. "I may not be as sharp as Machiavelli, but you're no stupid housewife either."

In the face of her better judgement, Tildy softened against him, let her fingers walk across his upper lip. "What will we do?"

"I don't know yet. But at least I know what kind of stakes we're playing for."

Elsewhere, the afternoon was running out like a slow leak in a tire.

"Another Gatortail sets sail," Karl sang to himself.

He was deep in the suds, and suspicious. What could Tildy be doing in there all this time? It had taken him a while, but he'd narrowed down the possibilities. She had to be showing that big-town slick something he shouldn't see. Either the box under the bed or herself on top of it.

"Some kinda way for a man to be treated under his own roof," he called out.

The silence came back down like a trap and Karl had to ask himself the really thorny question: What is it makes me such a pussy? Why can't I kick that door in and pull my wife out by the hair?

He could only ask, not answer. It hadn't always been this way. Once he'd been a death defyer in a cherry red race car, and any woman who went behind his back got popped in the chops— But jackshit! A man of his young age shouldn't be playing "those were the days."

He tottered to the window. There were those bitches he'd asked Tildy to do something about, and they were playing cards in their bras and laughing.

"Hey. Hey." He rapped on the glass. They took no notice, so he flung the window up and dangled himself out. "Hey, you fatbags gotta take off now. You see there, it almost be night." He pointed to where the sun was like a damaged eye socket on the western horizon. "Put on your pants and take off. . . . I said it right. Put on, take off."

"Pipe the fuck down," M.J. responded.

Karl swung at the air, spilled beer down his arm. "Pull your bags over here and we'll see 'bout it."

"Break it up, brats." Tildy had come out to see about the noise.

"Your husband can't hold his liquor. Don't get salty with us about it." Flora, nonetheless, was getting into her pants.

Tildy, pulling Karl aside, yelled back, "I'm sober and as anxious to see you gone as he is."

"What took ya so long?" Karl tried kissing her, missed.

"I overslept," she told him.

"What's this attitude for?" Flora said.

"For peace and harmony."

"Your problem, girl, is you forget who your friends are." M.J. hoisted herself up, toed a pillow like it was something not quite dead. "You practice loyalty, and in the end you thrive. Go your own way and you won't have shit to show for it."

"An attitude problem," Flora agreed. "It all stems from that."

"No sermons. Just get going."

"You wrote the ticket, just remember that." M.J.'s head vanished inside a Cougarettes sweatshirt, then popped free again. "Straight along to clown town."

"I'm sorry it had to be this kind of job," Flora said, "but I want that garage."

"What kind of job?"

All Tildy got for an answer was M.J.'s upraised middle finger as Flora slapped her car into reverse, cut past the Galaxie to the black-top; and then all six splatting notes of the custom installed "Charge!" horn.

"Should be some purple exhaust 'bout now," Karl said.

Christo came up behind them with a tube of olive loaf seated cherootlike in his molars. "So what's the latest?"

"Finally run them bags offa the property, din't we?" Karl missed another kiss and fell heavily among the Gatortail empties.

Tildy pictured transiently a famous tattoo: Born to lose. She was dazed but cognizant. Sparn had sent those two for bloodhounds. They'd report back now, if they hadn't already with that phone call from R.C.'s.

"I think we're in the crosshairs," she said. "I think we ought to pack a bag and go."

"Could you translate that?" Christo said.

"Just think the worst and you'll be there." She helped Karl to his feet. "Come on, kiddo. Help me sort through the drawers."

"Awful sudden ain't it?" Tildy herded him backward. "We goin' on a trip, I'd like to know where."

"Tarpon fishing in the Keys? Would you like that?"

"Honeyboat, you know I would. I'll be a fish-killin' fool for you."

"Where does that leave me?" Christo said.

Where it left him was right by the window and in a position to understand just a few minutes later that there wasn't going to be any fishing trip. The clock had run out and the exits were closed.

"A large black car just drove up on the lawn," he said. "Guy in a cowboy hat and a beehive blonde. They seem to be checking the place out."

Tildy rushed to join him, the confirmation of dread in some strange way a relief. Vinnie Sparn wore the cowboy hat and striding regally under the dome of glazed hair was Dolly Varden. Sundown tints blushed the waxed surfaces of the limo as Big Pete stepped out, buffing his lips with a monogrammed handkerchief.

"Isn't that the bozo who tried to grab you at the hotel? The one in the hat?"

"Yes, yes." Tildy pulled away from him. "I'm going out there."

"What good is that going to do?"

"Whozzat?" Karl, who had put on a hat adorned with lures, moved uncertainly out of the shadows. "You leavin' without me?"

"Don't worry," Christo said. "Nobody's leaving."

Karl shuffled forward and peered out. "Is it bad?"

Pete had spotted them, waved his hanky. "Hello, young people. A lovely spot you have here."

Tildy froze with her hand on the knob. "Ten more minutes," she said hopelessly. "Ten more minutes and we could have been gone."

Karl's lips began to tremble. "It's bad, isn't it?" In one horrible mental leap, he'd understood what this was going to cost.

Then Pete nodded to Dolly, who began to read expressionlessly from her stenographer's notebook.

"Florida statute number seven one six point zero one: 'It is hereby declared to be the policy of the State, while protecting the owners thereof, to possess all unclaimed and abandoned money or property for the benefit of all the people of the State. This law shall be liberally construed to accomplish such a purpose.'"

Sparn looked skyward and opened his arms like a crooner. "I come here today as a representative of the people, one citizen standing for all. In this capacity, it is my intention to recover the abandoned property of one Lester Clines, deceased, on behalf of the general public. The liquid capital subsequently transferred to me will then be sent through the pipelines of my various commercial holdings to trickle down and irrigate the economic community at large. I love Florida. I believe there is no better living anywhere on this planet. I've had many good years here. Profitable years, years of growth and family closeness. Now, in my own small way, I would like to offer recompense."

Christo whistled softly. "Somebody throw a net over this guy."

"Go home, Pete," Tildy said from the doorway. "There's nothing for you here."

"I have different information. According to a call I received this morning from a trusted employee—one, I might add, who believes in the team concept—the Clines bequest may be found in a footlocker under your marriage bed."

All Tildy could think of was: Why in God's name didn't we take a vault at the bank?

Finally, because something was required, she said, "If it was only a question of money, I'd say come on in. But see? I'm locking the door."

"If you like. I'm a generous man and I haven't forgotten the good times we had. Ah, how I favored you. A waste. But I will allow you a last thirty minutes to enjoy your ill-gotten wealth before you hand it over to me. Starting now." Sparn gave a limp salute and turned to his boy. "Vinnie, you may set the table."

"Righto, Dad."

Vinnie seethed with resentment. Set the table, Vinnie. Change the tire, Vinnie. Orders me around like one of his greaser caddies at the club. Like I don't have feelings.

He began removing things from the trunk, remembering the trip down and Pete making him call the radio station that was having the Mother's Day Mom-A-Thon. For a pledge of fifteen dollars or more to Children's Leukemia Research, they read your message on the air. To Mrs. Helen S. with love and admiration. Right there in front of Dolly; Pete had even handed him the dime. What could he do? Righto, Dad.

Vinnie set up the folding chairs, the card table. He fluffed the linen cloth, laid out plates and silverware, cheese and fruit and cold cuts. He lit the tall white candles.

"A toast," Pete said as he filled three glasses. "To better things for all of Florida's sons and daughters. And for Les Clines and his boys, our hope that the heat's not too terrible down where they are."

"This wine should have been chilled," Dolly said.

The siege was on.

"So?" Tildy's cigarette was the only light in the room. "Sorry you came, I'll bet."

Christo reached across her and took a puff of his own. "To be a part of this little pageant I would have come twice as far."

"I believe you."

"So where do we stand with our half hour?"

"They're still dining out there. Maybe his watch stopped."

The refrigerator door was audible as it opened and closed, its rubber gasket unpeeling, slapping; then came the clatter of an ice tray being emptied.

"Karl, are you mixing drinks?"

"Probably not a bad idea," Christo said.

They saw moving past them a vague shape which, as it neared the front window, turned out to be Karl cradling a bowl of ice.

"Cocksuckin' Sparn. Eat ice."

Before they could stop him, Karl began flinging cubes at the enemy. Hard white knots bounced in the grass, burst against the limo fenders. One, traveling straight as a clothesline, knocked the fork from Dolly's hand, and Karl gave out a long falsetto war cry.

Vinnie pulled open his suede jacket. In the hand that dipped under his heart was an oily black lump.

"Get back," Christo roared. "He's got a piece."

Karl said, "I ain't afraid of no popgun cowboy. Whyn't you come a little bit closer?"

Vinnie aimed and squeezed off a round: exploding glass and a shriek from Karl as the slug buzzed over him and buried itself in the wall. The recoil threw Vinnie's arm upward and his second shot hit nothing but sky.

"When are you going to learn to use both hands?" his father said.

Refusing until now to let go of old putty, a final wedge of glass fell and the sound made Karl duck and cover. Christo dragged him up and threw him angrily against the wall.

"Want to get us all killed? This is no playground fight, you jar-head. It's dead serious and we're all in the line of fire. Now, can you grasp that or not?"

"Okay, so I'm a jerk. But I don't need you to tell me what's serious. Who you think dug up that treasure chest they all want so much? Karl D. Gables, that's right. And ain't nobody got cause to take it from me. I figured where to look and how, and with my own wife disbelievin' me, I made it pay off. So you're damn right it's serious. Just as serious as my life."

"Not mine." Tildy was curled on the floor, as far away from everything as she could get. "I don't want to die for a box of jewelry. Let's give in to him. I want to see the end of this, that's all."

"Let's not go overboard," Christo said. "Maybe he'll take half."

"Ain't yours to offer, neither one of you." Karl tried to find his wife's face in the dark. "Don't do this to me, baby. You know it ain't right."

"Karl, didn't anyone ever give you the story on being a grown-up?"

Out of the murk, her hand slapped his face. He felt weak all over and an awareness of disgrace filled his brain, made him forget where he was.

"You've got to learn to compromise," Tildy said. She went swiftly to the window and called Pete over. "Let's deal."

He moved languidly, examining his hands front and back for traces of food. "Marvelous. We'll settle it now, and then everyone can have a slice of Dolly's blackberry pie."

"We'll give you half, Pete. Free and clear."

"Give?" Sparn's voice jumped an octave. "You'll *give* me half?"

"Seems more than fair to me. In a just world, a claim jumper like you would be hanging by his neck from the nearest tree."

Shooting his heavily starched cuffs, Sparn clucked sadly. "I am here to retrieve the contents of Lester's trunk. All of it. There is simply nothing more to talk about. No bargains, no trades. You'll have it ready as soon as I finish my dessert, clear?"

A nerveless fixity. A thick black line drawn flat across the air. Three sets of lungs worked in rhythm and three pairs of eyes kept closed. Man and wife and suitor sat in a row on the sofa like end-stage crackpots in the lobby of a welfare hotel, loitering without sentiment at the scene of their own ruin.

An auto horn fanfare, then Pete bellowing through cupped hands. "This is your last chance to cooperate. If you don't come out voluntarily, we'll have to force you out."

Tildy whispered, "He means it."

"Fuck him." Christo breathed deep. "We handled his Vinnie Winnie before, we can do it again."

"Absolutely the last call." Pete waited. "It's your choice then. I've done my best."

The green bottle in Vinnie's hand was filled with kerosene. He thumbed the wheel of his lighter, the rag wick flared and he started to run. Christo saw the orange streak first, screamed, and the others were already scrambling away as Vinnie hurled the firebomb. Flames spread across the floor and up the wall. As Christo retreated, one leg of his jeans caught. He dropped and rolled, smothering the burning denim with his hands.

"Got to contain it in this room." Christo sprang up, coughing. "Turn shower on. Soak down. Blankets, towels too. Go. Run."

With augmented strength from spurting adrenaline, he pulled furniture away from the front of the room where the blaze was worst. Heat was something alive on his skin and wanted to squeeze the breath out of him. Then Tildy was beside him with a wet towel in either hand, beating at a diagonal line of flame trying to skid behind their defenses. Ashes swirled in the air, all that was left of the curtains. Karl emerged from the haze with soaked shirts and a wastebasket of water.

"More, more. Fill pots, whatever you can find."

"I can't breathe," Tildy cried.

"Keep on. Push it back."

"Too fast. Coming too fast."

Christo flailed like a mad dervish at the oncoming wedge of flames. He was half blind and pain spread over his hands. They were losing ground. He knew very soon it would be time to run. Cold water exploding on his back and, through a chink in the smoke, Karl waving his arms.

"Found a piece of hose. Hook it to the sink, it might reach."

"Let's do it. Our only shot."

Karl jammed one end of the hose up inside the running faucet and made a seal of encircling fingers. Christo took the other end as far as it would go, had to press his thumb over the threaded socket and arc the spray to make it reach. But it did reach. Already the smoke was thinning. Tildy screamed his name.

"Over here. I'm over here."

She zigzagged in trying to follow his voice, finally tumbled at his feet, her black face twisted with retching. No time to soothe. Christo got her upright, gave her the hose, told her to keep it moving from side to side. Then he filled soup pots from the toilet and ran them to trouble zones; back and forth, his hands throbbing, back and forth, tripping and spilling, throat constricted, until he collapsed. Tildy aimed the hose at him and he wanted to swim up the stream, curl inside the tubing and sleep for days.

They'd done it. The fire was dead and gone, leaving only soot and blisters and nausea. But it had sucked their reservoirs dry, exhausted their resistance. Hearts ping-ponging, they lay on the wet floor awaiting the inevitable. This engorged playlet, delirious with its own simplicities of greed and power, would have its third act climax all over them.

On the other side of the charred wall, Pete Sparn swallowed a little brown hypertension pill and wondered aloud.

"It never crossed your mind to cut their power line so the water pump wouldn't function? It never crossed your mind to simply crash in through the back and get what we came for? I'm discouraged, Vincent. I consider all the time and care, everything I've invested, to produce the blundering simp standing before me and I'm deeply discouraged."

Snapping the spring clip into his weapon, Vinnie said, "I'm going to take care of it, Dad. I'm going to take care of it right now."

"Not that way. We've had enough fireworks for one night."

"Please. Let me show you what I can do."

"Unfortunately, you already have. And on the dubious assumption that you could carry the operation off, three dead bodies add up to a complication I don't need."

"Think about it, Dad. Who's going to give a rusty fuck for these zeros?"

"A corpse is a corpse and each one has to be accounted for," Sparn said wearily. "As usual you fail to use basic management principles in attacking the problem. No, I'm going to have to solve this one myself."

"I'm not letting you go in there solo."

"Just wait in the car, Son. Dolly needs the company."

Sparn would have knocked on the door, but it was giving off faint wisps of smoke and he was afraid he might burn himself.

"Aloha, young people. Your tenacity does you credit. All the same, this has turned into too long a night for my taste. Let's put a final period on it."

"Go on," Tildy rasped, knowing in her innards that they couldn't beat him. "Let the bastard in."

Christo limped to the door. "Come ahead, bossman. I've been wanting to get a whiff of you up close."

"Who are you?"

"Just a friend of the family."

"And where do you stand in all this?"

"Probably in your way. Come on, the kitchen's still basically intact."

Sparn picked his way through rubble, resigning himself to the defacement of his white loafers, and breathed with the PS handkerchief over his mouth. The sight of Karl and Tildy propped against one another startled him. Their unearthly zombie eyes. A nervous edge came on him.

"Glad you could make it, Pete," she said. "You'll have to excuse the mess."

"Yeah, too bad about that." With his back flush against the drainboard, he edged along to where he could keep an eye on all three of them. "But we can still resolve this without serious injury. How does that sound?"

"Preferable," Tildy said.

"You see how it is. We're all very tired and we can't stand the sight of each other. Be smart. Give me the fucking goods and we'll say goodbye forever."

"Just curious," Christo said. "You ever done time?"

"I'm a businessman. We don't do time. We smash it like the atom."

"Everything comes easy for you," Christo said. "It's not healthy."

Karl was trying hard not to listen. He filled his mind with pinups of fish. Grouper, scup, bonito, yellowtail; all arrested in midthrash, fins stretched and gills open. He felt his wife's flesh against him like the resistance of water and wished only to go deeper.

Sparn shifted from foot to foot, confident of his machinery, but wary. These people were crazy, unconditioned by basic management principles.

"Through that door, hmmm? Must be. I don't suppose I can lift it all by myself."

"Not quite."

Christo reached to take hold of him, but Sparn pulled away with considerable agility for such a round man. He clutched at the air like someone searching for a light switch in a dark room."

"Have a go, homeboy. I wouldn't mind."

Tildy let her eyes go gradually closed, popped them open again. "You men just won't stop chewing. You leave your teeth marks everywhere. I've had enough. My house is still standing, my husband is still lucid, my heart is still available and that's enough." She tugged on Christo with her eyes. "I know what I'm doing. Give him a hand."

266

Christo winced and blew air. "If you're sure."

He and Sparn went at the job without a word or look. They took narrow, sideways steps and had cleared the doorway when Sparn, with a slight alteration of balance, indicated they should set the cargo down. His mouth fell open and he made anticipatory tweeting noises as he fumbled with the lid.

"That crazy Lester."

Hands on knees, he leaned down for a closer look.

Into Tildy's blank mind, like napalm into a deserted village, there came an inspiration. It took hold of her and she took hold of it. She whipped off her belt and with the lightning first step that had stolen a thousand bases, reached Sparn before he had even registered the flash of movement. She twisted the belt around his neck and jerked back. He toppled, clawing at her, but Tildy maintained purchase, climbing onto his wide chest and twisting the belt again. Sparn began to go red; his eyes rolled. Stretching, Tildy crossed her shin over his throat and dropped all her weight. His larynx broke with a gelatinous crack. His legs twitched and the front of his pants slowly darkened.

"Stop. He's done." Christo had to lift her away.

"He would have killed us all," she said. "Eventually."

Karl stepped over the body as if it were a ditch and plunged both hands into his precious stones. "You had to be strong. I just knew it."

She tipped against him, pressed her cheek under his shoulder blade and just breathed.

Watching, Christo thought: She was protecting him, that's what it was really all about.

"Savor the win," he said. "I'll take it from here."

Fireman's carry, that was the answer. Christo's legs shook as he stood under the weight. He steadied himself, took a few experimental steps. Dead feet bounced behind his thigh.

"What are you doing?" Tildy said.

"Going to dump him. I want them to see."

"Vinnie. He'll shoot."

"I don't think so. Anyway, he can't hit the side of a barn."

Watching, Tildy thought: He's trying to impress me. How can I love a man who's as transparent as all the rest?

Swaying into the white flare of headlights, Christo dropped his burden and stepped back. Not bullets, but Dolly who came exploding out of the car, dove across her unreachable love, kissed his swollen mouth.

"I'm with you. I'm with you." She wept.

Vinnie advanced in shock motion, pausing between each step. Then, before he came too close, he stood as quiet and still as a snowman. Christo took the gun from his hand and threw it into the woods.

"I'll see you buried," Dolly hissed. Her face was all bone. "You killed the man, but not his power. That's mine now."

There was a quivering balloon of saliva on Vinnie's lip. He did not respond when Dolly asked him to help carry his father to the car. She had to do that on her own, dragging him by the heels in fits and starts, boosting and butting him onto the rear seat. Beehive lopsided and wobbling, she came back to take Vinnie by the elbow.

And just before she got behind the wheel, Dolly pointed with a trembling finger. "Whatever it takes, I'll see you buried. All of you. As Jesus Christ is my witness."

The limo fishtailed away, knocking over the card table and the remnants of dinner.

Christo stayed for a few minutes, listening to the night and feeling himself charge up for another, unexpected run.

He found Tildy and Karl puttering randomly in their fried living room. "Whatever you're thinking, we've got to get out of here now."

"Right, the Keys," Karl said eagerly. "I'll show you how to land the big ones."

"Not far enough," Christo said. "Let's see if I have a better idea."

He made a long-distance call.

"Jazzbo. I wasn't expecting to hear from you this soon."

"I'm all jammed up. Need to get out of the country. That shipment you were talking about, it's still on?"

They put on clean, dry clothes, took nothing but Karl's trunk and a thermos of screwdrivers out to the Galaxie. Christo tapped the face of the gas gauge, adjusted the mirrors.

"With any luck, we'll be meeting a boat in Cape May, New Jersey."

Further on, at a lonely crossroads under a canopy of pines, they passed a disabled vehicle with its hood yawning. Seated on a flat rock just beyond were Flora Pepper, the Submarine Queen pitching machine, and her Polish lover.

But there was no moon at all and nobody recognized anybody.

EPILOGUE

Go on, high ship, since now, upon the shore
The snake has shed its skin upon the floor
—*Wallace Stevens*, Farewell to Florida

A slender bird drops from a balsa tree and its belly is the same pale cloudy green as the river over which it swoops. A languorous river. A wide undulating stripe of water walled in by forest. This is dense and boundless forest, a thick vegetable custard poured over the land. Smooth trunks rise twenty and thirty feet, then spread decisively, foliage entwining to make a second sky. Light comes through slits in the canopy, slides down vines that spiral around each other like living cable, into the feathery arms of ferns on whose broad blades tiny mosses live—parasite on parasite on parasite—and finally strikes the spongy floor, heating the soup that nourishes vast root systems below. Sad, damp smells hover here like flies. There is a weak but steady hum as of concealed machinery, some remote device that irradiates this endless spectrum of greens.

With an escort of matted sticks, a lone rubber sandal floats on the sleepy current past overhanging bushes studded with fruit, past crocodiles basking stupidly on a brown beach. By a filmy pool just beyond, where the river has chewed on the soft bank, a vulture tears meat from a bloated coypu, backs away, and before eating shakes the water from its feet.

Narrowing some now, the river runs clear over white sand and white butterflies dart erratically over the surface. Here the trees have thinned out, are smaller; slim palms that rustle with each swell of the breeze, cast shadows slanted away from the river, falling in long parallel lines that by accident here and there merge with other palms. With more open space, undergrowth is thicker. Waxy leaves shaped like cups tremble and spill their cargo of reflected sunlight.

269

Tendrils, let loose, coil and slip into the water like snakes. The geography of light and shadow is more complex here. Colors mount and recede; background shapes bend and break.

Just ahead on the left, below a crude clearing where felled trees lie across one another like jackstraws, there is a beached canoe and next to it on a piece of canvas, a small outboard motor half disassembled. A few banana trees have been planted in giddy, spasmodic rows. Through the glutinous air, which up till now has held the suggestion of a snoozing cow's breath, come the sharp smells of smoke and charred herbs. A tight bend up ahead; the river picks up speed over sloping rocks peppered with mica. Accompanying the monotonous burble of the water is the sound of someone alternately sucking and blowing on a harmonica.

The shore is sandy and flat, wide open to a torrid but indifferent sun. There are perhaps sixteen huts clustered here, each one different from the others in size or shape or in the mix of building materials. A path, almost the suggestion of a road, leads into the pushed-back woods. On either side of it are scattered garden plots haphazardly fenced. Many broken stalks here, leaves brown and stiff. The soil is particular about the things it will grow. A small dog noses around lumps of trash at the water's edge, some of it delivered by the river, some of it drifted down from the settlement. The rubber sandal arrives now, bouncing off an outcropping stone, spinning in a gentle eddy until it comes to rest against a formation of rags and curved tin. The dog paws the sandal up onto shore and begins to chew, her jaws squeezing out the water it's soaked up. She sucks this rubbery tasting juice to the back of her tongue with great pleasure.

By the hut that is farthest from the others a cookfire burns, a blackened pot balanced over the coals. The woman peers into it, a broken piece of comb clenched between her teeth, then stands up again and plucks at the ragged fringe of hair over the man's ear. With finality, she twice clacks together the blades of the scissors she borrowed from Lita, whose son breathes the pain of his ulcerous legs into his harmonica, and pats the man's brown back.

"It's not exactly Charles of The Ritz," Tildy says, "but it's the best I can do."

Christo touches his bare neck. "I should have a real good sunburn back there by tonight."

"Well, at least you don't look like a hippie."

"That's great. Tomorrow I can go and apply for a job at the bank."

270

Tildy just smiles and backs away. She hardly notices his jabs anymore. Intimidation is pointless here. She squats by the fire and looks into the pot. In boiling gray water the chunks of armadillo rotate slowly. Karl was so proud when he brought it in that morning, the first thing ever caught in his traps.

"However it turns out, it won't be fish," Tildy says.

But Christo has gone down to the water to clean his teeth with salt and a green stick.

Tildy was ill almost all the way across. by the time they reached Boca Chica Bay, she had lost ten pounds and her skin was the color of slush. They had made a nest for her among the boxed television sets (Orozco always arranged for return cargo—life was too short, he said, to ever waste a trip running empty) where she shivered and heaved and never saw the sun. Being awake meant only pain and discomfort, but sleep, or the kind of lapsed consciousness that passed for sleep, propelled her into terrible dreams of suffocation or endless pursuit through empty and harshly lit rooms.

Christo and Karl both took their turns at work with the others up on deck, being cursed and jostled a good deal of the time. At night they ate watery beans and salt fish and slept without padding in the hold, the unavoidable rivet heads prodding their flesh. So there was misery enough to go around.

"Sure as fuck ain't been no pleasure cruise," Karl said when at last they came in sight of Cartagena, the oldest fortified city in the New World and the playground of smugglers and pirates for centuries, as he knew from his reading.

Here came Orozco with his jerked-beef face and sad thin smile to explain that slipping three fugitives into the country without papers would be most expensive. As to the televisions, well of course he had set two aside for the harbormaster, but this was another matter altogether, no? And then there was his own considerable trouble to count in. A favor to his good New York friend and customer, certainly, but after all . . . .

It was clear from his relentlessly insinuating manner that he had looked inside their trunk. Realizing they had left all choices back in Cape May—and there was a grim sort of comfort in that—Christo asked what he had in mind exactly. Orozco shrugged. What value could one give these things in a city where the children sold bags of raw emeralds in the streets like candy? But he was not a cruel man. He understood the pressures they were under and the difficulties they might face. He invited them, each one, to take a few pieces they liked, the prettiest ones, and he would take care of the rest. Then they would be free to go as they pleased. And freedom, was that not in the truest sense without price?

They carried Tildy down to the dock on a board.

The taxi driver who snapped them up could not have been more than fourteen years old. He sat on a heavy pillow in order to see over the pink furry dashboard of his '59 Chrysler Imperial and leaned on the horn as they crept through the overpopulated streets. He was disturbed that they wanted to be left off at a cheap hostel, but was more than happy to accept their U.S. dollars.

The room smelled like old clothes. From the café downstairs Christo brought bread and bottled water, got Tildy to eat a little, then laid himself out on one of the canvas cots, insensible to anything but the sound of his own breathing. It was too hot to think. At night it didn't get any cooler. Christo woke all at once in a wallow of sweat as jukebox music came palpitating up through the floor. He got up, peeling his shirt off, and caught Karl's anxious whisper in the dark.

"You got a plan?"

"A what?"

"Plan, a scheme, like. You got us here—okay. What're we gonna do now?"

"Stay alive."

Tildy slept off and on for a day and a half, slowly working her way along: a piece of fruit here, a hard-boiled egg there, and finally a bowl of meatball soup which Karl spoon-fed her like a baby, wiping her mouth with his cuff.

Christo meanwhile was out in the streets, looking to convert gold lockets and rings into pesos. Every town has its Broadway, never hard to find, and after a few circuits of the avenue where banks and airline ticket offices were grouped, he found a customer, a redheaded kid from Baltimore with a guitar around his neck. He said his name was Zane.

"My mom's gonna love this." He held the sapphire up to the light, fingered its delicate setting. "Last wedding ring she got went down the garbage disposal at home."

But this one-at-a-time groove was not the place to be; he'd attract attention before long. Christo needed to deal some fast quantity and get out of sight. He wandered along and found a shabby little park of patchy grass, flowerbeds, an equestrian statue coated with verdigris. Some local studs were gathered around a beer-fueled rhythm combo: congas, cowbell, maracas. Christo hung out for a while, blending into the scenery and waiting for someone to come to him.

The someone was well-dressed, on this set at least, and screened his eyes behind mirror-finish glasses. It took some time for Christo, in a kind of international hustler's pidgin, to establish that he was a seller rather than a buyer. He flashed a little yellow metal for the mirror man and said if he wanted to talk, they'd have to walk, not about to get down anywhere near all those hometown troops. The mirror man took his time thinking it over, looked in a dozen different directions, at his watch, at the cigarette he flicked in a hard straight line toward some dusty geraniums, before he motioned: Let's go.

He stopped after they'd strolled a couple of blocks and held out his hand. "Policarpo Fung. *Mi madre* of Hong Kong." Then, aiming an admonitory finger, "*Mi hermana,* she husband big police *aquí. Comprendo?*"

Christo dipped his head. Sure, *comprendo.* You want to run a bogus front page, here's one in my language. And he cranked out a story about looking after a lonely oilman's wife in Maracaibo, really looking after her, and after all those nights he'd had it coming. He flashed the goodies again, giving Fung a longer look this time. Fung loosened visibly, concluding exactly as he was supposed to that a man who made his living in the bedroom was soft as butter and no kind of threat.

Five minutes later, they closed the deal behind the pinball machine in a quiet bar. Playing it extra safe, just in case Fung had a buddy waiting out front, Christo went to the men's room and climbed through the window. He felt unbeatable as he jogged away with a solid wad in his pocket and under it the little bracelet he'd held back for Tildy.

He tried to get the most out of this sensation; didn't seem like he'd be feeling it again.

Tildy turned and twisted and tossed, but a comfortable position did not exist. In the lingering dementia of her illness, everything made sense: Karl sitting there prayerfully, the cooking smells that clung to the inside of her nose like nits, the long dreamy distance from anything real.

Karl's hand on her face was a chafing annoyance but she smiled anyway, cautious of him, wondering what he must make of the breakage and displacement of the last two weeks, or if at this point it

made any difference to him at all. Suddenly, without any real outward change, his touch became sexual and she, with the itchy desire
of recently fevered skin, took his hand and put it between her legs,
inside her drawstring pants, pressing it still for a long moment to
show that she wanted nothing more, only his firm presence there.
Karl obeyed, looking past her to the blotchy wall. It was nice not to
feel like a husband anymore; just someone taking care of her, a partner on this stealthy trip. On clear thread, a spider floated down from
the ceiling, swayed a little in free air, and disappeared out the window. That easy, out the window and gone?

"You know, I can feel your heartbeat all the way down here,"
Karl said .

"Is it fast or slow?"

"Just steady and light. Like rain."

They left the next morning, traveling by fumy yellow bus over
small roads, stopping at every hamlet and water hole so that it took
all day to go a hundred miles. The driver told jokes and sang and
whizzed around curves trimmed with little memorial crosses. They
reached Ingrato on the Rio Magdalena the following afternoon and
transfered to a boat. Right away a drizzle set in, more mist than rain.
Nowhere to really get away from it, so they stood in the center of
the broad, open deck and cooled their tired faces, watched droplets
mount up in each other's hair. The other passengers seemed unset-
tled by their presence, chattering in tight little groups, openly staring. One thin-lipped man who had been looking hungrily at the
pack of American cigarettes they passed back and forth (their last),
hurried away embarrassed when one was offered. Tildy made up a
slippery barefoot dance to go with the music from someone's radio
that just as soon turned into static. When the sun came back, Karl
took his shirt off and tied it to the railing to dry, too loosely apparently, since it slipped away somewhere when he wasn't looking. It
was the only one he had and later, sitting on a coil of tarry rope by
the bulkhead, his teeth chattered like castanets. The water was slow
and flat and there weren't any more people to wave and sing out
from shore. The loud engines frightened beautifully colored birds
out of the trees.

Little by little they lost all interest in time or destination. The
strange southern light coalesced into a wall impossible to see
through, beyond which there was nothing to see. And by now they
weren't fleeing anymore, had come so far there was no longer any-

274

thing to get away from, but still they could not stop. This movement was something past their control or choosing. It approximated some de-evolutionary process—a six-legged mammal crawling on its belly back to the swamps.

They reached the end of the line. Now a raft carried them, a raft equipped with a small square sail. Barely lifting his eyes from the water, without a word being said, the old man pushing and steering with a long bamboo pole knew just where they belonged.

The heat that beamed down all day now rises up from the ground. Dinner scraps hiss and smoke on the embers. Legs stretching out, head on a pad of moss, Tildy inhales and hands on the home-made cigarette whose bulbous coal is reflected as two orange dots in Christo's eyes when he turns his face to hers.

Christo has taken to rolling his tobacco in dry leaves. The results are sloppy, but better than buying cigarette papers from the Syrian. You do what you can, even out here. But he makes the rules, the Syrian, waiting in his dark store like a spider. His customers come in the evening, having put it off as long as possible, and he sells them crackers and sticks of chewing gum one at a time, measures out cornmeal with a teacup. Everyone hates the Syrian. It is the kind of intimate loathing usually reserved for a family member, the kind with its own unsmotherable voice.

Zarzuela and his obedient wife are fishing with handlines in the moonlight. He shows her a certain kind of tug to give the bait, and she looks like his granddaughter. Christo recalls asking Zarzuela why no one has done the logical thing and hacked the Syrian to pieces with a machete.

"Of course we think of it," the old man said. "But then where would we buy our rice?"

Tildy looks through the fire's languishing glow and sees Karl framed in the entrance to the hut. His back is turned as he repairs a tear in the palm thatch.

"It's easiest for him."

"What gives you that idea?" Christo says.

Her limp finger points: Karl looking intently into his hands where he is making some tool out of wire and a forked stick.

"He thinks he's at Boy Scout camp," Christo says.

"No, he doesn't have to think that way. That's why it's easier for him."

The cigarette has disintegrated on the ground at Christo's feet.

He lowers himself on his hands, crimps his mouth in an O to capture the last smoke. He blows some at her and in a childish voice sings, "'Tenting tonight, tenting tonight. Tenting on the old campground.'"

Odd, the ease with which they have been absorbed into the settlement. Invading gringos, two men and a woman, certain responses were to be expected. But from the first moments—the raftsman refusing to be paid, and wading in because he wouldn't take them any closer—they were greeted with universal inattention. No hostility or suspicion, no acceptance either, merely this passive absorption. Days and days before they found out that Zarzuela speaks English.

Don Alfonso, as he is invariably addressed, is mayor of this mute, shrunken paradise. He tells Christo things that gradually outline a solution to the riddle. The settlement is entirely made up of men and women who are fugitives. They have been on the run so long, all their lives in some cases, that they have lost fear. Hector deserted from the Guardia Nacional. Tito beat up a plantation owner. Luz escaped from a reformatory where she'd been sent for stealing hairpins. And Lita, Lita had a priest's baby and left Barranquilla before he was twenty-four hours old. This is the enclave they have found, the rock of their refuge. No more need be known or asked of people who come here than that they are here.

Still, there is a kind of normal life. Voices get louder at the smell of cooking meat. People go almost naked, but cover their fires when the rain comes. Lita, passing by with a load of wet laundry, will smile so brightly at Tildy, then lower her eyes the moment she is noticed. Normal life: These things are hard to interpret.

"There is no place like the jungle, my friend. No place where a man is so much in control of his future."

In the shade of his little porch, the Syrian fans himself with a wrinkled soccer magazine. The scroll of clouds that softened the morning heat has rolled itself up and Karl, stooping against the sledge handle, drinks the sweat that runs down to his lips. But the Syrian looks quite comfortable in his double-breasted serge suit with padded shoulders, his stiff white shirt and midnight blue tie. He begins to peel an orange and the smell wafts across the compound like the perfume of a woman who enters a cool bar after three sets of tennis. An orange! What is it that prevents Karl from diving at the bits of rind the Syrian tosses to the ground? Hard to say, but it's something other than pride. Karl's knuckles are swollen, his nails discolored from the stone wall he's building that will someday surround the entire compound. At this rate, in another two or three years.

"A little music, my friend? So you will forget the heat."

The Syrian cranks the Victrola, lowers the bamboo needle onto the record. Always the same record: "Velvet Moon" by Harry James and his Orchestra. The Syrian conducts with his magazine and the band follows perfectly, as always. One thing you have to say for him as a boss, he really works at it.

Karl shanks in one last wedge of stone and it's time to strap on the basket again and go scrounging for more. Every rock in the immediate radius has already been used. Sometimes he has to go clear back to the river for a full load. Is this the way they built the pyramids?

"No no, something else now." The Syrian motions him to put the basket down. "The shade is here, so be putting Xerxes to graze."

Xerxes is the donkey. High on his rump he still carries a bullet from the night when the Syrian, enraged at finding a case of white rum bought off a nigger sailor was nothing but water and white vinegar, emptied his antique revolver in the moonlight. Xerxes has his own house to live in. Not with furniture or anything, but it's one of the outbuildings with windows and a door.

"What you clean out of his room you can spread on the garden."

"Tell you what, I don't get something to drink I can't guarantee I'll be standin'. If I ain't standin', I can't be shovelin' neither."

"Fanta?" The Syrian brings out a warm orange drink from inside. Snapping his memo book open, moistening the tip of his pencil with a little kiss, he adds another five pesos to Karl's account.

Xerxes puts his puny head out the window. He brays noisily and goes back to chewing the sill. They are late letting him out today and he doesn't like it at all. The Syrian moves to the hollow gourd placed to catch the drip from his irrigation pipes. Two miles of bamboo irrigation pipe carved and laid by people from the settlement to work off their debts.

"*Para servir a tu, mi mozo.*"

He tilts the gourd, dribbles water along the donkey's lapping tongue.

Christo lowers the basket. He crouches by it at the edge of the path.

"You should rest, Don Alfonso. We've come a long way."

Zarzuela glances up, shrugs, stirs the brush with his long stick. They have been gathering vines most of the day. They have been hiking through the forest with eyes on the ground, attentive for the small white flowers that always grow nearby. The Father makes such signs for us to follow, Zarzuela instructs.

Many years ago there were missionaries on this part of the river. They had come all the way from Sedalia, Missouri, to translate the Bible into the language of the Indians and lead their souls to His everlasting mercy; three men and a woman who had never been further south than Memphis. Without Zarzuela they would all have died. He cooked their meals and washed their clothes and cared for them when they were sick. He built their shelters and the open-sided chapel. He rebuilt the chapel after it burned down. He quickly mastered their language, read the elevating texts of Schweitzer and Dr. Peale, sang hymns in a strong baritone. And when the woman looked at him with begging green eyes, he did not yield.

But he never believed in their God. Not for a second.

The sun is low when they reach the ravine. They climb along a shelf of rock to the cave where Zarzuela keeps his spirit devices: large brewing pot, striped blanket, leather pouch containing necklaces of teeth, dried paws, bundles of feathers. Christo is about to collect wood for the fire, but no, something else to be done first. Zarzuela leads him to a shallow stream. They bathe and put on the spotted skins. Zarzuela has the smooth taut complexion of a much younger man. His movements are soft, luxurious. In the bottom of the pot he places a flat white stone that gleams up through the water like an eye.

Chopped and split with a machete, the vines are pitched into the boiling pot. Soon a thick greenish scum brims over and sputters on the coals. While they watch and wait, squatting on the blanket amid bitter, clinging smoke, Zarzuela tells the story of the first woman in the world.

The daughter of the Master of Fish lived at the bottom of the river. She was young and restless and impatient with the cold darkness that surrounded her. One night she decided to swim up out of the black trench and explore other places. Down on the bank of the river the men had lit a great fire to prepare their *yagé*. The daughter of the Master of Fish was attracted by its glow and swam closer. Her father had warned her never to go near the surface of the water, but the closer she came to the light the brighter it became and the more it drew her on. The youngest of the men heard the disturbance in the water. He ran down to the edge and found the daughter of the Master of Fish floating on her side. She was helpless in this new world. The light blinded her and the heat of the fire dulled her mind. Using a thorned vine, the young man pulled her onto shore, lay down and possessed her. This was the first woman in the world.

Finally, satisfied that the *yagé* has brewed long enough, Zarzuela spits on his hands and lifts the pot away from the fire to cool. He brings out two wooden cups decorated with wavy black lines.

"You must give up all you know," he says, washing both cups with sand. "To the Father you must open yourself like a woman and wait for his touch."

Christo nods obediently. His mind has never been so empty.

"If you are lost, I will be here to guide you back."

"*Mil gracias*, Don Alfonso." Christo lifts the cup to his mouth.

Lita's boy has been brought outside on a pallet so that his sores can bake in the sun. He can watch the *téjo* from here. The harmonica is almost too hot for his lips to touch, but he blows a low note and prays for Tildy to win.

A wide board is propped against a tree. Near the top a circle has been drawn with charcoal and at its center, fastened with a bit of pitch, is the blasting cap. Tito has two boxes of them, which he keeps in a secret place. He worked on a road gang long ago.

Now the men are choosing their stones, passing a jug of cassava beer. Chewing on her nails, Tildy stands off from the others. She looks at the tipping hut made of cardboard and tin cans hammered flat; it belongs to the little man known as Señor Equis. He sits outside with the flat rock he has painted to look like a transistor radio. She can smell the strips of meat drying on his roof as he looks up, smiles, waves.

Tito paces off the distance and scratches a line in the dirt with his heel. The men jostle and manuever behind him, arguing over the order in which they will throw. Unregarded, Tildy is a shadow among them, weighing her three stones. It is not hostility they feel toward her, not complacence. She is just there, a part of the landscape that surrounds them but to which they have no real connection, like a bush whose name they do not know although they eat its fruit. Tito spreads his arms, nudging the others back to give him room. He sights along one pudgy finger, rocks back and throws the first stone. It strikes inside the circle but well away from the blasting cap. The next two are not as close and Tito is visibly annoyed, pushing the beer jug away when it is offered. Hector of the narrow shoulders and crooked lips has had more beer than anyone, which is okay since he made it. His first two throws don't even hit the board and Jaime says why doesn't he practice on something large like his wife's head. Hector aims his last shot at Jaime but hits a clay jar instead, breaking it. Brilliant, Jaime says. The throw of the year.

While everyone clusters around the broken jar to discuss what kind of restitution should be made to its owner, Tildy slides up to the line and lets go. The fat stone, vaguely triangular but smoothed by the action of the river, slams into the black, kicks up a tiny dust cloud. The next lands in almost the same place; a piece chewed out of the circle, two prongs that don't quite meet. Only Lita's boy is watching her. He thinks she is even more beautiful than the Virgin of Chinquinquira, whose picture is tacked up over his hammock. On her last try Tildy goes sidearm, pushing off with such force that her follow-through carries her halfway around and her back is turned to the quick bang like a bullwhip on stainless steel. Lita's boy honks jubilantly on his instrument. The applause of Señor Equis is so light and dry that only he can hear it. So she's done it again—the men spit and shake their heads. Anyway, it's kind of a stupid game. Hey, Hector, what do you say we break out another jug?

Tildy feels weak, needs to lie down. The queasiness is still with her from the morning. Like an oven inside the hut. Why didn't one of us think to cut a little window? She fashions a pillow out of the empty sacks (Karl brings them home from the Syrian's stuffed inside his pants) and drops her lids, realizing only seconds later that she has to pee. Botheration; she reaches behind her for a pan. It is customary in the settlement to deposit human waste directly into the river and allow the natural conveyor to carry it off. This is a problem for the more modest among them, Zarzuela's wife for example, who waits for the cover of darkness to empty her child's sand bucket girdled with red stars. And Christo relays the story of a safe-cracker full of *aguardiente* who went down by the river to ease his pressure, passed out and drowned in six inches of water. Improved technology is called for, a modernizing hand. That spot under broad-leafed trees at the downriver edge of the settlement, Karl could build a three-holer there, with a door you could latch. Think what this (probably all they can offer), could do for their standing in the community, for the goodwill of their artificial family. Family . . .

A thumping hose of blood circles Tildy's head. Family. A word she should have kept out of her mind. A conjuring word that makes bad dreams appear. A triad marriage blossoms in the wilderness where organisms feed constantly off one another and the rules and regulations of the past no longer apply. X plus Y describes the old world; X plus Y plus Z the new. Parasite on parasite on parasite. An overloaded structure like this runs itself. It generates excess energy that has to go somewhere.

Tildy has missed her last two periods. For a time she hoped it was the sudden transfer to a new environment that had upset her previously consistent cycle; a change in diet, exotic bacteria in the water. But she can't maintain doubt anymore. A little creature is stirring down there, pattering on the walls of its padded cell.

"I'm pregnant," she says experimentally, with the coy, sparkling-eyed delivery of distant suburban comedies.

She lifts her shirt, trails dry fingers across her abdomen. A vibratory warmth there, but it does not seem in any way distended. Still, she can keep her secret only so much longer. The problem is whom to tell, and how. She doesn't know which is the father. She has no intuition, no real preference. Mr. Y or Mr. Z? Karl with his genes of inertia and defeat? Christo with his genes of instability and deceit? It's a choice she'd rather not make.

Tildy flexes her knees, stretches, eases through the jagged doorway into air as heavy and predictable as the shadows. How quiet it is. Not a breath of wind. Two crested birds chase and plunge across low branches without a sound. The steamy, muffling atmosphere insists on quiet, disguises what is going on so feverishly here and in the distance. When she holds herself and sings part of a tune she cannot place it's like a curse thrown against the elastic disdain of the quiet. Hector passes without looking, a turtle shell dangling at the end of string wrapped around his hand. Her feet are white and sticky against the ground layered under her—crumbled minerals, ashes, powdered thorns and bones and bark. She curls and squeezes her toes in case anything is trying to crawl between them. The patchy black dog who has a dozen owners goes along dragging a back leg. Nearby, Lita is on her knees spreading a salve of fish oil and yam over the sores while her boy covers his eyes. Behind her there are other people moving, working. Of course, disintegration is quiet. And it is anywhere she might choose to look, sealed like a baby inside the concave blue muscle of the sky. She has a thirst like sand and her throat feels barbed all the way down. Arms extended, she walks as if on a rail down to the river. Something plops away, leaves a covering of bubbles and no more. It is hard not to think that the river runs in a circle, that the water passing returns and is always the same. She flattens her body over rocks and lowers her face into the water. She drinks until it aches, then pushes up with her hands and the droplets that fall from her chin send out rings from the center of her reflection. Into the multiplying rings comes a pointed green leaf. Its veins are thick and pearly, its serrations sharp. It is drifting. Drifting and drifting toward an unseen brink.